BRIGH

"I am not accustom[ed] ... am making love to ...

"Making love?" Gwenda gasped. "Dear heavens. Is that what you thought you were doing?"

His glare should have stopped her, but she could not let the poor man continue under such a delusion. "Oh no, my dear Lord Ravenel! I regret to tell you, but you were doing everything absolutely wrong."

"Indeed, Miss Vickers?" Ravenel said through clenched teeth. . . .

"I'll also wager you never looked at Miss Carruthers when you were proposing, which is a great pity. You have the most handsome pair of eyes."

THE SUGAR ROSE

"Why, you never taught me the proper way to kiss."

The instant the words were spoken, Aurelia flushed, regretting it. Everard's eyes narrowed to points of steel.

"Then by all means," he said, his voice low, dangerous. "Allow me to complete your education."

Before she could move or cry out in protest, his arms were around her. His mouth hovered above her lips for the barest instant, before crashing down to claim her lips. Aurelia was too stunned to put up more than a token struggle before she became lost in the bruising, sensual tempest of Everard's kiss. . . .

Also by Susan Carroll
Published by Fawcett Books:

THE LADY WHO HATED SHAKESPEARE
THE BISHOP'S DAUGHTER
THE WOOING OF MISS MASTERS
MISTRESS MISCHIEF
CHRISTMAS BELLES
MISS PRENTISS AND THE YANKEE
THE VALENTINE'S DAY BALL

BRIGHTON ROAD

THE SUGAR ROSE

Susan Carroll

FAWCETT CREST • NEW YORK

Sale of this book without a front cover may be unauthorized. If this book is coverless, it may have been reported to the publisher as "unsold or destroyed" and neither the author nor the publisher may have received payment for it.

A Fawcett Crest Book
Published by Ballantine Books

BRIGHTON ROAD copyright © 1988 by Susan Coppula
THE SUGAR ROSE copyright © 1987 by Susan Coppula

All rights reserved under International and Pan-American Copyright Conventions. Published in the United States by Ballantine Books, a division of Random House, Inc., New York, and simultaneously in Canada by Random House of Canada Limited, Toronto.

Library of Congress Catalog Card Number: 94-94027

ISBN 0-449-14924-2

All the characters in this book are fictitious, and any resemblance to persons living or dead is purely coincidental.

Manufactured in the United States of America

First Ballantine Books Edition: July 1994

10 9 8 7 6 5 4 3 2 1

Contents

BRIGHTON ROAD

To my good friend Linda Benjamin, for all her encouragement and support—this book is dedicated because very likely I will never write about a cowboy hero for her.

Chapter 1

Out of the mists he came—his windswept hair darker than a raven's wing, the pulse at the base of his throat throbbing with all the fury of the passionate Italian blood coursing through his veins. His scarlet-lined black cape swirled about his broad shoulders as he reached out his arms to her. Even though the castle ruins loomed behind him . . . even though its sinister shadow cast a blot upon the bright beauty of the moon itself, Gwenda felt safe as she hurled herself into his strong embrace . . . .

Lost in the depths of her dream, Miss Gwenda Mary Vickers stirred upon the hard wooden settle in one of the White Hart's private parlors. Her short chestnut curls tumbled over her spencer, the folds of the rose-colored jacket scrunched up to form a pillow. Gwenda clasped to her bosom the heavy volume she had been attempting to read when she had fallen asleep. Hugging the book tenderly, she mumbled, "Oh, Roderigo. Roderigo, my love."

His fingers, warm and rugged, crooked beneath her chin, forcing Gwenda to look up at him. Even as she did so, his features blurred, becoming obscured by the mists, but she sensed the full curve of his lips drawing closer to her own. . . .

With a low groan, Gwenda rolled over, still clutching the book. Balanced precariously on the settle's edge, she moistened her lips in eager anticipation of her dream lover's kiss.

His arms tightened about her. He pulled her closer, ever closer. She could feel the heat of his passion-drugged breath. His mouth was but a whisper away—

Thud! Gwenda tumbled off the edge of the bench, landing hard upon the inn's polished wooden floor. The fall jarred her instantly awake. Gwenda sat bolt upright, shoving aside the heavy book that had somehow landed on top of her. Before she could so much as draw breath, she heard a low whine, and then a warm, rough tongue shot out, bathing the side of her face with affectionate concern.

"Down, Bertie," Gwenda commanded firmly, thrusting aside a large, lean dog, his glossy white coat spotted with black. She rubbed her bruised hip and blinked, trying to get her bearings.

Her gaze traveled upward along the coaching prints set upon stout oak walls, the fireplace swept clean of ash for the summer, the mantel laden with plates and mugs of gleaming copper and pewter. From outside the open window she could hear the clatter of iron-rimmed wheels and horses' hooves announcing more arrivals and departures from the ever-bustling inn yard.

Aye, she was in a private parlor of the White Hart. On the floor, to be precise. She had been cooling her heels here for the past three hours, ever since her carriage had snapped a brace a few miles outside the village of Godstone Green. The Hart's congenial landlord had very kindly offered her a book with which to pass the time. What was it now? Gwenda consulted the book's title page. Daniell's travelogue, *Views of the East*. Mr. Leatherbury's tastes in literature did not quite match her own. Small wonder that she had fallen asleep. Then she had begun to dream, only to fall off the high-backed settle just as . . .

Gwenda's green eyes darkened; her usually good-humored countenance tensed into a scowl. Fending off further attempts of her dog to console her, she heaved herself to her feet and plunked back down upon the settle.

"Damn!" she hissed. Her brother, the most holy Reverend Thorne Vickers, would have blanched with horror if he had heard her, but Spotted Bert was far more forgiving of her vagaries. The dog merely cocked his head to one side, arching a disreputable-looking ear that was much the worse from too many encounters with ill-mannered cats.

" 'Tis too provoking to be endured, Bertie," she said. Bert emitted a sympathetic bark and thrust his head upon her lap. Gwenda absently scratched him behind the ear. "I suppose I could have been in the throes of the most hideous nightmare and I might have slumbered through the day undisturbed. But let me be caught up in the most delicious of dreamings and it never fails. I always wake up at the best part."

Her hand stilled, coming to rest upon the dog's head. She sighed, feeling bereft, as though she truly had been deprived of Count de Fiorelli's kiss. Although she could never bring his features clearly into focus, she knew his name well. The Italian no-

5

bleman had appeared in far too many of her fantasies, both sleeping and waking, besides having emerged as a character in many of the novels she wrote for Minerva Press. He might have borne a different name and title in both *The Mysteries of Montesadoria* and *The Dark Hand at Midnight*, but he was still, as ever, her Roderigo: brooding, passionate, and courageous.

Gwenda half smiled at her own nonsense, ignoring Spotted Bert as he nudged her hand with his cold nose, indicating his earnest desire that she resume the scratching. Although she had been writing Gothic tales of love and terror for the past three years, she would have stoutly denied she was a romantic. Nay, confirmed spinsters of one and twenty years were not supposed to give rein to flights of fancy. But there was always one foolish corner of her heart urging her to allow the bright colors of her imagination to splash over drab reality. Even now she was tempted to stretch back out upon the bench, shutting her eyes tight and seeking to recapture the dream. But experience had taught her that that never worked. It was possible to drift right back into nightmares, but never dreams. She would have to content herself with falling back upon her imagination.

But that was the difficulty. Her imagination never balked at conjuring what it would be like to have one's side skewered by a villain's sword, but that soul-searing kiss always eluded her. Despite two broken engagements, she had never experienced anything like it. Both Sir Jasper Pryor and Lord Marlon Lambert had been content to kiss her hand. Mayhap that was why she had never married either one of them.

Only once had she ever been kissed upon the

mouth by a man, and that had been by her cousin Wilfred, the Christmastime she was fifteen. For a wager, her youngest brother, Jack, had made Wilfred do it by holding a sword to his back. With Wilfred's mouth so cold with fear, his hands clammy, his embrace had reminded Gwenda of a dead mackerel.

She could have *used* that dream kiss, Gwenda thought, to bring greater authenticity to the romantic scenes in her books. But there . . . She shrugged. She scarcely could spend the rest of the day moaning about it.

She reached down to pat Bert but found him gone. The animal's attention had been claimed by something he had spied through the window. His entire body taut with anticipation, a low, joyous growl erupted from Bert's throat. Gwenda recognized the sound only too well. It was a warning the dog reserved especially for his feline enemies.

"Bert!" she said, attempting to collar the dog. But it was too late. With a bunching of his powerful hindquarters, Spotted Bert cleared the sill and bounded outside. Gwenda reached the window in time to see a barking flash of black and white tearing between horses' legs in hot pursuit of a caterwauling fluff of gray.

She started to shout but immediately recognized the futility of the effort. Bert would not pay her the least heed. He would return when he was ready, to lament fresh scratches or with his tail wagging with victory at having forced his opponent to take refuge in a tree.

Gwenda scanned the crowded inn yard, hoping for some glimpse of her own coachman bringing her the welcome intelligence that the carriage would be ready soon for her to continue her trip to Brighton.

Her family would be expecting her by five at the house Papa had rented in the Royal Crescent, and as matters now stood, it would be long after dark before she arrived, especially since she saw no sign of Fitch or her footman.

The inn yard appeared in more of a state of confusion than usual. A stage from London had just arrived, letting down its passengers for their twenty minutes of rest and refreshment. Just behind them an elderly gentleman was demanding a mug of ale and a change of horses for his post chaise. But more of the uproar stemmed from a large party that had just rattled into the yard, consisting of several carriages, a low perch phaeton, and some young bucks on horseback, all obviously traveling together on some sort of excursion. As the ladies were handed down from the coaches, waiters, ostlers, and postboys flew in all directions to provide the Hart's customary lightning service.

Even the host himself appeared harried. Mr. Leatherbury combined the mannerisms of a jolly country squire with a brisk efficiency in dealing with his guests. He mopped his cherubic countenance with a large kerchief as he bent his rotund frame into a bow to a tall man wearing a curly-brimmed beaver who alighted from the phaeton.

In the midst of such bustle, Gwenda did not doubt that the landlord had likely forgotten about the lady he had ushered into the private parlor hours before. She thought of sending her maid to make inquiries about the progress of repairs to her carriage, but as usual the pert French girl was nowhere to be found. Colette was likely off flirting with one of the handsome young waiters again.

Gwenda drew back from the window, eyeing with little enthusiasm the book that lay discarded upon

8

the floor. If she didn't want to spend the rest of her afternoon absorbing more details about Indian mosques, mayhap she had best go to check on the carriage herself.

Returning to the settle, she retrieved the spencer that had served as her pillow and attempted to smooth out the rose velvet garment whose pile had been sadly crushed. She shrugged herself into the short-waisted jacket, then eased it over her traveling gown of dove-gray jaconet. She buttoned the frog enclosure, noting with a grimace how the spencer appeared to band tightly over the curve of her bosom, as all her apparel did.

Gwenda had oft heard herself described as "a handsome figure of a lady." She had always supposed that meant she had a chin a little too forthright for her to be considered beautiful, was too tall, and had full breasts. Her mother was forever reminding her not to hunch her shoulders forward. It was an old habit that had evolved from her youthful self-consciousness over being buxom when her friends yet appeared boyishly slender. Her mama had tried in vain to help Gwenda correct her posture. "A general's granddaughter," Prudence Vickers would remind her sternly, "should always maintain a proud military bearing." But Mama, not quite so amply endowed, had no notion of how self-conscious one felt. Those high-waisted clinging gowns that were now the fashion made Gwenda frequently feel like the figurehead on the prow of a ship.

Remembering her mother's admonishment, however, Gwenda did try to straighten a little. Without benefit of a mirror, she attempted to fluff some order into her wayward mass of curls, then headed for the door.

But she had not taken two steps when she realized she had forgotten something. Rather guiltily, she glanced down to where her stockinged toes peeked out from beneath the hem of her gown. It was another of her bad habits: forever discarding her shoes, then forgetting where she had put them.

In the sparsely furnished inn parlor, it took her little time to locate one of her Roman sandals by the settle. She sat down, then slipped her foot into the soft blue leather, quickly crisscrossing the lacing up her calf and tying it into a neat bow.

But the second sandal proved more elusive. She finally found it dropped behind the fireplace andirons as though someone had sought to hide it. She could well believe that *someone* had. Gwenda pursed her lips as she examined her footgear. The leather bore signs of many teeth markings, and the damp, frayed lacing was nigh chewed through. Now she knew how Spotted Bert had whiled away his time when she was napping.

"Blast you, Bertie," she muttered as she sank down on the settle, trying to figure out how she was going to wear the mangled sandal. She had hoped the dog had finally outgrown his penchant for gnawing on any unguarded shoes he could find. When the lacing broke off in her hand, she stifled an oath of vexation just as she heard the parlor door open behind her.

Gwenda hoped it would prove to be the errant Colette. Knowing that because of the settle's high back she could not be seen from the door, she started to peer around the wooden side to make her presence known. But instead of her maid it was the plump landlord who bustled in, saying, "Right this way, Lord Ravenel, and I shall have some refreshments sent in immediately."

To Gwenda's embarrassment, Mr. Leatherbury ushered in a strange gentleman who was so tall he had to duck to avoid banging his head on the oak lintel of the door. She shrank back behind the settle, quickly pulling her skirts down. Thus composed, she prepared to call out and alert the host to his mistake: that this parlor was already occupied.

But before she could do so, she heard the man who had been addressed as Lord Ravenel say, "Refreshments will not be necessary. I only require the use of this room for but a few moments."

Gwenda heard Mr. Leatherbury's puzzled "Oh," then could almost imagine his shrug as he added, "Very good, my lord." He bustled out again, doubtless relieved to be able to attend to his more demanding guests.

As the door clicked shut, Gwenda realized she had been left alone with the stranger. Grimacing, she regarded with little relish the prospect of now limping out half-shod to announce her presence. But she was consumed with curiosity as well. Why on earth would someone desire the use of a private parlor for only a few moments? Before revealing herself, she cautiously risked a peek at Lord Ravenel, who stood just inside the door, briskly stripping off his gloves like a man marshaling himself for some grim and difficult task.

He certainly had to be one of the largest gentlemen she had ever seen, and all of him solid muscle, she would have wagered. From the heels of his gleaming Hessians to the crown of his glossy ebony hair, he stood well over six feet. A navy-blue frock coat molded perfectly a most unyielding set of broad shoulders. The cut of his immaculate cream-colored breeches and waistcoat were plain, with naught of the dandy about him; his neck was half

11

strangled in a stiff collar and a cravat tied with mathematical precision. But the starched neckcloth appeared no more rigid than the cast of Ravenel's swarthy countenance. His features were rough hewn, from the square cut of his jaw to the harsh planes of his cheeks. Forbidding black eyebrows shadowed eyes as dark as the thick lashes framing them.

Not in the least shy or timid, Gwenda yet felt a trifle reluctant to point out to this formidable-looking man that the parlor was already occupied. Her hesitation proved costly. The next she knew, the door opened a second time. Her situation became more awkward when a waiter stood back to allow a lady to enter. Gwenda judged the lady to be not much older than herself, but far more elegantly gowned in corn-yellow satin, her fair ringlets wisping from beneath a poke bonnet. The waiter discreetly retired as the beautiful young lady regarded Ravenel through violet eyes gone wide with surprise.

"Lord Ravenel," she protested. "There was no need for you to bespeak a private parlor. We are all going to dine outside. The landlord has some tables arranged for our party beneath the trees. It will all be most charm—"

"I know that, Miss Carruthers," Ravenel said, sweeping her objections aside with a brusque motion of his hand. "But I wanted the favor of a few moments alone with you before we part."

Just the right amount of blush filtered into Miss Carruthers's cheeks to highlight her eyes. "That sounds most improper, my lord," she said, dimpling with a tiny smile. "Mayhap I had best summon my aunt."

No more improper than her own position,

12

Gwenda thought, mentally cursing the folly that had caused her to delay in speaking up. It would be dreadfully embarrassing for her to pop out now, but she had no desire to witness whatever sort of tryst was about to take place. And yet Ravenel's dark eyes looked more impatient than amorous. Gwenda crouched farther back on the settle, hoping that the lady might persuade him to leave, but his lordship appeared to be not the most persuadable sort of man.

"Of course I intend no impropriety," Ravenel said. "And your aunt would be very much in the way. Now sit down. Please."

Even when Ravenel added "please," it still sounded like a command. Gwenda heard the scrape of a chair and then a rustling of silk, which told her that Miss Carruthers had complied.

"Oh, blast!" Gwenda whispered to herself. Now what was she going to do?

Miss Carruthers said, "Surely, Lord Ravenel, whatever you have to say to me could wait until we meet again in Brighton."

"No, it cannot. I feel I have waited too long already."

Miss Carruthers's heavy sigh carried clearly to Gwenda's ears. Squirming at the plight in which she found herself, Gwenda eyed the open window through which Spotted Bert had vanished and wondered what her chances were of clambering through it unnoticed. But after risking another peek around the settle, she quickly abandoned any such notion. Miss Carruthers's chair was drawn up in the far corner of the room, closest to the door. Although Ravenel loomed over her, he did not look at the young lady. Rather, he seemed to be staring out the window, an absent expression in his eyes as he

mustered his thoughts. Despite the discomforts of
her situation, Gwenda could not help being caught
up by the picture that the two of them made, somewhat like the hero and heroine of her latest novel—
Miss Carruthers, so angelically fair; Ravenel, so
dangerously dark. Except that the backdrop was all
wrong. Gwenda would have opted for walls of stone
with rich Italian tapestries and velvet curtains of
royal purple fringed in gold. Miss Carruthers's
blond hair should have cascaded down her back instead of being arranged à la Sappho, and Gwenda
would have rounded her eyes, gotten rid of that cat-
like slant. As for Ravenel, he would appear to better advantage in a crimson doublet, with a sword
buckled at his waist. His hair should have flowed
back from his brow in midnight waves rather than
been cropped into the severe Brutus cut so popular
among the gentlemen.

Linking his hands behind his back, Ravenel drew
himself up to his full height. Mama, Gwenda
thought, would greatly have approved of his lordship's posture. The man looked as though he had
been born with a ramrod affixed to his spine. He
said abruptly, "I see no reason to waste any more
time, Miss Carruthers. I have your father's permission to address you, and I am sure you have been
expecting me to do so."

Good heavens! Gwenda could scarcely credit her
ears. The man could not possibly intend to deliver
a proposal of marriage, not here at an inn.

But her own dismay was nothing compared to
Miss Carruthers's. Dropping her manner of placid
gentility, she half started from the chair, irritation
and alarm chasing across her delicate features. "Oh
. . . oh, no. I—I wasn't expecting—Please, Lord
Ravenel. Desmond. 'Tis yet too soon."

Desmond! Gwenda stifled the desire to shriek. She was not so unreasonable as to expect to find men named Roderigo or Antonio outside the pages of her books, but *Desmond* . . . How could his parents have been so utterly unfeeling?

" 'Tis not too soon," Ravenel snapped. "I have received enough encouragement from you, Belinda, that I think I may make bold to speak what is in my mind."

In his mind? What about his heart? Gwenda thought. She realized she had been staring so long that, despite her concealment, she marveled that they did not feel her eyes upon them. Both Ravenel and Miss Carruthers appeared so caught up in their own drama that neither seemed to suspect that they were not alone.

All the same, Gwenda cautiously drew farther behind the settle. Resigning herself to the fact that she was now cornered until the end of this painful little scene, she eased into a more comfortable position as Ravenel launched into his proposal. He had a magnificent voice, deep and full-timbred. But his delivery—Gwenda winced. He might have been addressing a meeting of Parliament. She could almost picture his rigid stance, one hand resting upon the lapel of his jacket. He detailed quite logically and clearly for Miss Belinda Carruthers all of the advantages of becoming Lady Ravenel. These seemed to consist chiefly of estates in Leicestershire, a house in town, and an income of twenty thousand pounds a year. He was also prepared to generously overlook Miss Carruthers's own lack of fortune.

Gwenda shifted on the settle, having to bite her tongue to overcome the urge to interfere. Ravenel was doing it all wrong. Not that she was insistent that a man go down upon one knee. But at least he ought to clasp Miss Carruthers's hands between his own and forget all this rubbish about estates.

"In conclusion," his lordship said, "I believe our similarities of tastes and interests make for the likelihood of us achieving a most comfortable marriage."

Gwenda smothered a groan against her hand.

Ravenel added, almost as an afterthought, " 'Tis only for you, madam, to name the day that will make me the happiest of men."

A pause ensued at the end of his speech, which drew out to such lengths that Gwenda could not forbear sneaking another look even if it meant risking detection. Miss Carruthers appeared tormented with indecision, her pretty face not so much flustered as gone hard with calculation. The only thing Gwenda could liken the woman's expression to was when she saw her brother Jack contemplating some desperate gamble.

"No!" Miss Carruthers finally blurted out. "I—I mean yes, I cannot . . ." She flounced to her feet. "I mean I—I am deeply sensible of the honor you do me."

Not half as sensible of it as he was, Gwenda thought wryly as she noted Ravenel's brow furrowing with the weight of a heavy frown. Then she realized her interest in the situation was causing her to lean too far forward and pulled herself back.

"I beg your pardon," he said. "But am I to understand that you are refusing my offer?"

"No!" Belinda cried. "What—what I truly feel is that I cannot marry you . . . not—not at this time."

"My dear Belinda," he began again, but his growing irritation robbed the endearment of any effect. "Do you wish to marry me or not? A simple yes or no will suffice."

16

What a passionate attempt at persuasion that was, Gwenda thought, rolling her eyes. How could Miss Carruthers possibly resist!

"If you would only wait until I come to Brighton," Belinda faltered. "Just give me a little more time . . ."

"A little more time in Lord Smardon's company?" Ravenel said. "I am not a complete fool, Belinda. I am fully aware that the *friend* you intend to visit on the way to Brighton is the Earl of Smardon. You are hoping to marry him, are you not? That is why you will not return a round answer to my proposal."

"Oh, n-no. I don't mean to marry anyone." Belinda's voice dropped so low, Gwenda had to strain very hard in order to hear her. "There—there is another reason for my reluctance. You see, I was once engaged to a young officer, er, ah . . . Colonel Adams of the Tenth Cavalry. He—he died fighting in Spain. I fear I have not quite gotten over my Percival's death."

" 'Once engaged'?" Ravenel echoed. "You never mentioned anything of the kind before."

With good reason, Gwenda thought cynically. There was a note of insincerity in Belinda's voice that made the whole thing sound like a hum.

"I hope I am not the sort of lady who goes about wearing her heart on her s-sleeve." Belinda's voice broke.

When Gwenda next peeked at the couple, she saw that Belinda's eyelashes batted, fighting back the tears that made her eyes sparkle like jewels. Appearing damned uncomfortable, Ravenel dredged up a linen handkerchief, which he thrust at her. Gwenda wondered why the young lady's distress roused no sympathy in her. Rather, she felt as though she

17

had stumbled into the second act of a very bad melodrama.

"Thank you, Lord Ravenel," Belinda said, dabbing at her eyes with the linen. She gave a brave little sniff. "I am sure you understand now why I wish you to give me more time."

"But—" Ravenel began.

"Pray don't distress me by saying more just now. I will give you my answer in—in Brighton." Miss Carruthers at last managed to skirt past him. She bolted through the parlor door, fairly closing it in his face when he tried to follow.

Gwenda waited tensely for Ravenel's reaction. He did not look like the sort to slap his forehead or tear his hair and lament. For a moment he stared at the closed door, looking rather nonplussed. Then he scowled, his eyes seeming to grow darker and darker until Gwenda thought even the most black-hearted villain she had ever created would have thought twice about trifling with his lordship in his present mood. She half expected he would swear and drive his fist against the door panel.

But although his jaw set in a hard, angry line, Ravenel merely snatched up his gloves and put them on again with sharp, savage tugs. Gwenda held her breath for fear he might yet take a notion to walk farther into the parlor. When he reached for the door handle, she had to smother a sigh of relief. She sank back, congratulating herself on escaping undetected, when she heard a sharp bark. The next instant Bert jumped back through the window, his muddied paws skidding on the wooden floor.

With an inward groan, Gwenda flattened herself against the settle as Bert galloped over to where she sat. She shooed the dog frantically with her hand, hissing, "Go away, Bertie." But Spotted Bert was entirely impervious to such hints. He barked and wagged his tail as though he had not seen her for a twelvemonth, then assaulted her hand with rough, affectionate licks.

"What the deuce!" Gwenda heard Ravenel exclaim. With a sinking heart, she listened to the sound of his boots striding across the room. She had not a chance to move so much as a muscle before his lordship was bending over the settle and peering directly into her face.

"H-hullo," she said with forced brightness as she struggled to fend off Bert.

Never had she seen a man look more thunderstruck. Ravenel's expression was exactly what she had been trying to achieve in her last book for Count Armatello when he saw the ghost of his murdered sister rise up before him.

Ravenel's astonishment quickly gave way, his face suffusing with a dull, angry red. Gwenda could see the storm brewing in those brilliant black eyes and hastily sought for words of explanation and apology, but before she could say another word, Bert began sniffing at Ravenel's sleeve.

Ever a sociable creature, her dog took a sudden, violent fancy to his lordship. His tongue lolling out, Bert leaped up, trying to lick Ravenel's chin. With a muttered oath, Ravenel tried to thrust aside the eager, panting animal.

"Oh, no! Bad dog. Heel, Bertie!" Gwenda cried.

But Bert never heeled. He continued to leap up as though determined to scale Ravenel, scraping his muddy paws clean upon the length of his lordship's immaculate cream-colored breeches.

"Down!" Ravenel said sternly, collaring Bert and forcing the animal back upon all fours. The dog whined and fidgeted while looking adoringly up at Ravenel.

Gwenda saw in Bert's intrusion a chance for her to escape from what promised to be a most unpleasant confrontation. She stood up, reaching for Bert's collar and said, "I do apologize for Bertie's behavior, sir. If you will permit me, I'll just be taking him—"

"Sit!" Ravenel thundered.

To Gwenda's mortification, she obeyed the command with more alacrity than the dog did. She plopped back down upon the bench. Spotted Bert gave in reluctantly, lowering his hindquarters to sit on her feet. To her astonishment, he remained seated even after Ravenel released his collar.

"That's absolutely amazing," Gwenda could not help exclaiming. "Bertie never listens to anyone."

"A trait that his mistress apparently doesn't share." With a look of disgust at his breeches, his lordship brushed at some of the mud stains with his gloved fingers.

Gwenda had the grace to blush. "I am so dreadfully sorry, Lord Ravenel. I did not mean to eavesdrop, but indeed I can explain why I did so."

He folded his arms across his chest. "I am all eagerness to hear your reason, madam."

Gwenda thought he looked far more eager to throttle her, but she continued in a rush, "You see, I was waiting in here while my carriage is being repaired, but the landlord forgot I had already claimed the use of the parlor and he—"

"And I daresay you experienced a sudden loss of voice that prevented you from speaking up."

"Everything happened so fast, and then—"

"And then you decided it would be far more interesting to skulk behind the bench and listen."

20

Gwenda eyed him in frustration. "For someone who claims to be so eager to hear what I have to say, you have an annoying habit of interrupting me."

Ravenel silenced her with a lofty wave of his hand that Bert took for encouragement to assault his lordship again. After subduing the dog with another curt command, Ravenel fixed Gwenda with a stern eye. "Upon my word, madam. You should have had the delicate sensibility to make your presence known instead of spying upon a man like— like some chit of a schoolgirl."

Gwenda could have endured him railing or even swearing at her, as her brother Jack would have done, aye, and considered she deserved it. But when Ravenel lectured her in that stuffy manner, he reminded her of her odious brother Thorne.

"I am rather afraid I don't have any delicate sensibilities," she said.

"Nor scruples!"

"No, I am not overburdened with those, either," she agreed affably. "I do think you might have had more sense than to go about proposing to people in a public place like an inn. But, I daresay," Gwenda added, trying to be charitable, "that you were too worried that Lord Smi—Smardon, or whatever his name is, was going to steal a march on you with Miss Carruthers."

Ravenel's jaw dropped open in an outraged gasp. "Why, you—you impertinent little—"

"And it is only natural your lordship should be feeling a little surly—"

"Surly!" Gwenda thought he would choke on the word.

"Pray accept my heartiest condolences upon your

21

recent disappointment," she concluded magnanimously.

"My recent disappointment is none of your affair." His voice started to rise, but with obvious effort he brought it back down again. "I do not even have the *honor* of your acquaintance, madam."

"Oh, so you don't. I am Miss Gwenda Mary Vickers." She swept to her feet and made him her best curtsy, but the regal effect was somewhat spoiled when she accidentally trod upon Bert's tail and he let out a reproachful yelp. As she bent down to soothe the dog, she realized Ravenel was regarding her with a mighty frown.

"Vickers? You are not—not by any chance one of the Bedfordshire Vickers?"

"Yes. Of Vickers Hall, just outside the village of Sawtree." She straightened, offering him her hand.

He didn't take it. A visible shudder coursed through him as he muttered, "Good Lord. One of the Sawtree Vickers. That explains everything."

Gwenda was not certain she liked his tone. She tipped her chin to a most belligerent angle. "And exactly what is that supposed to mean?"

"Nothing. Only that I have heard of your family before." Ravenel gave her one of those wary looks generally reserved for village idiots and the hopelessly insane. His eyes raked over her as though seeing her for the first time. Gwenda thought he dwelt on the curve of her breasts a little longer than he should have. She fought down a blush. Her Roderigo would have been far too high-minded for that.

Altogether she did not believe that his lordship was behaving with much gallantry, but she was willing to make allowances for a man who had been so recently crossed in love.

22

Once more she nobly tried to apologize for her intrusion. "Pray do not feel embarrassed over what I just witnessed, my lord. I assure you I am the soul of discretion."

His thick eyebrows arched up in sardonic fashion. " 'Tis difficult not to feel embarrassed. I am not accustomed to having an audience when I am making love to a lady."

"Making love?" Gwenda gasped. "Dear heavens! Is that what you thought you were doing?"

His glare should have stopped her, but she could not let the poor man continue under such a delusion. "Oh, no, my dear Lord Ravenel! I regret to tell you, but you were doing everything absolutely all wrong."

"Indeed, Miss Vickers?" Ravenel said through clenched teeth. "What a pity I hadn't realized you were present. I could have consulted you first."

"You should have been telling her something far more passionate than that you want a *comfortable* marriage. I'll also wager you never looked at Miss Carruthers when you were proposing, which is a great pity. You have a most handsome pair of eyes."

"Of all the arrant nonsense—" Ravenel began, turning an even deeper shade of red.

"There is still time for you to make amends. You could go after Miss Carruthers even now, take her in your arms and say—"

"Miss Vickers!" he snapped.

"No, I don't think she would like it if you called her by my name," Gwenda continued, undaunted. However, the black look Ravenel shot her did cause her to retreat a step. She could not help admiring the way his eyes smoldered when he was angry. Gwenda stared as if mesmerized into those raging dark depths, wondering rather breathlessly what he would do if he lost his temper. She had never been menaced by a man, as her hapless heroines were by the villains in her books. Obviously she could expect no help from Bertie. The dog had rolled over onto his back and was shamelessly begging to have his stomach scratched.

With one powerful leap of her imagination, Gwenda conjured up images of everything from Ravenel's gloved fingers reaching for her throat to his restraining her ruthlessly against him. She felt vaguely disappointed when he merely drew himself up stiffly and said, "Since there is not the least likelihood we shall ever meet again, Miss Vickers, I have no intention of discussing my personal concerns with you any further. But, in future, let me advise you not to listen in on private conversations. Other men might be lacking in my considerable self-restraint."

"And let me advise you, my lord," Gwenda said, never able to refrain from having the last word, no matter what the risks, "that the next time you propose to a young lady, you find one that does not make you feel quite so *comfortable.*"

Ravenel compressed his lips as though not trusting himself to reply. He spun on his heel and stalked over to wrench open the door. But this time he forgot to duck as he stomped across the threshold and slammed the top of his head against the door frame. The cracking sound was enough to make Gwenda wince in sympathy just hearing it. He reeled back, clutching his head, obviously seeing stars, the string of curses he wanted to utter trembling on his lips.

"Oh, damnation. Go ahead and say it," Gwenda urged impatiently. "I haven't any delicate sensibilities to offend, remember?"

She heard the indrawn hiss of his breath. His mouth clamped into a stubborn white line, but his snapping dark eyes did the cursing for him. Then he exited from the room with the most incredible forbearance Gwenda had ever witnessed in a man that furious. He didn't even slam the door behind him.

Gwenda let out her breath in a long sigh. "Well, of all the toplofty men I have ever met!" She bent down beside Bert, obliging him by scratching him at last and rendering the dog into a state of bliss with his eyes closed tight.

Gwenda tried to put the stuffy Lord Ravenel out of her head, but she could not help thinking about his lordship's broad shoulders, his raven's wing hair, and those marvelous flashing dark eyes so at odds with his rigid manner.

" 'Tis a great waste, Bertie," she said mournfully, shaking her head. "A great waste."

Chapter 2

Desmond Arthur Gordon Treverly, the sixth Baron Ravenel, stormed down the inn corridor, seeking the White Hart's landlord. He fully intended to collar Leatherbury and inform the man that when his lordship requested a private parlor, by God, he expected it to be just that—*private*.

But he had to check his pace as he passed the coffee room and the stage passengers swarmed out. The twenty minutes allotted for their stopover had obviously come to an end, and if they did not resume their places, they would likely find themselves left behind. As this group tumbled out of the door, Ravenel glimpsed the apple-cheeked landlord about to rush in.

"Leatherbury," Ravenel shouted angrily, but the landlord paused only long enough to sketch a quick bow.

"I will be with you in a moment, your lordship," he said, huffing with great indignation. "There are some travelers who arrived on foot attempting to bespeak dinner in my kitchens and, I assure you, here at the Hart we do not cater to *that* sort of person."

Leatherbury's round face quivered with outrage, as though he placed walking in the same category as horse thieving. Then he bolted into the coffee room before Ravenel could say another word.

The baron considered it beneath his dignity to chase after the man. In any case, he was fair enough to concede that the affronts he had just received in the parlor were not precisely Leatherbury's fault. No, the blame must rest entirely with that extraordinary creature with the impudent brown curls and too candid green eyes.

"Making love? Is that what you thought you were doing?" The memory of Gwenda Mary Vickers's astonished gasp stung Ravenel worse than Belinda's not consenting to marry him. How dare that impertinent chit address him in such a manner! How dare she presume to eavesdrop, then to criticize him!

The floorboards trembled beneath Ravenel's feet as he stomped out through the inn's main door and into the bright sunlight. But the heat suffusing his face had naught to do with the warmth of the summer's day. Above his head, the inn's sign creaked, the white stag that had been the badge of Richard the Second authenticating the inn's claim that it had been built in the fourteenth century. Before him stretched the cobblestone street dotted with white-stone cottages baking in the afternoon sun. A line of fat geese waddled across the village green.

But both the bucolic charms of Godstone and the ancient timber-frame inn were entirely lost on Ravenel as he continued to fume over his recent encounter with Miss Vickers.

Aye, as soon as he had heard her name, he had been well aware of what sort of behavior to expect. The Vickers family comprised the most notorious collection of lunatics to be found outside the confines of Bedlam. The insane exploits of Mad Jack

Vickers were legend: shooting the currents beneath London Bridge, hiding inside a coffin to prove that he could survive being buried alive, balancing on one leg atop Lord Marlow's old coach horse. Mad Jack, the baron supposed, must be brother to the young lady he had just met. And as for the father! Ravenel grimaced. Never would he forget the time Lord Vickers had swept into the House of Lords clad in a Roman toga and delivered a speech more fit for Drury Lane than the august halls of Westminster. The mother, Lady Vickers, was said to be constantly besieging the Duke of Wellington with letters, telling him how he ought to be conducting the campaign against Napoleon.

Gwenda Vickers reportedly had some eccentricity, too, although at the moment Ravenel could not recollect what it was. Certainly a penchant for spying on total strangers must be numbered among her peculiarities. Doubtless she had a tongue that ran like a fiddlestick as well and would report his humiliation over half of England.

The prospect only aggravated Ravenel's ill humor. His gaze swept toward the distant spot where the rest of his traveling companions were seated upon benches beneath a large oak tree, a generous repast spread out on the table before them. But the baron felt no temptation to join them, not even when Miss Carruthers waved gaily and beckoned to him as though nothing had happened. He gave her a stiff nodd, then turned away, still smarting from her recent rejection of him. Belinda had not said no precisely, but she wasn't exactly falling over herself to marry him, either. Although Ravenel would not have described himself as being heartbroken, his pride had been dealt a severe blow.

As he stalked around the side of the inn, heading

for the stableyard, Gwenda Vickers's voice seemed to echo in his mind once more. ". . . you were doing everything absolutely all wrong . . . even now, you could go after Miss Carruthers, take her in your arms . . ."

"Bah!" Ravenel muttered under his breath. "What romantic piffle." Imagine offering such personal advice to a man she had never met before! Miss Vickers must be all about in her head, the same as the rest of her family. And yet he could not help mentally reviewing his wooing of Belinda, wondering if he had proceeded amiss. No. He shook his head. He could not concede that he had. He had conducted his courtship with the same seriousness and propriety he brought to all of his duties as Baron Ravenel. And in his thirty-second year, one of those duties was clearly to get himself a wife, then an heir.

Miss Carruthers had seemed such an ideal choice: a duke's granddaughter, a lady of breeding and refinement, intelligent and accomplished, not given to any wild whims of behavior—at least not until today.

Lost in his reflections, Ravenel drew back instinctively as the stage rattled past him away from the inn, the outside passengers clinging precariously to the top rail. So Belinda still mourned this—this Colonel Percival Adams who had died in Spain. Doubtless a cavalry officer with a fine pair of mustaches, and excessively dashing, which Ravenel was fully aware that he was not. "Sobersides"—that was the sobriquet bestowed upon him by the London wits.

The baron's jaw tensed. Not that he cared a jot what such society fribbles thought of him, nor that many wagers had been laid at White's betting that,

29

despite all of Ravenel's assets, the fair Belinda would never have him. Likely she would choose his nearest rival, the Earl of Smardon, a golden-haired Corinthian of the first stare of elegance. A swaggering, muscled dolt with more brawn than brains, Ravenel thought scornfully, but his sneer quickly faded to a frown.

He fared ill by comparison to Smardon. The baron was well aware that he had not the least reason to be conceited over any of his personal attributes. He deplored the bronzed cast of his complexion that made him look more like some rascally buccaneer than a gentleman. But he also knew his own worth in terms of lands and the position he had to offer a lady. All during the London Season, Belinda had afforded him every encouragement, giving him reason to think his addresses would be acceptable to her until Lord Smardon, the only other eligible bachelor whose holdings rivaled his, had appeared on the scene.

Although Ravenel was loath to admit it, Miss Vickers had been right when she had accused him of worrying that he would be cut out by Lord Smardon. His anxiety on that score had, mayhap, led him to commit the first breach of propriety in his life, proposing to Belinda at a common inn. And only see what humiliation that had brought him!

So unnecessary, too, for it seemed his rival was not Smardon but a soldier long dead. Odd. Never once had Belinda mentioned any such thing as being haunted by memories of a fiancé killed in the war. But, of course, a gentleman did not question the word of a lady, so Ravenel quelled all of his suspicions that Belinda was merely keeping him dangling, making a fool of him.

No, he had made up his mind to have Miss

Carruthers for a wife, and have her he would. The Ravenels were excessively stubborn when it came to obtaining what they wanted. He would renew his addresses with more persistence when Belinda had finished junketing about with her aunt and arrived in Brighton.

This resolution took some of the edge off his anger and disappointment, but he still felt in no humor to make pleasant conversation over luncheon with his other traveling companions. Their destination was Tunbridge Wells; his was Brighton. He had only come with them thus far because of Belinda's presence in the party. But it would do the lady no harm to fret and fear she had displeased him.

Ravenel saw no reason why he should not continue on with his journey immediately. It was merely a question of collecting his elderly valet, Jarvis, from the coffee room and ordering his groom to have the phaeton brought round at once.

But his anger flared anew when he espied his new carriage drawn up before the stables, his prime pair of blooded bays pawing in the traces, completely unattended. With a low growl in his throat, which boded ill for the negligent Dalton, the baron hastened in that direction, barely avoiding being knocked down by a curricle departing from the inn yard.

Ignoring the driver's curses, Ravenel closed the distance between himself and his own rig. Not that he was that particular about the phaeton, but he took fierce pride in his cattle. He never trusted his bays to an ostler, no matter how high the inn's reputation. His groom, Dalton, was paid a handsome wage to see to the horses and make certain they were not so much as touched by any clumsy stable boy. The man had only been in Ravenel's employ a month, but he had given complete satisfaction up until now. The baron trusted that Dalton would have some good excuse to offer for his neglect.

Unfortunately, when he located Dalton just inside one of the empty horse stalls, the groom did not seem of a frame of mind to offer any excuse. From the hazy look in his eyes, Dalton appeared incapable of even pronouncing his own name.

Backed against the side of the wooden stall, the short, wiry groom seemed about to go limp at the knees from the caresses of a petite, dark-haired wench with full, pouting red lips. Dalton stood scarcely over five feet high, and the girl was about his equal in height. Ravenel felt like a giant bearing down upon them.

The girl leaned forward until her bosom brushed against Dalton's thin chest. "Ooh, la, *monsieur* must be very brave to drive such wild horses."

Dalton blushed and stared down at the wench's clinging bodice front. " 'Tis really nothing, miss. 'Tis naught like 'is lordship owns one o' them 'igh-perch phaetons the sporting gentlemen drive. Something of a slow-top 'is lordship is."

As the girl giggled, Ravenel felt his cheeks begin to burn.

"The—the slow-top?" she repeated. "*Ça, c'est drôle. Monsieur* is so clever."

"So clever," Ravenel bit out, startling the couple into leaping apart, "I hope *monsieur* has no difficulty in finding himself a new position."

"Lord R-Ravenel." Dalton's eyes grew wide with guilt and dismay. He started to stammer out an apology, but the baron had already turned to stride out of the stables. Dalton followed after him, whining excuses.

Ravenel, although an exacting master, was usually most generous about giving erring servants a fair hearing and a second chance. But he felt he had borne enough insults this day. By God, he was not going to start tolerating insolence from his own hirelings.

Although it nigh killed him to do so, he ordered one of the ostlers to see to his bays. He cut off Dalton's blistering protest by drawing forth his purse and stuffing some pound notes into the groom's leathery hand.

"Your wages, sir," Ravenel said, eyeing the groom in a fierce manner that had cowed men far braver and more importunate than Dalton. "You may keep the boots, but, of course, you will return the livery."

"Aye, my lord," the groom said sullenly, scuffing his toe in the dirt.

The baron thrust a few more coins at the man. "And here is a little extra to cover your expenses back to London. I will even furnish a reference as to your skill in handling horses, but as to your reliability . . ."

He left the sentence incomplete, his scornful tone making it clear what he thought. Although Dalton pocketed the money, he did not trouble himself to conceal a look of resentment.

Ravenel dismissed the man's lowering expression with as much contempt as he did Dalton himself. Heading back toward the inn he nearly collided with the cause of this recent trouble. The French girl deliberately thrust herself into his path, her heavy perfume filling his nostrils even above the odors of the stableyard.

Ravenel's nose crinkled with distaste. He by far preferred the smell of his horses. When the girl fluttered her lashes, showing every sign of being prepared to take up with him where she had left off with Dalton, his lordship gave her a wide berth.

As the baron stomped toward the inn door, he could only wonder at what was happening to the White Hart. Once the most respectable of hostelries, today the place was absolutely crawling with brazen females. Not that he was so unjust as to classify a lady such as Miss Vickers with the likes of that French doxy. But both women had managed to embarrass him in the short span of an hour and Ravenel looked forward to the prospect of never setting eyes on either again. He would round up Jarvis at once and be gone from this infernal place.

Despite the bustling atmosphere of the White Hart's coffee room, the waiters yet found time to pay Sebastian Jarvis the same amount of deference as he would have received at home. As the baron's eldest and most trusted servant, he was accorded a respect little short of that shown the master, a respect that his presence seemed to command wherever he went.

He was a distinguished-looking old gentleman with flowing white hair and keen blue eyes that no amount of years could dim. The lines upon his profile were finely stitched as though Time had become a seamstress, her needle gently fashioning an age-worn face mended with dignity. Jarvis bore more countenance than did most dukes who traced their ancestry back to the time of the Conqueror.

"More rum and milk, sir?" The young waiter hovered respectfully at Jarvis's elbow, ever ready to refill his mug.

"No, thank you, lad," Jarvis replied in his soft, courteous voice. Indeed he was not sure he should have had the first one. He had hoped the toddy might soothe the ache behind his eyes. What did ladies do when they got the megrims? Jarvis would have been mortified to ask.

When another waiter hustled forward to set a sizzling beefsteak before him, Jarvis regarded his meal with little appetite. He could not believe he had another of those wretched headaches.

But it seemed he acquired one every time he rode out in the hot sun with Master Desmond in the open carriage. Jarvis passed his hand across his brow with a small sigh. And to think of the way he used to ride on horseback all day, accompanying the present baron's grandfather in the most blistering summer weather. He stared mournfully into his empty cup.

"You're getting a little long in the tooth, Jarvis old man," he murmured. Aye, so he had been doing, these past ten years and more. His wry smile was reflected back at him in the cup's bottom.

But this time his discomfort was not entirely due to the heat of the day. Fretting over his young gentleman had done little to ease the steady throb behind Jarvis's temples. There was little about Master Desmond that he didn't know. Hadn't he acted as valet to the lad ever since he had been left an orphan at the tender age of nine, when typhus carried off the late Lord and Lady Ravenel? He was fully aware of all of his lordship's moods and therefore knew perfectly well why Master Des had disappeared into a private parlor and that Miss Carruthers hard after him. He ought to be wishing his young master every success and yet . . . Jarvis heaved a heavy sigh. There was something about that Miss Carruthers, something cold and sly that kept Jarvis hoping the match would not come off, despite his master's wishes. The lady simply did not seem right for his Master Des.

But when Jarvis had ventured to utter even the slightest criticism of the lady, his lordship had flown up into the boughs. So, despite the familiarity that his long acquaintance with Master Desmond gave him, Jarvis had been wise enough not to offer any more unsolicited opinions, but that did not prevent him from continuing to worry.

When Ravenel finally made his appearance in the coffee room, Jarvis anxiously scanned his lordship's countenance for some sign that his fears had come to pass: Master Desmond was now engaged to Miss Carruthers.

But the baron's heavy brows were drawn together like a thundercloud hovering over the stormy darkness of his eyes. His mouth was set into a hard line. It would be obvious even to those who did not know Master Desmond well that something had happened to vex his lordship.

She must have refused him, Jarvis thought. Intermixed with his relief was a perverse anger at the lady who could thus have the bad taste to reject his fine young gentleman.

As Lord Ravenel strode toward his table, Jarvis pushed back his chair in order to rise. His lordship placed a restraining hand upon his shoulder. "Sit, Jarvis, and finish your meal."

Ravenel flung himself into the chair next to him and sent one of the waiters to fetch him a glass of ale. While he waited for it to be served, he drummed his fingers impatiently on the table. "As soon as you have finished eating, we'll be off."

"Very good, Master Des—" Jarvis broke off. Even after all these years, he sometimes forgot to call his gentleman by his proper title. "Very good, my lord," he amended.

While he picked at his beefsteak, he covertly studied the baron, hating the unhappy frown that carved deep ridges into Ravenel's brow. His lordship stared moodily out the window. Beyond the latticed panes, Jarvis could see the party of the baron's friends yet making merry beneath the oak tree, Miss Carruthers the merriest among them.

His master spent too much of his life peering out windows, Jarvis thought sadly. He was suddenly haunted by the memory of a much younger Master Desmond, trying conscientiously to grapple with learning to manage a vast estate, all the while stealing wistful glances to where his cousins played cricket upon Ravenel's lawn.

Jarvis coughed softly into his napkin and cleared his throat. "I—I could not help noticing, my lord," he said diffidently. "Am—am I not to wish you joy?"

"No, I am afraid not, Jarvis," Ravenel said, his frown deepening. He took a large pull from his mug of ale, then wiped his lips with a napkin, looking as though the brew had left a sour taste in his mouth.

"Never you mind it, Master Des," Jarvis said, just as he had done so many times before when his lordship's odious cousins had refused to include him in one of their escapades. He added, "There is many a young lady who would consider herself fortunate if you—"

"I doubt that," Ravenel said with such a bitter twist to his lips that it struck up a dull ache in Jarvis's heart. "In any event, I have not given up on Miss Carruthers yet."

"Then you mean to go with the others to Tunbridge Wells after all," Jarvis said. Despite the pain in his head and his uncertainty that his master's pursuit of Miss Carruthers was the best thing, he brightened. His master did not enjoy himself in the company of other young people half enough.

But Jarvis's hope was quickly dashed. "No, I am still going straight on to Brighton. I told you that my man of business is going to meet me there."

"So you did, my lord," Jarvis said, crestfallen. Business, 'twas always business with Master Des. His lordship had been drilled with a sense of responsibility far too early in life, with never a chance to enjoy all the follies of youth.

"Miss Carruthers will be in Brighton herself within a sennight." Ravenel frowned again as though the prospect did not entirely give him pleasure. He startled Jarvis by asking him abruptly, "Have—have you ever proposed to a lady?"

"Me, my lord? Good gracious, no."

The baron looked rather disappointed. "Then I suppose you have not the least notion how to go about it."

Regretfully, Jarvis did not. An inveterate old bachelor, it distressed him to feel he could be of so little use to his master on this score. After much thought, he ventured, "I suppose the direct approach would be the best. Put the question plain and proper."

His answer seemed to please Master Desmond. "That's what I thought, too," Ravenel said, nodding his head in satisfaction as though somehow vindicated.

"Aye, my lord," Jarvis continued. "If the young lady cares at all about you, she should not need much by way of persuasion."

The rest of his answer did not seem to delight Master Desmond as much. As his lordship became lost in another brown study, Jarvis bit back the urge to say, Forget that blond minx, Master Des. Miss Carruthers was such a cold sort of beauty with her pale-colored hair and winter-blue eyes. Master Desmond needed a lady with all the riot and warmth of springtime. But that was not the sort of poetic sentiment a dignified valet should be expressing, not even if he had served the family through three generations.

Ravenel tossed off the last of his ale and then rose with his characteristic abruptness. "Well, Jarvis, if you are done harassing that unfortunate beefsteak, we'd best be off. I should like to make Brighton well before dark, especially since we will be traveling alone. I have dismissed Dalton."

Over the years Jarvis had trained himself not to show surprise. "Indeed, sir?" was all he said.

"Yes, the fellow was too impudent by half."

Although Jarvis heartily agreed with him, he yet felt a little disturbed by the tidings. It was not like Master Desmond to act so quickly and out of hand. He should not like to think his lordship's recent disappointment was starting to cloud his judgment.

He stood up to follow Ravenel from the coffee room, not looking forward to an afternoon of the hot sun beating down upon his already aching head. But he had barely taken a step when the floor seemed to rock beneath his feet, the paneled walls of the coffee room spinning before his eyes.

"Jarvis!"

He caught a flash of Ravenel's face gone pale with concern. His lordship's strong arm eased Jarvis back into his chair.

After a few moments with his eyes closed, the world around him resumed its normal steady balance. " 'Tis—'tis nothing, my lord," he said. "Except a drop too much rum."

"The devil it is! The heat has been bothering you again and you never said a word to me."

"N-nonsense. Fit as a fiddle, I assure you." Jarvis would have attempted to rise again, but Ravenel refused to let him.

"Well, that settles it. We shall spend the night here and go on to Brighton in the morning."

"Never, my lord," Jarvis quavered with indignation. "Certainly not on my account."

"To own the truth, I am feeling rather exhausted myself."

Jarvis knew a plumper when he heard one. He could not remember the day his lordship had ever admitted to feeling tired. Besides, Master Des had a trick of not quite meeting one's eye when he was being less than truthful. However, before Jarvis could protest, the baron rushed on, "Besides, I fear one of the bays might be straining a fetlock. That was why I dismissed Dalton—for neglect. No, I think we should all do better for an afternoon's rest."

Jarvis grumbled, "Well, the bit about the horse is a far better tale than that nonsense about you being fatigued, my lord—"

"Good. I am glad you liked it." Ravenel flashed one of his rare smiles. "You wait here for a moment. I shall bespeak rooms for us and see to it that the bays are properly stabled."

"Master Desmond!" Jarvis made one last attempt to protest, but the baron was already striding from the room. He knew there would be no dissuading his master now. Obstinate he was, once he got a notion in his head, like all the Ravenels before him.

Jarvis's shoulders slumped with dejection. What a worthless old stump he was, delaying Master Desmond this way. His lordship needed one of those smart young valets who could keep pace with him and rig him out in dashing style, make that Miss Carruthers suffer a few pangs of regret over trifling with Master Des's feelings.

The bleakness of Jarvis's reflections increased when he later peered through the coffee-room window and saw that the rest of Master Desmond's friends were departing for their carriages. Although his lordship was there to bid farewell to Miss Carruthers, she was too busy flirting with one of the other young bucks to even offer her hand to be kissed. When the coaches rattled away down the street, followed by the young men, laughing and shouting, on horseback, all gaiety seemed to have fled with them. Ravenel was left standing in the shade of the oak tree, his hand raised in a gesture of farewell that no one appeared to notice. Alone, Jarvis thought with a heavy heart. As ever, Master Desmond was alone.

As the sun set over Godstone's red-tiled roofs, Ravenel watched Jarvis light the candles in his bedchamber. The room was comfortable enough as inn rooms went, with a large four-poster bed, although Ravenel could have done without the lavender scented sheets.

For about the dozenth time, the baron started to pace, then checked himself, struggling not to reveal his restlessness to Jarvis. He could have been in Brighton by this time, he thought, then was immediately ashamed of himself. Nay, what did one more day matter? He had already been inconsiderate enough, not noticing that the heat had been making Jarvis ill. The valet had been part of the fabric of his life for as long as Ravenel could remember, as much a solid, comforting presence as the baron's beloved home. He kept forgetting that the old man must be well into his seventies.

Studying the elderly servant's face as he laid out the baron's night things, Ravenel mentally applauded his decision to break the journey. Jarvis was looking much better for an afternoon spent resting within the cool confines of the inn. The pinched whiteness about his mouth and the lines of strain feathering the corners of his eyes had been eased. The delay in his traveling plans was a small price to pay, Ravenel reflected, to see Jarvis looking much more the thing again. After a good night's sleep, the elderly valet should be restored to his invincible, stately self.

Although he did not feel in the least tired, Ravenel feigned a yawn. "Well, I think I shall be turning in early, Jarvis, and I suggest you do the same. I mean to be off at cock's crow tomorrow."

"Very good, my lord. I'll just polish your Hessians and then—"

But the baron moved more quickly than the valet and snatched up the soiled leather footgear before Jarvis could reach them.

"There is no need for you to bother about that. I will simply send them belowstairs to the boots. That is what those fellows are hired for after all."

"The boots, my lord?" Jarvis gasped, his features settling into an expression of dignified horror. "You—you would trust your Hessians to a common servant at an inn?"

"Why not? You know I am no dandy, Jarvis. It makes no odds to me whether I can see my face reflected back in a bit of leather."

"But, my lord—"

"And," Ravenel continued, his eyes skating away from any direct contact with his valet's outraged blue ones, " 'tis now the fashion to have one's footwear sent down to be polished by the boots."

It was a damned clumsy lie and Ravenel greatly feared he was wreaking havoc with Jarvis's pride, but he would not have the old man sitting up to polish the Hessians when he should be in bed. The baron strode firmly to the door. Ravenel flung it open, preparing to summon one of the inn servants.

Instead of one of the maids, he saw the lanky figure of the boots himself just a few doors down the inn corridor. The boots was squatting down to pat the head of a familiar black and white dog, and standing next to him was an all-too-familiar dark-haired lady.

Good lord, Ravenel thought, freezing on the threshold of his chamber. That Vickers woman was still running tame at the White Hart. He had assumed her carriage had been repaired and she had departed hours ago.

At the present moment, she was thanking the boots for returning her dog. "I am pleased to hear that you think Bertie such a friendly creature. Indeed, he is most sociable, but I ought to warn you. I fear he has not been bearing you company out of entirely disinterested motives."

The boots appeared as bewildered by this strange statement as Ravenel himself, overhearing it. But he was not going to risk another encounter with Gwenda Vickers merely to satisfy his curiosity as to what she was talking about. He attempted to step back quietly and close the door.

But it was too late. The incorrigible Bertie had already spotted him. With a joyous bark, the animal came loping toward him as though Ravenel were his long-lost master. The baron braced himself for the assault, but handicapped as he was by the

Hessians still clutched under his arm, he had to endure several licks sweeping from the tip of his chin up to the bridge of his nose before he could collar the dog.

"Heel, you infernal hound!" he said as Gwenda hastened over to intervene. "Miss Vickers, have you no control over this wretched animal?"

"None whatsoever, I'm afraid," she said cheerfully. Ravenel thought she might at least appear a little uncomfortable to encounter him again, considering the circumstances of their last meeting. But far from appearing disconcerted, she seemed absolutely delighted to see him.

"Lord Ravenel. This *is* splendid," she said. "I thought you had gone. I was going to post it to you, but now I shan't have to. Just wait here. I won't be a second."

Before the baron could protest or even inquire as to what the deuce *it* was, Miss Vickers spun about and raced off down the corridor. She was already whisking into one of the rooms when it occurred to him that she had left him to struggle with her dog.

"Miss Vickers," Ravenel fumed as her bedchamber door clicked shut with an ominous finality. Bertie was showing a strong desire to bolt inside Ravenel's own room and make Jarvis's acquaintance.

"Oh, no, you don't," he muttered, although it took a great deal of his strength to dissuade the friendly animal. He managed to ram his Hessians into the hands of the boots, who had stood watching the entire scene with a huge grin on his face.

"Would yer lordship be needing a bit of a hand?" the boots asked.

"No!" Ravenel said, having succeeded in thrusting Bertie back along the corridor. "You just look after my Hessians. I'll be wanting them first thing in the morning." And to Bertie he commanded, "And you! Get along. Follow your mistress."

Bertie whined. Wagging his tail, he gazed soulfully at the baron. Hardening his heart against the dog's mournful look, Ravenel retreated into his room and slammed the door. He released his breath in a gusty sigh and proceeded to straighten his cravat, which had gone askew in the struggle with the dog.

He turned to meet Jarvis's questioning look. "My lord, whatever is—"

But the elderly valet's question was cut off by the sound of a light rapping on the door. The dog couldn't knock. Ravenel assumed it had to be *her*.

He grimaced and closed his eyes. Would Jarvis think he had run completely mad if he told the valet to pretend that he wasn't here? No, it wouldn't serve. Nor could he permit his venerable valet to open the door and be flattened by the exuberant Bertie.

"Never mind, Jarvis," Ravenel said, moving with a quickness that belied his weary tone. "I'll deal with this."

Cautiously he inched open the door, but there was no sign of the dog, only Miss Vickers. She appeared completely unruffled, as though it was the most natural thing in the word for an unescorted lady to knock at the chamber door of a strange gentleman.

Balancing three slender leather-bound volumes in her hand, she said reproachfully, "Lord Ravenel. You didn't wait."

Before he could reply to this accusation, she added, "Have you got Bertie in there with you?"

45

"No, I most certainly have not!" Ravenel snapped.

"Blast! Then I suppose he has gone following the boots again." She added darkly, "As if I didn't know what mischief that dog is plotting." She glowered in the direction that Bertie had presumably disappeared.

The baron shifted impatiently. "Miss Vickers, was there something you wanted of me?" he asked in accents of the most awful civility.

"Oh, yes. Yes, there was." His question seemed to snap her attention back to himself. Ravenel found himself staring into her wide green eyes. He noted that they were not precisely green. They had flecks of gold in them. Or was it that she had golden eyes with flecks of jade? 'Twas difficult to tell. Her eyes seemed to have a trick of changing according to the lighting and her mood. Also, she had the most absurdly long dark eyelashes he had ever seen.

". . . and I treated you very badly this afternoon."

With a start, Ravenel realized Miss Vickers was apologizing to him.

"I had no right to be eavesdropping and thrusting myself into the midst of your affairs. It was abominably rude of me—"

"Miss Vickers, please!" The baron held up one hand to stem this breathless flow of words. "I think the less said of this painful matter, the better. I have no desire except to forget it ever happened."

"But I cannot forget. Not until I make you some amends. I have a gift for you and I hope you will accept it."

A gift! Ravenel bit back a shocked exclamation. Did this young lady have any notions of propriety? "Really, Miss Vickers," he said. "I don't think that you should—"

"Oh, please," she begged, extending the stack of books to him with a wistful smile. Ravenel would not have said Gwenda Mary Vickers was a beauty, but he was forced to admit that she had an unusually appealing smile. It was not coy or of a forced politeness; it was warm and genuine.

He shuffled his feet uncomfortably. "Well, I . . ."

His hesitation was all the encouragement she needed to eagerly thrust the books into his hands. With some trepidation, he stole a glance at the title. *The Dark Hand at Midnight* in Three Volumes, by G. M. Vickers. Good God! Ravenel stifled a groan. Now he remembered Miss Vickers's peculiarity. She wrote those blasted Minerva Press novels, which were all about swooning women, family curses, men dashing about with swords making cakes of themselves, and ghosts and villains popping out of the wainscoting.

As the baron sought for some civil way to toss *The Dark Hand* right back at Miss Vickers, he felt something brush against his sleeve and was startled to see Jarvis attempting to peek past him into the corridor. Never in his life had Ravenel known his valet to display such a vulgar emotion as curiosity.

Gwenda Vickers dipped into a curtsy and beamed at Jarvis. "Good evening, sir," she said. "I assume you must be Lord Ravenel's uncle?"

"Why, no, miss."

"This is my valet," the baron filled in drily. "Jarvis."

"Oh!" Miss Vickers did not look in the least disturbed by her mistake. "How astonishing, for there is such a remarkable resemblance between you. Although not the same color, you both have remarkably handsome eyes."

It was the second time Miss Vickers had made that idiotic remark about his eyes being handsome, Ravenel thought irritably. It was high time this awkward and exceedingly improper interview drew to a close. He supposed the quickest way to do that was to graciously accept the wretched book. He shoved the volumes at Jarvis and then turned to thank Miss Vickers in his most rigid manner.

"Not at all," she said. "I only hope you enjoy the book. I have marked one particular passage for you in the second volume. It is where Antonio, Count Delvadoro, passionately proposes marriage to Lady Emeraude."

"Miss Vickers!"

The lady seemed totally oblivious to his warning growl.

"I don't mean to press the point," Gwenda said, "but I really do feel you are in want of just a few suggestions."

"Not from you!" Ravenel pressed his lips together, waiting until he felt his rising temper was more under control before he continued. "I beg your pardon, Miss Vickers, but fiction is one thing, reality quite another."

"Pooh! Why should it be?"

"Why should it—" Ravenel choked. Then he realized his mistake. He was trying to reason with Miss Vickers as though she were a sane person and not a Vickers at all. He sighed. "I shall try to find time to read the book, Miss Vickers. Now you really should not keep standing about in a drafty inn corridor."

"And if you will most particularly note that one passage—"

"Yes, yes. good night, Miss Vickers." He eased the

door closed, hearing her muted "Good night, Lord Ravenel" through the heavy portal.

He stood by the door, listening for the sounds of her retreating down the corridor. He frowned. A lady of quality should not be wandering about alone at an inn like that. For all of Miss Vickers's unusually forward behavior, Ravenel sensed a certain childlike innocence about her. The lady was clearly not up to snuff and required some sort of a keeper.

In spite of a voice sternly reminding him that it was none of his concern, the baron could not refrain from inching the door open a crack and peeking out to make sure she had gone safely back to her room.

He saw Miss Vickers about to cross her own threshold when her head snapped toward the end of the hallway where the stairs led up from below.

"Colette!" Miss Vickers said in a tone of mild exasperation. "I was wondering where you had gotten to this time."

Colette. So Miss Vickers did at least have some sort of a female traveling companion, Ravenel thought with an inexplicable sense of relief. But his relief quickly changed to dismay when he saw the pert female who approached Miss Vickers. Damnation! It was that French doxy he had caught practicing her seductive wiles upon Dalton in the stables.

"Pardon, *mademoiselle*," Colette said. "I was but fetching your warm milk from the kitchens."

She bobbed an insolent curtsy and handed the glass to Miss Vickers. Something in the Frenchwoman's expression as she followed Miss Vickers into her bedchamber disturbed Ravenel. Colette's sinister smile would have done credit to a Lucrezia Borgia.

The chit was obviously a person of no character, a scheming lightskirt. Miss Vickers ought to be warned and—And what the deuce was he thinking of?

The baron closed his door, appalled by his own fanciful notions. He was permitting his imaginings to run away with him on the basis of witnessing one sly smirk, harboring thoughts more worthy of the whimsical Miss Vickers than of his own orderly mind. Ravenel passed a hand over his brow, wondering if lunacy could possibly be contagious.

In any event, the lady and her maid were none of his affair. He was trying to curtail all future acquaintance with Miss Vickers, not entangle himself further with the lady.

The Dark Hand at Midnight, indeed, he thought contemptuously. He would make sure to instruct Jarvis that those volumes should be conveniently forgotten when they left the White Hart tomorrow.

But when Ravenel turned, he was appalled to discover that Jarvis—that most correct and sensible of gentlemen's gentlemen—had donned his spectacles and was already deeply engrossed in Volume One.

Chapter 3

The morning sun streamed through the windows of Gwenda's room, patching the bed with squares of light. She could feel the warmth upon her face, but she could not seem to force her eyes open to confront the breaking of day. Nor did her limbs seem to want to move, either. She felt as though she had been swathed in cotton batting from head to toe with some of the fluffy whiteness actually stuffed inside her head. A low groan escaped her lips, some part of her mind registering the fact that she had just passed a very strange night. It was not natural for her to sleep so heavily, so deeply without dreams. She always had some sort of dreams.

With great effort, she at last managed to shift her legs from beneath the coverlet. Something warm and moist was licking the soles of her feet. Gwenda struggled up onto one elbow and regarded the black and white blur at the foot of her bed through bleary eyes.

"Bertie," she tried to call but scarcely recognized her own voice. When had her tongue gotten to be so thick?

The dog stretched, then ambled along the length of the bed. She patted him, coming slowly more awake as he nuzzled her.

"That'll do, Bertie." She chuckled when his rough

tongue tickled her ear. She caught the dog's head firmly between her hands and mumbled, "I trust you will be a good dog today and behave more civilly if we chance to meet Lord Ravenel again."

Bertie gave a sharp bark as though he understood.

She yawned, scratching his ear. "Aye, like all rogues, you are most quick with your promises, sir."

She knew full well Bertie would conduct himself as outrageously as he always did. Not that it mattered. She supposed there was little likelihood they would see Lord Ravenel again. Even if he hadn't gone, she sensed that his lordship would dodge her company. Why could she simply not leave him alone? It was one of her own principles to avoid rigorously any gentleman with too much starch in his collar. She had too oft found it denoted a most humorless outlook on life.

She might certainly have put Ravenel down as the stuffy lord he appeared to be, striking eyes or no, if she had not chanced to be walking toward the front of the inn at a particular moment yesterday afternoon. It was then that she had seen Ravenel as he stood and waved good-bye to Miss Carruthers. He must be more in love with the lady than Gwenda had at first supposed, for he had appeared not so much high in the instep as unhappy and vulnerable. Gwenda's intuition told her that Lord Ravenel was a lonely man, and she could not bear to see anyone left lonely. But what could she do to alter Ravenel's case? He was obviously not the sort of man to accept anyone's advice.

"I doubt my interference did any good at all, Bertie," Gwenda murmured to her dog. "Most likely he used my book to light the fire as soon as I was gone, and the next time he woos Miss Carruthers or any other lady, he'll make the same mistakes all over again."

Gwenda sighed, then shrugged. At least she had the satisfaction of knowing she had tried. She swung her legs over the side of the bed. Through eyes yet dulled with sleep, she squinted at the small china clock ticking on the mantel. Good heavens! Five minutes after the hour of ten. If that time were correct, then the morning was more advanced than she had at first supposed. She was not ordinarily a late sleeper.

"Colette?" Gwenda called, stretching her arms over her head and suppressing another yawn. She spoke more sharply when she received no answer. "Colette!"

There was still no response from the adjoining chamber.

"Rot that girl. Sleeping in again and deaf as a post besides. I tried to tell Mama she would never do." Grumbling, Gwenda pushed herself to her feet and was surprised to feel that her legs were a little wobbly. Even the swat of Bertie's tail against her calves seemed enough to unsteady her. She staggered to the white porcelain washbasin. She strained to lift the heavy pitcher and splash a small quantity of water into the bowl.

Taking a deep breath, she heroically dashed some of the cold water onto her face. Although she gasped with the shock, it felt good, setting all her pores a-tingle, and driving off the last wisps of fog that clouded her brain. As she reached for a linen towel to dry herself, her gaze fell on a soiled glass left on the nightstand.

Her nose crinkled at the curdled remnants of the milk she had drunk last night. Beastly stuff. She would not have bothered with it if Colette had not pestered her so. The milk had had the most peculiar undertaste. She must remember to speak to Mr. Leatherbury about it.

But the first order of business was to rouse Colette to help her dress, then make inquiries as to whether that dratted coach brace had been mended.

Gwenda shuffled barefoot across the carpet to the door of the small chamber that adjoined hers and rapped loudly. "Colette!" This time she did not wait for any response before unceremoniously shoving the door open. The sight that met Gwenda's eyes momentarily drove all thoughts of her errant maid from her head. She gave a tiny gasp and stood frozen in the door frame.

Her portmanteau, which had been arranged so neatly along the wall of Colette's room, were now tumbled about the room. The lids were flung open, the trunks empty except for a few trifling articles of clothing strewn over the floor.

It took Gwenda's stunned senses a few moments to recover before her mind assimilated the truth.

"Why, I . . . I've been robbed," she whispered, a sick feeling striking in the pit of her stomach. But how and when? She could not forbear a nervous glance about her as though she might find the thief yet lurking behind the curtains or beneath the bed.

No, she was being nonsensical. The deed had obviously been done under cover of night. She bent down and righted the small casket that had contained her jewels, now distressingly empty.

Her shock slowly faded, with anger taking its place. "The wretched villain," she cried, "sneaking in here while I slept but yards away." The mere idea of such a thing caused a shiver to work its way up her spine.

She turned to glare at Spotted Bert. "And you, Bertie! A fine watchdog you are! It would not surprise me if you had licked the villain's hands and then helped retrieve things to put into his sack."

Bertie cocked his head, appearing to be confused by the reproachful tone.

"You might at least have barked. Goodness knows, you are never quiet on any other occasion."

Gwenda broke off her scolding as a thought struck her. Mayhap Bertie had barked and she had been so deeply asleep she hadn't heard him. But what about Colette? Surely she must have noticed something was amiss.

Gwenda's eyes traveled toward her maid's cot and she stiffened. So startled had she been upon first entering the room to find her trunks rifled, she had not noticed the smooth linen sheets turned carefully back, the feather-tick pillow plumped to perfection. It was obvious Colette's bed had not even been slept in last night.

As Gwenda stared at the cot, unwelcome suspicions began to sift into her mind. The untouched bed, the odd-tasting glass of milk Colette had pressed upon her, her heavy sleep that was almost as though she had swallowed a good dose of laudanum or some other drug.

Feeling much troubled, Gwenda sank back on her heels and wrapped her arms about her dog's neck. "No, it won't do, Bertie, to go leaping to conclusions without proof. I know it looks bad that Colette is not here, but then she never is when I want her. Why, for all I know the poor girl could have been kidnapped by the thieves. As Mama would say, a good general would never court-martial anyone without first obtaining all the facts."

Gwenda rose thoughtfully to her feet and walked back to her own room. At least her wrapper was still there, laid out over the back of the chair. She tugged the soft peach-colored robe over her linen nightgown and looked for her slippers, but they were gone.

"I do trust that was the thief at work," she said sternly to her dog, "and not you, Bertie."

Spotted Bert allowed his tongue to loll out, assuming his most innocent expression.

Gwenda strode past the dog. Opening her door, she stepped into the corridor and was fortunate enough to encounter one of the inn's chambermaids, a strapping country lass with blooming cheeks and a cheery smile. She bustled past with an armload of fresh towels. Gwenda, who had a knack for recalling names, even down to the lowest menial in the kitchens, remembered that the girl's name was Sallie.

She summoned the girl to her side and asked, "Sallie, have you seen my maid belowstairs this morning?"

"Mamzelle Colette? No, miss. I'm sure I haven't." The girl sniffed. There was a disdainful edge in her voice that Gwenda had oft heard from other female servants when they spoke of Colette.

"Oh, dear," Gwenda said. "Well, I'm afraid something dreadful has happened." She beckoned for the girl to follow her into Colette's room, where she exhibited her empty trunks.

"You will perceive," she said calmly, "that I have been robbed."

Gwenda was completely unprepared for the maid's spectacular reaction. Sallie emitted a small shriek and dropped her towels. Turning pale with horror, she shrank back against the wall, clasping her hands over her bosom.

"Oh, lawks, miss. Lawks!"

"You needn't act as though I've just shown you a dead body," Gwenda said, growing a trifle impatient with these Cheltenham theatrics. "Though I will admit the thought of a sneak thief is most distressing. And the disappearance of my maid only further complicates the matter."

"Oh, miss!" Sallie exclaimed again.

"And I am not quite sure how I ought to proceed," Gwenda said, thoughts of constables and Bow Street Runners chasing around in her brain. In any event, she saw that the excitable chambermaid was not going to be of much help beyond wringing her large hands and moaning "Oh, miss! Oh, miss!" at suitable intervals.

Gwenda supposed she could begin by determining exactly what had been taken. As she squatted down, she thought ruefully that that was not going to be difficult since, in truth, not much of her belongings had been left. The jewels and money, of course, were gone and most of her clothes except for her second-best bonnet and a drab merino traveling gown. She could not help reflecting on how Colette had always regarded those particular articles of her clothing with scorn.

Aside from that, she found the copies of her novels scattered by the bed, her chipped ivory hairbrush, and a pair of stockings with a hole in it. But just beneath the stockings she saw the glint of an object that made her cry out with joy.

Her pearl-handled pistol! The thief had somehow missed or discarded it. It had been a special gift from her mother.

"A general's granddaughter ought to know how to

use a weapon, Gwenda," Mama had said. "Those
books you write are quite entertaining, all about
how the dashing hero rescues the fair lady at the
last possible moment. But the sad truth is, my love,
that a gentleman can never be depended upon to
arrive for anything on time."

Dearest Mama. Always so practical, Gwenda
thought as she scooped up the pistol. Somehow the
loss of everything else did not quite matter so much
now. She raised the pistol in her hands, cocking
back the hammer, and lovingly tested the balance
of the finely wrought weapon.

She momentarily forgot the presence of the jit-
tery chambermaid, nor did it occur to her that she
was leveling the muzzle directly at Sallie until
the girl let loose an ear-splitting scream.

Only minutes earlier, several doors down, the
newly arisen Ravenel, garbed in his scarlet brocade
dressing gown, had lathered his face with shaving
soap. Bending toward a small cheval glass, he cautiously wielded a straight-edged razor beneath his
chin.

It had been some time since Jarvis's hands were
steady enough to perform this task for his master.
It stretched the baron's ingenuity considerably to
find excuses why he should shave himself, invent-
ing other pressing duties for Jarvis that would salvage the old man's pride.

This morning Ravenel had been unable to think
of anything else better than expressing an earnest
desire that Jarvis read aloud to him. Regrettably,
the only material available for such an exercise
seemed to be Miss Vickers's wretched book. Jarvis
appeared momentarily astonished by the request,
but then he obeyed with alacrity, intoning Miss

Vickers's nonsense as though he were reading a sermon from the pulpit.

" '... and the dismembered hand crept nearer and nearer to the terrified maiden, a trail of blood dripping from its severed stump—' "

"Good Lord!" Ravenel muttered. What a ghoulish imagination Miss Vickers had. He wasn't certain he cared to hear about blood and dismemberment when he was wielding a razor so close to his own throat. "Er, Jarvis, skip that bit. Go further ahead."

"Very good, my lord."

Was it Ravenel's imagination or did his valet sound disappointed? As his lordship negotiated the sharp steel over the curve of his jaw, he heard the rustling of pages.

"This part in Volume Two must be of exceptional quality, my lord," Jarvis said. "I see that Miss Vickers has taken some pains to mark it."

The baron opened his lips to protest, but Jarvis had already begun to read. " 'Count Delvadoro drew the fair Emeraude against his manly bosom. The soft glow of adoration in his handsome blue eyes made the lady long to weep for joy.' "

Ravenel pursed his lips. That Vickers woman was always going on about eyes, he thought, remembering her comment about his own. He couldn't refrain from stealing a furtive glance into the mirror, studying the skeptical dark depths reflected back at him. Did she really think that his eyes were ...

Ravenel drew back feeling sheepish and disgusted with himself.

" 'The count pressed his lips fervently against Emeraude's fingertips,' " Jarvis read in bland tones. " ' "Oh, my heart's treasure," said he. "If you will not consent to be my own, I shall—" ' "

The count's intentions were lost in the next instant, interrupted by the sound of a woman's muffled scream. Ravenel was so startled that he very nearly sliced off his nose.

"What the devil!" He swore and grabbed a handkerchief to stem the drops of blood where he had nicked himself. His eyes met Jarvis's alarmed gaze.

"I don't know, my lord." The valet rolled his eyes to the book in his lap as though he half feared the sound had emanated from the pages of *The Dark Hand* itself.

Ravenel heard a flurry of movement in the corridor beyond. As he strode toward his door, he could not begin to guess what the commotion was, but he harbored a dreadful certainty that he was going to find Gwenda Mary Vickers the source of it.

He flung open the door and stepped into the hall, only to be nearly knocked down by a fleeing chambermaid gibbering like a terrified monkey.

"Come back here at once, you goose," a familiar feminine voice shouted at the maid.

Miss Vickers erupted from her room, brandishing a pistol.

Good God, Ravenel thought as the chambermaid dove behind him with a frightened squeak. That Vickers woman was more crazed than he had feared.

As she waved the pistol at his chest, Ravenel sucked in his breath, bracing himself for a loud report and the feel of a ball searing through his flesh.

Miss Vickers's eyes flashed scornfully as she peered past him at the cowering chambermaid. " 'Tis not loaded, you idiotic girl." Her assurance did nothing to calm the maid, who went off into hysterics, but the baron sighed with relief.

All the same, he caught Gwenda's wrist and carefully forced her to lower the weapon to her side. "What the deuce are you doing with a thing like that?" he growled.

"My mother gave it to me," Miss Vickers said, as though that explained everything. "It was a present for my last birthday."

Ravenel swallowed an urge to point out to her that most mothers gave their daughters gifts like pearls or parasols. "No. I meant, why are you—"

But his question was broken off since by this time the other guests staying at the Hart came rushing out into the hallway: a stout dowager clutching her wrapper about her, her scrawny daughter hard on her heels; several elderly gentlemen still wearing their nightcaps; and from Ravenel's own room, Jarvis, adjusting his spectacles to peer with interest at Miss Vickers. Everyone spoke at once, demanding to know what had happened in varying tones of fear and indignation. To add to the din, the chambermaid continued to wail and Miss Vickers's dog leaped about, setting up a fearful barking.

Mr. Leatherbury charged onto the scene, his round face flushed red from the unaccustomed exertion of running up the stairs.

"What?" he said, huffing. "What is the meaning of all this?" His gaze traveled from the pistol still gripped in Gwenda's hand to Ravenel's face. The baron became conscious of a fresh trickle of blood going down his chin and groped for his handkerchief again.

"Miss Vickers!" the landlord said in shocked accents. "Never tell me you have gone and shot at his lordship."

"Don't be preposterous," Ravenel muttered from behind his handkerchief.

61

"Certainly not," Miss Vickers said. " 'Tis just that I have been robbed."

Her blunt statement caused a fresh sensation: more outcries from the other guests, more sobs from the chambermaid, and more barking from Bertie.

"Robbed?" Leatherbury said, his face turning purple with outrage. "Here at the White Hart? Impossible, Miss Vickers. Quite impossible."

"It is very possible, you silly man," Gwenda retorted. "You have but to go look in my room."

In the face of Leatherbury's obvious disbelief, even the imperturbable Miss Vickers began to get a trifle agitated. A most spirited quarrel developed between her and the host of the White Hart. Several of the waiters and the boots came crowding into the corridor to add their voices to the hubbub.

"Eh? What's happened here?"

"Dunno . . . think one of the guests has been robbed."

"Brigands!" the dowager shrieked. "We might all have been murdered in our beds."

"Nonsense. Utter nonsense," Leatherbury replied huffily.

Ravenel had had all that he was prepared to endure. He was not accustomed to tolerating confusion, especially not in the morning before he had even had his coffee and beefsteak.

"Quiet!" he thundered.

The authoritative tone of his command immediately reduced everyone to silence. Even Bertie subsided after one more small yap. Ravenel took advantage of the hush to snap out a series of brisk orders that sent the waiters back to their posts and the other guests scurrying for their rooms. He had the boots lead away the sniveling chambermaid and put Jarvis in charge of Bertie. Strangely enough, even the dog seemed to recognize the dignity of Jarvis, for Bertie went quietly without offering to leap upon him.

Then the baron strode back to Gwenda and Leatherbury. All traces of her annoyance with the landlord had faded, and she greeted Ravenel, her eyes glowing.

"Well done!" she said, clapping her hands with enthusiasm. "You're so awfully good at that."

"Good at what?" he asked, taken aback.

"Ordering people about, taking charge. You were just like some magnificent Turkish despot in your scarlet brocade. You looked most formidable rapping out commands even if there is still a small bit of shaving soap clinging to your chin."

Ravenel wondered if she was mocking him, but there was no doubting the sincerity of her admiration or the warmth of her smile. He flushed, his fingers moving self-consciously from the lapel of his dressing gown up to wipe at his chin. Damn the woman. She had a positive talent for disconcerting him.

He chose to ignore her comments, saying gruffly, "Now, Miss Vickers. What is all this nonsense about being robbed?"

" 'Tisn't nonsense. Follow me and I'll show you." Gesturing with her pistol, Miss Vickers led the way back to her room. The baron followed her, with Mr. Leatherbury hard after him, still mumbling, "Ridiculous. Impossible. Not at my inn."

But the landlord's manner changed rapidly when they stood looking down at the overturned trunks in the maid's room. He blanched and stammered, "B-but ... I can scarcely credit my eyes. I—I ... my dear, dear Miss Vickers. Do forgive me. That such a thing should have happened to you *here* at the White Hart."

Leatherbury proceeded to ply her with everything from a glass of wine to sal volatile. But the landlord looked in far greater need of smelling salts than Miss Vickers did. Ravenel could not help noticing that even under these trying circumstances Miss Vickers had a most becoming tint of rose in her cheeks. She waved aside all of the landlord's solicitude.

"You needn't worry, Mr. Leatherbury. I have never swooned in my life—not even the time my brother shot me in the foot with an arrow."

Ravenel, who had begun to make a cursory examination of one of the trunks, paused. He knew he would be better off not inquiring further into this startling statement, but his curiosity got the better of him.

"Your brother shot you with an arrow?" he repeated.

"It was over a wager. Jack thought that if I held a quill pen between my toes, he could nick off the top of the feathers." She sighed. "Of course, that was a long time ago, but I've never since had quite the same confidence in Jack."

"I—I daresay," Mr. Leatherbury said faintly.

Miss Vickers brightened. "But my father has bought Jack a commission in the army. I hope he will learn to have better aim with a musket."

Heaven help the British army, Ravenel thought, turning his attention back to the matter at hand. The maid's bed was obviously unslept in, the trunks opened by someone who had access to the keys and didn't have to force the locks. The conclusion was obvious to him, but all he said was, "And where is your maid this morning, Miss Vickers?"

"I don't know." She added, almost too quickly, "But that doesn't necessarily prove anything against her."

Ravenel thought it proved a great deal. He said, "I suggest we take steps to find the girl immediately. Leatherbury, you might begin by making inquiries among your servants. And the constable had best be sent for."

"Aye, at once, my lord." The distracted host appeared only too eager to be doing something. He rushed out still lamenting, "A robbery! Here! At my inn!"

Miss Vickers sank down upon the cot, ruefully biting her lip. "The poor man. I feel quite guilty somehow for having brought this distress upon him."

"You might have had the consideration to be robbed elsewhere, Miss Vickers," Ravenel agreed drily. "Most unkind of you."

She regarded him in surprise, then her ready smile flashed up at him. "Why, Lord Ravenel. You do possess a sense of humor after all."

His lips twitched in response to the marveling tone of her voice. It occurred to him that Miss Vickers looked rather charming for a lady who had just tumbled out of bed. Her chestnut curls danced about her flushed cheeks in appealing disarray, nigh tempting a man to smooth back the silken tangles from her brow. The peach-colored wrapper but served to highlight the creaminess of her skin along her delicate collarbone and graceful neckline. And as for the way the soft lawn night shift clung to the full curve of her breast . . .

Ravenel averted his gaze, embarrassed by the direction his thoughts were taking, and suddenly aware of the impropriety of their situation: alone in the maid's room, neither of them decently garbed.

The baron tugged at the sash binding his brocade dressing gown and cleared his throat. "Ahem. Well, you'd best summon that wilting chambermaid to help you dress. You do have something left to wear, don't you?"

"Yes." Gwenda plucked a drab-looking gown from the floor, regarding it with little enthusiasm.

"Then I will meet you belowstairs and we can decide how best to proceed."

Her dark lashes swept up as she shot him a look of mingled astonishment and gratitude. "Thank you, Lord Ravenel. 'Tis most gallant of you to concern yourself in this matter."

"Not in the least," he muttered, and then exited somewhat awkwardly from the room. If Gwenda was surprised by his behavior, Ravenel was astounded. What was he doing meddling in this business when his only desire was to avoid the eccentric Miss Vickers? He put his interference down to an irrational feeling of guilt. He could not help remembering that look he had seen on the maid's face the night before, the impulse to warn Miss Vickers that he had suppressed.

Not that he intended to be drawn too far into this affair. No, he would simply see to it that some responsible person was put in charge of helping the lady and then he would be on his way to Brighton.

After returning to his own room, he explained briefly what had happened as Jarvis helped him to dress. The old man clucked his tongue sympathetically. "Poor Miss Vickers."

"Yes," Ravenel agreed with an absent frown, noticing for the first time that Bertie was still in his room. The dog had made himself quite comfortable, falling asleep on the baron's bed. Bertie didn't stir until Ravenel made ready to leave. Then the dog stood up, yawned, and followed him.

Anyone would think the beast belonged to *him*, Ravenel thought, grimacing, as he made his way downstairs. He found Miss Vickers already there, ensconced in the same private parlor that had witnessed their first unfortuitous encounter the day before.

Garbed in that unbecoming maroon gown, she sat in a straight-backed chair fingering her bonnet with a most forlorn expression on her face. She scarcely took notice of the cup of tea the solicitous Leatherbury placed upon the table beside her.

When Ravenel entered, the host met his questioning look with a frown. "The maid seems to have vanished, my lord, and Miss Vickers has been telling me her fears that a sleep-inducing agent was introduced into her milk last night. We have no choice but to conclude that Mademoiselle Colette was the culprit."

This information occasioned the baron no surprise, but Miss Vickers's expression did. Earlier she had not been in the least perturbed to find her belongings plundered; now she appeared excessively troubled.

She fetched a heavy sigh. " 'Tis not that I mind so much about my things—'twas only a parcel of frocks and fripperies after all. But it is most distressing to be hoodwinked by a person one knew and trusted."

Aye, thought Ravenel. Miss Vickers, for all her grim imaginings about villains and evildoers, was exactly the sort of lady who would trust everyone, who cherished complete faith in her fellow creatures. As he observed the puzzled hurt welling in her luminous green eyes, he was astonished to feel a strong urge to find that ungrateful French trollop and wring her neck.

He strode up to Gwenda, took her hand, and patted it. "My dear Miss Vickers, a dishonest wench like that is hardly worth fretting over. I am sure it will be only a matter of time before she receives her just punishment and your belongings are returned."

Gwenda glanced up at Ravenel, astonished by both the gesture and the gentleness of his tone. The kindness and sympathy on his face did much to mitigate the natural severity of his features. She wondered if the man had any notion how devastating his eyes were when they glowed softly like that. His hand was quite large and strong, engulfing her slender fingers in a warm clasp. She felt oddly breathless and had difficulty concentrating on what he was saying.

"Mayhap there might be some clue in your maid's background, Miss Vickers. Who referred her to your service?"

His palms were slightly callused, very likely from riding. She could picture him masterfully gathering up the reins of a fiery black stallion, its glossy mane the same midnight color as his hair.

"Miss Vickers?" Ravenel prodded gently.

Gwenda came out of her daydreaming with a start. He had been asking her something. What was it? Oh, yes. Colette's character reference.

"She didn't have one."

"Didn't have one!" the baron echoed, looking nonplussed.

"No, we met her one day in a millinery shop. Mama hired her because she spoke such beautiful French."

Neither Ravenel nor Mr. Leatherbury appeared to be following her logic, so Gwenda explained patiently, "My mother is deeply concerned about Napoleon, the threat of a French invasion. She thought it would be good if we perfected our command of the language."

"But—but," Mr. Leatherbury protested, "why didn't she engage a tutor?"

"I didn't need a tutor," Gwenda said. "I needed a maid."

Ravenel's mouth snapped shut. He dropped her hand as though she had suddenly contracted some contagious disease.

"Of all the cork-brained—" He drew himself up erect and fixed her with a stern eye. "Are you giving me to understand that you simply plucked this woman out of the streets?"

"Not out of the streets," Gwenda said, resenting his tone. "Out of a hat shop."

He shook his head in disgust. "Then I fear you have gotten exactly what you deserved, Miss Vickers."

Gwenda was stunned by his change of attitude. But if he had suddenly lost all sympathy for her, she was beginning to feel quite out of charity with him, especially when he launched into a long homily about the folly of hiring servants without references.

This was Lord Ravenel at his positively most stuffy, Gwenda thought. When he squared his shoulders in that pompous manner, she longed to stick a pin into him. She crossed her arms over her chest, wondering how such a man could ever have made her heart skip a beat, even for the barest instant.

The baron was so caught up in lecturing her that

he appeared not to notice the ostler who slipped into the room and beckoned to Mr. Leatherbury. Whatever the burly groom whispered to the landlord, poor Leatherbury went chalk-white, darting a glance of terror at his lordship.

". . . and I have never had a servant in my employ," Ravenel was saying, "upon whose character I could not stake my own reputation."

"M-my lord," Leatherbury said. He approached the baron with all the abject timidity of a rabbit coming to impart bad tidings to a fierce-maned lion. When the host momentarily lost his power of speech, Ravenel prompted impatiently, "Yes, man. What is it?"

"M-more misfortune, your lordship." Leatherbury swallowed. "W-we now know how the wench made her escape. S-she t-took your phaeton and . . . ," the host concluded in a voice that was barely audible, "your bays."

"My bays?" Ravenel choked, then repeated in a much louder voice, "*My bays!* Your grooms allowed that scheming baggage to take my horses!"

Leatherbury cowered away from him. Even Gwenda felt herself tense at the fury vibrating in the baron's voice. So that was how a man looked when he is enraged enough to commit murder with his bare hands. She had gotten that all wrong in her second book.

The ostler spoke up. "Nay, me lud. 'Twas one o' the young stable lads wot made the mistake. 'Twas during the confusion when the night stage was coming through. The girl had yer ludship's tiger with her, a-wearing yer own livery and he says as how they was off to fetch a doctor fer yer ludship."

"My tiger?" Ravenel repeated numbly. "Dalton?"

"Aye, the same, me lud."

Gwenda tried to remain nobly silent but couldn't. "How shocking! I suppose the man had a great many character references, Lord Ravenel?" she inquired sweetly.

His lordship spun around, the fierceness of his gaze causing Gwenda to shrink back in her chair. "It so happens I dismissed that man from my service just yesterday, Miss Vickers. But as to character, Dalton was quite satisfactory until your doxy of a maid got her hooks into him."

"I suppose Colette abducted your Dalton and forced him to steal your horses and ..." Gwenda paused in the midst of her indignant little speech, and mulled it over in her mind. "Goodness, that would be a diverting twist to a tale, wouldn't it? I wonder what my publisher would think."

She wasn't sure, but she could tell full well what Ravenel thought. His mouth was pinched together in a thin white line to keep from cursing aloud.

"Where the dev—Where is that constable, Leatherbury?"

"I-I'll just find out what's keeping him, my lord." Leatherbury scuttled out with Ravenel hard upon his heels. Gwenda bit back a smile. She liked the baron much better when he was on a rampage than when one of his stuffy spells came over him. She supposed it was too bad of her to have teased him. The loss of some small change and clothing was nothing compared to the loss of a fine pair of blooded horses.

But she doubted a village constable was going to prove of much help to his lordship. He would be better off pursuing the miscreants himself or hiring a professional thief-taker.

The only bright spot of the morning came when her footman James sought her out to tell her the

71

carriage brace had been fixed. She could depart for Brighton any time she was ready, which was not likely to be long, Gwenda thought philosophically. It was not as though she had a great deal to pack.

With Bertie whisking by her side, Gwenda was on her way upstairs to do so, when the boots passed by her, going down. The lanky young man appeared just as agitated as the rest of the inn staff by all the untoward happenings.

"Ain't it just awful, miss?" the boots moaned. "Such doings at the White Hart I never thought to see. And to top it all, someone's gone and pinched one of them Hessians his lordship gave me to polish. I ask you, what would anyone want with just one boot?"

Thankfully, the man rushed on his way without waiting for an answer, as Gwenda felt a flush steal into her cheeks. She froze upon the stair, glancing down at her dog. "Oh, Bertie," she whispered. "You didn't."

The innocent wag of his tail told her nothing, but she knew Bertie could contrive to look unconcerned even with bits of leather sticking between his teeth. With a sinking feeling she returned to her own room.

She finally located Ravenel's boot under the bed she had slept in. The rolled-down leather top looked as though it had been attacked by a party of rabid squirrels.

"Bertie, how could you?" Gwenda moaned. "Out of all the guests at this inn, why did you have to single out Lord Ravenel's boot?"

Bertie whined and hung his head, looking suitably ashamed.

"I've seen that performance before," she said bitterly. "Half the actors at Drury Lane should do remorse so well. No, get away. I will not pet you, sir. You have sunk yourself completely beneath reproach this time."

She snatched up the boot and thrust the dog out of her path. Bertie trailed after her as she marched into the hall, squaring her shoulders. Well, mayhap if she was lucky, she would find Jarvis first. She had a feeling the elderly valet would accept the return of the Hessian much more kindly than Ravenel would.

But her luck was out. There was no sign of the dignified valet. The baron was far more easy to locate. Gwenda discovered him in the stableyard, shouting at the unfortunate Leatherbury.

"What do you mean there are no post-horses available?"

The landlord's cherubic face quivered. He appeared about to burst into tears. "I am sorry, my lord, but there isn't a one. I don't even have a horse of my own to lend you. The best I could do is a farmer's donkey or . . . or if you would care to wait, something might be had from the next village."

"I don't care to wait. Between your ostler's carelessness and that fool of a constable, I have been delayed here long enough."

Gwenda crept up behind Ravenel, holding the boot behind her back. Now she understood how poor Mr. Leatherbury must have felt earlier when he had to tell his lordship about his stolen bays.

"Lord Ravenel!" she called.

He stiffened at the sound of her voice. Then he spun about and favored her with an impatient glance. "What is it, Miss Vickers?"

"I—I found your other boot."

"I wasn't aware the blasted thing was missing."

73

She nodded unhappily and fetched the Hessian from behind her back.

"Thank you," he said curtly, taking the boot and starting to tuck it under his arm. He paused, his eyes arrested by the teeth marks on the top. Then his gaze shifted from the ravaged leather to where Bertie stood beside her panting, his tongue hanging in a foolish dog's grin.

Ravenel clenched his jaw until it quivered. Something seemed to explode inside of him.

"Damnation!" he bellowed.

So the man could swear after all, Gwenda thought, taking an awed step backward. "I—I am so sorry."

"Sorry!" His lordship strode a little away from her, his hands tightening on the boot as he strove to compose himself.

"Please. I know you've had an absolutely beastly time of it and 'tis partly my fault," Gwenda said, following him. "If you would only allow me to make amends. I could not help overhearing Mr. Leatherbury just now about the post-horses. My carriage is repaired. I could take you—"

"Certainly not," Ravenel ground out between his teeth. "I desire nothing except that you should keep your distance from me, madam. You—you are the absolute mistress of disaster!"

Gwenda flinched as if he had struck her. Before he said anything more that he would regret, Ravenel stalked back inside the inn, where Jarvis awaited him in the private parlor.

The baron plunked the damaged boot down. "Get rid of this thing."

Jarvis said nothing but quietly disposed of the Hessian. "I have ordered your lordship's breakfast."

"I am not in the least hungry," Ravenel snapped.

Indeed, he had a strong suspicion that even the most delectable beefsteak would have tasted like old shoe leather at that particular moment. He knew he was behaving like a temperamental schoolboy, and that realization did naught to soften his mood.

Not that he truly cared a damn about what that blasted hound had done to his boot. It was just the final blow to an already foul morning. Not only was his journey delayed another day, but he had lost his bays. He had been quite proud of those horses. Perfectly matched, they had cost him a tidy sum.

But he wasn't even sure if it was their theft that gnawed at him as much as knowing what a prize fool he had been made to look. Lecturing Miss Vickers about her servant and then to have one of his own commit a far greater crime . . .

Jarvis's gentle voice broke into his disquieting reflections. "You had no luck then, my lord, in obtaining another conveyance?"

"None, unless you wish to jog along by common stage or in a cart behind a farmer's donkey."

"I should not mind it, my lord," Jarvis said valiantly.

"But I should."

No, as much as Ravenel loathed the prospect of lingering about the White Hart, he knew he could not expose his valet to the hardships of the stage or the donkey. "Of course, we could always take Miss Vickers up on her generous offer," he said sarcastically.

"What was that, my lord?"

"To travel with her in her carriage."

To Ravenel's extreme consternation, Jarvis looked pleased by the suggestion. "That would be most kind of your lordship," the valet said. "I own

I have been concerned about that unfortunate young lady. Losing all her money and now no maid in attendance, left to travel all on her own."

"You might as well be concerned about Boadicea, the warrior queen." Ravenel snorted. "I'll wager she left far less havoc in her wake."

"The young lady does seem to have a penchant for getting into trouble, my lord. All the more reason she should not be permitted to journey to Brighton alone."

"That is her family's responsibility—not mine."

"Very good, my lord," Jarvis said. There was a shade of disapproval in his valet's eyes that Ravenel had never seen there before.

He squirmed, made most uncomfortable by it. Blast it, Jarvis didn't even know the half of it. Ravenel had never sworn or behaved with incivility to any female before. Miss Vickers had induced him to do both within twenty-four hours of her acquaintance.

Disquieting memories of the recent scene in the inn yard flashed through his mind. Gwenda meekly offering him the boot, trying desperately to apologize; the look of hurt in her eyes when he had lashed out at her. He would have to beg her pardon for that, but as to traveling with her . . . No, if for no other reason, it would be dashed improper.

He had an impulse simply to pen her a note of apology. It would be so much safer than going near the woman again, but his conscience would not allow for any such shirking.

At first he hoped—nay, *feared*, he amended—that she had already gone. But he encountered her coming down the inn stairs, swinging what was obviously an empty bandbox. She was wearing a bonnet that was nigh as hideous as her dress. The huge

76

poke seemed to swallow her head, making the piquant face sheltered beneath it seem absurdly youthful, like a little girl got up in her mother's things. Her usually candid green eyes regarded him with a wariness that made him feel even more of a perfect brute.

He approached her stiffly. "Miss Vickers, I want to apologize for my behavior in the inn yard just now."

She gave him an uncertain half smile. "Oh, no. You had every right to be angry. It was terrible of Bertie, and I would be only too happy to pay—"

"I had no right," he said firmly. "You have suffered as much by these recent events as I have, and much more graciously, I might add. Please say that you forgive me."

"Of course I do." She held out her hand, her smile broadening into her customary expression of good humor. Ravenel thought it was rather like watching the sun breaking through the clouds on a dismal day and was astonished at the poetical turn his mind seemed to have taken of late.

Instead of merely shaking her hand, he carried it to his lips and brushed her long, slender fingertips with a kiss, thus surprising himself again. It was a gallant gesture he rarely felt comfortable according any lady.

Miss Vickers neither blushed not simpered in the annoying way of most society misses. Her green eyes sparkled with pleasure.

She gave his hand a squeeze. "Good. I am so glad we are friends again. Now mayhap you will reconsider my offer to make use of my carriage."

" 'Tis very kind of you, but it would not be proper," he explained patiently as though to a child. "You see, you have no female companion with you."

"But we would be in Brighton before nightfall. And if anyone asked"—Gwenda nodded toward a point beyond his shoulder—"we could tell them that your Jarvis there is my uncle. Such a distinguished-looking man. I should not mind at all claiming him for my relative."

Ravenel glanced around to see that Jarvis had come up behind him. The elderly manservant was blushing like a peony.

Ravenel shook his head. "No. I fear, Miss Vickers, such proceedings would be most unwise."

"Oh, please. At least let me convey you to another inn where you could hire a post chaise. I do feel so wretchedly responsible for the fix you are in."

The baron prided himself on being rigid to the point of inflexibility once he had made a decision. But he had never in his life encountered such wide, pleading green-gold eyes. Well, he thought, relenting, what harm could it do to go at least part of the way with Miss Vickers and make sure she was headed safely on the way to her destination this time.

"Very well." He sighed. "If you do not mind waiting a few moments while I gather up my things."

Jarvis looked pleased, Miss Vickers delighted. The only one yet suffering from qualms was Ravenel himself. But what could possibly happen between here and the next town?

He clung to that sanguine opinion until he saw Miss Vickers's equipage being brought around. It was a spanking new coach, and smart enough. But the footman who tossed the baron's portmanteau up onto the back was a scruffy, ill-favored lad, half drowning in a livery too large for him, the sleeve of which showed signs of being employed as a handkerchief.

Yet it was the coachman, Fitch, who was Ravenel's chief concern. The man perched upon his box. Beside him Spotted Bert panted as though eager for the journey to begin. The dog looked far more ready than Fitch. The poker-stiff coachman's tensed hands knotted about the reins in a way that Ravenel knew marked the most amateur of whips.

As for the team, his lordship's expert eyes knew a mismatched set when he saw it. He would have wagered his last groat that those restive wheelers were beset with a tendency to break into a gallop every chance they got.

This is a grave mistake, a stern voice warned him, but Miss Vickers was smiling up at him, waiting to be handed into the coach. Ravenel had no choice but to do so, then spring up after her, as he wondered what he had let himself in for now.

Chapter 4

As the carriage lumbered away from Godstone, Gwenda settled back against the squabs, wondering why she felt so absurdly pleased with herself. Mayhap it was a sense of satisfaction from having persuaded one of the stubbornest men in England to change his mind; mayhap it simply soothed her conscience to help to make some amends to his lordship after all the difficulties she had brought down upon him: the eavesdropping, the stolen bays, the ravaged boot.

But it was a satisfaction his lordship obviously did not share. Tensed into an attitude of pained resignation, Ravenel sat opposite her, his broad shoulders braced against the gentle sway of the well-sprung carriage. The reed-thin Jarvis appeared quite lost in his master's shadow, as Ravenel's large frame seemed to dominate the coach. Gwenda was conscious of her knees almost brushing against his, of the tight-fitting doeskin trousers that emphasized the muscular outline of his legs.

Gwenda was obliged to admit the real reason she took pleasure in Ravenel's accompanying her. The man intrigued her, with his stiff mannerisms so at odds with his gypsy-dark eyes, the humor and the temper that he took such pains to suppress even if it well nigh choked him, the gruffness that concealed a shyness, an uncertainty she found rather endearing in such a formidable-looking gentleman. Before they arrived at their destination, Gwenda resolved to coax him into relaxing the rigidity that threatened to carve premature age lines about his mouth and eyes and to wring at least one smile from the man.

As though becoming aware of her earnest regard, Ravenel shifted uncomfortably on his seat and then stared out the window with frowning concentration. His long fingers drummed upon his knee, beating out an impatient rhythm.

"Miss Vickers, I don't wish to sound as though I'm complaining," he said, "but if we continue along at such a snail's pace, I doubt any of us will reach Brighton this side of Michaelmas."

"Certainly we will. We always travel this slowly and still arrive well before nightfall. You see, Fitch—" Gwenda broke off and coughed discreetly into her hand. She had been in Ravenel's company long enough to realize he might find it unsettling to be told that her coachman was afraid of horses. She continued, "Fitch is a most cautious driver because my dog oft gets down to run with the carriage. Our nearest neighbor, Squire Bennington, tried to train Bertie as a coaching dog, but I am afraid he found Bertie rather lacking in—in *gentlemanly reserve*, so he gave the dog to me."

A chuckle escaped Gwenda. "Sometimes Bertie even—" She halted again. She'd best not mention that, either—that instead of running beneath the rear axle, her reckless dog would insinuate himself under the pole tip and race the forefeet of the wheelers and the leaders' flying hooves, wreaking such havoc on poor Fitch's nerves that he needed a drop of whiskey to steady himself. No, that bit of information would not help Ravenel to relax. His lordship already had little cause to be fond of Bertie.

But she had paused so long in her answer, she found the baron regarding her rather suspiciously. She swallowed and then concluded brightly, "Ah, sometimes Bertie runs the longest distances. You would be quite astounded."

"I sincerely trust not, Miss Vickers," Ravenel said with some feeling. "I have been astounded enough for one day."

"Of course," she said demurely, folding her hands in her lap and reassuring herself how right she was to withhold certain facts from his lordship. After all, Fitch had faithfully promised after the last time that he would never get foxed again.

The next instant the coach veered sharply to the left. Gwenda bumped her shoulder against the side and straightened, rubbing her bruised arm. She was well accustomed to the peculiarities of Fitch's driving.

Ravenel, however, appeared a little alarmed as he eased back Jarvis, who had thumped against him. His lordship peered out the window again, exclaiming, "What the deuce is your coachman doing, Miss Vickers? Why has he taken this turning off the main road?" Ravenel started to thump on the roof to get Fitch's attention, but Gwenda caught his sleeve.

"No, 'tis quite all right, Lord Ravenel. We always travel by the old route through East Grinstead, Uckfield, and Lewes."

"That's the longer way," he protested.

"Aye, but the road is in excellent condition and there is much less traffic."

And much less chance that Fitch would get them lost if they stuck to the old route. But Gwenda buried that thought behind an ingenuous smile. "Don't worry so, Lord Ravenel. I promise you we shall all be making merry in Brighton before the sun sets. I am sure you can hire yourself a rig as easily in East Grinstead as anywhere else."

"I suppose so." The baron settled back uneasily. "But I would think that Lord and Lady Vickers—at least *most* parents—would be concerned about their daughter after such an unexpected delay. I cannot think what they are about, letting you travel alone."

There it was again—that certain sharp edge, that hint of criticism that came into Ravenel's voice whenever he mentioned anything about her family.

"I am not alone." Gwenda bridled. "I have Fitch and James and Bertie, and I did have Colette. 'Twas only to have been a simple day's journey from my aunt's home in Richmond."

She winced at the memory. "I am fond of my Aunt Lucinda, but a more dreary house party you could not have imagined. There was a young man present who was about to write a book. I always seem to be introduced to someone who is just about to write a book. Mr. Pomfret spent hours regaling me with the plot—" Gwenda halted as a horrible fear struck her.

"You do not, by any chance, write, do you, Lord Ravenel?"

Ravenel's mouth twitched. "No, Miss Vickers. Naught but business letters."

"Thank goodness," she breathed. "Now if Jarvis does not, either, I shall feel quite safe."

The valet assured her most gravely that he was not that clever. For the first time, she noticed that among his lordship's belongings—his whip, riding gloves, and hat—that Jarvis had taken personal charge of, the first volume of her novel was included.

Gwenda glanced at Ravenel. "Oh! So you have been reading the book I gave you?"

There was a long pause and then he said, "I scarcely have had time to look at it. Quite frankly, Miss Vickers, I am not much interested in fiction, but Jarvis has been finding it most entertain—"

"Why, my lord," Jarvis interrupted. "Begging your pardon, sir, but you had me read you some of it only this morning."

Gwenda beamed at Ravenel in triumph. He shot his valet a quelling frown, but unperturbed, Jarvis continued, "Your lordship did not much care for the part where the hand was running amok, but you appeared to enjoy the scene where the count offered for Lady Emeraude."

"The marriage proposal?" Gwenda exclaimed with delight. "I knew your lordship would find that bit fascinating. Of course, it is somewhat exaggerated for the purposes of fiction, but it does give you some idea how you ought to go on with Miss Carruthers the next time—"

"Miss Vickers!" Ravenel's face suffused a dull red. If he had been relaxed at all, he was immediately all stiffness again. "If you do not mind, I have no desire to discuss my personal affairs."

Gwenda's gaze shifted from his lordship's crimson-stained cheeks to the valet, who was also looking slightly discomfited. "Oh, I see. I am sorry for having mentioned it. I naturally assumed Jarvis knew. My brother Jack confides everything in his valet, and Jarvis certainly looks the sympathetic sort to whom I would tell all my darkest secrets if—"

"Miss Vickers!" The baron let out an exasperated sigh. "Can you not get it through your head? It is you I object to discussing my affairs with. *You!* Besides being practically a stranger, I cannot see where you have had the experience to be offering me advice."

What! Did the man think simply because she was unwed that she had never had an offer? Gwenda drew herself up primly. "Indeed, I have, my lord. It so happens I have been engaged twice."

"Twice!" his lordship and Jarvis both gasped in the same breath. Ravenel's lips parted as though he meant to ask something. Then he appeared to change his mind and feigned a deep interest in the distant farmhouses snuggled into folds of green pastureland.

"Then what—" Jarvis began, then stopped, looking appalled at himself. "I beg your pardon, miss. I never intended to be so forward as to pry. I'm sure there must have been some great tragedy . . ."

"Nothing so dramatic," Gwenda said with a tinkling laugh. "I jilted them."

From the degree of shock that registered on the faces of both men, Gwenda felt she'd best hasten to explain. "I was very young the first time I fancied myself in love, barely sixteen. Jasper was such a delightful companion, but the minute we were engaged, he developed the most distressing habit of sighing and acting like a great cake over me."

"I thought you approved of men who behave so," Ravenel said, rather acidly.

"I like a man to be romantic, not silly. When Jasper took to writing poetry, I simply couldn't bear anymore."

His lordship appeared intrigued in spite of himself. "And the second one? What was his folly?"

"Marlon? His error was even worse." Gwenda offered him a smile brimming with mischief. "The minute the betrothal ring was slipped upon my finger, he started trying to change *me*."

Ravenel regarded her sternly, struggling to keep a straight face. But his mouth quivered, finally breaking into a grin that softened his harsh features. He chuckled. "Miss Vickers! You truly are the most abominable young lady. What shocking bad manners. Ending engagements, leaving a trail of broken hearts . . ."

"But you are laughing," she pointed out.

"So I am," he said, shaking his head at himself. "Much more time in your company and I fear you will have corrupted every notion I have as to what is sane and proper."

"Mayhap you set too high a value upon sanity, my lord."

"Mayhap, I do," Ravenel conceded with another smile.

"And as to broken hearts, both Marlon and Jasper are now quite happily wed. I did them the greatest kindnesses by releasing them." Gwenda became serious suddenly. "There is no greater tragedy than a loveless marriage. I hope that you—" She stopped, for once catching her wayward tongue in time. If she expressed her hope that Ravenel would make sure he was most sincerely in love with Belinda before proposing once more, Gwenda would only set his back up again, which would be a great pity. His lordship looked so devastatingly handsome when he smiled.

Curbing her urge to interfere, Gwenda steered the conversation into safer channels. She soon had both Lord Ravenel and Jarvis chuckling over her trials and tribulations as an authoress. They seemed to find particularly amusing how she had given herself the jitters when writing *The Dark Hand*. It hadn't helped matters the least bit when her brother Jack had suspended a stuffed glove on the end of a broom handle and tapped her on the shoulder with it. He had laid a wager on how far she would jump.

Thus merrily occupied, the time seemed to fly past, and before Gwenda realized it, the carriage had lurched to a halt and James was letting down the steps to help her alight into the stableyard of the Dorset Arms in East Grinstead.

Ravenel sprung down after her with his elderly valet following at a more sedate pace. Although Jarvis had greatly enjoyed all of Miss Vickers's lively chatter, he had spent the last mile puzzling over the lady's exact relationship to his young master. That his lordship appeared to find Miss Vickers a great nuisance was undoubtedly true, but it had been a long time since Jarvis had seen his master unbend enough to laugh so freely or even to indulge in a fit of temper.

Jarvis judged that Miss Vickers had a way of exploding into a man's life like a burst of fireworks, but he didn't think it would do Master Des any harm to have an occasional skyrocket erupting in his path. For all of Miss Vickers's little oddities, Jarvis quite liked the young lady.

It was with great regret that he watched his master hustle Miss Vickers into the Dorset Arms and settle her into a private parlor before excusing himself to see about the hire of a carriage.

As Ravenel bowed his way across the threshold, Jarvis managed to catch his lordship's eye.

"It does seem such a shame, sir," he whispered, "to be leaving the young lady alone—"

"Don't you start that again," Ravenel hissed. "Miss Vickers will be just fine. 'Tis only another three or four hours to Brighton from here—well, mayhap six the way her coachman drives. But she will arrive at dusk, and I have no intention of dawdling away the rest of my afternoon in this fashion."

Ignoring Jarvis's reproachful look, the baron closed the parlor door and went in quest of the landlord. For the first time since he arose that morning, luck seemed to be with him. The Dorset Arms could indeed provide his lordship with both a curricle and a spanking pair of grays.

Ravenel made arrangements to hire them immediately, steadfastly suppressing all notice of Jarvis's disapproval. By God, that Vickers woman seemed to have done a thorough job of bewitching his valet. Normally a stickler for the proprieties, why couldn't Jarvis see that it simply wouldn't do for the baron to keep trailing about with an unchaperoned lady? It was not as though he were her brother or even a distant cousin.

Besides that, he had all manner of pressing business awaiting him in Brighton, to say nothing of the need to engage some competent person to track down that rascal Dalton before the trail became completely cold. No matter how entertaining Miss Vickers might be—and Ravenel was prepared to concede that at times she was—he simply had no more time to waste.

With such thoughts churning in his head, the baron strode back briskly to the inn parlor to convey his thanks to Miss Vickers for having brought him as far as East Grinstead and to take his final farewell of the lady. He was even feeling gracious enough to express a polite wish that they might meet again one day.

His graciousness vanished when he swung the door open and found the private parlor empty. The luncheon he had ordered for Miss Vickers yet stood upon the oak table untouched.

"Blast the woman!" Ravenel muttered. "Can she never once be doing what is expected of her?"

He swiftly collared one of the waiters only to obtain the vague information that he believed the young lady "was wandering about out in the back somewheres behind the taproom."

Ravenel's mouth pursed into a grim line. Well, it seemed instead of a cordial farewell, he would be obliged to treat Miss Vickers to a lecture on the impropriety of unescorted females roaming too freely at public places.

Exiting through the front door, he quickly directed his footsteps toward the side of the inn opposite the stableyard. Fortunately for his temper, he had no difficulty finding the troublesome female. She was walking through the vegetable garden just outside the kitchen door. Shading her eyes with one hand, she peered at a distant line of birches as though she were looking for something.

The baron squared his jaw and strode purposefully in her direction. But before he had taken many steps, he saw a slim dandy emerge from the taproom. Garbed in a riding cloak with a ridiculous multiplicity of capes, the ginger-haired fop swaggered toward Gwenda, casting her a killing glance through his quizzing glass.

Damnation, Ravenel thought, clenching his teeth as he recognized the Honorable Frederic Skeffington. What perverse mischance of fate had planted that empty-headed swell here in East Grinstead at this most unfortunate moment?

" 'Pon my soul," Freddy drawled, sweeping into Gwenda's path, "I heard that Kent is called the garden of England, but I never expected to find a rose amongst the cabbages."

Instead of retreating or even offering the man a chilling stare, Gwenda merely politely requested Skeffington to move out of her way. "You see, I am looking for—"

The dandy smirked. "And you have found him, my dear."

"How could I possibly be wanting to find you? We are not even acquainted, sir."

"That situation is easily remedied."

Ravenel came up between them just in time to prevent Freddy from slipping his arm about Gwenda's waist. "You're going to be in need of a far different sort of remedy, Skeffington," he growled, "if you don't take yourself off at once."

Startled, the dandy drew back, eyeing his lordship from toe to crown through his quizzing glass. "Sobersi—I mean, Lord Ravenel! I thought you were still in London. Well, dish me!"

The baron's hands clenched into fists as he felt himself more than ready to comply with this request. Freddy's gaze settled on his lordship's knuckles, and the young man flushed with dismay, the glass slipping from between his fingers to dangle by its ribbon. "S-steady on, Ravenel, old man. If—if I had any notion the wench was already bespoken—"

"I am here to escort the *lady* back to her aunt," the baron ground out.

"Her aunt? Quite so." The dandy looked abashed.

"I completely misunderstood. I trust you will forgive me, Miss—Miss . . . ?"

But before Gwenda could supply her name, Ravenel took a menacing step closer to Skeffington.

"Yes, yes, I—I'll just be going," Freddy concluded. "P-pleasant seeing you again, my lord." The dandy took to his heels and fled back to the inn.

Ravenel battled an urge to charge after him and give him the thrashing he deserved. Freddy Skeffington had ever been a insolent dog. At the very least, Ravenel should have drawn his cork and—Suddenly appalled by his own thoughts, the baron allowed his hands to uncurl. What in the blazes was the matter with him? Although he frequently enjoyed a bit of exercise with his fists in the privacy of Gentleman Jackson's salon, never had he come close to doing anything so vulgar as actually engaging in a brawl. He had the feeling that he had just made a complete spectacle of himself. To add to his sense of mortification, he spun around to find Gwenda nearly doubled over with the effort to suppress her chuckles.

"Don't you dare laugh at me." Furiously, Ravenel shook one finger at her. "As usual, this entire wretched scene is your doing, laying yourself open to the advances of one of the most unprincipled rattles in England who—who . . ." His words trailed off, becoming incoherent when she startled him by seizing his hand and pressing it between her own. Her mirth faded; her smile waxed more gentle.

"I wasn't laughing at *you*, Lord Ravenel," she said earnestly, a soft light coming into her eyes. "I must confess I didn't think that Mr. Skeffington appeared much of a dangerous rakehell, but all the same you were perfectly splendid. No knight charging to the rescue of his lady could ever have appeared more fearsome."

"That will do, Miss Vickers. No need to turn this into a scene from one of your novels." The baron hastily disentangled his hand from hers. He was not accustomed to being admired by a lady, and never had any shown a tendency to see him in the role of a knight errant. Rather sheepishly, he had to admit the image was not entirely displeasing.

"You will at least allow me to thank you," she said.

"The best thanks would be if you could contrive to stay out of trouble for five minutes." He attempted to maintain a stern front. "You shouldn't go about risking your reputation by drawing the attention of strange men, especially one the cut of Freddie Skeffington."

"Why? Is he really such a loose screw?"

"You should not use such cant terms, either, but yes. That is exactly what he is and—"

"He did have the most interesting cloak," Gwenda interrupted.

"I was not discussing his cloak, Miss Vickers, but your habit of—"

"You would look well in a cloak like that." She tipped her head to one side in a thoughtful, considering manner. "Of course, not with such a ridiculous number of capes. Two or three tiers would suffice."

"Miss Vickers!"

"Yes, two capes would accent the width of your shoulders nicely."

Ravenel resisted the ungentlemanly urge to clap a hand over her mouth so that she would be forced to listen to him. "Would you kindly stop changing the subject," he said irritably. "What were you doing out here alone, anyway?"

"I was looking for Bertie. He has run off again."

"That cursed dog! Whose shoe has he pinched this time?"

"No one's. He spotted a cat to chase." She shrugged apologetically. " 'Tis Bertie's other fatal weakness."

His lordship heaved an exasperated sigh. Seizing her by the elbow, he started to propel Gwenda back toward the inn. "You might have asked me to look for the infernal creature instead of waltzing about where you could be accosted by any ruffian chancing through here for a glass of ale."

Although she went along meekly enough, Gwenda voiced a mild protest. "I assumed a spinster such as myself would be safe, especially while garbed in this mousy gown. I am hardly a green girl anymore, you know."

Ravenel snorted. "Miss Vickers, you are just about as green as those eyes of yours. As for that gown, dismal as it is, that sheer fabric does nothing to disguise the fact . . ."

He slowed his step as his gaze was drawn involuntarily to the outline of Gwenda's hips, the tantalizing curve of her bosom. A lovely pink blush stole into Gwenda's cheeks, which only served to emphasize the impression the lady gave of wide-eyed innocence.

Damn! The baron swore under his breath. She would never be safe left on her own. The lady was too heedless, too trusting, and far too attractive. She strolled about with her head poked somewhere in the clouds with little notion of either the conventions or the perils of the real world.

He halted in his tracks, the decision looming up

before him like a tangible barrier, the decision that was as inevitable as the payment of land taxes or the occasional visit to the toothdrawer. His shoulders slumped with resignation.

"Come along," he said. "It is high time we returned to the carriage."

"We?" Gwenda asked, angling a surprised look up at him. "You mean to say there is no conveyance for you to hire here at East Grinstead, either?"

"No." Ravenel averted his eyes as he uttered the bald lie. " 'Twould seem I must impose upon your hospitality a while longer. At least as far as Lewes."

Aye, Lewes. There he could hire a rig and follow her the rest of the short distance to Brighton. They would not be seen to arrive together and he could still be sure she was deposited safely upon her family's doorstep, thus satisfying all that conscience, honor, and Jarvis could possibly demand of a fellow.

The baron cut off all of Gwenda's assurance that she would be delighted to have his continued company and hustled her toward the stableyard.

When Jarvis was informed of the change in their plans, he replied in wooden accents, "Very good, my lord." But Ravenel thought the old man had a most disquieting twinkle in his eye as he followed the baron and Miss Vickers toward the coach.

"But what about Bertie?" Gwenda asked, trying to hang back.

"I'll find him. You wait inside the coach. If Skeffington spots us together again and realizes you don't have an aunt, you won't have a shred of reputation left."

Gwenda dug in her heels even as her footman moved to open the carriage door. "You should have told Mr. Skeffington I was with my uncle and then Jarvis—"

"Skeffington would have no difficulty in recognizing Jarvis as my valet. *Get in*, Miss Vickers." Ravenel braced his arm about her waist and all but lifted her bodily into the vehicle.

"And don't let her escape," he ordered Jarvis, "before I get back with that blasted dog."

He did not wait for any acknowledgment of his command. He started off at once in pursuit of Spotted Bert. The task did not take him as long as he feared, for he had not gone many steps when Bertie came loping around the side of the stables. But he was obliged to waste considerable precious time removing some burrs from the animal's smooth coat.

"Serves you right," Ravenel muttered as Bertie let out a yelp when one prickly thorn stuck a little deeper than the rest. "Mayhap next time you'll think twice before you . . ." Horrified, he let his words trail off. Damn it, now *he* was starting to talk to the dog in much the same manner as he oft heard Gwenda do.

Ignoring Spotted Bert's licks of gratitude, the baron shooed the animal up onto his perch beside Fitch. Upon second inspection of Miss Vickers's coachman, his lordship decided he was no more impressed with the fellow than he had been earlier. Granted, Fitch appeared a little more relaxed, but his face was flushed and sweaty, his eyes shifting in a most guilty fashion away from Ravenel's when he informed the man they were finally ready to depart.

His sense of unease was not mitigated by noticing that the sun seemed to be slowly vanishing. Gray clouds scudded over the day's previous brightness; ominous shadows darkened on the horizon. If

Ravenel's own coachman had been sitting on the box, he would have directed him to spring the horses in order to gain some time before the rain broke. But with Fitch, Ravenel issued a stern admonition for him to drive with care.

"Shurtainly, my lord," Fitch mumbled, tipping his hat with a bovine smile. Then he gathered up the reins, his deep baritone voice breaking into a loud chorus of "The Girl I Left Behind Me."

As the baron took his seat in the carriage, he wondered in what unlikely place the Vickerses had found Fitch, but he was afraid to ask. The coach lumbered down the rutted lane, leaving East Grinstead behind them.

The gathering gloom beyond the carriage windows seemed to cast a pall over their party. They had not gone many miles when Gwenda felt her eyelids growing heavy despite the increased jouncing of the coach. After her drugged sleep of the night before, one would have thought she would feel well rested today. Instead, she somehow waxed more tired than usual. She struggled to stifle a yawn, but it was not easy, especially watching Jarvis nodding off in his corner.

She thought it would be intolerably rude of her to do likewise, but then Ravenel did not seem at all inclined for conversation. He was far too preoccupied with stealing frowning glances up at the sky and checking his pocket watch at periodic intervals.

Nestling her head against the squabs, Gwenda regarded the baron dreamily through half-lowered lids, her mind reverting to the incident in the garden of the Dorset Arms. Ravenel had been a sight to stir any maiden's heart: charging to her rescue with that fiercely protective light in his eyes, every muscle in his formidable masculine frame tensed for battle.

She had never been rescued before, Gwenda reflected with another yawn, had never had reason to be. It would have all been so perfect if, instead of a mincing, ginger-haired fop wielding a quizzing glass, Freddy Skeffington had been a shade more villainous, satanically dark, his cadaverous fingers gripping a twisted dagger. With such thoughts teasing her imagination, Gwenda's eyes drifted closed. . . .

. . . she was running across the deck of a ship, the tall masts lost in a ghostlike mist, her heart thumping in terror. Hunched beneath his layering capes, Captain Frederici was but a breath behind her. Risking one glance over her shoulder, she saw the glint of the evil pirate's single eye, heard his chilling laugh as his bony fingers reached out to grasp her arms. . . .

"Oh," Gwenda moaned, slumping down farther on the carriage seat. "Roderigo . . . help me!"

Even as she struggled in Frederici's cruel grip, another dark form leaped down from the rigging, the familiar scarlet-lined black cloak sweeping back from stalwart shoulders. Strong hands reached out to pluck the villain away from Gwenda, hurling the fiend into the sea. With a glad cry, Gwenda flung herself against her rescuer's chest, burying her face against stiffly starched white linen. . . .

Gwenda's nose twitched as she mumbled, "Roderigo, what are you doing with that cravat?" Her sleep-smoothed brow furrowed with confusion.

*The mists seemed to part, for once clearly reveal-
ing to her the features of Roderigo, Count de
Fiorelli. She caught a glimpse of a hard angular
jaw and cheekbones, a full, sensual mouth, and
flashing dark eyes set beneath heavy black brows—
all somehow disturbingly familiar. But the next instant his face vanished as the deck pitched beneath
Gwenda's feet, the ship heaving in the grip of the
storm. Roderigo lost his balance and fell on top of
her. . . .*

"Ow," Gwenda breathed, her eyes jerking open.
Wide awake, she was astonished to find herself still
pinned beneath Roderigo's hard-muscled frame. No,
it wasn't Roderigo at all. It was Ravenel who was
struggling to ease his weight from her—not an easy
task considering the way the coach was rocking
and swaying like a small ketch caught in a tidal
wave.

"What . . . what?" she faltered.

"It's that blasted coachman of yours," Ravenel
grated, managing to wrench himself to his feet.
"He's been picking up speed the last half mile or
so." Bracing himself, he strove to help Jarvis whom
Gwenda suddenly realized lay tumbled on the floor.

She snatched at the back of the seat to prevent
being tossed about any more than she already was.
From the slant of the carriage, she realized they
must be thundering up a hill at an appalling rate.
Through the window, she obtained a rollicking
glimpse of what seemed a world gone gray.

After hauling Jarvis back onto the seat, Ravenel
tried to bang on the coach roof and was nearly
overset on top of her once more. "That fool can't
take a hill at such an out-and-out clip," he shouted

at her, "or he'll never be able to check the team going down."

"I know that," Gwenda screamed back. "What do you expect me to—oh!"

Her reply was cut off as the carriage crested the hill and started on a mad downward plunge. As Ravenel collapsed on top of his valet, Gwenda lost her grip on the seat and tumbled across the baron's lap. For the next terrifying seconds, she, Ravenel, and Jarvis seem naught but a bruising tangle of arms and legs.

With a muttered oath, the baron shoved her ruthlessly off him. As Gwenda hit the coach floor with a jarring thud, she brushed the hair from her eyes to glare at him.

Ravenel had somehow gained his feet. "Damned fool," he muttered. "Got to do something before he kills us all." His jaw steeled with grim determination, he reached for the coach door.

With a flash of horror, Gwenda realized what he was contemplating. Her heroes often did such mad feats as climbing out of a racing coach to do battle with villains or to halt a runaway, but to see the baron about to attempt such a thing in earnest caused her heart to give a wild leap of fear.

"Ravenel! No—" she started to cry out, but a cracking noise split the air and the coach gave a sickening lurch to one side. The door was flung open, and before Gwenda's terrified gaze, Ravenel lost his balance and pitched out into the blur of dust beyond.

Chapter 5

Green . . . Ravenel's startled gaze registered a splash of green bare seconds before his body struck the ground. But it couldn't be grass, the ridiculous thought flashed through his mind. Grass couldn't possibly be so—oof!—damned hard.

The impact of his fall drove the breath from his lungs and sent him rolling over and over until he at last thudded to a halt. Closing his eyes tight, he attempted to dispel the black webbing that danced before him, to banish the ringing from his ears. His mind was a blur of confusion, except for the urgent need to draw a gulp of air into his pain-racked chest.

Several shuddering breaths later, the world finally seemed to stop spinning beneath him. He was lying flat on his back and something cold was brushing against his face. Forcing his eyes open, Ravenel focused on Spotted Bert's nose but a fraction from his own. The dog whined, then licked his cheek.

With a low groan, he shifted onto his side and cursed, trying to prevent Bertie from nuzzling his ear. One hand crushed a dandelion. He glanced down at it, his mind yet numbed with shock, trying to make some sense of his surroundings. He appeared to be sprawled in a pasture, marooned in the middle of nowhere with nary so much as a cottage visible or another living thing except Miss Vickers's dog.

Miss Vickers! The carriage. Memory sliced through his throbbing head like the cold, sharp edge of a razor. He had been thrown from the carriage just as . . .

Regardless of the pain that spiked along his bruised flesh, Ravenel jerked up onto one elbow, his gaze whipping down the narrow ribbon of dirt road to a point some hundred or so yards distant. His blood froze when he saw the carriage tipped into a ditch, the only figure in sight that fool of a coachman weaving on his feet as he struggled to cut the snorting, plunging horses free of the traces.

But where was Miss Vickers? Jarvis? Dreadful imaginings jolted through the baron, of both the lady and his valet yet trapped inside the coach, possibly bleeding and unconscious. Spurred by panic, he managed to drag himself to his feet. He limped from the meadow with Bertie trailing at his heels.

As soon as he drew near the road, much to his relief, he espied Miss Vickers and Jarvis helping to ease the footman on the grassy bank just above the ditch. James was wailing in a most unmanly fashion.

When Bertie barked, Miss Vickers's head snapped in Ravenel's direction. Releasing her hold on James, she came running down the road, her bonnet flying back, held only by its strings. Ravenel was excessively grateful to note that except for the pallor of her cheeks and the tear at the waist of her gown, she seemed to have no ill effects from the accident. As Bertie raced toward his mistress, the baron paused, expecting that Miss Vickers, overjoyed to find her pet unharmed, would embrace the dog.

He was therefore unprepared when she shoved past Bertie and flung herself against him, the fierceness of her hug nearly sending them both tottering over backward.

"Thank God," she cried, muffling her face against his chest. "I thought you must have been killed."

"Er, yes," Ravenel said gruffly to conceal how moved he was. He could not recall anyone ever becoming distraught over the prospect of his death. There was no doubting the genuineness of her distress. She was making no attempt to weep prettily, as Miss Carruthers would have done. Her breath came in great gulping sobs as she wreaked absolute havoc upon what remained of his cravat. His arms closed about her and he patted her back. "There now, Miss Vickers . . . Gwenda, my dear. Please, you must not upset yourself."

"B-but you terrified me half to d-death." She sniffled. "What—what possessed you to—to try such a mad thing?"

"I will admit it was not the most prudent thing I have ever done," he agreed soothingly. He cradled Gwenda closer, finding the sensation of her soft curves molding against him very agreeable.

But his sense of propriety and responsibility all too quickly reasserted itself. He could scarcely stand here in the middle of the road embracing Gwenda while Jarvis stood anxiously awaiting him, the footman continued to howl, and that dolt of a coachman was doing God knew what to those horses.

Ravenel eased Gwenda away from him. She wiped her eyes with her knuckles, looking a little flustered and mortified by her own tears. " 'Twould seem the only one injured is poor James," she said with a quavery smile. "What good fortune we have had."

"A-aye," he agreed, somewhat dubiously, rolling his eyes skyward. If this was Gwenda's notion of good fortune, she was going to be positively ecstatic when those stormclouds gathering over their heads broke. He turned and strode toward the embankment as quickly as his bruised hip would allow.

For a moment Ravenel feared even his stately Jarvis meant to fall upon his neck and weep for joy to find his "Master Des" yet in one piece. But although appearing much shaken, the old man as ever maintained his dignity. Gwenda skirted past Ravenel to bend down beside the footman, who sniveled and clutched his ankle.

Encouraged by Gwenda's murmur of sympathy, James wailed, "Ohhh, 'tis me leg, miss. I've broken it sure."

"Nonsense," she said bracingly. "If you had done that, the shaft of the bone would likely be protruding through your flesh and—"

Before she could reduce the lad to total hysterics, the baron nudged her aside and made a cursory inspection of James's foot himself. It was not easily done since the footman screeched like a banshee before Ravenel had laid so much as a finger on the injured area.

At last he pronounced, "No, 'tis not broken. Most likely the bone is but chipped, or 'tis a very nasty sprain. As soon as we—"

Ravenel broke off as another squeal pierced the air, but this one did not originate from the unfortunate James. Rather, it was an equine cry of fear. The horses and Fitch. The baron straightened abruptly, beginning to feel a little harried.

He spun about to peer at the front of the upset carriage. Fitch had managed to cut the horses loose, but now as the overexcited animals milled about, the coachman cowered back, wielding his whip as though surrounded by a pack of savage beasts.

"Stop that!" Ravenel bellowed, heading toward the man, but Fitch had already caught one of the leaders on top of its nose. The horse reared back and then charged down the road, rapidly followed by the other three.

"No! Damnation!" The curse escaped from Ravenel before he was aware of it. Although every muscle in his body shrieked in protest, he leaped down the bank and over the ditch and tore off after the horses. But even if he had been in top form, the pursuit would have been futile. The last horse he had backed at Newmarket should have set such a pace as those four, Ravenel thought bitterly.

He staggered to a halt, clutching his side, and watched their only hope of riding for help vanishing in a cloud of dust. Gwenda drew up breathlessly at his side, holding up her skirts.

"W-well," she said brightly. "At least we know that none of the horses were injured, either. We really have been remarkably lucky. I—I am sure the team will not go far and we will have no difficulty finding them."

The glare Ravenel shot her caused even Gwenda's unquenchable smile to waver. He thought he had held up well until now, considering he was not in the least accustomed to being flung out of carriages or finding his traveling schedule overset by unnecessary accidents. But this last bit of idiocy on the part of the Vickerses' coachman was entirely too much for any sane man to bear.

"Madam," he growled, "if I were a horse, I would flee all the way to hell before I let that cow-handed fool come near me again."

Whipping about, Ravenel advanced on Fitch, his wrath swelling with every painful step. But the coachman showed not the least sign of alarm, not even when the baron seized him by the collar of his driving cape. Rather, it was the baron who recoiled at the heavy odor of stale gin reeking from the man.

Despite the goose egg forming on his forehead, Fitch was obviously feeling no pain. He went limp, directing a muzzy smile past Ravenel at Gwenda.

"Was brave thish time, Mish Vickers," he mumbled. "Took care 'o the 'orses to the lasht."

With that, Fitch rolled up his eyes and sank against the baron in a heap. Ravenel lowered him to the ground none too gently, but the man still curled up on the stone-strewn road as blissfully as though it were a feather bed.

"Oh, dear." Gwenda sighed. "Fitch has shot the cat. Again."

The word *again* went through Ravenel like a cannon blast. "Again?" he asked with a most deadly calm. "Miss Vickers, what do you mean 'again'? Are you telling me that your coachman has a habit of drinking?"

"Well, I would not call it a habit, precisely. But he does like a drop now and again to steady his nerves because . . ." She faltered in the face of his furious stare, then concluded meekly, "Because he's afraid of horses."

"Afraid of horses?" Ravenel said through clenched teeth. It was probably ridiculous to even ask for an explanation, but for the sake of his own sanity, he felt he had to know. *"Then why the blazes did you allow him to drive your coach?"*

"It's rather a long story. You see, Papa organized this musical society and Fitch has the most wonderful baritone for singing catches and glees—"

"Perdition, madam!" Ravenel roared. "Do you people never hire your servants for normal, sane reasons like everyone else does? Did it never occur to your father that a coachman should have some experience, should feel comfortable handling a team?"

Gwenda's chin jutted upward in a defensive manner. "Papa always says that lack of experience should not bar a man from obtaining a situation. If everyone thought the way you do, my lord, how would anyone gain any experience to begin with?"

She sounded so entirely reasonable; it was he who was shouting like a lunatic. That realization did nothing to help Ravenel curb his temper. He raised his hands in a gesture rife with frustration.

"You and your entire family are stark raving mad. And I must be madder still to have ever traveled one inch in your company."

Gwenda flushed bright red, but before she could voice whatever comment trembled on the tip of her tongue, Jarvis appeared, wedging himself between them.

"That will do, Master Desmond," he said sternly, making Ravenel feel all of nine years old again. "I scarcely see that shouting at the young lady will do aught to remedy our situation."

"There is not much else to be done," the baron said, "when here we are, left stranded in the middle of who knows where."

Gwenda bent sideways around Jarvis to glare at Ravenel. "I know precisely where we are. Or—or almost. There is an inn not more than a mile from here. I shall walk there and fetch help."

"Hah!" Ravenel snorted. "You'll do nothing of the kind. Do you think I would set you loose upon an innocent countryside?"

"Master Desmond!" Jarvis looked positively scandalized.

But the baron felt pushed well past the brink of civility or any kind of gentlemanly behavior. Considering the condition of the coachman and James's injury, it was patently obvious to him who would be obliged to go trudging in search of aid. But Miss Vickers hotly refuted the suggestion.

"You? You could not possibly find the place. I have only the vaguest notion myself and would have no way of giving you directions."

"And *this*," Ravenel sneered, "from the woman who declares she knows precisely where we are."

As Gwenda bristled with indignation, Jarvis quickly interposed, " 'Twould seem that the most sensible solution, my lord, would be for you to escort Miss Vickers—"

"I should as lief be escorted by Bertie," Gwenda said.

The baron also voiced his own objection to this scheme. "No, Miss Vickers must stay with you, Jarvis. Do you expect me to leave you alone to cope with one man injured and another drunk?"

Jarvis drew himself up to his full dignity. "I have been coping with all manner of disasters since well before you were born, Master Desmond. But if you now think me such a feeble old man, mayhap it is time I served you notice."

Ravenel bit back an oath. To add to all the other disasters, now he had offended Jarvis. He paced a few furious steps down the road, experiencing a discomfiting feeling of having no control over the situation. At last he conceded with bad grace, "Very well, I shall take you with me, Miss Vickers—"

"How utterly noble of you," Gwenda interrupted in a voice dripping sarcasm.

"—because I am sure Jarvis will be far safer if I do."

"Why, you—you—"

But his lordship did not give Miss Vickers a chance to think up a name bad enough to call him. He moved quickly, dragging the inert coachman off to the side of the road. He examined the wrecked carriage to see if it would prove steady enough to provide some sort of shelter and then settled Jarvis and James inside, making them as comfortable as possible. With a mighty heave, he managed to thrust Fitch's unconscious form onto the coach floor.

He paused briefly in the midst of these exertions to warn Gwenda, "We are going to have to hasten. The next we know, we shall be caught in a thunder shower."

"It is not going to rain," she said loftily. "I have seen those sort of clouds frequently before. They may threaten all day, but the storm never breaks until well after dark."

An hour later, Ravenel, Gwenda, and her dog were yet shuffling wearily down the road, the woodland thickening around them and overshadowing their path.

The baron hunched down, drawing up his collar. "It is starting to rain, Miss Vickers," he informed her in long-suffering accents.

"I am perfectly aware of that, my lord," Gwenda snapped, feeling one large drop splash and trickle down the back of her neck. Even Bertie's tail drooped, the water starting to bead on his glossy black-and-white coat.

Gwenda, accustomed to meeting the direst of calamities with a philosophical good humor, felt more cross than she could ever remember. Step after wretched step they had traveled, with no sign of the inn or the village she had sworn was there. Ravenel said nothing, but from his grim expression she knew it would be only a matter of time before she was treated to another of his long homilies on her scatter-brained ways. Her anticipation of this did little to soothe her temper.

She wrapped her arms about herself as the rain started to come down harder, shivering with the knowledge that she would soon be soaked to the skin. Ravenel stripped off his coat. But the gallant gesture was somewhat diminished by the manner in which he thrust it at her.

"No, thank you," she said. "After everything else, I should not like to have you blaming me if you get a chill."

She gasped when he seized her by the arm and halted her in the middle of the road. He roughly whipped his coat about her shoulders. When she started to discard it, he caught her hand.

"Miss Vickers. Attempt to remove that frock coat and I shall not be answerable for what I might do. Until I met you, I would have sworn that I would never shout at, curse, or strike a lady. You have already provoked me into the first two. . . ." He let the sentence trail off in ominous fashion.

With two brothers Gwenda had learned long ago not to allow herself to be bullied, but Ravenel made a most formidable figure towering over her. Some elusive memory tugged at her as she studied the piercing light in his dark eyes, the rainwater glistening on his swarthy skin, his wet garments outlining the stalwart set of his shoulders like some storm-swept buccaneer. Then, with a jolt, she realized what it was. Dear heavens, Ravenel looked just like Roderigo had in her recent dream. Or had it been that Roderigo resembled Ravenel? Either way, it was a most disconcerting discovery to make at this particular moment.

"Thank you," she grumbled, allowing the coat to remain around her shoulders. "But, in the future, I wish you would have the goodness to stay out of my dreams."

The baron looked startled, but to Gwenda's relief he merely shook his head and did not question the strange comment she had let slip. As they resumed their trek, he lapsed into his own dark thoughts. After a time, Gwenda saw his lips move as though he were counting something.

"If you have aught to say"—she winced as she trod in a puddle, the water seeping inside her already damp slipper—"I wish you would just say it. It is an odious habit of yours—thinking so loudly."

"I was merely making a tally, Miss Vickers. In the last twenty-four hours I have witnessed the loss of six horses and two carriages. It staggers the imagination."

"*My* carriage is not lost! I know exactly where it is."

"Just as you knew exactly where this elusive inn was to be found."

"We might have stood some chance of finding it if you had let me inquire at that farmhouse we passed awhile back." The miserable way in which Gwenda's sodden skirts were beginning to cling to

110

her legs inspired her with an unreasonable urge to shift all the blame for their trouble on to Ravenel.

"It is a peculiarity of men I have frequently noticed," she said. "You can never bear to ask directions or admit when you are lost."

The baron slicked back his rain-soaked dark hair. "At that farmhouse all you would have achieved was the farmer's wife setting her dogs upon us. We are not precisely the most reputable-looking couple, Miss Vickers."

As Ravenel plodded along, he drew himself rigidly upright. Gwenda set her teeth, knowing what was coming.

"If you had not been so insistent in the first place that you knew the way, I would have felt more of a need to make inquiries. But then it is all of a piece with your manner of conducting a journey, ill-conceived and ill-advised—"

"Kindly do not start doing that again!" Gwenda stomped her foot, which had the effect of pelting them both with an additional spray of water.

"Doing what?" his lordship demanded.

"Lecturing me in that pompous manner. It is another annoying habit of yours. Anyone would think you—you were some aged grandsire tyrannizing over a flock of unruly grandchildren."

"Not grandchildren, Miss Vickers, but as the head of my family I do have responsibility for many dependents, younger cousins whom I frequently have had to *lecture*, as you put it."

"*That* must make them all positively dote on you."

Ravenel flinched as though she had hit upon some painful point, but the expression was so fleeting she might well have imagined it. She nearly regretted her spiteful remark, but he quickly

111

recovered himself and began to intone, "One's duty is not always pleasant, either for—"

"Oh, do stop! You are beginning to remind me of Thorne again."

Ravenel shot her a questioning glance from beneath his rain-drenched brows.

"My eldest brother, the most holy, the most God-fearing Reverend Thornton Vickers. Jack and I always call him Thorne because that's what he was—a thorn in our sides, forever prosing on and tattling on us. It is very irritating to be in the company of someone who always considers himself so superior."

Even in the gloomy half light, Gwenda could see how Ravenel flushed. Although he appeared chagrined, he said, "I suppose you think I should find that comparison unflattering. But it so happens I do not. It is most heartening to hear that at least one member of your family is respectable. Where does Reverend Vickers hold his living?"

"He doesn't have one anymore." A hint of wicked satisfaction crept into Gwenda's tone. "Thorne ran off to become a Methodist. He does most of his preaching in sheep pastures these days."

Lord Ravenel made no effort to stifle his groan.

"Aye, even Thorne is but another one—" What had his lordship called her family earlier? "—one of the *raving mad* Vickers," Gwenda filled in, somewhat bitterly. "I daresay you think the whole lot of us ought to be locked up in Bedlam."

The baron hunched his shoulders, looking uncomfortable, but his jaw squared stubbornly as he replied, "Even you must confess that your family does not exactly march in tune with the rest of the world."

"I thank God that they don't!"

112

"And that any sort of common sense, notions of propriety, or a well-ordered existence—"

"In my family, enthusiasm and dreams and . . . and imagination have always been valued above your odious common sense. As for your stuffy notions of order, they don't seem to have done much for you. You are one of the most unhappy, bad-tempered men I have ever encountered."

"I had not the least problem with my temper, Miss Vickers, until I—"

"I know! Until you met me." Gwenda choked, an unaccountable lump rising into her throat. She had never felt the need to defend herself or her family before. But his lordship's critical attitude was beginning to raise doubts in her own mind about the delightful skimble-skamble household in which she had been raised, doubts that were far more dampening to her spirits than the rain weighting down her skirts.

His lordship drew up short. "Well, my *odious common sense* tells me we may as well turn back. There is obviously nothing down this road but more trees."

"There is nothing back the way we came, either." Gwenda stubbornly kept on going. When she became aware that Ravenel was not following, she turned to glance impatiently at him. She was annoyed to see that Bertie had halted as well, hanging about his lordship's heels. Even when she called his name, the disloyal hound refused to come to her.

"We are turning back, Miss Vickers," Ravenel said. "We need to find some sort of shelter immediately. I thought I heard thunder just now, and if lightning starts up, I don't care to be walking anywhere near you."

He had said worse to her, but for some reason this last comment brought an unexpected moisture to Gwenda's eyes that had naught to do with the rain. "What a p-perfectly mean thing to say." She whipped about so that he would not see her foolish tears. "You may do as you please, my lord. But *I* am going on."

Gwenda had scarcely taken more than a half-dozen steps when she heard him coming after her. She dashed rain and salt water from her eyes, then stiffened, fully prepared to resist if he attempted to turn her about by force. To her astonishment, he merely proceeded to arrange his coat more firmly about her—a ridiculous gesture, for the garment was as sopping as her gown beneath.

"You are right, my dear," he said softly. "It *was* mean. I have been behaving in a most boorish fashion and I do beg your pardon."

Gwenda tried to harden her heart against him, but it was difficult to do so when the harsh planes of Ravenel's face were gentled by the hint of warmth in his eyes. As she falteringly accepted his apology, she found that she could not meet his gaze. He astonished her further by tucking her arm firmly within the crook of his and guiding her down the road with as much solemn gallantry as though they were taking a stroll through St. James's Park. Although the rain descended upon them in even harder gusts and a threatening rumble of thunder shook the sky, Gwenda experienced a strange feeling of being warm and secure.

Then, as if by some kind of fairy's magic, when they rounded the next bend of the road, she espied the outlines of a building set back amidst the trees.

"Ravenel, there it is," Gwenda said excitedly. "The inn I told you about." Her spirits soared as she felt vindicated. She had been leading the baron in the right direction all the time.

She was pleased to see his lordship looking considerably heartened. Giving her hand a squeeze, he said, "My dear, dear Miss Vickers. Pray forgive my ever having doubted you. May wild horses tear me in two if I ever cast aspersions upon your judgment again."

She giggled when, despite the rain beating down upon them, he paused to sweep her a mock-gallant bow, exhibiting a playful side to his nature that she would never have dreamed he possessed. For once Ravenel seemed to share her feelings of being nigh giddy with the relief of seeing their ordeal about to come to an end, with the prospect of a warm fire, a dry shelter, and a place to rest aching feet.

Linking arms once more, Gwenda and Ravenel splashed through the puddles like a pair of rowdy urchins. Bertie raced ahead of them, barking, showing more frisk than he had the past mile and more. Gwenda's mood of exhilaration did not abate until they slogged through the mud of the yard itself. But as she glanced about her, her heart slowly sank with dismay. This was not any inn she had ever patronized and she found herself wishing she was not about to do so now.

The tumbledown stables appeared fit for nothing but sheltering the most spectral sort of horses. Far from the comforting bustle to be found at the White Hart, not so much as one carriage, one groom, or one ostler was to be seen. The puddle-soaked yard appeared so deserted that Gwenda jumped at the loud banging of a stable door. Her flesh prickled with the uncanny sensation of being watched. And Bertie, her friendly-to-a-fault Bertie, emitted a low growl from his throat.

She all but flung herself against Ravenel's chest when the inn itself was illumined by a jagged flash of lightning. If she had been designing a roost for bandits or a home for wayfaring ghosts, or even conjuring up an isolated spot for murder to be done, her imagination could not have produced anything that would rival this place. It was a most decrepit-looking Tudor structure: the wooden beams projected an aura of decay, the mullioned windows glared like baleful dark eyes. The inn sign creaked in the wind, its chipped paint depicting a scantily clad prizefighter, its faded letters proclaiming *The Nonesuch*.

Ravenel eased Gwenda away from him. The rain pelted his face as he tipped back his head to glance at the sign and she could tell he had already forgotten his recent vow not to cast any more aspersions on her judgment. His whole manner was one of insufferable resignation, as though he had been expecting all along that she would bring down some fresh calamity upon his head.

"It is much more congenial on the inside," Gwenda said, feeling her defensive hackles start to rise.

She watched the baron reach for the wrought-iron door handle and had to fight back an urge to stop him. But what could she say? That the Nonesuch gave her a very bad *feeling*? Ravenel would only fancy her a bigger fool than he already did. She had no choice but to suppress her forebodings.

The rusted iron hinges screeched like an evil bird of omen as he thrust wide the inn door.

Chapter 6

. . . the castle walls, cold and bleak, closed about the Lady Emeraude like a well of doom. The stones themselves seemed wrought of evil, mortared with the blood of innocents, weathered by fingers plucking at them in despair. . . .

"Miss Vickers! You are cutting off the flow of blood through my arm."

The baron's protest jarred Gwenda out of her imaginings. She suddenly realized how tightly she had been clutching him as they crossed the threshold of the Nonesuch.

"S-sorry." She forced herself to release him, then nearly tripped over Bertie, who bounded in ahead of her. As his lordship slammed the door closed behind them, she thought she knew how her poor heroine Emeraude must have felt when thrust into the evil Armatello's lair. Gwenda resolved never again to treat her heroines so shabbily.

Not—she was obliged to admit—that the taproom before her resembled in the least the Gothic splendors of her villain's gloom-ridden *castello* except perhaps in its starkness. The inn's walls were unadorned but for some bits of cracking plaster; the taproom housed an oak bar counter and a few crude tables and rough benches. A feeble effort at a fire smoked and hissed upon the blackened stone hearth. The logs had been recently kindled and were yet damp, Gwenda judged, from the way they crackled. The room was unoccupied, but along the far wall a door stood ajar.

"Hallo!" Ravenel called. "Is anyone within?"

His inquiry was met with naught but the rain lashing against the windows.

"No one is here," Gwenda whispered. She looked for some sign that Ravenel shared her uneasiness, but his lordship merely appeared annoyed that his summons had not been answered forthwith.

"Of course someone is here," he said. "That fire did not build itself."

What an unfortunate way of putting it, Gwenda thought. She envisioned a pair of disembodied hands stacking the wood. That was one of the dreadful things about having a lively imagination, she had long since discovered. At times, it could be most inconvenient. She could not restrain a shiver that had little to do with the wet gown clinging to her skin.

"Come over by the fire," Ravenel said. "You are soaked through."

"As if you are not!"

But he ignored her retort. Showing no concern for his own discomfort, the baron proceeded to remove his drenched coat from her shoulders. His strong fingers untied the wet strings of her bonnet, then tugged it from her head, brushing aside the damp tendrils of hair from her forehead.

"There. Now mayhap you can start to dry out a—" Ravenel broke off as Bertie shook out his coat, spraying them both with a shower of droplets.

"Blast that dog!" But there was more of exasperated tolerance in his lordship's voice than any real

118

anger. Gwenda noted with astonishment that the irascible Lord Ravenel was accepting this latest disastrous turn of events with much better humor than either she or Bertie.

While her dog suspiciously snuffled one of the benches, Gwenda's eyes roved about the room, coming to rest on the mantel where a large, sinister spider was about to feast on the blood of a beetle caught in its webbing.

"'This place has an aura of evil about it,'" she said, quoting the heroine of her last book, "'. . . an odor of death and decay.'"

The baron sniffed the air and crinkled his nose. "That's frying onions," he said. "I'll check the kitchens for the landlord."

Before he could stir a step, Bertie suddenly flattened back his ears, a deep-throated growl escaping him. Gwenda resumed her grip on Ravenel's arm as the door at the end of the room began to creak open slowly.

She sent a silent prayer that the Nonesuch's landlord would prove to be a round, jolly sort of fellow like Mr. Leatherbury. Even better, he might have a plump, apple-cheeked wife to fuss over Gwenda and chase all these nonsensical fears out of her head.

But as the host made his appearance, wiping bony hands on a soiled white apron, she let out a quavery sigh. It could not be worse than if she had strayed into one of her own novels. With stooped shoulders, a hooklike nose, squinty eyes, and coarse black hair, the wretch might as well have had "villain" inscribed all over his sallow skin.

"What's toward—" he started to snap with a heavy frown but was cut off by Bertie. The dog charged forward, barking and baring his teeth.

"Eh! Get back, you flamin' brute." The man retreated and snatched up a cudgel from behind the bar counter.

"No! You monster!" Gwenda cried, rushing forward as he threatened to bring the heavy wood crashing down upon Bertie's head. "Don't you dare!"

But Ravenel moved faster, catching hold of Bert's collar and dragging the snarling dog back out of harm's way.

"Down, Bertie!" Ravenel thundered. "Quiet!"

Spotted Bert stopped barking but continued to growl. The hair at the back of his neck bristled as at the next instant a set of whiskers emerged from behind the bar. A fat black cat tore off for the kitchen at a waddling run.

The host stepped forward, brandishing his cudgel at all of them. "Clear out! The pair of you and take that slaverin' beast with you afore I bash his skull."

If Gwenda had had any misgivings about the Nonesuch and its host before, Bertie's reaction to the man only served to confirm it. "We shall be only too happy to do so," she said, reaching for Bertie's collar.

"No we won't," Ravenel said, although he released the dog to her care. "I have no intention of being thrown back out into the storm."

He turned the full weight of his formidable stare on the landlord. "If this is how you treat your customers, I am not surprised to find your establishment empty."

"I'm closed t'dy," the man grumbled, but he lowered the cudgel. "And I never have aught to do with beggars."

"We are not beggars but victims of a coaching accident," Ravenel said in his most lordly tones.

"What's that to me? I don't repair coaches here. Be off with you."

"We are not seeking repairs, my good man, but a place of shelter. Then I need some horses and a coach to be sent to fetch the servants and baggage we were forced to leave behind. The lady and I will require some dry clothes, and later, a bit of supper."

Gwenda, struggling to keep a grip on Bertie, blinked at the baron in astonishment. He rapped out his commands as though he truly expected this surly rogue to obey him.

"Lady?" The man's squinty eyes flicked over Gwenda. "That's rich, 'pon my word."

Ravenel moved so quickly that Gwenda scarcely had time to gasp. He wrenched the cudgel from the host's hands and fairly lifted the weasely fellow off his feet by his collar. It took all of Gwenda's strength to restrain Bertie, who seemed eager to join his lordship in the assault.

"The lady," the baron repeated with stony emphasis. "My sister, Miss Gwenda . . . Treverly, and I am Lord Ravenel. We are both accustomed to being accorded a little more respect."

Although the man's gaze roved fearfully up the baron's towering length, he choked out, " 'Twouldn't matter if you was the Prince Regent hisself. There's naught I can do for you. This inn is closed."

"Mayhap I can persuade you to open it." Ravenel released the man. The host staggered, one bone-thin hand snaking up to rub his unwashed neck. His lordship groped for his waistcoat pocket. He took great pains to display both the chain of his gold pocket watch and the ruby signet ring he wore as he drew forth a thick wad of damp bank notes and flicked them.

Gwenda made a small sound of protest, which

went unheeded. She could not believe the sensible Lord Ravenel could be so foolhardy. Did he not see the gleam of greed in that villain's eye? Did he not notice the furtive licking of the lips? Scarcely realizing what she did, she bent down beside Bertie and huddled the dog protectively closer.

With a feeling of dread, she noted the immediate change in the host's manner. Rubbing his bony hands together, he whined, "Well, there might be somewhat I could do. Never let it be said that Orville Mordred turned his back upon fellow creatures in distress."

"Mordred? His name would be something like that," Gwenda muttered into Bertie's ear. The dog growled as though in agreement.

Mordred scratched his long, pointed chin. "Happen to have an ostler I could send off with my own rig to fetch your servants."

"Good. Make arrangements to do so at once." Ravenel complacently returned the money to his pocket, seemingly blind to all of Gwenda's efforts to catch his eye. "And if you have a woman on the premises who could attend to my sister . . ."

"Alas, no, there isn't." Mordred attempted an ingratiating smile that revealed two brown stumps where his front teeth should have been. "My missus was called away unexpected-like to her mother in Leeds."

More likely he murdered his wife and stuffed her up the chimney, Gwenda thought. That's why it doesn't draw properly. Feeling that she had kept silent for far too long, she straightened and cleared her throat.

"M-my lord." Belatedly, Gwenda remembered the relationship the baron had bestowed upon them. "Brother dear, might I have a word with you?"

Ravenel looked startled, then quickly recovered himself. "Oh. Er, certainly, my dear sister."

As he approached, Gwenda caught him by his wet sleeve and tugged him closer to the fire. She stole a glance at Mordred. Although the man appeared nonchalant enough, she could have sworn the villainous rascal's ears grew by several inches in an effort to hear what she whispered to the baron.

Gwenda kept her voice so low, Ravenel was obliged to bend his tall frame to the point where the curve of his cheek was but a breath away from her lips.

"Lord Ravenel, I—I must tell you the truth. This was not the inn I was looking for. I have never been to this place in my life."

"I rather guessed that, my dear." The baron's brief smile would have been intolerable if not for the unexpected gleam of tender amusement in his eyes.

Her pulse gave a little flutter, but she ignored the sensation as she whispered urgently, "We—we cannot stay in this dreadful place. That fellow is likely plotting to slit both our throats."

"Miss Vickers! This is not the time to let your imagination—"

" 'Tis not my imagination. You have only to look at that man to see what a scoundrel he is." She gestured vigorously to where Mordred leaned against the bar, feigning to remove some of the dirt from beneath his nails with a small jackknife. "He has mean eyes and," she added, as a triumphant clincher, "Bertie growled at him."

Ravenel sighed with weary patience. "Bertie was growling at the cat."

"He was not! That was not Bertie's cat-chasing

growl. He—" Her protest was cut off by Ravenel's laying his fingertips upon her lips.

"I perfectly agree with you, Gwenda," he said gently, lowering his hand. "I am sure Mordred is a rogue, but the worst I anticipate is his charging me thrice for whatever miserable service he offers."

"But—"

"And we have no choice. The storm shows no sign of abating and I am worried about Jarvis and the others with only that broken-down coach for shelter."

"Oh. A-aye, the others," Gwenda said in a small voice. A guilty flush mounted into her cheeks. She had been so caught up in her own apprehensions, she had nigh forgotten the unfortunate circumstances in which they had left James, Fitch, and the baron's elderly valet.

Ravenel's hand enveloped hers in a reassuring squeeze. "Trust me. Everything will turn out all right."

Gwenda trusted him completely. It was Mordred she had her doubts about. But his lordship was correct. They had no choice.

When the baron turned back to the landlord, Mordred straightened immediately, all servile attention.

"I'll have a look at that carriage of yours now," Ravenel said, "as soon as my sister is settled into a private parlor."

"Alas, my lord, we don't have such a thing here. But I would be only too pleased to let the young lady have the use of my missus's sitting room."

All traces of his former insolence gone, the host could not have been more cloyingly polite. But as Mordred flashed her a crocodilelike smile, Gwenda thought she by far preferred it when he was surly.

As the man bowed her through the open doorway, she was reminded of the large black spider yet busily spinning its web on the mantel.

Mrs. Mordred's sitting room proved a most curious chamber, small and narrow. The cozy homespun rug, overstuffed horsehair sofa, and battered tea table were jarringly at odds with the collection of blunderbusses and muskets mounted upon the wall. The sight of these weapons made Gwenda wish she had had the foresight to bring along her own pearl-handled pistol.

The baron eyed the room with great disfavor but muttered, "Well, at least there is a better fire here than in the taproom. You stay close to the hearth and try to get some of the dampness out of your dress. I will not be gone long."

"Of course," she said dolefully. Here Ravenel was, preparing to leave her alone in the very heart of a murderer's den, and he was worried she might be taking a chill. But Gwenda managed to put up a brave front, not wishing the baron to think her a complete ninnyhammer.

Only when the door had closed behind his lordship did she rub her arms and glance about her with a tiny shiver. Bertie was restless, too, sniffing in every corner. He seemed to be particularly fascinated by an old pianoforte shoved against the wall. When Gwenda drew tremblingly closer to investigate, she saw that the dog had discovered nothing more than a mouse hole. Next to it was a large workbasket, presumably Mrs. Mordred's.

She must be a strange sort of woman, indeed, for beneath the stack of sewing Gwenda could just make out the top of a bottle of gin. Her mind began to conjure up images of guilt-ridden consciences, murders ages old, mayhap someone walled up alive in the chimney bricking, a family accursed, the present generation driven to madness and strong drink.

With a tiny sigh, she located a small three-legged stool and ensconced herself on it by the blazing logs on the hearth. There was naught left for her to do but wait for Ravenel and allow her imagination to run riot.

The baron stood in the inn doorway, anxiously drumming his fingers as he watched the Nonesuch's ancient coach lumber out of the stableyard, vanishing behind dark sheetings of rain. Never in his life had he found himself in such a quandary. He had longed to return with the coach and seek Jarvis out himself, but it would have been unthinkable to drag Miss Vickers back out into the storm or to abandon her in such dubious quarters as the Nonesuch.

At least the groom Mordred had produced from the stable had seemed a sturdy, sensible fellow, kindly despite his rough accent. But in this foul weather, even if the groom carefully followed the directions given him, Ravenel could not expect to see the carriage return with Jarvis within the next few hours.

And even if Mordred could be persuaded to hire out the vehicle, it would be close to midnight before the baron ever deposited Miss Vickers safely in Brighton. A heavy frown creased his brow. Who was he trying to fool? There was no possibility of traveling any farther this day. No matter what time the carriage returned, his elderly valet was certain to be done in by the afternoon's events, and there was also the footman's injured ankle to be dealt with. No, he might as well face the fact. They were all going to have to spend the night in this wretched place.

As Ravenel closed the door, shutting out the patter of the rain, his soft curse echoed about the empty taproom. Miss Vickers might be fretting and conjuring up all sorts of faradiddles about their host's murderous intent, but she obviously failed to see the true nature of their predicament.

They were apparently the only guests at the Nonesuch, she without any sort of chaperone or female traveling companion. If it ever became known—and experience had taught Ravenel that such mishaps usually had a way of leaking out—there would be the very devil of a scandal. Her reputation would be utterly ruined.

Not that it was in any way his fault, the baron thought, but it was not precisely hers, either. The lady could not help it if she had been born a Vickers, taught to hire baritones for coachmen and French trollops for maids. But, blast it all, no Baron Ravenel had ever been involved in scandal, and he was not about to be the first. If he had to, he would even . . .

He clenched his eyes tight, a shudder coursing through him. No! He could not possibly be thinking of *marrying* Miss Gwenda Mary Vickers.

"Your lordship?"

Ravenel's eyes flew open to find Mordred at his elbow. The fellow did have a most nasty manner of creeping up on one. The baron had not even heard him enter the taproom.

"What is it?" Ravenel snapped.

"I was only wanting to know if I should be preparing a room for your lordship . . . and your sister?"

The baron battled an urge to smack the sugges-

127

tive leer from the man's face. It was obvious the innkeeper had not believed the sister-brother Banbury tale. But, then, who would? Ravenel wondered gloomily, his shoulders sagging.

"No. That is . . . yes. We will require *two* rooms—one for myself and my valet, another for the lady."

The man's eyebrows rose even in the face of Ravenel's challenging stare, then Mordred merely shrugged and went to carry out his lordship's bidding, leaving Ravenel to find his own way back to the sitting room.

Just beyond the taproom, a pair of rickety stairs led up to the second floor. In the corridor beyond the stairs, he saw two doors but could not quite remember behind which one he had left Gwenda. He tried the first one; the handle would not turn. Before he could apply more force, he heard Bertie's bark in the opposite room. He supposed this particular door led to the kitchens or the cellar, but how strange that Mordred should keep it locked.

The baron felt far too preoccupied to give the matter more than a passing thought. As he strode toward the other door, his mind revolved with schemes to render his situation with Gwenda innocuous, more proper, to find some way to spare her reputation without sacrificing his own sanity. But at the moment his brain seemed too numbed with weariness to function clearly.

Rubbing his brow, he pushed his way into the sitting room. Gwenda sat huddled near the fire, her bedraggled skirts appearing to have reached the same state of semidamp discomfort as his own garb.

Bert yipped with joy to see Ravenel, but his lordship discouraged any warmer tokens of welcome. He forced the dog to lie down on the rug before

128

turning his attention to Gwenda. Faced with the prospect that this woman might well have to become his wife, Ravenel found himself studying her more intently than he had ever done before. Of course, Gwenda could scarcely be expected to be looking her best under the circumstances. But that was the curious thing. The baron, who had ever preferred a lady to be neat and precise, thought that Gwenda had never looked more charming than now, when her face was framed by a riot of chestnut curls drying into the most tousled disorder. The heat from the hearth had brought a becoming blush of rose into her cheeks; her green eyes reflected the gold of the firelight. The velvety outline of her mouth was enough to invite any man to—

Ravenel checked his thoughts when Gwenda's gaze shifted in his direction, almost as though she had felt the weight of his stare. He flushed guiltily, then rubbed his hands together in a too hearty manner.

"Well, the coach is on its way," he said in what he felt was the most foolish manner possible. After all that had passed between himself and Gwenda, why was he suddenly feeling so awkward with her, so acutely aware of their situation . . . alone . . . together. To conceal this inexplicable attack of nervousness, he stomped about, blustering, "That rogue Mordred has not done one thing to see to your comfort. He could at least have managed a cup of tea."

Although Gwenda protested she wanted nothing, Ravenel flung open the sitting-room door and bellowed for the innkeeper. But his summons was answered by a youth who identified himself as Rob.

"Mis-ter Mordred . . . bade me . . . wait . . . upon

you . . . and the lady," Rob intoned, like a child who has been taught to say his piece by rote.

The lad both looked and smelled as though his customary place was in the stables, but nonetheless the baron asked what the inn could offer by way of a supper.

"L-leg of mutton . . . fried rabbit . . . spitchcock eel," Rob recited.

Ravenel did not feel as though he could quite face a spitchcock eel, but he put in an order for the mutton. Gwenda did not appear to notice what was taking place. She was so unusually silent, he felt his own sense of discomfort increase. As soon as the boy had scurried out of the room, Ravenel stole another furtive glance at her.

He noticed the fear shading her eyes, the way her hands trembled. Of course. She, too, must at last be realizing the nature of their plight. He cursed himself silently for an inconsiderate fool. So caught up in his own feelings, he had given no thought to what Gwenda's must be. Besides worrying about the prospect of her own ruin, she might well be harboring other terrors. After all, their acquaintance was brief. She might be supposing him the sort of bounder who would take advantage of this situation.

A rush of tenderness surged through him, a protective urge to draw her onto his lap and . . . No, what was he thinking of? That would scarcely be likely to reassure her.

Instead, Ravenel pulled up another stool beside her and reached for her hands. Despite the fire, they felt slightly chilled.

She gazed at him, her brow furrowing. "Oh, Lord Ravenel, I have been thinking. . . ." Her lashes swept up so that he was staring full into those

130

ever-changeable green-gold eyes. He wondered if it really would be such a terrible fate to have to wed Gwenda Mary Vickers.

"Yes?" he prompted gently when she hesitated.

"Do you . . ." Her voice quavered. "Do you believe in ghosts?"

"Do I what!"

This question was so far from anything Ravenel had expected that he was torn between an urge to shake her and to laugh aloud. He released her hands, saying tartly, "I have never given the matter of ghosts much thought."

Gwenda's eyes shifted fearfully about the room. "What would you do if one were to rise up before you this very minute?"

"I would tell it to go away. I object to being haunted before I have had my dinner."

A reluctant smile quivered upon her lips, drawing forth the most appealing dimple. "Aye, I daresay you would."

Ravenel could see clearly what had been taking place in his absence. When Gwenda should have been agonizing over the prospect of her social ruin, the same imagination that had fashioned the terrors of *The Dark Hand* had been busily at work instead.

Before the baron could scold Gwenda for her nonsense, a timid knock sounded on the door. It was Rob returning to lay covers on the tea table. Ravenel was relieved to see that although Bertie sniffed at the lad's thick hobnail boots, the dog did not take the same exception to Rob that he had to Mordred. Gwenda, however, was another matter. She regarded the stable boy with an expression of horror.

When the lad had gone, she turned to Ravenel

and gasped, "You couldn't possibly be thinking of eating anything!"

"Well, yes. That was largely my intent." His lordship lifted the cover off one of the dishes. The mutton looked overcooked, but he suddenly realized he was famished. He had had nothing to eat since breakfast.

When he invited Gwenda to join him, she vigorously shook her head.

"You must suit yourself, my dear," Ravenel said, too weary to coax her and too exhausted to stand on ceremony. He sat down at the table, but before he could raise one bite to his lips, Gwenda rushed across the room and all but snatched the fork from his hand.

"Don't! It might be poisoned."

"Gwenda—"

"No, truly! Pray listen to me, Lord Ravenel. There are worse possibilities than ghosts. I have heard of obscure inns where the unwary are lured in and poisoned or clubbed over the head . . ."

The baron leaned back in his chair with an exasperated sigh. "We were not lured in. The landlord did his best to get rid of us."

"That's exactly what I mean," Gwenda said, making his head nigh ache with her vehement illogic.

Still, he might have humored her and set aside his plate, no matter how hungry he was, if he had believed her to be genuinely distressed. But he detected a certain sparkle in her eye and began to suspect that she actually enjoyed terrifying herself with all these imaginings.

He wrestled his fork from her grasp and stubbornly attacked the food on his plate. But it was difficult to eat with any great relish with Gwenda on one side of him, looking as though she expected each mouthful to be his last, and Bert on the other, regarding him with pleading canine eyes.

Ravenel's appetite rapidly diminished. He flung down the fork in disgust and lowered his plate for Bertie, who devoured the remainder in two great gulps. The baron then had to spend several minutes convincing Gwenda that he had not just poisoned her dog.

The only tolerable part of the meal was the surprising quality of the brandy, which Rob served after clearing the dishes away. Ravenel had a hard time persuading Gwenda to let him drink it, but the struggle was well worth it. He had not sampled such fine spirits since he had drunk the last bottles he had been able to obtain from France.

He wished Gwenda would toss off a bumper herself. It would do her a world of good, help her to relax. Ravenel feared if he did not soon give her something else to think about besides ghosts and murderers, she would drive him to distraction. If her mind worked in the manner of an ordinary sort of young lady, he would not have to be racking his brains for some way to make her understand the real problem that faced them. As it was, he could think of no easy way to introduce the unpleasant subject.

He set down his brandy glass and took to pacing the narrow room. Unfortunately, Gwenda did the same and they frequently had to come to abrupt halts to avoid colliding. The only one behaving sensibly, Ravenel noted wryly, was Spotted Bert. The dog yawned and watched their progress from a cozy spot where he was curled up before the fire.

Ravenel stalked over to the windows, the sky pitch-black beyond, but at least the rain had nearly ceased. The carriage sent to rescue Jarvis would likely return soon. That would be a great relief, but it scarcely did anything to alter the situation with Gwenda. The baron glanced over his shoulder and noted that the lady had paused in her perambulations long enough to poke the fire.

How would she react when he told her she would likely have to marry him? Gwenda was so unpredictable, there was no telling. Scarcely thinking what he was doing, he hovered nervously near the pianoforte. He didn't realize he had begun to plunk out a tune on the keys until Gwenda replaced the poker and exclaimed in surprise, "I didn't know you played. I—I mean, I never fancied that *you* would—"

"I don't." Ravenel flushed, quickly drawing back his hand. "That is, I never had lessons. I play a little by ear."

"But what a remarkable talent to waste. Why did you never have a tutor?"

He shrugged his shoulders in a manner that was a shade too offhand. A childhood memory he had thought long forgotten surfaced in his mind: the stern uncle who had been his guardian actually locking the door to the music room at Ravenel so that the baron could not succumb to temptation.

He unconsciously repeated his late uncle's words. "Playing the pianoforte is not something the Baron Ravenel is expected to know."

"But—but if you are fond of music . . ." Gwenda faltered, looking thoroughly confused.

And so she would be, Ravenel suddenly realized. He could almost hear her saying again, "In my family, enthusiasm and dreams and imagination have always been valued above your odious common sense."

He suppressed a strange twinge of envy as he

tried to explain to her, "My being fond of music is all the more reason I should avoid it. A man in my position cannot afford foolish distractions."

He did not truly expect Gwenda to understand this point of view, but neither was he prepared for the sympathy that shone so warmly from her eyes.

It both embarrassed and disconcerted him. Why the deuce should she be feeling sorry for him, when it was she who was hovering on the brink of social disaster? He said gruffly, "There are far more pressing matters for you to worry about than my lack of music lessons, matters that do not seem to have occurred to you."

"Such as?"

"Such as the fact that we have been pitchforked together in the most devilish manner. You and I—we . . ." To his annoyance, Ravenel felt his face growing red, his tongue seeming to tie itself in knots.

"We what?" Gwenda asked, crinkling her nose.

Her air of innocent bewilderment snapped the last of his patience. He crossed the room and roughly seized her upper arms. "Damn it, Gwenda. You have to marry me."

Her eyes widened; her mouth dropped open. She had never found her imagination lacking before, but not even in her wildest dreamings had she ever thought of Ravenel clasping her in such a passionate manner, demanding that she be his wife. Nor had she imagined what her own reaction would be. She blushed. She trembled. Her heart pounded so loudly she could scarcely hear her own tremulous breathing.

"Oh, Roderi—Ravenel," she stammered. "I—I never dreamed that—that you would feel this way."

135

"Of course I would. I am a man of honor, after all."

"So you are," she murmured shyly. "My chivalrous knight."

"I could scarcely just ride away after I had compromised you, no matter how unwitting it was on my part. As a Ravenel, I could not tolerate that sort of scandal."

The hand that Gwenda had been reaching up to stroke the rugged line of his lordship's cheek froze in midair. "What?" she asked faintly. "What are you talking about?"

He shot her a look more impatient than loverlike. "My dear, you will be utterly ruined if it is known you spent the night at the same inn as I, unchaperoned. That is why I have no choice but to marry you."

The rose-lined cloud upon which Gwenda floated dissolved from under her feet. Ravenel did indeed bear a most heroic cast to his countenance at this moment, but it was more of the nobility of one about to bravely embrace a firing squad than his lady. She squirmed free of his grip.

"Oh. I see," she said dully, surprised by the keenness of her disappointment. "How—how utterly *honorable* of you. But as a Vickers, I didn't think you believed I had a reputation worth saving."

The baron looked momentarily shamefaced, but he recovered himself. "We are not discussing any remarks I might have made previously about your family. When we are wed, I assure you I would not be so ill-bred as to utter any further criticisms. No matter what should happen, I would never be so uncivil as to blame you—"

"Please." Gwenda groaned. "Do not start making any speeches. You presume entirely too much, my

136

lord. I have no intention of accepting your *generous* offer."

"I was not offering. I was telling," he said, his voice rising with every word. "You have to marry me. As a Ravenel—"

"Exactly whose good name are you trying to protect?" she interrupted acidly. "Yours or mine?"

"Yours! If you but had the wit to know it. And though I do not expect you to feel in the least grateful."

"Grateful!" Gwenda's own voice became successively more shrill. The sound of their quarrel roused Bertie enough so that he opened one eye to regard them sleepily.

She shouted, "How dare you talk of gratitude when you inform me you must marry me, with your face looking grim as death."

"Forgive me if my manner offends you," Ravenel bellowed back. "But in the past eight hours, I have been thrown from a carriage, nigh drowned in a thunderstorm, given indigestion from overcooked meat—"

"I told you not to eat it!"

"—which is not calculated to put a man in the most gallant frame of mind."

Gwenda rubbed her arms where her flesh had recently felt the strong pressure of his fingers. "Well, I will say one thing," she flung out. "At least this proposal is somewhat of an improvement over the one you made to Miss Carruthers."

The dangerous spark that flared in Ravenel's eyes should have caused Gwenda to fall silent. But Thorne had always told her that her besetting sin was never knowing when to hold her tongue. She continued, "I would never marry you, not even to save my reputation. No, not even if I was to be branded for a trollop and dragged to the pillory tomorrow."

A muscle twitched along Ravenel's jawline. He approached her with an ominous deadly calm that was far more devastating than any outright show of anger. Gwenda had enough sense to retreat behind the tea table.

"So you would never marry me?" he hissed in accents of soft menace. "I daresay you don't find me romantic enough. A most boring, stuffy man."

"I—I did not mean that, precisely," she said, wondering exactly what he intended to do when he got his hands on her.

"Old Sobersides Ravenel. Not in the least like any of those dashing heroes you write about."

"I—I never said that."

Indeed, if Ravenel only knew how exactly like one of her heroes he did look at this moment, stalking her around the tea table in his weather-stained white shirt, his undone cravat revealing the bronzed flesh of his neck, his dark eyes raking her in a manner that both threatened and tantalized. How often had Roderigo appeared thusly in her dreams, only moments before he would attempt to bestow upon her that elusive kiss that never seemed to materialize.

Gwenda stopped in her tracks, tracing the sensual outline of Ravenel's mouth with her gaze. What was she doing? Here might be the perfect opportunity to find out about that kiss, and she was nearly flinging it away by retreating. But no. She blushed to the roots of her curls. What a scandalous notion! She couldn't possibly demand of Ravenel a thing like that. But if she didn't, she might never in her life have such another chance.

The words seemed to spill from her lips of their

own accord. "Ravenel. Have—have you ever kissed a woman before?"

"Have I—" Her question brought him to an abrupt halt, bare inches between them. "Of course I have." He added bitterly, "Though I daresay you'd tell me I don't do that right, either."

"I have no way of judging unless you do so."

Despite his angry mood, Ravenel looked a little taken aback.

"And you can hardly expect me to marry you unless you kiss me first," Gwenda said, entirely forgetting that she had just told him she would never marry him on any account.

Ravenel appeared far more likely to box her ears. But he grabbed her by the shoulders, hauled her forward, and planted a kiss on her lips that was swift, hard, and far from satisfactory. But as he was pulling back, their eyes met and some lightning awareness seemed to spark between them.

He drew her into his arms more gently this time. Gwenda came without resisting until she was pressed so close to his chest, their bodies seemed to melt together. His head bent toward hers, his hand cradling the back of her neck. The moment stretched out forever, as in one of her dreams, and as Gwenda stared deep into the night-dark pools that were Ravenel's eyes, she was certain she would wake too soon, as she always did.

But then his mouth covered hers, tenderly at first so that she could savor the warm texture of his lips. Gwenda tried to capture her feelings at this moment, but it was impossible. As Ravenel deepened the kiss, all thought sifted through her mind like quicksilver until she held no memory of aught save Ravenel and the wondrous, fiery sensation of his lips on hers.

He pulled back, his mouth parting from hers with a lingering reluctance. His voice was husky. "My—my dear Gwenda. I should not. I am taking the most shameful advantage of your inno—"

"Don't waste time apologizing," she begged. "Just kiss me again." She flung her arms about his neck. Ever a quick study, Gwenda proceeded to demonstrate to Ravenel just how much she had learned from their first embrace. She pressed her mouth to his in an ardent kiss that was even sweeter, headier than the last one had been. Ravenel crushed her hard against him, returning her passion with fervor, when suddenly he wrenched himself free.

"Miss Vickers!" he gasped. This time it was the baron who retreated around the tea table. When Gwenda murmured in protest and attempted to follow him, he held up one hand to ward her off.

"No, no more of that," he said, panting. "Not until we are married."

She could not tell whether he appeared more shocked by his own behavior or hers. The warm glow enveloping her faded, leaving her overcome with feelings of shame and misery.

She pressed her hands to her flaming cheeks. "We are not getting married. I—I have been kissing you under false pretenses ... b-because you look like him and—and he looks like you. I never knew how R-Roderigo ought to kiss before, but I never thought ... And how could one begin to describe such a devastating experience in a book, anyway?"

Since she concluded this rather incoherent speech by bursting into tears, it did not surprise her that Ravenel should look thoroughly confused. He kept a most wary distance between them.

"We are both more than a little overwrought from the day's events," he said. "You should retire. I'll just go and inquire if your room is ready, and we'll settle this matter in the morning." The baron spun on his heel and retreated briskly from the room.

" 'Tis s-settled now! I am not m-marrying you," Gwenda cried, but the door had already closed behind Ravenel.

Bert stood up, stretched, yawned, and ambled over to nuzzle Gwenda's hand sympathetically. She gave a doleful sniff and patted the dog. "Oh, Bertie! If he had any doubts before, now I have thoroughly convinced him that I am a lunatic." She stomped her foot. "As if I give a fig for his opinion or his beastly honorable proposals!"

She wiped her eyes angrily on her sleeve and managed to compose herself by the time his lordship returned with the young waiter, Rob, bearing a candlestick to light her way.

Ravenel bade her a curt good night and promised to have her trunk sent up as soon as it arrived. "And be sure to keep your door locked" were his final words to her, before retreating to the fire and presenting her with the rigid outline of his back.

Gwenda glared at him through her tears and followed Rob from the sitting room, Bertie trailing after them. As they mounted the creaking stairs to the upper floor, the candle flame cast eerie, flickering shadows upon the inn's ancient, gloomshrouded walls. Under other circumstances, she would have permitted herself a delicious shiver, allowed her mind to conjure up all sorts of sinister images. But at the moment her thoughts were too full of the recent tempestuous scene with Ravenel.

The boy indicated the door to the chamber that was to be hers, but when she moved to sweep past him, Rob suddenly blurted out, "His lordship never said a truer thing!"

"What?" Gwenda asked sharply, wanting only for the boy to be gone so that she could be alone.

"About keeping your door locked, miss." Rob leaned forward, lowering his voice to a frightened pitch. "And not venturing out of your room tonight, not under any circumstances."

It was the kind of dire warning she had often used in her books, but she scarce heeded the sense of what Rob was saying.

"Of course," she said, giving the boy an impatient, weary smile. Taking the candle, she whisked into her chamber and fairly shut the door in Rob's anxious face.

Chapter 7

"That woman *is* going to marry me," Ravenel muttered, clenching his jaw to an almost painful state of stubbornness.

"Of course, my lord," Jarvis said. He had lost track of the number of times he had uttered that soothing phrase since his arrival at the Nonesuch a half hour ago. Never had he seen his young master in such a pelter. From what few mumbled words he caught, Jarvis supposed his lordship to be fretting over Miss Carruthers and her rejection of him. But why, in the wake of everything else that had happened, should such a thing now be preying upon Master Des's mind? The only likely explanation was that his lordship was overwrought. It behooved Jarvis to get him into bed as quickly as possible.

The valet rolled back the coverlet and eyed the sheets with great disfavor. Yellowed, threadbare, they appeared apt to come apart at the slightest touch. He clucked his tongue. "This bed is very likely full of vermin, my lord."

"Good," his lordship replied in abstracted fashion. "Make sure there are at least two. I shall never get to sleep otherwise."

Jarvis swiveled his head to stare at Ravenel in astonishment, then realized that his lordship had scarce heeded a word said to him. By the light of an

143

oil lamp, its glow obscured by a dusty globe, his lordship pawed through one of his trunks. He found his dressing gown, which he proceeded to don inside out.

You have had a very long day, Master Des, Jarvis thought. He had been worried about his lordship and Miss Vickers ever since he had watched the young couple vanish down the road and saw the rain coming on. But his anxieties would have been tenfold worse if he had known they had fetched up in this dirty, tumbledown inn.

"It would have been far better if I had come and rescued you, my lord." Jarvis could not help voicing this opinion for mayhap the dozenth time. A grunt was his only reply.

Jarvis felt he had fared much better than Lord Ravenel and the young lady. The rain had barely begun when a farm cart had happened by. If only they had known there was a snug cottage within walking distance a bare quarter of mile beyond the field where his lordship had been flung.

After hailing the cart, Jarvis had soon had the drunken coachman and the poor young footman comfortably settled in the cozy farmhouse with plump Mrs. Ladbroke fussing and plying them with hot tea. With her help, Jarvis had bandaged James's ankle and sobered up the coachman. Jarvis would have been well content if not for his nagging fears over Lord Ravenel's continued absence. When the carriage from the Nonesuch had arrived in search of him, Jarvis had been most eager to leave. Not so Fitch or James, he thought with disapproval. They were too selfishly concerned with their own ailments to stir a step for their mistress. These young servants nowadays. It would have taken more than a sprained ankle or a raging headache to keep Jarvis from Master Des.

Through all this Jarvis was a trifle ashamed to feel a twinge of smugness. The young master oft seemed so sure his poor old valet was beyond coping with any disaster. Jarvis thought he had done rather well today, shown his lordship he was not completely past it. Had he remembered to tell Master Des with what foresight he had left a note pinned inside the wrecked carriage, otherwise the groom from the Nonesuch never would have found him at Mrs. Ladbroke's cottage?

"Yes, Jarvis. You told me. Several times," was his lordship's disgruntled reply.

While Ravenel took to pacing again, Jarvis hunted for a warming pan to take some of the dampness from the sheets, then he thought better of it. Any friction would likely cause that worn linen to disintegrate entirely.

The baron brushed past him, grumbling under his breath, "Blasted woman. Not one grain of common sense beneath all those curls. But I know my duty."

Jarvis paused in his efforts to plump up the pillows to study Ravenel anxiously. It was always a bad sign when the master began to pace. And was the look in his eye a trifle feverish?

"I trust you have not taken a chill, my lord."

"No, Jarvis," Ravenel said with barely concealed impatience. A permanent frown appeared creased between his brows.

If not ill, Jarvis concluded, the master was in a devilish bad skin over something . . . something more than all these traveling mishaps or the conditions of this dreadful inn. Jarvis knew his lordship and Miss Vickers had not set out today on the most amiable terms with each other. Still, Miss Vickers was such a good-natured young lady. Jarvis could not believe she had plagued his lordship with either tantrums or hysterics.

He cleared his throat and ventured sympathetically, "It has been a most trying day, my lord. I daresay you and Miss Vickers had a monotonous time of it, waiting here at this rundown inn."

"Monotonous!"

To Jarvis's surprise and alarm, Master Des halted in his tracks and emitted a bark of wild laughter. "No, Jarvis. Miss Vickers might inflict many torments upon a man, but monotony would never be one of them."

The words were no sooner out of Ravenel's mouth than he wished he had returned a more noncommittal answer. Jarvis was regarding him with renewed uneasiness, the scrutiny of his still keen blue eyes probing deep enough to render the baron mighty uncomfortable. He felt himself coloring and returned to rummaging through his trunks, demanding what had become of his tooth powder.

Jarvis located it for him in a trice. "I am glad to hear my lord was not bored. I trust you at least passed your evening with some degree of comfort?"

The valet's concern and curiosity irritated Ravenel's taut nerves to the snapping point. He straightened, brandishing his toothbrush. "If you must know, Jarvis, Miss Vickers and I spent our time inspecting the food for poison and waiting for ghosts to whisk down the chimney. That is, when we weren't engaged in shouting matches and chasing each other 'round the tea table."

To say nothing of the kissing, he added to himself, an embarrassing flush of heat rushing through

146

his loins at the memory. And to think nothing of it, either, if he wished to get any sleep at all tonight.

He continued, scarce giving Jarvis time to register his dismay. "But I suppose these events will become everyday occurrences when Miss Vickers and I are married. I shall soon grow to regard them as commonplace."

If he had expected to shock the imperturbable Jarvis, Ravenel was disappointed. Although the old man exclaimed, "Marry Miss Vickers?" he appeared more worried than startled. "But, my lord, what about Miss Carruthers?"

"Miss Carruthers? What the deuce does she have to do with any of this?"

"I thought that you were wanting to marry her only yesterday morning."

Yesterday morning? Ravenel marveled. Aye, so it had been, and yet the scene with Miss Carruthers seemed as hazy in his memory as though it had taken place in another lifetime. The only part that remained clear to him was bending over that settle and finding tumbled brown curls, abashed green eyes, a pixieish smile. Was it truly only yesterday that Gwenda Mary Vickers had erupted into his life? It seemed more like years since he had last bade good-bye to a sane existence.

He said curtly, "I asked Miss Carruthers and she turned me down. So now I am going to marry Miss Vickers."

Jarvis's fine white eyebrows jutted upward in disapproval. "Miss Vickers is indeed a charming young lady, but 'twould seem your lordship's decision is rather sudden."

"Damnation, Jarvis. You of all people should understand why I am doing this. Honor demands it. I

147

could scarcely allow her reputation to be ruined owing to this little escapade."

"Is not your lordship being a trifle rash? Chances are that matters might be arranged so that no one would ever know about this mishap."

Ravenel found himself unexpectedly irritated by Jarvis's well-meant comments. "No, the affair is quite hopeless. I must marry her, and that's flat."

"And what is Miss Vickers's opinion?"

As usual, Jarvis had an uncanny knack for cutting through to the heart of the matter. The baron thought of Gwenda's insistence that she would never wed him, and his mouth set into its former obstinate line.

"Miss Vickers's impractical opinions are of no consequence. She has no more choice than I. I will make her marry me. I see my duty quite clearly."

With that, Ravenel flung down his toothbrush. There was no water in the chipped porcelain basin, anyway. He stalked toward the bed, the silence into which Jarvis had lapsed becoming more unnerving with each passing second.

"Well?" Ravenel rounded on his valet. "You never liked Miss Carruthers in any case. So are you not going to wish me joy?"

"Not yet, my lord." Jarvis's cryptic remark and sudden smile were both equally annoying. Ravenel decided he had had all he could possibly endure for one day.

When Jarvis helped him out of his dressing gown, he flung himself into bed. Catching the edge of the sheet, he gave it an angry jerk and rolled over in accompaniment to the sound of tearing linen.

"I am not going to marry that overbearing man, Bertie," Gwenda declared to her dog, who was attempting to arrange himself on the window seat. Silhouetted against the glass, Spotted Bert issued a mournful whine like some hound of dire prophecy.

Beyond the latticed panes, the moon made a ghostly glow cresting the night-beclouded sky. Upon the nightstand, a candle burned low in its socket. A draft whistled past the window, causing the flame to waver, sending shadows leaping up the dark-paneled walls of the chamber.

Amid the moth-eaten velvet splendor of the bedcurtains, Gwenda tossed and turned on the lumpy feather-tick mattress. The room must once have been the finest the Nonesuch had to offer, but now its decay was worthy of any ruined castle whose mortar had ever dripped from the ink of Gwenda's pen.

The door didn't latch properly, either. Gwenda had discovered that earlier when she had answered a timid knocking. It had been Rob bringing up the trunk with her meager belongings, which Jarvis had had the forethought to see recovered from the wrecked coach. After the lad had gone, Gwenda had realized there was no way to lock the door, leaving her prey to whatever might be creeping abroad tonight in the corridor.

Never in her life had she so much scope for her imagination to run rampant, and never in her life had she been so indifferent to it all.

Despairing of ever finding a comfortable position, she sat bolt upright in bed, hugged her knees to her chest, and complained, "Ravenel might have delivered the trunk to me himself. Along with an apology. The effrontery of the man, Bertie! The insufferable condescension. As though he were doing me the greatest of favors. The high-and-mighty

Lord Ravenel stooping to wed one of the half-mad Vickers. As if I would ever consider his odious proposal."

Did she fancy it or was there a rather accusing gleam in Spotted Bert's eyes? Gwenda squirmed. "Well, I might have been carried away for just an instant. When he first spoke of marriage, he seemed so much like I had envisioned Roderigo."

Gwenda closed her eyes and touched a trembling finger to her lips, yet tasting of the fiery passion of Ravenel's kiss. She groaned. "Ohhhh! How can any man so—so positively stuffed with duty, honor, and pomposity kiss that way?" She pummeled her pillow in frustration. "It isn't fair, Bertie. It simply isn't fair."

She ceased the assault when she saw some of the feathers flying out.

Bertie gave a soft, reproachful bark. He crouched down on the seat, burying his head beneath his paws almost as though trying to shut out some of her grumblings.

"I do beg your pardon, Bertie," Gwenda said bitterly. "Pray excuse me for having troubled you with my trifling problems." She rolled over with one last parting shot. "But I'm not going to marry that man. I'll be hanged if I do."

She drew the musty coverlet up to her ears, but with such thoughts churning in her head, it was some time before she drifted off to sleep. Even then it was a most restless slumber, with disturbing snatches of dreams.

She stumbled through the mist-obscured ruins, pursuing an elusive, ever-familiar stalwart figure garbed in a black cape. . . .

"Roderigo," Gwenda groaned into her pillow. "Wait for me, my love."

Running so fast, her heart seemed ready to burst. She could never quite catch up to the raven-haired man or make him hear her. Then, as from a great distance, she heard . . . barking?

Gwenda tossed from side to side. Bertie! What was he doing here at the castle?

Her dog was growling, attacking the edge of the dark-cloaked man's cape. Gwenda staggered forward, begging Bert to stop. No! Heel, Bertie, heel! It is Roderigo. It is . . . The man turned slowly around. It was Lord Ravenel. His strong arms reached out for her, the sensual curve of his lips curved into a mocking smile, the dark glow of his eyes seeming to mesmerize, to draw her on. . . .

"Stop it," Gwenda mumbled. "You are not Roderigo. You are not."

It took every ounce of resistance she possessed to wrench herself awake. She sat up, breathing hard, brushing back damp tendrils of hair from her eyes.

"Damn that man, Bertie!" she gasped, directing her gaze toward the window seat. "I told him . . . I did—"

She broke off, her words faltering. Although the candle had long ago guttered out, the pale glow of the moon was enough for her to realize the window seat was empty. Gwenda groped about in the darkness, expecting to find Bert curled up at the foot of the bed, but her hands encountered nothing but the rumpled coverlet.

It was then she noticed the shard of light slicing

its way across the floor, light that emanated from the crack where the door to her bedchamber stood ajar.

Gwenda's hands tightened on the sheet as she hugged it to her breast.

"B-Bertie?" she called softly. There was no answer. She called louder, a little more urgently. "Bert!"

Still no response. But it was nothing to be alarmed about, she tried to assure herself. Bertie was frequently given to nocturnal wanderings. He might have scented that black cat again or—Gwenda grimaced at a less comforting thought—or Mordred.

Shivering, she swung herself out of bed. She located her wrapper and tugged it on over her nightgown. Padding cautiously to the door, she peeked out. There was no sign of Bert or anyone else in the corridor beyond. But someone had left a candle burning in the old-fashioned wrought-iron wall sconce.

"H-here, Bertie." Gwenda tried to whistle, but she was so nervous she couldn't pucker. A heavy thud issuing from the lower story of the inn nearly caused her to jump from her skin. The noise was followed by the unmistakable creak of footsteps.

It must be well past midnight, she told herself. Yet someone was up and stirring. Someone or *something*.

She swallowed hard, trying to ignore the uncomfortable pounding of her heart.

"Blast you, Bertie," she whispered, wishing the dog was safe in her room, wishing her room had a bar a foot thick. Her gaze traveled wistfully toward a closed door only two down from her own room—

the door that Rob had informed her earlier led to Ravenel's lodging.

But no. Gwenda could well imagine what the baron's scathing comment would be if she roused him in the middle of the night to go searching for Spotted Bert. As if she needed his lordship's help in any case, she thought, stiffening her spine.

She was sure Bertie hadn't gone far. Most likely that was him she heard below in the kitchens, knocking things over, making a nuisance of himself.

"W-won't I give him a dreadful scold when I find him," she said with a quavery laugh. Of course, Ravenel was right about one thing. There was not the least reason to be frightened. The Nonesuch was naught but a neglected old building.

All the same, Gwenda first took the precaution of fetching her pearl-handled pistol from the trunk. She set it to one side while she searched for something to put on her bare feet, pleased to find that for once she had not mislaid her slippers. Shoving her feet into the soft leather, she stepped out into the hallway. With trembling hands, she removed the candle from the sconce and used it to light her way down the stairs.

The wretched steps did have to creak so, shrieking her approach to whomever might be lurking— No. Gwenda set her lips resolutely. She could not allow herself to think such ridiculous things. There was no *whomever*—only Bertie.

When she reached the lower floor, she raised the candle and glanced nervously about. All seemed quiet and yet. . .

The darkness itself, the inn's very walls seemed to have taken on life. The hair prickled at the back

153

of Gwenda's neck. She could feel a presence, eyes watching her.

Then she heard another floorboard creak—and she hadn't moved. "Oh, Bertie," she quavered. "Please let it be you."

But the prayer had scarce left her lips when a hand shot out of the shadows behind her, gripping her shoulder. Gwenda screamed and spun about like one demented. She flailed the candle before her like a sword, spattering hot wax on her knuckles.

The light flickered across Ravenel's brocade dressing gown as he flung up one arm to shield his face. "Damme, Gwenda! Stop that before you set me on fire."

"R-Ravenel?" Gwenda sagged back against the wall, just barely managing to steady the candle while she pressed her other hand over the region of her wildly thumping heart.

His lordship cautiously lowered his arm. "What the deuce are you doing here, Gwenda?"

"What am I— What are *you* doing creeping up on me in that fashion? 'Twas enough to send me into a fit of apoplexy."

"I could not sleep. I went into the taproom to see if I could find a spot more of that brandy." His lips compressed in a stern manner that by now Gwenda found all too annoyingly familiar. "Now, madam. You will please account for your own presence."

All traces of Gwenda's recent fright faded before a rush of anger. She said, "If it is any of your concern, Lord Ravenel, I am looking for my dog."

"The dog be damned! I will not have you chasing about this place in the dead of night garbed only in your bed clothes. Go back to your room at once."

"I will do no such thing." Gwenda bristled at his

proprietary tone. The temerity of the man. He behaved as though he were already her husband. In any case he was a fine one to talk of being garbed only in night clothes. 'Twas obvious that beneath his robe his lordship wore naught but his breeches. The opening in the brocade revealed glimpses of a hair-roughened chest. Gwenda had the grace to blush when she realized she was staring at the contours of his muscular frame a little too intently.

"Are you not afraid of encountering any cutthroats, or worse, down here in the dark?" Ravenel asked, a wicked glint coming into his eye.

Gwenda could see clearly what he was about. If he could not bully her into obeying his commands, he meant to frighten her. She raised her chin defiantly. "I am not in the least afraid. After all, I have ..." Her haughty words faded to silence as she groped with one hand in the pocket of her wrapper and found it empty. She had been so pleased with herself for remembering her slippers, she had forgotten the pistol.

Her face flushing with chagrin, she lowered her gaze. Not about to admit her absentmindedness or her qualms to Ravenel, she declared stoutly, "Now if you will excuse me, I am going to find Bert."

She spun on her heel, and marched down the hall, but she immediately heard Ravenel coming after her.

"I will find the wretched animal," he began.

"No, thank you. I want no more of your *chivalrous* gestures."

Gwenda paused outside the door that led to the kitchens and reached for the handle.

"Of all the ridiculous notions. You'll never find him in there," the baron said. "I tried that door earlier and it is kept locked."

155

When the handle turned easily in Gwenda's grasp and the door creaked open, she could not forbear shooting him a look of triumph. She herself doubted that Bertie had come this way, but she was not about to give Ravenel the satisfaction of admitting that.

Tiptoeing into the kitchen, she sensed him close behind her. As she softly called Bertie's name, the light from her candle spilled over a grease-laden iron stove stacked high with dirty pots that looked as if they had not been cleaned at any time during this century. A plump rat stood sampling something from an unwashed plate, but when the light fell upon it, it quickly vanished behind the stove.

Gwenda shuddered. "And to think you actually ate something prepared in here," she could not refrain from reminding Ravenel.

He grimaced, but all he said was, "I hope you are satisfied. You can see Bert is not here. The sensible thing for you to do is—What the deuce!"

He broke off, staring past her with an arrested expression on his face. Gwenda glanced somewhat nervously behind her to see what had caught his attention.

It was the door that led into the kitchens from the yard outside. It was flung wide open, the night breezes and pale moonlight contriving to make sinister rustling shadows of the trees beyond.

"There's something out there," Ravenel muttered.

"Bertie?" Gwenda asked weakly, feeling her heart begin to sink down to her toes.

"I don't think so. Give me the candle, Gwenda."

She did as he asked but whispered anxiously, "What for?"

"I am going to see what's out there."

This notion seemed so far removed from

Ravenel's usual good judgment that Gwenda started to protest, but his lordship was already striding purposefully forward. He flung a curt command to her to remain where she was, but she took no heed of that and followed, clinging to his arm. She could feel the tension cording his muscles, making them whip-taut.

"Gwenda, I told you— Damme!"

She heard Ravenel crack his knee against something, then he staggered, nearly oversetting them both. When he regained his balance, he bent to rub his leg, cursing softly. Then he held the candle so as to illumine the object that had blocked their path.

Gwenda stared in frowning surprise at a pile of small wooden casks piled willy-nilly just inside the kitchen door.

"What is it?" she breathed. "Gunpowder?"

The baron made a closer inspection of one of the kegs, then a slow smile spread across his face. "No, not gunpowder, my dear. Brandy."

"Brandy!"

"Aye," he said. "I don't wish to alarm you, Gwenda, but I believe we have stumbled upon a bit of smuggling."

Far from being alarmed, Gwenda was flooded with a sense of keen disappointment. "Smuggling? Is that all?" she asked.

"I am afraid so, my dear."

"And after all my lovely conjectures about murders and—and family curses and ghosts!"

Although Ravenel regarded her solemnly enough, Gwenda had the curious impression that he was being hard-pressed to maintain a straight face. "Mayhap we had better—"

But Gwenda never knew what Ravenel was

about to suggest. A tall shadow suddenly loomed in the kitchen's open doorway. Gwenda gave a terrified gasp and dove into Ravenel's arms. She could feel his own heart give a lurch as he tensed to confront the intruder.

But the moon-silhouetted figure on the threshold appeared as alarmed as Gwenda.

"Oh, lordy," Rob yelped, nearly dropping the cask he was carrying as Ravenel directed the light from the candle full in his face.

For several seconds, none of them moved. As Gwenda caught her breath, she watched Rob's Adam's apple bob up and down.

"Miss. Y-your lordship," he stammered. "You shouldn't be down here." He set the cask down with a dull thud.

"Neither should you," the baron said pleasantly enough, although Gwenda felt him tighten one arm protectively about her waist.

"I—I—was just doing a bit of work for Mr. Mordred," the lad said, twisting his hands. "M-moving some molasses down into the s-storeroom."

"Molasses, indeed. More like smuggling a bit of brandy."

They might well have been the king's soldiers, Gwenda thought, about to clap irons upon the unfortunate young man from the way Rob's teeth began to chatter.

"Oh, no, m'lord! 'Twarn't me. Me and Mr. Mordred don't do no smuggling. 'Tis old Tom Quince that does that and he—he brings the stuff up from the coast for us just to pass 'round the neighborhood."

Gwenda squirmed away from Ravenel to lay one hand reassuringly on the boy's arm. "Goodness.

Don't put yourself into such a taking. We weren't spying on you—only looking for my dog."

"Oh!" Rob's expression of relief was quickly replaced by a furtive one of guilt.

"Have you seen the dog, lad?" Ravenel asked.

Instead of answering, the boy hung his head. Gwenda felt a sudden squeezing of fear inside her.

"Rob, what has happened to my dog?"

"Nothing so terrible," Rob mumbled. "B-but Mr. Mordred—he made me do it."

"Do what?" Gwenda cried.

"Well, you see, miss, your dog came sniffling around outside and when he saw Mr. Mordred—he went for him. Dogs don't seem to like Mr. Mordred noways. Your Bert . . . he took quite a chunk out of Mr. Mordred's leg—"

"Astonishing," Ravenel interrupted. " 'Twould seem that hound does possess some sense of discrimination."

Gwenda gave him a reproachful look before prodding Rob. "And then?"

"I had to do something, miss, or Mr. Mordred would have shot the dog sure. I tied him up in the stable, and to keep him quiet I—"

"Tied him up!" Gwenda exclaimed, allowing Rob to explain no further. Why, Bertie had never been so abused in his life. Never had he been thus confined. She could well imagine what poor Bert must be feeling: confused, terrified at being shut up in those dark stables.

"We've got to let him out at once," she said indignantly. She shoved past Rob and was halfway out the door when Ravenel caught her roughly by the arm.

"Are you mad?" he asked. "You can't go charging

out there. There's a band of smugglers creeping about."

"Only two," Rob interposed. "Mr. Mordred and old Tom Quince. But truly, miss, it would be better to wait until morning."

Gwenda might well have been persuaded, but at that moment a low, piteous howl carried from the direction of the stables.

"Bertie!" she cried. "Don't be afraid. I'm coming."

Wrenching free of Ravenel, she tore off, running around the side of the inn and heading for the stableyard. Mud splashed against her legs from the puddle-soaked yard, but she had no thought for anything but rescuing her dog. Gwenda heard the baron's furious hiss as he came charging after her, but she, far lighter on her feet, managed to outdistance him.

Not stopping to draw breath, even when she reached the stables, she drew aside the bar and flung wide the heavy door. Bursting inside, she found Bert cowering in the first empty stall. His moist eyes gleamed up at her through the dark. He whined, attempted to stand, and then flopped back on his haunches.

"Bertie! What have they done to you!" Gwenda dropped to her knees in the straw and flung her arms about him. Bert's head sagged against her chest.

Ravenel burst through the stable door. He paused a moment, gasping, before starting to scold, "Gwenda, you little fool—"

"Bertie is hurt." She cut him off, choking on a half-sob. "He cannot even stand."

The baron frowned and knelt down beside her. Bertie squirmed with his usual delight to see his lordship. But when he attempted to greet him, the dog's head lolled to one side. Bertie's tongue shot out to lick Ravenel's cheek and missed.

The baron sniffed the air and then grimaced. "Damnation. That boy must have given Bert some of the brandy to quiet him. The dog's not hurt. He's as drunk as your coachman."

"Don't be ridiculous. Bertie couldn't possibly—" Gwenda recoiled as the dog panted in her face and she smelled it, too: the reek of strong spirits.

"Oh, Bertie," Gwenda groaned. The dog regarded her muzzily through half-closed eyes. "Whatever am I going to do with him, Ravenel?"

Ravenel got to his feet, dusting wisps of straw from the knees of his breeches. "You will simply have to let him sleep it off."

"I'm not leaving him tied up here in the stables! Not with that dreadful Mordred likely to come back." Gwenda began struggling with the knot of the rope looped around Bertie's neck, a difficult task in the semidarkness.

The baron caught her by the elbow and tried to haul her to her feet. "I will take care of Bert, Gwenda. But I want you to slip back to your room before someone catches . . ."

He allowed the sentence to trail off at the sound of a heavy footfall just outside the stable door. The next instant light flashed into Gwenda's eyes, momentarily blinding her. She heard the sharp intake of Ravenel's breath. Stifling her own shocked outcry, she saw that it was Mordred. He walked with a pronounced limp, his breeches torn presumably by Bertie's teeth. In one hand he held a horn lantern, in the other an upraised pistol. The baron stepped in front of Gwenda so that the muzzle was aimed directly at his chest. He mentally cursed himself for a fool. At the first hint of anything amiss, he should have forced Gwenda back to her room.

"You two!" Mordred blanched with dismay, then spat in disgust. "I might have known. I should have chased the pair of you and that damned dog back into the storm. But my generous nature is always getting the better o' me. I had a bad premonition about letting you stay."

Despite how pale and frightened she looked, Gwenda inquired, "Oh, do you have those, too?"

Ravenel spoke up in his best voice of authority. "See here, Mordred. Don't be a fool. Smuggling is one thing, but—"

"Quiet!" Mordred snarled, his thumb clumsily struggling with the hammer as he attempted to cock the pistol.

Ravenel prudently held his tongue. He could tell from Mordred's awkward handling of the weapon that he was a rank amateur, far more dangerous than a man who possessed any skill. If Ravenel could only contrive to knock the pistol aside, his and Gwenda's situation would not be entirely hopeless. He was confident he could handle Mordred and then there would only be the boy, Rob, and the one referred to as old Tom Quince.

While the baron assessed their chances, a rough voice called out, "Eh, what's happening here, Mordred?"

A hulking figure lumbered out of the shadows to stand beside the innkeeper. Ravenel's hopes plummeted at his first view of "old" Tom. Quince was a giant of man with coarse skin, a broad crooked nose, and a thatch of salt-and-pepper hair.

"Nothing's amiss. I can handle it," Mordred said, although fine beads of sweat had broken out on his brow. "Just finish unloading those casks and get out of here before anyone else sees you."

Tom Quince did not appear in the least perturbed by this surly command. His eyes traveled contemptuously over Ravenel, taking in his brocade dressing gown.

"Flash cove." He sniffed. Then his gaze moved to where Gwenda knelt on the stable floor, her arms clutched around Bert's neck. The dog's tongue hung out, his bark issuing in a foolish-sounding grr-uff.

A sudden gleam sparked in Tom Quince's eye, which the baron much misliked. The smuggler's mouth split in a gap-toothed leer.

"If this be not Tom Quince's lucky day." The burly man licked his lips. "What a prime bit o' goods. Just what I've been hankerin' fer."

Ravenel saw his own dread mirrored in Gwenda's terrified eyes. He shouted at Quince, "You lay one hand on her, and by God, you'll regret it." He started toward Quince, forgetting the weapon trained upon him.

"You! S-stay where you are," Mordred said, the pistol trembling in his hand.

"I allers wanted me a fancy coachin' dog like that 'un." Quince hunkered down and proceeded to scratch Bert behind his ear.

So certain had Ravenel been that Gwenda was about to be ravished by this great brute, it took him several seconds to realize it was the dog Quince desired and not her.

Gwenda smacked the smuggler's hand away from Bert. Dragging the dog with her, she inched farther back into the stall. "N-no. You leave Bertie alone."

"Quince, you damn fool," Mordred cried. "What are you doing? Forget about that cur before you queer everything."

But Quince ignored him, continuing to advance on Gwenda. "Now, little lady, don't raise a fuss. Old Tom ain't goin' to hurt you. Just be a good gel and give me the nice doggie."

"No!" Gwenda crouched back, her eyes turning in desperate appeal to the baron.

There had been times during the past two days when Ravenel thought he would have gladly surrendered Spotted Bert to the devil himself and said good riddance. But he took one look at the tears spilling down Gwenda's cheeks and an unexpected rage surged through him.

He plunged in between her and the smuggler, driving his fist into Quince's stomach.

"Stop before I fire," Mordred warned, taking aim.

Although Quince bent over and grunted, Ravenel's blow hardly seemed to affect the large man. He neatly blocked Ravenel's next punch, a toothy grin spreading over his face. "Oho, would you look at this struttin' gamecock? So it's a mill ye're after, laddie? Fine wit me. Ain't been no trouble wit the excisemen of late. Gettin' a mite dull. Want to fight me for the dog?"

"Be only too happy to oblige," Ravenel grated.

"Are you mad, Quince?" Mordred stepped forward with the pistol trying to take charge, but Quince jostled him aside.

"Ah, shut yer bone box. I got to show this fancy gent'mun here the proper way to throw a punch."

Before Gwenda's stunned senses could even register what was happening, Ravenel had stormed from the stable with Quince, Mordred trailing behind, still grumbling. Gwenda settled her bleary-eyed dog back down into the straw and got to her feet, scrambling after the men.

When she emerged through the stable doors, she

saw Quince in the middle of the yard, yanking off his coat. He spit on both his palms and doubled up his fists. The baron quickly rid himself of his brocade dressing gown, stripping down to his breeches. Moonlight skated off the hard contours of his chest and arms as he assumed the fighter's stance.

Gwenda could only gape at his lordship in horrified astonishment. Merciful heavens! What the devil had gotten into the man?

"Ravenel!" she shrieked. But her outcry proved a mistake. By distracting his lordship, she enabled Quince to land the first blow. He caught Ravenel square in the eye, sending him flying backward into the mud.

Gwenda winced and started to run to him, but Ravenel was already jerking to his feet. He charged forward and got off a solid punch at his opponent's nose, succeeding in drawing his cork.

Quince gave a snort of surprise, then the fight commenced in earnest, blows flying left and right, both of them slipping and sliding in the mud. Gwenda stuffed her hand against her mouth, fearful of crying out again and breaking the baron's concentration. She sucked in her breath each time Quince's meaty fist connected with Ravenel's flesh.

Completely forgetting they were on opposite sides, Gwenda turned indignantly to Mordred. "Don't just stand there. Make them stop."

"I would if I could get off a clear shot," Mordred blustered. "Don't know why they're fighting over that vicious brute, anyway. Just look what he did to my leg."

But he got scant sympathy from Gwenda. She wrung her hands and thought of rushing in between the two men, but they were like a pair of raging bulls. Never had she seen Ravenel look so wild, a nigh savage light in his eyes, the sweat glistening on his muscular chest. His breath was coming hard; his knuckles were raw and bleeding. Yet Gwenda had the strangest notion that he was somehow actually enjoying this horrid contest.

So desperate was she that Gwenda began to think of rushing back to the inn to retrieve her pistol and rouse Jarvis, when she saw Quince waver slightly. Ravenel's next blow dropped the big man to his knees. Although his own chest was heaving, Ravenel yet held his pose waiting for Quince to get up.

The man turned his head to one side and spit out a tooth. He flung up one hand and gasped. "E-enuff."

Gwenda expelled her breath in a tremulous sigh, not quite trusting this capitulation. But the smuggler staggered to his feet, his split lip twisting into a lopsided grin as he held out one callused palm.

"Here. My hand on it. Never thought to see the day one o' the gentry could match Tom Quince. A pity ye be a lord, so it is. What ye might have done in the ring."

Gwenda watched in mute astonishment as the baron slowly shook hands with the smuggler and then Quince was pressing a flask of brandy upon him.

"Enough of this nonsense," Mordred shouted, marching forward and waving his pistol at Ravenel. "I want him locked up in the stable before he gets loose and fetches the excisemen—"

"His Nibs would never do that. 'E's a gent'mun. Somethin' you know nothin' about," Quince said loftily. "Now give me that 'ere afore you hurt someone." With that, he wrenched the pistol away from the abashed Mordred and tucked it into his own belt.

The entire scene grew hazy before Gwenda's eyes. As her disordered senses took in the fact that the fight was indeed over and it seemed that

Ravenel had won, she felt nigh giddy with relief. She swayed on her feet, as close to fainting as she ever had been in her life.

Then a strong hand closed upon her shoulder, steadying her.

"Gwenda! Gwenda, are you all right?" Ravenel's deep voice sounded close to her ear. Someone pressed a flask to her lips, forcing a fiery liquid down her throat.

She sputtered and choked on the brandy, but the light-headedness left her. Her world snapped back into focus. Her gaze traveled up to Ravenel's face. His brow was furrowed with concern. His cheek was turning purple, one eye was almost swollen shut, and he was asking *her* if she was all right.

"Oh, R-Ravenel!" she said, her breath catching on a sob.

Quince regarded her with pained surprise as he recorked his brandy flask. "Here now, there be no need to start a-snifflin' again. Tom Quince allus honors his word. You get to keep your dog. You can thank your man there for that. He certainly strips to advantage."

"I—I know." Some of the color flooded back into Gwenda's pale cheeks. "I—I mean I do . . . I—"

At that moment, the moon drifted from behind the clouds, illuminating her expression. Her gaze met Ravenel's, her green-gold eyes shining soft with gratitude and admiration.

It was most strange, Ravenel thought, staring back at her, suddenly conscious of being half-naked, his breeches mud-stained, his face battered. But for the first time in his life, Desmond Arthur Gordon Treverly could imagine what it was like to be a dashing knight, garbed in a silver coat of mail shining bright as the sun.

Chapter 8

The late-afternoon sun charted a downward course by the time Ravenel spotted the rooftops of what had once been the sleepy fishing village of Brighthelmston, now a bustling fashionable resort owing to the Prince Regent's patronage.

His lordship slapped down on the reins of the hired tilbury, but the gray mare pulling the carriage set its own pace regardless. He did not attempt to urge the horse again and settled lazily back against the seat. He was not in a hurry for once.

"Brighton, Miss Vickers," Ravenel said, drawing in a deep breath, already scenting the salty tang of sea air. "I do believe we might make it this time."

His remark coaxed only a brief smile from Gwenda. She had been quiet and unusually solemn ever since they had set out from the Nonesuch at noon. Ravenel dragged his gaze from the road winding ahead and regarded her rather anxiously. He didn't care at all for the deep shadows under her eyes. She appeared like some pale waif garbed in that overlarge frock that belonged to Mordred's wife. Although he had to admit the green shade was becoming to her eyes, they seemed so lackluster. And he could wish for a little more color in her cheeks.

The baron trusted that a good sleep would restore her to her irrepressible self again. Goodness knows neither of them had gotten much of that last night. The only one who seemed unaffected by the previous eve's events was Bert. The dog wedged himself in between Ravenel and Gwenda, making a nuisance of himself by thrusting his head into Ravenel's line of vision and barking to be let down for a run. He appeared none the worse for the amount of brandy he had lapped up.

I should have such a hard head, the baron thought wryly.

When he was obliged to shift over on the seat to make more room for Bert, Ravenel winced. Damn! Was there any part of his anatomy that was not bruised from Quince's fists?

His lips parted in a rather painful smile. What a glorious fight it had been! The sparring he enjoyed at Gentleman Jackson's seemed staid by comparison, he mused, yet marveling at his own recent behavior.

In the early hours of the morning, he had recounted every detail of the fight with almost boyish enthusiasm to Jarvis. The old man ought to have been appalled to discover that his master had been brawling in the mud with a smuggler, then staying to tipple brandy with the rogue. But there had been a certain indulgence in Jarvis's manner, merely adjuring Ravenel to hold still as he had applied beefsteak to the swollen eye.

Not even as a lad had the baron ever so forgotten himself as to engage in boisterous wrestling or bouts of fisticuffs like his school fellows or cousins frequently did. Always he had been conscious that such ungentlemanly conduct was beneath the dignity of the Baron Ravenel.

Then what had become of his dignity in the stableyard of the Nonesuch? Ravenel still didn't know. Some ages-old constraint inside him seemed to have snapped, and he had made up for all the mischief denied him in his lost boyhood in a single night. Stranger still, he harbored no remorse, no self-recriminations at his lapse of reason. If anything, he felt amused recalling the episode with Tom Quince. When the man's wagon had finally been unloaded, the baron had shaken the smuggler's hand as though parting with an old friend.

And Mordred . . . Ravenel chuckled to himself at the memory, stopping abruptly at the twinge of pain in his sore jaw. Mordred had fallen over himself to be obliging, frightened that the baron might decide to hand him over to the authorities. Besides turning up with the gown for Gwenda, the innkeeper had offered his coach to convey Jarvis and the baggage to Ravenel's lodgings in Brighton. By some magic the host had also produced a tilbury for Ravenel to drive Gwenda home in, all this without asking for a single shilling in payment. Always eager to help a fellow creature in need, Mordred had crooned, and surely his lordship was not the man to hold a grudge against a poor innkeeper? So much for Gwenda's desperate, murderous villain. The baron wondered what she would say if he told her that he had discovered later that the man's pistol had not even been loaded.

He stole a speculative glance at his companion but could scarce see her face. Her head drooped forward, her bonnet and curls shading her eyes. She truly was exhausted, he thought, wishing he could draw her head down onto his shoulder. She had fallen asleep in such an awkward position.

But Gwenda was not asleep. She suffered not so

much from exhaustion as from a severe attack of
guilt. She could scarce bring herself to meet
Ravenel's gaze all morning, astonished that he appeared so cheerful, what with those shocking
bruises on his cheek, to say nothing of his poor eye.

It was all her fault. If she had listened to him
and returned to her room, not dragged him out into
the night looking for Bert, none of last night's escapade would ever have occurred. She had expected
Ravenel to deliver a lecture that would last all the
way to her parents' doorstep or at least to put on
his martyred look.

How utterly unfeeling of the man that he chose
to do neither! Here she was in the throes of remorse, willing, nay eager, to listen to a scolding in
noble silence, and what must Ravenel do but sit
there, looking so confoundedly nonchalant.

With the exception of his shocking black eye, he
was rigged out in his usual manner, with stiff-
starched cravat, somber-colored waistcoat and
breeches, his curly-brimmed beaver perched upon
waves of neatly combed ebony hair. But his behavior was most . . . most un-Ravenel-like. The man
acted as though he had not a care in the world but
to enjoy the drive, the brightness of the day after
last evening's storm. Why, at the moment, he was
even softly whistling some tuneless ditty.

Unfortunately, Gwenda could think of only one
way to account for his uplifted spirits. He had to
be rejoicing in the knowledge that he was soon to
be rid of her. Not that she could blame him, but the
notion only added to her misery. Had she not
brought disaster to him, from the moment she had
thrust herself upon his notice at the White Hart,
attempting to meddle in his relations with Miss
Carruthers and involving him with stolen phae-

tons, chewed boots, coaching wrecks, treks through rainstorms and smugglers? Everything Ravenel had ever said about her was correct, Gwenda thought with a heavy sigh. Shatter-brained, heedless, impractical ... And to climax everything, he had been obliged to engage in a vulgar brawl to save her dog. Gwenda was certain that was an affront to his dignity that the baron would never forget.

She quickly blinked back the tear that threatened to trickle down her cheek. At least one good thing had come out of it all. The baron obviously had given over his foolish notion that he had to marry her. He had not mentioned it once this morning. Last night's affair must have brought him to his senses. Not even his lordship's rigid code of honor would require such a sacrifice, that he should tie himself to a female absurd enough to run abroad in her nightgown and become entangled with smugglers, a woman so sadly wanting in the sort of propriety and good sense Ravenel would demand of his wife.

She was glad of this, Gwenda told herself stoutly, for of course it was not as if she wanted to marry him. Just because the man did at times appear in her dreams as Roderigo, she certainly hadn't been so foolish as to fall in love with him. No, how utterly absurd that would be.

The tilbury gave a sudden jolt, which forced Gwenda to sit erect and clutch the side of the carriage. She realized with a start that they were rattling over the cobbled streets of the town itself and only his lordship's expert handling of the reins had prevented their locking wheels with a phaeton driven by some reckless young buck.

Even this did not serve to ruffle Ravenel's temper. With some amusement, he pointed out to Gwenda the distant outline of the Regent's whimsical pavilion. She eyed with little interest the classical villa with its central rotunda encircled by six Ionic columns. Beyond that a glass dome topped what was surely the most lavish structure ever built to stable horses. But the sight of the palace only served as a melancholy reminder to Gwenda that she and Ravenel were approaching the end of their journey.

All too soon the tilbury jounced along the Marine Parade toward that fashionable area of Brighton known as the Royal Crescent. The town house her family had rented proved to be one of the newer ones with charming wrought-iron balconies and canopied bow windows. The walls were glazed with black tiles to withstand the gales and salt spray of the sea.

As Ravenel reined in the shuffling gray mare, Gwenda prepared to jump down before his lordship could come around to assist her.

"I have given you enough trouble," she said primly. "But before we say farewell, I must tell you how much I . . . how truly grateful—"

"There's no need to go into that now. I am coming in with you." His lordship leaped somewhat gingerly from the carriage, wincing as he held a hand to his ribs. Bertie bolted right after him.

When Ravenel came around to hand her down, Gwenda shrank back. "Oh, n-no. I know how tired . . . how eager you must be to get to your own house. There is not the least necessity for you to come in with me."

"Indeed there is. I have to speak to your father."

Gwenda's eyes widened in dismay. "About what?"

" 'Tis customary to consult a lady's father in

these delicate affairs. I need to assure him that I am going to marry you."

So Ravenel's mind had not altered. He was still insisting that she be his wife. A curious sensation of gladness stirred inside Gwenda, but she quickly suppressed it, recalling Ravenel's reason for doing so.

She answered rather sharply. "I told you you are not obliged to do that. I am willing to risk my reputation rather than enter into such—such an undesirable union."

For a moment, she fancied she saw a shading of hurt in his dark eyes, a pain that had naught to do with his bruised flesh. "I had rather hoped you were starting to reconsider—" He broke off. "Never mind. I know what is proper. If you won't be sensible, I would as lief refer the matter to your father's judgment."

His cheerful manner vanished as he squared his jaw in a stubborn manner. He reached up, his hands spanning her waist. He lifted her rather forcefully from the tilbury so that she tumbled against him.

Gwenda quickly pulled herself back from the all-too-welcome support of his strong arms. " 'Tis you who won't be sensible. You have made your chivalrous offer; I have refused it. You ought to be satisfied."

"I won't be satisfied until I have talked to Lord Vickers."

Gwenda started to argue, but it was difficult to do so while fighting an unaccountable urge to burst into tears.

"Very well," she said. "If there is no other way to appease your infernal conscience! But I know full well how Papa will handle the matter."

Gwenda flounced away from him. While Ravenel consigned the horse and tilbury to the care of a groom, she marched up the town-house steps with Bert frisking alongside, swatting at her skirts with his tail.

The baron joined her at the door, his expression a mingling of obstinacy and trepidation. He might well have been a visitor contemplating his first excursion inside Bedlam, reluctant but manfully determined to face the ordeal ahead.

Knowing the contempt in which Ravenel held her family, Gwenda anticipated the forthcoming introductions with dread. Lord knows, she was not ashamed of her family, but at times they could be so—so *enthusiastic* and Ravenel so stiff-necked.

She thought again of trying to turn him aside from his purpose, but the oak portal was already being swung open by a servant whose familiar tanned features seemed out of place in butler's garb.

"F-Fitch!" Gwenda gasped in utter astonishment.

"Miss Gwenda," the coachman exclaimed. "Praise the Lord!"

She could only stare at him, recalling that the last time she had seen the man Ravenel had been stuffing his unconscious form inside the coach.

"Fitch, what are you doing here?"

"The master gave over trying to make a coachman of me. He said I should try butlering—"

"No," the baron interrupted, looking equally astounded. "She means, how the deuce did you get here ahead of us?"

"Ah, Master Jack found me and James and fetched us here late last night." Fitch stepped back to allow Gwenda and Ravenel to enter the foyer. Before Gwenda could demand any further details

175

from her erstwhile coachman, another male voice called out, "Fitch. Who is it?"

Gwenda tipped back her head, her gaze traveling up the marble staircase to the regions above. A youth attired in scarlet regimentals leaned over the gilt railing. So dashing, so manly did he appear in uniform that it took Gwenda a second to recognize her scapegrace brother until Jack's face lit up at the sight of her.

"Gwenda, you madcap!" He tore down the steps at such a rate he appeared certain to fall and break his neck.

"Oh, Jack! Jack!" With a glad outcry, Gwenda flung herself into his arms, momentarily forgetting everything but her joy in being reunited with her favorite brother.

They hugged while Bert leaped up at them barking, then both began to talk breathlessly, scarce giving the other a chance to reply.

"Damme, Gwen. Father's had me searching all over Kent for you . . ."

"Oh, I'm so sorry if I've worried everyone."

". . . and even after I found the wrecked carriage and that great looby Fitch, he had no notion where you'd got to—"

"I've been quite safe. But, Jack! Your new uniform. You look so smart!"

" 'Tis nothing to cry about, for mercy sakes. You already appear enough of a fright. Where'd you get that hideous dress?"

While in the midst of these greetings, a door off to Gwenda's right opened and other familiar, well-loved voices were heard.

"Jack? Did I hear Bertie's bark?"

"Is that our Gwennie come back?"

The next instant a short, plump woman rustled

forward. Dear Mama, her military-style spencer and skirt as ever neat and precise. And just behind her, Papa, his dreamy eyes already filling with tears of gladness. Gwenda had not a chance to utter a word before her parents swept down upon her, embracing her.

Lingering upon the threshold, his presence gone unnoticed, Ravenel shifted his feet, beginning to feel a trifle awkward. With some hesitation, he removed his hat and handed it to Fitch. Studying the trio surrounding Gwenda, he had no difficulty recognizing Lord Vickers. The man's leonine mane of silver hair was a familiar sight at the House of Lords. The woman with the lace cap and unruly curls, of course, had to be Gwenda's mother, Lady Vickers. And as incredible as it seemed, the jovial, harmless-looking lad must be the infamous Mad Jack.

Yet even without observing the Vickerses all together, Ravenel felt he would have instantly known the members of Gwenda's family. It was not so much a strong facial resemblance they shared as it was that exuberance of manner that was so much a part of Gwenda's charm; an unaffected display of warmth and affection that marked them all as belonging together.

The baron took a step backward, suddenly feeling like an intruder here. He was on the point of taking back his hat and slipping quietly away when a lull finally occurred in all the hugging and exclamations.

"My dear child," Lord Vickers said to Gwenda, blowing his nose into his linen handkerchief. "I thought you were dead."

"Stuff, my dear!" Lady Vickers exclaimed. "Why must you always be thinking people are dead? One cannot be five minutes late coming back from the dressmaker's without you working yourself into a fret."

" 'Twas more than five minutes." Her husband raised his hand with a dramatic flourish. "To have one's only daughter vanish from the face of the earth! To find naught but the wrecked remains of her coach—"

At this juncture, Fitch startled them all by bursting into a loud lament. "Oh, 'twas all my fault, sir. That accursed drink. You should turn me off without a character, so you should."

In his fit of remorse, Fitch twisted and crushed the brim of the baron's hat. But before Ravenel could rescue his much-abused headgear, the butler turned and stumbled off toward the servant's stairwell, taking Ravenel's hat with him.

"Fitch!" Lord Vickers called. "Oh, the poor fellow. Fitch!"

"Let him go, my dear," Lady Vickers said. " 'Tis best he retires below until he composes himself. One cannot have a hysterical butler answering one's door, can one?"

It took the startled Ravenel a moment to realize her ladyship had directed this last comment to him.

"Oh! Er . . . no, it would not do at all."

Lady Vickers nodded in approval. "Such a sensible man. So good of you to call. 'Tis always so delightful to receive unexpected visitors. . . . Who are you?"

Her ladyship's acknowledgment of Ravenel's presence had the effect of also turning her son's and husband's attention upon him. To Ravenel, it seemed he was facing a veritable sea of curious green-gold eyes. He had never before experienced any difficulty in pronouncing his own name, but he found himself stumbling over it.

Gwenda came to his rescue. She pushed her way to his side, looking a little nervous and breathless herself. "This—this is Lord Ravenel, Mama. He—he is the gentleman who has been looking after me and has rescued me several times and—and risked his life fighting with smugglers and all manner of brave things."

Ravenel felt his cheeks wash a dull red. He wished Gwenda would have given him a more ordinary sort of introduction. He started to disclaim, but the Vickerses were already upon him, pumping his hand with enthusiasm: Lady Vickers reiterating her conviction that he was a sensible man, Jack terming him a "brick," and Stanhope Vickers declaring what a pleasure it was to meet the preserver of his most beloved daughter.

"I am your only daughter, Papa," Gwenda reminded him.

"So you are, my pet. So you are." Stanhope Vickers clapped his hands together. "Well, Lord Ravenel. We must adjourn to the parlor at once, and you and Gwennie can regale us all with an accounting of your adventures. Prudence, my own, mayhap a spot of tea—"

"No, sir. Please," the baron said quickly before he found himself entirely carried away from the purpose of his visit. "If it would be at all convenient, I would like the favor of a few words with you . . . alone."

Lord Vickers's surprise seemed to spread to the rest of his family, with the exception of Gwenda, who leveled a deep frown at Ravenel, which he steadfastly ignored.

"Why, certainly, sir," Lord Vickers said. "If that is what you wish."

"Oho! What mischief has Gwenda been about this time?" Jack Vickers called out gleefully.

"Be quiet, Jack," Lady Vickers said. She disconcerted the baron by offering him a glance of unexpected shrewdness as her eyes traveled from him to her blushing daughter. She briskly shooed her son toward the door. "I am very sure you have some business that requires your attention elsewhere. And as for Gwenda, she is all done in. She should go upstairs for a hot bath and liedown. I will send Colette—"

Her ladyship paused a moment to frown. "Oh, no, that is right. Fitch told us Colette has run off. So sadly unreliable, but she did speak French so prettily."

"Mama, please," Gwenda said as soon as she could get a word in. "I am not in the least tired. I should like to wait—"

But her mother swept her protests aside. "As your grandpapa the general always said, a soldier is of no use in battle unless she has had the proper rest."

Ravenel had no chance to so much as speak to Gwenda before her mother was marching her up the stairs, gently straightening her daughter's shoulders as they went. Gwenda shot one anxious glance back at him, her look half pleading, half indignant.

Damn it, Gwenda, Ravenel wanted to shout. I am insisting upon this marriage for your own good.

Then he caught a glimpse of himself in the cheval glass mounted on the wall and saw that he looked every bit as tense as she did. He followed Lord Vickers into the study for what he feared was

180

going to prove the most awkward interview of his life.

". . . and that is the whole of the matter. So you see why I must marry your daughter," Ravenel concluded.

"Dear me," Lord Vickers said. "You and Gwennie certainly have had a most unfortunate time of it."

Considering Lord Vickers's usual flair for the dramatic, the baron found this a rather surprising bit of understatement. He wondered if Gwenda's father had understood one word of all that he had just related.

Seated behind a desk littered with rumpled parchment, half-mended quill pens, and dripping inkwells, Lord Vickers rocked back in his leather-covered chair, bridging his fingertips beneath his chin. He shook his head and blessed his own soul several times.

"So do I have your permission to go ahead with the marriage banns?" Ravenel prodded.

"I don't quite know what to tell you, young man." A gentle frown creased Lord Vickers's long forehead. "Any practical considerations of my daughter's future, I usually leave to her mother. We had much better consult her."

Without waiting for Ravenel's agreement, Lord Vickers snapped to his feet with surprising quickness. He strode to the door, flung it open, and called for his wife.

Very shortly, Prudence Vickers poked her head in the doorway, a pair of wire-rimmed spectacles perched on her nose. "What is it, my dear? Are you ready for your tea?"

"Not just yet, my love. It would seem Gwennie has gotten herself into some sort of a coil. Last night she and Lord Ravenel were stranded together at an inn . . . er, the Nonesuch. By the by, it sounds rather quaint. Remind me to stop over there the next time we are traveling through Kent."

"Certainly, my dear."

The baron bit back an impatient oath. "The point is, my lady, that your daughter was unchaperoned and—"

"And so Lord Ravenel feels he ought to marry our Gwen," Lord Vickers finished.

Lady Vickers studied Ravenel over the top of her spectacles. "Oh? Is that your only reason for wishing to do so?"

The baron squirmed uncomfortably. If he had any other reasons, he was not quite ready to examine them. "It seems to me reason enough."

"And Gwenda?" Lady Vickers asked. "Is she enthusiastic about this notion?"

"N-o-oo," Ravenel said reluctantly. "I admit that she is not. But under the circumstances—"

"Then under the circumstances, she had better not do it."

"That is your opinion, is it, my dearest heart?" her husband asked.

"Indeed it is. Stanhope, only consider. Gwenda has already betrothed herself twice and broken it off because the affection was found wanting. A third time and it could develop into a most disagreeable habit."

Lady Vickers gave Ravenel an amiable smile so very much like Gwenda's. "Thank you all the same for your offer, my lord, however misplaced it may have been. I am sure in all other respects you are a most sensible man. Now do forget all this, and hurry along for tea."

With that, her ladyship popped back out again.

The baron rubbed the back of his neck, thinking ruefully that Lady Vickers was certainly her daughter's mother. He heaved a deep sigh and made one last attempt to reason with Lord Vickers.

"Sir, with all due respect, what you and your wife don't seem to understand is if this tale leaks out, your daughter will be ruined. Society may begin to say a deal of other things about Gwenda, things far less pleasant than whispers of broken engagements."

"Shall they?" Lord Vickers asked. "Well, I think it far more important not to force two delightful young people into a marriage neither wants rather than take heed of idle gossip."

Ravenel opened his mouth and closed it again. What was he to say in the face of such impracticality?

Lord Vickers smiled and continued, "Lady Vickers and I only want our daughter to be happy."

"But, my lord—"

"In truth, those who love Gwenda, who value her as they ought, would know she could never have done anything bad. The opinion of the rest of the world simply doesn't matter."

Ravenel could only stare at the man. This was utter folly. He knew it was and yet . . . There was a soft glow in Stanhope Vickers's eyes as he pronounced these words, and a quality to his voice infusing it with wisdom, a gentle, loving wisdom that made the baron's own notions of duty and propriety ring quite hollow.

Mayhap it was not the Vickerses who were the half-mad fools, but himself and the rest of the world. Ravenel ran one hand across his brow in confusion.

"There, there, young man." Lord Vickers patted

him on the back. "You come along with me. Things always seem much clearer after one's had a cup of tea."

The fiery ball that was the sun poised on the verge of dipping below the sea, the ever-darkening waves frothed against the shore, and the twilight sky streaked with rosy ribands of sunset.

"Blast!" Gwenda hissed, letting fall the delicate organza curtain. She had only laid down upon the bed for a few minutes, never intending to fall asleep. What if Ravenel were already gone?

She stumbled to the French gilt wardrobe and found a simple white muslin gown, which she donned. Barely taking the time to tame her mop of curls, she flung an Indian shawl about her shoulders and raced out of her bedchamber.

She rushed to the gilt railing and was about to tear down the stairs when she noticed the tall, broad-shouldered figure pacing the hall below.

Ravenel. She breathed a tiny sigh of relief. So he had not already fled the Vickers household in horror. He appeared to have survived the talk with her father, although exactly what had passed between the two men Gwenda could not tell from Ravenel's expression. He looked neither relieved nor disgusted, merely thoughtful.

When Gwenda began to descend the stairs, he glanced up at her, his mouth tightening with a wry grimace. "You need not look so apprehensive, Gwenda. 'Tis all over."

Gwenda paused at the foot of the steps. "And?" she asked anxiously.

"Your father has convinced me you were right to refuse my offer. I have no intention of troubling you any further." He drew himself up stiffly and

Gwenda thought she detected a flash of hurt in his eyes. For the first time, it occurred to her how she must have wounded Ravenel's pride.

She wished she could think of something soothing to say, but ended by blurting out, "Then why are you lingering here in the hall?"

"I was on the point of leaving." He gave an exasperated laugh. "But it seems Fitch has misplaced my hat. Your family is tearing apart the servants' quarters looking for it."

Gwenda blushed with mortification. "Oh, Ravenel, I am so sorry—" she began, then stopped. "No, I am not. I am glad of it, for otherwise I should have missed you." She added accusingly, "You were going to leave without saying good-bye."

"Of course I wasn't! That is . . ." He took a few steps away from her. "You were resting. I did not want to disturb you. Now you look . . ." He paused to glance back at her, a warmth coming into his eyes. Then he quickly averted his gaze. "Much better," he concluded.

Gwenda felt her blush deepen and she fretted the ends of her shawl. This was absurd, she thought, after all that she and Ravenel had been through together, for both of them to be behaving so shy and awkward now.

She cleared her throat, preparing to say what she had attempted to earlier in the tilbury. "My lord, I want you know how grateful I am for everything—"

"Please! No speeches, my dear." A mischievous smile tipped Ravenel's lips, as devastatingly charming as it was unexpected. It was the way he had always been meant to smile, Gwenda thought sadly, not in that constrained manner she knew he would adopt as soon as he set foot out the door.

She tried to assume a cheerful manner. "Well, I daresay you will find yourself quite busy. All those business affairs you have had to neglect because of me and—and . . ." She faltered. "Miss Carruthers will likely be in Brighton soon."

"I suppose she will." The baron appeared to sober somewhat at the mention of Belinda's name, although he asked teasingly, "Any more advice for me, Miss Vickers?"

Gwenda started to speak, then firmly shook her head. At that moment Jack came bursting into the hall, carrying Ravenel's hat.

"Fitch locked it down in the wine cellar!" Her brother rolled his eyes. "I am not certain how well he is going to serve as a butler, either."

Ravenel merely smiled as he took the curly-brimmed beaver from Jack. He asked Gwenda to express his thanks to her mother and father, then shook hands with Jack. Under her brother's curious eyes, Gwenda thought Ravenel would do the same with her. But when she offered him her hand, he carried it to his lips and pressed a fervent kiss upon her wrist. He turned and strode out the front door, without glancing back.

He had not taken five steps away from the house when he heard someone call his name.

"Ravenel?"

He turned quickly at the sound of Gwenda's voice. She stood silhouetted in the doorway, the simple white muslin accenting her curves. The breeze ruffled her soft curls, her ever-changeable eyes assuming the green luster of the sea.

"Yes?" he asked hopefully.

"I—I do have some advice." She drew in a deep breath. "I—I hope that sometimes you will remember to be just a little improper."

Ravenel playfully tipped his hat in acknowledgment of her words. She withdrew into the house, the door inching closed. As soon as she was gone, his smile faded. He grasped his hat, heading toward where one of Lord Vickers's grooms had brought around his tilbury.

The baron was somewhat amused to see Spotted Bert waiting there in the gathering dusk. The dog barked at his approach, charging forward and wagging his tail.

"What! Did you think I was going to leave without saying good-bye to you, either?"

He bent down to scratch Bert beneath the chin, but he found his gaze traveling past the dog to the sea, which was wide and mysterious, lapping against the shingled beach, so empty, so wretchedly lonely.

Ravenel jerked to his feet, saying sharply to the dog, "Damn it, Bert. What a fool I am! I didn't have to marry her. I wanted to. That's why I've been going on and on about duty, making such a pompous ass of myself. I'm in love with the woman."

He started purposefully back toward the house, only to halt again. He glanced down at Bert padding by his side. "But 'tis of no avail, is it? She doesn't want to marry me. There is no reason that she should."

He thought of his title, his twenty thousand pounds per annum, the vast cold manor in Leicestershire. He stared at the Vickers town house where the lamps were already being lit, the light glowing warmly beyond the panes of glass. Through the open window he could hear the sounds of singing, laughter.

"I don't really have anything to offer her, do I?" Ravenel murmured, his shoulders sagging.

He replaced his hat on his head and turned to go, pausing to pat the dog one last time. "You will look after her, though, won't you, Bert?"

The dog cocked his head to one side. Bert's only reply was a low, mournful whine.

Chapter 9

Gwenda dipped her quill pen in the ink and scratched it laboriously across the page. For nearly a week she had been closeted in her room, seated at the small desk by her window overlooking the sea. If she ventured out at all, it was only for her brief visits to Donaldson's Lending Library. But *The Sepulchre of Castle Sorrow* had not advanced much beyond the first chapter.

> *The wind whistled past the velvet curtains. The candle flickered and went out in a hiss of smoke. Roderigo felt the chill of the grave pervade the castle walls, the stench of decaying flesh, crumbling bones, and the dark deed long forgotten—*

The last word trailed away in a smear of ink as Spotted Bert nudged his cold nose against Gwenda's elbow. He thrust his head in her lap, whining, rolling up his eyes in mournful fashion.

"Bertie, please!" Gwenda forced the dog back. "How am I ever to accomplish anything with you moping all over me?"

Her exuberant Bertie did not seem to be himself ever since their arrival in Brighton, the day that Rav—Feeling a small twinge in her own heart, she suppressed the thought. No, likely it was only that the sea air did not agree with Bert. She blotted the ink and reached for her pen once more.

> *The shade of an ancient warrior rose up before him, its bloodstained visage awful to behold. "Roderigo!" quoth the ghost in dire accents, which would have caused a man of less fortitude than the young count to swoon. "Roderigo! Arise. The time hath come to address the wrongs done me by your family."*
>
> *Roderigo staggered back, flinging one hand across his noble brow. "Before tea!"*

Gwenda flung down her pen in disgust and tore the parchment in two. The pieces joined the others that littered the soft carpet at her feet. She started to lean her aching head against her hands when Bert startled her by springing up. Thrusting his head through the open window, he gave a series of short, joyous barks.

She stood up herself to peer out. But she saw nothing in the stream of fashionable coaches, gigs, and phaetons making their way along the Marine Parade to have aroused such excitement in Bertie.

She was about to haul the dog back from the sill when she spied the tall man walking along the grassy enclosure, his features obscured as he bent forward to keep his curly-brimmed beaver from being snatched by the stiff breeze. Gwenda's heart quickened only to plummet with disappointment when the man doffed his hat to a passing carriage. Not glossy strands of ebony but only an unfamiliar dull brown.

Spotted Bert's barking faded to a chagrined whine.

"Oh, Bertie!" Gwenda snapped. But her vexation

had little to do with the dog. "Go on. Get out of here. Find a cat to chase."

Although Bertie hung back, she managed to thrust him out her bedchamber door, then slammed it behind him. But she immediately felt ashamed for being so short-tempered with Bert. Truthfully, these past days, she had been as bad as the dog, ever hopeful of catching a glimpse of a cravat with a little too much starch, a swarthy-looking man constraining his hard-muscled form beneath the stiff garb of a most proper gentleman. Yet if Ravenel ever was abroad, enjoying the Brighton sunshine, he never passed by her window.

"Anyone would think I was in love with the man," Gwenda grumbled as she sat back down at her desk.

That thought had been occurring to her all too often of late, a most frightening, distressing thought. Romantic as it was in books, Gwenda did not care for the notion of pining away from unrequited passion. She would much rather have a love that was returned, so that she might be comfortable and happy.

With Ravenel, that was too much to hope for. By the end of their journey, he seemed to have learned to tolerate her, to even be civil to her family. But that was a far cry from the warmth of feeling Gwenda would require in her lover. She had not heard so much as a word from his lordship in the past week.

Gwenda reached for another sheet of paper, then sat staring at the blank vellum. This foolishness would pass, she assured herself. Had she not fancied herself in love twice before? She had been much younger then, barely seventeen that disastrous season. She could smile at her youthful self now, all those torrents of emotion, the conviction that her heart would be broken in two if she was not able to marry Jasper. She had survived that only to be equally certain she would go into a decline and perish if she did not become Marlon's bride.

She did not experience any such violent fancies about Ravenel, only the feeling that as each bright sun-kissed day passed without his presence, the summer sky seemed permanently washed in gray.

Gwenda thrust the sheet and ink pot away from her. She was doing no good here. She might as well round up Bertie and take him out for a walk. She retrieved her bone-handled parasol, then descended belowstairs, whistling for Bert. The lower floor of the house basked in the afternoon silence, except for the distant strains of Papa practicing at the pianoforte.

Fitch informed her that the master had already demanded Spotted Bert's eviction. The dog always howled when her father sang, so Fitch had been obliged to chase Bert outside.

But although she stood on the front steps and called, Bert seemed to have raced off out of earshot. Gwenda could not face the prospect of returning to her lonely room, so she opted to venture on her walk without the dog. Yet her listless footsteps got her not much farther than the seven-foot-tall statue of the Prince Regent mounted in front of the Royal Crescent. Disgraceful thing, Gwenda thought. The buff-colored stone had been eroded by sea squalls until one arm broke off. Most mistook it for a likeness of Nelson.

She leaned against it, poking the tip of her parasol in the grass. A party of ladies and gentlemen rattled along the Parade in their carriage, all of them laughing, apparently bent on some excursion of pleasure. Then Gwenda watched a family with a large brood of children go past, likely off for some sea bathing. Why did the rest of the world always seem to be having a wonderful time when one was at one's most miserable?

"Hallo there! Gwenda!"

The sound of her brother's voice snapped her head around toward the distant line of town houses. Jack bounded down the steps and raced toward the grassy enclosure, waving something.

He came up to her, panting with indignation. "That blasted dog of yours is moving on from boots to belts now."

He thrust a strap of chewed leather in her face. Gwenda pushed it aside weakly, mumbling that she was sorry.

Her brother, obviously bracing himself for a heated exchange, snapped his mouth closed and blinked. "What?" he asked. "No 'Plague take you, Jack' or 'If you didn't leave belts lying around, Bertie couldn't get them, Jack'?"

"I am not in the humor for quarreling." Gwenda sidestepped her brother. She tried to open her parasol, but the breeze coming off the sea was a shade too brisk. Abandoning the effort, she trailed away from Jack, heading for the shingled beach.

Her brother caught up with her and fell into step. "You are not in much of a humor for anything since you came to Brighton. I never saw such moping, unless it was that silly dog of yours. 'Tis beginning to put me in the hips just watching the pair of you."

Jack scuffed the toe of his boot along the beach, sending up a spray of smooth, shiny pebbles. "As if I didn't already have enough to make me blue-deviled. Thorne is about to descend on us *and* Papa's cousin's from Cheapside. They all want to see me before I leave to join my regiment."

"That's nice, Jack," Gwenda murmured.

He caught her by the elbow, swinging her about. "I say, Gwenda. I've got a notion. Why don't you come to watch the military review on the Bluffs with me and my friend Neville Gilboys. He's a first-rate fellow. His family made him join the army, but he really wants to be a playwright. He's perishing to meet you and tell you all about this tragedy he means to write someday."

In her present mood, Gwenda shuddered at the thought of meeting an eager would-be writer.

But her brother persisted. "Do come! Neville's devilish handsome. Just like that Roderigo chap you're always dreaming about with blond hair and a trim mustache—"

"Roderigo doesn't have a mustache. He has ebony hair and dark eyes." Dark as the sea at midnight, Gwenda added to herself. Hugging her skirts close against the wind, she stared forlornly at the waves breaking over the shore.

Jack vented his breath in a frustrated sigh. "What's amiss with you, Gwen? I've never seen you like this before."

When she didn't answer, he planted himself in front of her. "I won't go away until you tell me." He injected that cajoling note into his voice that only he knew how to use so well. He always managed to wheedle her secrets out of her, and Gwenda knew she would be given no peace until she confided in him.

"I—I think I have fallen in love," she said.

"Not again!"

Gwenda did not appreciate his brotherly frankness, not when she had just bared her soul to him. "If you are going to take that attitude . . ." She began to walk back up the beach, but he caught her, forcing her to halt.

"No, no, Gwen. I am sorry. Come back. Who are you in love with this—" He amended hastily. "I mean, who is the lucky devil?"

She tried to maintain a stubborn silence, but instead she found herself resting her head against Jack's shoulder, tears beclouding her eyes. "Lord Ravenel," she whispered.

"Ravenel!" Jack croaked, although he patted her back.

Gwenda straightened immediately, her cheeks firing with indignation. "Aye! Why did you pronounce his name in that odious manner?"

"I—I didn't mean anything by it. 'Tis just that he does not seem in your usual line, Gwen. Although he behaved splendidly fighting that smuggler for Bert, his lordship is not the most dashing sort." Jack hesitated, then blurted out, "In fact, there is rather something about him that reminds me of Thorne."

"Ravenel is not in the least like Thorne!" Gwenda bristled, then remembered that she had once told the baron the same thing. "Well, mayhap only a very little at times. But Thorne would feel quite self-righteous if one got hurt doing something wrong. Ravenel *is* the sort of man who, if I accidentally set the house on fire, would give me a blistering scold. But first he would make sure I hadn't been burned."

"I see," Jack said, then infused his voice with a generous enthusiasm. "Of course. The very sort of thing to make a girl dote upon a chap."

"You don't see at all." Gwenda shifted her gaze to

the sea as though somewhere on the bright sparkling waters she would find the words to explain it to him. "Beneath his starched cravat, Ravenel *is* dashing. When I have dreams about Roderigo now, 'tis always Ravenel that I see coming through the mist. He has the most handsome eyes and when he ki—" She broke off, heat rushing through her at the memory. She stumbled on. " 'Tis not any grand gesture that makes him heroic, but all manner of foolish little things like—like tucking his coat around my shoulders in the rainstorm even when he was angry, and saving Bert even after Bert had chewed up his boot, and asking me if I was unharmed after his own head had nearly been broken by Quince's fist."

"You must be in love." Jack nodded solemnly. "You are not making any sense. If you care so much for him, why did you let Papa send him away when he had offered for you?"

"He does not love me." Gwenda sniffed. "There is someone else. Not that I believe he is in love with Miss Carruthers, either, but she is so much more proper than—"

"Belinda Carruthers?" Jack interrupted.

"Aye. Have you met her?"

"No, but I know *of* her. I ran into old Huddersby at the Ship Tavern just yesterday. Poor fellow was badly cut up; lost a big wager. It seems he had bet this Carruthers chit would wed the Earl of Smardon, but the earl didn't come up to scratch."

"And now I suppose Belinda will be only too pleased to receive Ravenel's addresses." Gwenda flushed with anger. "She has treated him so shabbily, keeping him dangling, telling him she is recovering from a broken heart. Some tale of being in mourning over a . . . a"—Gwenda searched her memory for the name Belinda had mentioned that day—"a Colonel Percival Adams of the Tenth Cavalry."

"The Tenth?" Jack said. "That's Neville's regiment."

Gwenda scarce heeded him as she added bitterly, "Somehow I never believed a word of what she said."

"Then, my dear sister, the thing to do is to eliminate this unworthy Miss Carruthers as a rival."

Gwenda slowly shook her head. She was not sure that Ravenel would care how sly Belinda was, merely that she would know the correct way to conduct herself as the future Lady Ravenel. Even without Belinda, Ravenel would not willingly consider Gwenda for that role. What had his lordship called her once? "The mistress of disaster."

Her shoulders sagged, her eyes once more filling with tears. This conversation with Jack had only succeeded in lowering her spirits. Debating the matter with her brother had done naught but to convince her how very much she was in love with Ravenel, and how hopeless it all was.

"It was most kind of you to listen, Jack," she said. "But there is naught to be done. I—I assure you I will recover." This time she turned and hurried back to the house, not giving him a chance to overtake her.

As Jack Vickers watched his sister racing along the beach, he made no effort to follow. She would recover, Gwenda had declared, but her brother was not so sure. He had never seen that kind of dull pain in her sparkling eyes before, a heartbreakingly wistful kind of despair.

"Damme!" he muttered. "How can I just march off to enjoy myself shooting Frenchmen, leaving poor Gwen in such a state? My only sister, after all."

Thoughtfully he walked along the sands, letting the water froth to the very tip of his boots. But the somber mood didn't last long. His spirits were as ebullient as the waves. Mad Jack Vickers never accepted any cause as hopeless. There was always *something* to be done.

Chapter 10

Donaldson's Lending Library was a gathering place for the haut *ton* that flocked to Brighton for the summer: a place to hear the latest gossip, to play at cards, to try out some new sheet music upon the pianoforte—in brief, to do anything but select a book to read. Or so it seemed to Gwenda.

She irritably brushed past the group of ladies crowded upon the veranda, smoothing out their light muslins, chattering about how positively dowdy Mrs. Fitzherbert had looked while attending the theater last night.

Inside the library itself was no better. To even reach the book stacks, Gwenda first had to skirt by three dandies studying copies of the latest caricatures by Gilray through their quizzing glasses.

"Dashed amusing, 'pon my soul," one of them drawled. "Depicting that rascal Bonaparte as a pygmy. What will Gilray think of next?"

The dandy's voice sounded oddly familiar to Gwenda. She angled a glance from the corner of her eye and was horrified to recognize the Honorable Frederic Skeffington, the man who had accosted her in the inn yard of the Dorset Arms. Mindful of Ravenel's admonishment that Skeffington was a "loose screw," Gwenda for once behaved in a prudent fashion. She ducked behind one of the bookshelves before Skeffington spotted her yet again without any female chaperone.

While waiting for the three gentlemen to move on, she feigned to examine Volume Four of the latest edition of the *Encyclopaedia Britannica*, never intending to eavesdrop on the conversation. But when she overheard one of them mention Ravenel's name, her heart skipped a beat and she could not help listening more intently.

"Yaa-ss, Sobersides Ravenel has been behaving in a damned odd manner of late." There was a pause, then a loud sniff. Gwenda realized that the speaker had stopped to take a pinch of snuff and waited in an agony of impatience for him to continue.

"Met him along the Steine the other day when me and Froggy Blaine were comparing times of our last run to Brighton. Did it in four hours, fifty-two minutes, I said. Then I asked Ravenel most civilly how long it had taken him. 'Three days,' said he, and broke into hysterical laughter."

Gwenda bit back a rueful smile of her own, but she heard Skeffington and the other man exclaiming in shock.

"Sobersides? Laughing?"

" 'Pon my word, who would have thought it?"

"And there is worse," the first man said. "I chanced to make some little jest about that old fool Stanhope Vickers and Ravenel glowered at me like a mad dog. Said if I had half as much wit as Lord Vickers, I might know when to keep my mouth shut."

Gwenda, as astounded as the others to hear this, dropped the encyclopedia volume on her toe. Stifling an outcry of pain, she bent to retrieve it. It might well have been Skeffington's other friend who had been struck, however, for the man gave a low moan.

"That tears it, then. I was one of the few who wagered Belinda Carruthers would have Sobersides in the end. But if Ravenel is going to start acting as queer as Dick's hat band . . ."

"Your chances have been quite scotched in any case, old boy." Skeffington spoke up. "I happened upon Ravenel myself while traveling to Brighton last week. He was in the company of some pretty little thing making the journey with her aunt. When I uttered a few pleasantries to the lady, he behaved very much like a jealous lover. Nearly gave me a leveler."

Skeffington's companions gasped:

"Dear me!"

"Extraordinary!"

Gwenda thought so herself, and the book nearly slipped from her grasp a second time. Ravenel, a jealous lover? She had never considered his actions in that light. But she immediately quashed the tiny flicker of hope, telling herself Freddie Skeffington was a great dolt.

She leaned up against the bookshelf, waiting anxiously to hear what else might be said. The three men had fallen so quiet, she began to wonder if they had moved on. She peeked cautiously around the side, then choked back a small outcry as she saw the reason for the dandies' sudden silence.

The object of their conversation himself had just walked through the library door, Belinda Carruthers draped upon his arm. Gwenda's pulses gave a leap, part joy, part dismay, as her hungry gaze drank in the sight of Ravenel. Every detail of him, from the broad outline of his shoulders to that

201

overstarched collar, from the brilliant dark eyes to the stubborn line of his jaw, seemed so inexpressibly familiar and dear to her heart.

She looked for some sign of the change in him that the dandies had been discussing, but she could detect nothing odd in Ravenel's manner. He stood as stiffly, as formally erect as ever. If anything, his reserve appeared more pronounced, his movements more perfunctory, as though he was not capable of taking pleasure in anything.

It hurt Gwenda to see that as much as it did to watch Belinda cling to Ravenel in that proprietary way. Gwenda swallowed the lump rising to her throat and shrank back behind the shelves.

The baron did not notice her skirts whisking from sight as he nodded his head in curt greeting to Freddie Skeffington and his two companions. They barely acknowledged it, smiling nervously and skittering by him as though he had the plague. Ravenel gave a slight shrug. Skeffington and his lot had always been a parcel of fools.

With great effort, Ravenel kept his gaze from sweeping about the rest of the library. He could not help telling himself that if there were any chance of encountering Gwenda in Brighton, it would most likely be here at the circulating library. But even if he chanced to see her again, what would that do but make him feel more empty and lonely than he already did?

"My lord?"

He felt Belinda tug at his sleeve and glanced down at her with some impatience.

"I would far rather have gone to the card assembly at the Old Ship. But since you insisted upon coming here, are you not going to at least select a book?"

There was a certain waspishness in Belinda's usually dulcet tones. As though she realized it herself, she was quick to flutter her eyelashes and add, "I know what a busy man you are. Indeed I was surprised and so flattered that you were able to spare the afternoon to escort me at all."

It would have been difficult to do anything else, Ravenel thought wryly. He had been deluged with missives from Belinda ever since her arrival in Brighton, assuring him that he was quite free to call upon her any time he wished.

As she flitted away from him to effuse greetings over some portly dowager and her freckle-faced daughters, Ravenel noted the high bloom in Belinda's cheeks. He thought sardonically how remarkable the sea air in Brighton must be for mending broken hearts. Belinda had never looked better and had not mentioned anything more about being in mourning. Perhaps the cure came less from the sea than from the tidings being bruited about that the Earl of Smardon had become engaged to his cousin.

Ravenel checked his cynical thoughts. In truth, he scarce gave a damn about any of it. While waiting for Belinda, he ran his fingers listlessly over some volumes arranged on a shelf, barely registering the titles until he came to one neatly tooled in red leather.

The Castle of Montesadoria by G. M. Vickers. Ravenel eased the book almost reverently off the shelf, then thumbed through the pages, one particular line catching his notice. His lips curved into a tender smile as he read, "The count was a gentleman of most noble mien with handsome dark eyes."

What a flood of memories those words unleashed,

memories that were sharply dispelled by the sound of Belinda's voice close by.

"Ravenel!"

The petite blonde peered past his shoulder and cooed, "What have you found that has you so absorbed?" When she saw the book, she broke into tinkling laughter. "My dear Ravenel, you surely don't read that sort of book?"

He glared at her, not feeling at all like "her dear Ravenel."

"What, pray, is wrong with this sort of book?"

"Why, 'tis the most arrant sort of rubbish about ghosts and—"

"Until you are clever enough to write one, you should not feel so free to criticize."

Belinda's violet eyes widened. She looked as taken aback by his rudeness as Ravenel was feeling himself. Coloring, she said, "Naturally I would never do anything so vulgar as to write for money." She added with a self-deprecating smile, "Of course, I do dabble a little with poetry."

"I detest poetry." Ravenel closed the book with a snap and replaced it on the shelf. What was amiss with him? It was as though he were deliberately trying to provoke a quarrel with Miss Carruthers.

Not that there appeared any likelihood of that. If Belinda was offended, she quickly concealed it behind a coaxing smile. She tucked her hand through his arm, gushing, "Much more pleasurable than any sort of literature is music. I do so dote on music. Let us see what new songs there are."

She swept over to the pianoforte, quickly sifting through the sheet music, asking for Ravenel's opinion of which she should try. She could have played "Rule Britannia" for all he cared. He scooped up one sheet and handed it to her, having no idea what he had selected as she arranged her skirts on the bench.

Belinda played well, or so most of society would judge, Ravenel mused. But he found her performance wanting in any spark of genuine feeling for the notes she thumped out with such precision. She knows nothing of—of *enthusiasm and dreams*, Ravenel thought, recalling Gwenda's words. Miss Carruthers appeared far more concerned with how well she looked seated at the instrument, tossing her golden curls, her dainty fingers rippling down the keys.

In that instant Ravenel knew he would never marry Miss Carruthers or any other society miss like her. His duty be hanged! He had cousins enough to make up for his own lack of heirs. He would spend the rest of his days at Ravenel, alone. On a cold winter's eve by the solitude of his hearth, he would take out the memory of three glorious days in his life spent in the company of a green-eyed wood sprite who both vexed and amazed and made every moment one of wondering surprise. The baron doubted that he would ever experience anything unexpected again.

This dismal thought had no sooner occurred to Ravenel when the door swung open, nearly slamming Freddie Skeffington against the wall. An officer in a cavalry uniform swaggered through the door.

"So sorry, old chap," he said, doffing his tricorne to the outraged dandy.

Freddie, prepared to sputter and take umbrage, stopped in midsentence, gaping at the soldier. Ravenel could not blame Skeffington. The colonel was a most extraordinary-looking individual. His hair appeared darkened with some strange substance that plastered it to his skull. A mustache of the same startling shade of black appeared shoved beneath his nose. His shoulders, which Ravenel could tell had been padded with buckram wadding, shifted, becoming uneven.

With a final nod to Freddie, the officer set some young ladies by the watercolor books to giggling when he paused to shoot them a killing glance. Ravenel had an odd feeling he had seen this person somewhere before. But surely he would have remembered anyone who looked that peculiar.

The soldier halted in midstep as he spied Miss Carruthers at the piano. He clasped one hand to his heart and strode over. "Belinda, my darling. It is you!"

Belinda's playing stumbled to an abrupt end. She stared up at the officer bending over her and said in affronted accents, "Sir! I do not believe that I have the honor of—"

"Belinda, it is I. Percy!"

"P-Percy?" Miss Carruthers said faintly.

"Aye. Your lost love, Colonel Percival Adams, whom you believed killed in the wars."

"I . . . I . . ." Belinda shrank back, turning as white as her muslin gown. Ravenel, equally astonished, stared at this apparition supposedly returned from the dead. So this was Belinda's Colonel Adams, he thought with a shake of his head. He had never thought Miss Carruthers a brilliant woman, but he had given her credit for having some discernment.

"There—there must be some mistake," Miss Carruthers babbled.

"The only mistake, my dearest, was my taking so long to rush back to your side," the colonel declared. He seized Belinda's hands and planted a fervent kiss upon each of them, which had the effect of knocking his mustache slightly askew.

Peering closer to look beneath the soldier's downswept lashes, Ravenel glimpsed mischievous green-gold eyes. As the jolt of recognition flashed through him, his lordship straightened, groping frantically for his handkerchief. He doubled over, apparently seized by a fit of choking.

By this time most of the other occupants of the library realized that something strange was occurring. Some listened with their heads discreetly averted, while Skeffington and his cronies gawked shamelessly.

Yet huddled behind the encyclopedias, Gwenda wondered in despair if she would ever be able to escape without the pain and embarrassment of encountering Ravenel and Miss Carruthers again. At the last glance she had stolen, they had seemed rooted by the pianoforte for the remainder of the afternoon.

But it gradually became borne in upon her that the music had stopped, that the hum of conversation in the library had grown strangely quiet.

"No!" Miss Carruthers's shrill outcry split the air. "You stay away from me."

"Forgive my impulsiveness, Belinda, my darling," a man's upraised voice said, "but we have been separated for so long."

A most familiar man's voice, Gwenda thought, freezing. With a feeling of dread, she inched out from behind the books and stared toward the pianoforte.

It would have taken more than boot blacking in the hair and a false mustache for Gwenda not to have known her own brother. A soft groan escaped her as she watched Jack pursuing the frantic Miss

207

Carruthers around the pianoforte where she sought to take refuge behind Ravenel.

"I've been a prisoner of the French. With amnesia," Jack declared. "But as soon as I got my memory back, I escaped and returned so that we could be married."

"I am not engaged to you! I have never been engaged to anyone," Belinda shrilled. "I don't even know any Colonel Percival Adams." She appealed desperately to Ravenel. "My lord, save me from this madman."

But Ravenel seemed strangely quiet, muffling his face behind his handkerchief.

Gwenda had no difficulty guessing what her brother was attempting to do. Her face heating scarlet with misery and humiliation, she rushed forward to stop him.

"Jack!" she said, jerking roughly at his arm.

Her brother paused in his pursuit of Miss Carruthers to glance down at her. He pulled a fierce face.

"You are mistaken, miss. I am Colonel Percival—"

"Stop it!" Gwenda choked. She reached up and wrenched off the false mustache.

"Ow!" Jack cried, clapping a hand to his upper lip. He eyed her reproachfully. "This would be the one day you'd decide to come out of your room—just in time to be here and ruin everything."

Gwenda turned brusquely away from him. She could not raise her eyes to face either Ravenel or Belinda. "M-Miss Carruthers. I-I am so sorry for what my brother—"

But she got no further, for Belinda expelled her breath in an angry hiss. "Then this has all been some sort of horrid prank at my expense." She whipped about, clutching at Ravenel. "My lord, I have been insulted. I demand you call this rogue out at once."

Up until this time, Ravenel had been trying most heroically to contain himself. But Belinda's final dramatic appeal put the finishing touch on this farce. The laughter erupted from his chest until tears blurred his eyes. His mirth spread quickly among many of the other library patrons who had been staring until the entire room seemed to ripple with laughter.

Belinda's face stained scarlet. She slapped Ravenel hard across the cheek with the full force of her palm. "You! You are as vulgar as that scoundrel."

Her venomous glare shifted toward Gwenda and her brother. "And—and as for the pair of you, you should both be flogged and never permitted near decent society again!"

She whirled on her heel and stormed from the library, nearly oversetting Frederic Skeffington, who had the misfortune to be lingering in the doorway.

Ravenel could not seem to stop laughing, even while rubbing his stinging flesh, until he focused on Gwenda's face. One sight of the tears streaking down her cheeks put an abrupt end to his merriment.

"How—how could you, Jack!" she whispered brokenly.

Jack Vickers crossed his arms over his chest, looking somewhat abashed but defiant. "What did you expect me to do? I couldn't let my only sister die of a broken heart. I thought if I could only get rid of the Carruthers wench . . ." Jack glanced earnestly at Ravenel. "My lord, surely you can see that you oughtn't to marry a lady who has already begun to tell you lies. I know my sister can be a bit of a nuisance at times, but at least she is honest and she loves—"

"Be quiet, Jack! I shall never confide in you again as long as I live." Gwenda's tear-dampened lashes swept up and for one moment Ravenel stared deep into her eyes so full of despair, so full of . . . yearning.

"Gwenda," he breathed.

But she was already fleeing from him, rushing toward the door of the library. This time Skeffington had the wit to dive for safety as Gwenda plunged past him.

Ravenel took several steps after her, then stopped, judging it best to let her go for the moment. His mind was yet reeling, wondering if what he had thought he had seen shimmering in her eyes could possibly be true. He turned back to confront her brother.

Jack nervously straightened the hem of his scarlet coat. "I—I think I'd just better be getting along myself." He gave the baron a brief salute and tried to inch past him.

But Ravenel caught him by the sleeve. "Not just yet, my dear Colonel Adams. You and I needs must have a little talk."

A heavy fog was rolling in from the sea, seeming to bring the summer's day to an early close. As Gwenda took Bertie for his evening walk along the beach, she wished she could simply be swallowed by the mist forever.

Still reliving in her mind the whole disastrous episode at Donaldson's that afternoon, she could think of no better fate than to be buried in the sands and have the tides wash over her head.

Jack had knelt outside her bedchamber door begging for forgiveness through the keyhole until Mama had finally made him go away and leave Gwenda alone. Gwenda tried to remind herself that Jack had acted out of deep affection for her, but if only he would stop to think before plunging into one of these outrageous schemes.

His bungling had only made her life ten times more miserable. Not only had he involved Lord Ravenel in the sort of public scene that she knew so well he detested, but with half of the *ton* looking on, Jack had blurted out to Ravenel that Gwenda was in love with him. Although she would pen his lordship a note of apology, she would never, never be able to face the man again.

Gwenda sniffed, then quickly wiped her eyes on her sleeve. One would think she'd be cried out after the amount of weeping she had done that afternoon. She took a deep breath and tried to derive some pleasure from the walk with Bertie. But, at the moment, even the sea looked cold and gray.

Bertie barked and leaped at her skirts as though attempting to cheer her. She picked up a piece of driftwood and flung it far down the beach for him to chase. He quickly plunged after it and scooped it into his mouth. But while Bertie might have learned to do that much, he could never quite grasp the fact that he was supposed to bring the stick back.

He tore off with it, expecting Gwenda to chase him. As her dog rapidly disappeared into the fog, Gwenda began to fear that mayhap throwing the stick had not been such a good idea. She was in no mood to play hide-and-seek.

"Bert!" she called. But the fog muffled her voice and she heard no answering bark. The thick salt spray of the sea seemed to hang in the air, chilling her. Gwenda wrapped her arms about herself, wishing she had remembered to wear a shawl. She walked on a little farther until she heard a noise. It was as though pebbles on the beach had been dislodged.

"Bertie?" She squinted, peering along the hazy shoreline. She thought she could just discern the outline of someone approaching. Too big to be a dog. It had to be . . . Gwenda tensed, her lips parting in apprehension. It had to be a man. . . .

Out of the mists he came, the sea breeze ruffling his midnight-dark hair, a black cape flowing off his broad shoulders.

Gwenda froze in her tracks, wondering if she was dreaming. She pinched her arm until she knew a great bruise had to be forming and yet the stalwart figure approached until he stood within an arm's reach of her trembling hand.

Ravenel. Gwenda could not even persuade her numbed lips to form his name. The only thing that prevented her from sinking to her knees was her noticing that he looked as gruffly shy and embarrassed as she.

"My dearest—" He broke off, ruefully raking his hand back through his hair. "Damme! I spent all afternoon trying to memorize that passage, and I still cannot remember how it goes."

"Passage?" Gwenda asked weakly, her mind struggling to grasp the fact that he truly was here and wearing a cape, a black cape with three tiers and a scarlet lining.

"The passage from your book. You see, Jack wasn't able to give me enough details about how the dream was supposed to proceed."

Gwenda wrenched her eyes from her wondering

inspection of Ravenel's new cape. She did not even need to ask what dream. Jack might well be her favorite brother, but she was going to kill him.

Gwenda backed away from Ravenel, her throat constricting with misery. "Oh, no-no, you needn't try to ... because Jack told you ... and now you feel s-sorry for me. Th-that entire scene at Donaldson's—"

"Forget what happened at Donaldson's," Ravenel said huskily, taking a step closer. "You need to tell me what Roderigo usually says when he comes out of the mist."

"He—he never says anything. He just—" Gwenda's voice cracked and she was unable to continue.

"He does something. Something like this?"

Gwenda's heart pounded as the baron slipped his arms about her waist.

"Y-yes," she whispered. Her gaze came slowly up to meet his, the intensity in his night-dark eyes taking her breath away. He gathered her closer, molding her against the hard plane of his chest.

As Ravenel's mouth moved to claim her trembling lips, a familiar bark sounded out of the fog. Gwenda groaned softly as she heard her dog come bounding along the beach. As Ravenel drew back, hesitating, Gwenda saw Bertie leaping up on his hind legs, the driftwood in his mouth. For the first time in his life, Spotted Bert had decided he was going to come back with the stick.

Why now, Bertie? Gwenda could have groaned.

At the sight of Ravenel, the dog dropped the wood and gave a joyful bark. Ravenel cursed under his breath as Bertie launched himself at them, leaving a trail of wet sand along the baron's cape.

Ravenel released Gwenda as he struggled to restrain the exuberant dog. "Not now, Bertie, old chap," he said through gritted teeth.

"Th-throw the stick and he'll chase it," Gwenda advised.

Ravenel snatched up the driftwood and flung it away with all his strength. Bertie gave another excited bark and pelted after it, spraying pebbles as he disappeared back into the haze.

But the romantic moment was entirely spoiled. Gwenda shivered, rubbing her arms.

"Damnation, Gwenda," Ravenel scolded. "What are you doing out here without a shawl? Do you want to catch your death?"

He swept the magnificent cape off his own broad shoulders and began to wrap it around her.

Gwenda tried to resist. She forced a tremulous smile, saying, "No, Ravenel. Y-you really must not go about thinking 'tis your duty to look after every woman who falls in love with you."

"My duty be damned!" He swept her up in the cape and caught her hard against him, his lips crashing down upon hers in a fiery kiss that left her mind reeling, her knees feeling weak.

He drew back long enough to breathe in a fierce whisper, "I love you, you little fool. Will you be my wife?"

It was the most wonderful proposal that Gwenda had ever heard. But she tried to retain enough good sense to protest. "You—you couldn't possibly mean that—"

He silenced her with another kiss, his lips sending such a rush of heat through her veins that she had no more need of the cloak.

It was several long, blissful moments before he would permit her to speak again.

"Oh, Ravenel," she said, burying her face in the

lee of his shoulder. "Are you certain? After all the terrible things I've done to you. The first day you ever met me, you—you lost your most prized horses—"

"That was the most fortunate day of my life." He pressed a number of kisses against her curls, the top of her brow. "I wish Dalton much joy of the wretched beasts."

Gwenda clearly saw there was no reasoning with a man whose mind was as far gone as that. She ceased to try, merely turning her face up so that Ravenel's lips could continue his feverish explorations. She waited breathlessly as he prepared to kiss her again, but he suddenly became solemn.

His mouth quirked into a sad half-smile. "I cannot entirely deceive you, Gwenda. I fear I will always be something of a . . . a sobersides, tempted to make speeches and lecture you—"

"Just as I will always be a little shatter-brained." She sighed. "And there is my family—"

"No. Your family is completely charming. I was a pompous ass to ever say otherwise."

"You won't find Thorne charming," Gwenda warned him, resting her forehead beneath Ravenel's chin. "Or the rest of Papa's cousins who have just gotten out of debtor's prison or the uncle who likes to keep his sheep in—"

But Ravenel laughed shakily and embraced her again, bringing an end to this daunting list. Locked in each other's arms, they gave over trying to convince each other why they should not be married. He cupped her chin between his fingers and fiercely demanded her answer.

"So, will you marry me, or do you intend to condemn Jarvis and me to a lifetime of utter propriety?"

"Oh, no, I would never do that. I—I mean, yes, Ravenel, I will marry you."

The completely unrestrained smile of joy that he gave her caused Gwenda's heart to ache with loving him.

"My darling," he said, crushing her tightly against him, then added after a brief pause, "Under the circumstances, could you not begin to call me Desmond?"

"I could never call you that under any circumstances," Gwenda said firmly. Then she sighed. "Roderigo."

"Oh, no!" Ravenel shuddered. "Absolutely not."

"My love," Gwenda amended.

Since Lord Ravenel had no objection whatsoever to this manner of address, the pact was sealed with a kiss.

The moon rose slowly in the night sky, its gentle white light parting the mists to shine softly upon three figures yet silhouetted by the sea . . . the lady Gwenda strolling by the side of her dark-haired lover. And, of course, her dog.

THE SUGAR ROSE

To Kim Ostrum Bush,
a talented writer and good friend, in grateful ac-
knowledgment of all those late-night phone calls that
helped put the starch into Everard's cravats.

Chapter 1

"Aurelia Sinclair loves Lord Justin Spencer." The heat of a blush coursed into Aurelia's cheeks; her green eyes widened in mortification when she realized she had absentmindedly scrawled those words onto the flyleaf in her latest volume of Byron's poetry. Bad enough to indulge in such romantic nonsense when she was only fifteen, but at the sensible age of three and twenty, she ought to know better.

Justin, she reminded herself sternly, had not ridden to Sinclair Manor this morning to propose marriage as a result of any passionate devotion. No, he came only to do what had been long expected of him by both the Sinclair and Spencer families. If Aurelia looked for any warmer emotion from him other than friendship, then she was a fool.

"Giddings will be showing Lord Spencer upstairs at any moment now." The reedy voice of her elderly companion, Mrs. Elfreda Perkins, startled Aurelia from her unhappy thoughts. "Are you ready, my dear?"

Thrusting the book deep inside her workbasket, Aurelia straightened, raising one hand to the back of her head. Not so much as a strand of silken auburn hair escaped the crown of tightly woven braids. She tugged at the high-standing frills of her lace collar and shook out the folds of her saffron morning dress, wishing she had worn her comfortable, plain gray serge gown. The gossamer yards of clinging yellow furbelows did little to enhance her figure. But then, Aurelia thought with a grimace as she placed her hands upon her plump waistline, the fabric had yet to be woven that could accomplish that feat.

"I suppose I am as ready as I ever shall be." Her heart did a nervous flutter.

"Good. Then I shall whisk myself out of here," Effie said, tittering. She raised her brows in a look that was meant to be arch, but gave her more the appearance of a surprised owl. "I should be infinitely *de trop* when Lord Spencer drops to one knee and asks a certain question."

Effie stood on tiptoe to give Aurelia a swift kiss before skipping out of the sunlit music room. Aurelia winced. She thought it bad enough that Justin's mama had dropped "just a hint" to Aurelia herself to expect his lordship's proposal directly after breakfast, but it seemed that everyone from Effie down to the lowliest cook-maid was also privy to the secret that his lordship was *finally* coming to the point.

The sound of footsteps on the marble landing outside the door alerted Aurelia to the nearness of Justin's approach. Quickly she sat down upon the high-backed red velvet sofa, dragging her embroidery frame from her workbasket in an attempt to appear as if nothing occupied her mind except for the altar cloth she stitched to donate to the church.

If you had an ounce of pride, Aurelia Sinclair, she thought, you would refuse him. A man that comes to you at his mother's bidding!

But all such notions fled when the door swung open and she saw Justin's tall frame silhouetted in the entry. He grinned at her; his brown hair bleached light by the sun made a pleasing contrast to his bronzed skin.

"Good morning, Aurelia."

Before she could reply, Giddings pressed forward into the room, an affronted expression crossing his stately features. He announced in his frostiest accents, "Lord Spencer, miss."

Her pulses racing, Aurelia half rose, extending her hand.

"And," Giddings continued in tones of strong disapproval, "Mr. Everard Ramsey."

Aurelia sank back, as dismayed as Giddings by the sight of the immaculately tailored, dark-haired gentleman who followed Justin into the room. How often had Justin regaled her with tales of Everard Ramsey, whose meticulousness in matters of dress was only matched by his recklessness at the gaming tables! But why was Justin's friend so perverse as to call upon her this morning of all mornings, when Justin meant to propose?

Justin, however, did not appear in the least discomposed by Ramsey's untimely arrival. As he turned to greet his friend with every evidence of pleasure upon his handsome countenance, Aurelia struggled to suppress her own sense of bitter disappointment.

"I tried to keep the fellow out," Giddings said in an overly loud whisper. "But when he came tooling into the yard, he saw Lord Spencer's horse and knew that you were receiving—"

"Thank you, Giddings," Aurelia said quickly, fearful that Ramsey would overhear. "Would you please see to refreshment for my guests?"

"Certainly, miss." The old man made a dignified exit, muttering how a nice glass of arsenic would do for *some* persons who had not the wit to realize their timing was most inopportune.

Aurelia directed a weak smile at the two men. "I—I fear Giddings grows more eccentric with age."

Completely disconcerted by this unexpected turn of events, she shook hands with Justin before turning to murmur a greeting to Mr. Ramsey. She had taken a marked dislike to the man, although she had met him only the night before at supper. The London dandy had inspected her across the table through his quizzing glass, studying her until Aurelia had been provoked into saying sweetly, "Pray, Mr. Ramsey, are you feeling quite the thing? My own dear papa was always wont to stare in just such a glazed fashion when he was about to suffer an attack of the gout."

The man hadn't even had the grace to blush, but her remark had had the effect of making him turn his gaze elsewhere, although she had the uncomfortable feeling that he followed every word of her conversation with Justin, her dinner partner.

After such an encounter, she would have thought that calling upon her would be the last notion to occur to Mr. Ramsey. 'Twas evident by his presence that she was quite wrong.

Ramsey executed a brief bow, his hooded blue eyes containing a hint of mockery. His perfectly formed jawline, his high cheekbones, his dark, arched brows gave the man an expression of carefully schooled arrogance. "I see my visit has taken you quite by surprise, Miss Sinclair." He produced a folded fan from the pocket of his flowered silk waistcoat. "You left this at my aunt's last evening, and she insisted I see it returned to you."

"What! The orderly, efficient Miss Sinclair forgetting her belongings." Justin chuckled. "That is most unlike the Reely I know."

Aurelia smiled at his teasing, but she felt her cheeks turn pink. Would she ever be able to persuade Justin to stop calling her by that dreadful childhood nickname?

"Thank you, Mr. Ramsey," she said, her hand clamping around the ivory handle. "But you need not have put yourself to such trouble, returning the fan immediately. Especially when I am sure you must have so *many more important matters* to attend to this morning."

"Here in the wilds of Norfolk, Miss Sinclair?" One of Ramsey's dark eyebrows shot upward. "No, I assure you I have no pressing business whatsoever. In fact, my entire day is at your disposal."

He strode further into the room, stripping off his yellow kid gloves, giving every impression of intending to make a very long stay. His blue eyes glinted with what Aurelia would have called pure mischief if it had been anyone else but the stiffnecked Mr. Ramsey.

Justin pressed a small parcel into her hands. "A trifling gift," he said, "but 'tis something I know you like above all things."

When Aurelia undid the string and the tissue wrapping fell away, she discovered a box of chocolates. Sweetmeats were ever a weakness with her, but her stomach was so knotted with apprehension and frustration, she had difficulty regarding Justin's gift with any sort of enthusiasm. Did Justin truly believe that was what she valued most in the world, sweetmeats? 'Twas obvious the insufferable Mr. Ramsey thought so from the way his cynical eyes shifted from the box to her waistline. In sheer defiance, she popped one of the sweet confections into her mouth before proffering the treat to the gentlemen, both of whom declined.

Ramsey held up his hand, feigning a shudder. "No, thank you, Miss Sinclair. So early in the day! Incidentally, I do hope you do not find our calling thus soon after breakfast *inconvenient*?"

Hardly that, Aurelia felt like snapping. She had only been waiting five years for Justin to declare himself, ever since her father's death had left her orphaned. It seemed that, thanks to Mr. Ramsey, she must perforce wait a little longer.

"Inconvenient? Not at all, Mr. Ramsey," she forced herself to reply. She focused her attention upon Justin, affording him her most gracious smile. " 'Tis prodigiously good to see *you* at any time, Justin. Pray, be seated."

"I told you, did I not, Ev," Justin said, "that Reely would not be like one of your London belles, still languishing in bed at this hour of the day."

"One of *my* London belles?" Everard said so softly, Aurelia nearly did not catch the remark.

Justin glared at him, before favoring Aurelia with another of his heart-stopping smiles. He seated himself astride the reading chair, leaning his arms with careless grace upon the back of the book rest.

Was is truly so absurd, Aurelia thought wistfully, to hope that Justin did not view the prospect of marrying her with complete repugnance, that once wed, his childhood friendship with her might develop into emotions a trifle warmer? If there were any chance at all . . .

But her contemplation of Justin was seriously disturbed by Mr. Ramsey, who had chosen not to seat himself. What must the man do but pace about, examining the appointments of the room through his quizzing glass. As he regarded the faded Tree-of-Life wallpaper, the worn carpet, Aurelia almost wished she had elected to receive the gentlemen in one of the coldly elegant drawing rooms decorated by her mother. But of all the parlors in the rambling manor house, this was the one she had always considered peculiarly her own, where she felt the most secure. The massive fireplace mantel was not a showpiece designed by Adams, Gibbons, or anyone of note, but was constructed of good, plain oak, as were much of the room's furnishings. Best of all, the room had no mirrors to reflect back to her the imperfections of her less than willowy form.

Aurelia tossed her head. As if she cared a fig for Mr. Ramsey's opinion. Let him turn up his nose at her taste in decorating if he wished.

"I believe Trueblood strained a fetlock on our canter over here," Justin was saying. "I consigned him to the care of your head groom but I could scarce credit it. You still have old Harley working down in the stables. Why, he must be upward of seventy years old by now."

"O-oh, at least." Aurelia was vexed to discover she could not concentrate on Justin's words, so uncomfortable was Mr. Ramsey making her. After he trailed his fingers along the keys of the ancient rosewood pianoforte, his inspection of the room brought him over to the fireplace, in such close proximity Aurelia had to gather in her skirts to keep them from being trodden upon by his immaculate black Hessians. His cream-colored kerseymere trousers brushed up against her billowing yellow silk. With such closeness, Aurelia could not help remarking how his navy coat with mother-of-pearl buttons molded perfectly to his frame. Although he was not as tall and muscular as Justin, 'twas obvious the man had no need to resort to padding to fill out his shoulders.

"Don't you remember that, Reely?" Justin's impatient voice cut into her thoughts.

"What—I—I didn't quite hear you," she said. Embarrassed that Justin should find her so inattentive, she nervously ate several more chocolates.

"I was speaking of the time old Harley nearly took a switch to me, the time I stole a ride on your father's best hunter."

"Oh, that. Truly, Justin, you were always involved in so many pranks, 'tis difficult for me to remember them all."

Justin looked remarkably handsome as he threw back his head in a hearty laugh, but Aurelia was unable to enjoy fully the effect. The devil take Mr. Ramsey! If he must ruin everything this way, the least he could do would be to sit down and direct his supercilious stares from some forgotten corner. She noted with dread he was now examining the horrible collection of China jade figures assembled on the mantel.

"This fellow looks rather like a rabid bulldog. What is it for, Miss Sinclair? To ward off evil spirits?"

"If it is," she sighed, "it obviously does not work."

The corner of Ramsey's well-formed lips quivered, a ghost of a smile tipping his mouth. Then his features hardened into their customary sardonic expression.

Justin yawned. "Oh, do sit down, Ev, and let us talk about something else besides bric-a-brac."

"I should be only too happy to oblige," Ramsey drawled, "but I do not recall that I was ever invited to have a seat."

"Why, Mr. Ramsey, I—" Aurelia began indignantly, then halted in confusion. She *had* all but shown him the door when he arrived. Even considering her disappointment, such behavior was inexcusable.

She began to frame an awkward apology, when Justin interrupted, "Don't be such a cod's head, Ev. You needn't stand on ceremony here. Don't you know your aunt is Aurelia's godmama? Why, both the Foxcliff and Spencer families have been acquainted with Reely forever and ever."

She grimaced. "Yes, I am just like the Tower of London. An ancient, well-known landmark."

Everard Ramsey emitted an odd, strangled sound. He muffled a sudden fit of coughing behind his hand.

"Oh, you know what I meant, Aurelia." Justin gave her a look of smiling exasperation.

"I am afraid I do," she murmured. "Please forgive me, Mr. Ramsey, if I have been remiss in my duties as hostess. Of course, you are quite welcome to sit down."

Indeed she was beginning to feel a little ashamed of herself for her uncivil behavior. The emotion quickly vanished when Mr. Ramsey ignored all the bandy-legged Queen Anne chairs and settled himself beside her on the sofa. The quizzing glass that had been fixed upon the mantel ornaments was now trained as mercilessly upon her face.

She gulped down two more chocolates and hauled her stitchery up onto her lap in an effort to maintain a calm demeanor. How piercingly blue the man's eyes were, the deep vivid blue of the sky on a crisp autumn afternoon. And his hair. Strange that she had not remarked it before. Those glossy midnight waves absolutely refused to remain swept into the neat Brutus style so popular amongst the gentlemen. It must be a source of deep chagrin to the particular Mr. Ramsey.

"Your ability with the needle is remarkable, Miss Sinclair." The sound of his voice startled her. "However do you contrive to take such delicate stitches without looking at your work?"

Aurelia nearly stabbed herself as she realized she had been staring at him as intensely as he regarded her. She lowered her eyes, but she determined not to allow Ramsey to intimidate her further.

" 'Tis all a matter of practice," she said. "Just as I am sure that is how you acquired your skill with a quizzing glass. Could I persuade you to level it at the carpet? I seem to have dropped one of my needles."

"Alas, Miss Sinclair, you overrate my ability. I have never been good at retrieving lost articles." But he did lower his glass, dangling it by the ribbon between two of his graceful, tapering fingers.

From across the room Justin muffled a yawn. Aurelia feared he was bored by the conversation, but she saw that he scarce attended to herself and Mr. Ramsey. Justin's gaze traveled to the tall windows, and Aurelia knew instinctively he regarded the fields, the woodland beyond. 'Twas perfect hunting weather. He shifted restlessly in his seat. It would not be long before he would be making his excuses, drawing his visit to a close.

Plague take Everard Ramsey! Aurelia forcefully jabbed her needle into the linen cloth and reached for another chocolate. She almost wished Giddings *would* slip a little arsenic into the man's Madeira.

Ramsey leaned forward for a closer inspection of

her work. "What is that you are sewing with such great energy?"

She was seized by a strange urge to shake him of his air of imperturbability. " 'Tis a shroud," she said primly.

Her words had the desired effect. Ramsey jerked upright, his eyes widening. "I—I beg your pardon? Er, sewing shrouds—surely that is a rather unusual occupation for a young lady?"

"I like to be prepared. One never knows when there will be a sudden demise in one's circle of acquaintance."

The elusive smile played across his features. "If you are thinking of me, then you had best be like Penelope and take your time about it. I am made of sturdier stuff than you might imagine."

"I may follow her example and unravel a little each night," Aurelia conceded. "But I refuse to stretch it out twenty years for you."

Despite herself, she was beginning to enjoy the verbal sparring, when Justin rose abruptly to his feet, stretching his long limbs. "I warn the two of you, if you commence talking about a bunch of musty Romans, I will be off at once."

"Greeks, my dear fellow," Ramsey said. "The story of Penelope and Odysseus is from Greece."

Justin shrugged. " 'Tis all one to me. I think it much better if we get to the purpose of my visit." He fished inside his waistcoat pocket. A look of annoyance crossed his tanned features. "Hang it all. I have forgotten the ring."

Aurelia froze, her needle poked halfway into a stitch, a rising sensation of horror taking possession of her. No! Surely not! Justin could not be meaning to carry on with his proposal, not under the critical eyes of Everard Ramsey.

After patting his coat pockets, Justin threw up his hands. "Oh, well, I can always bring the ring by another day. The important thing is to settle when the banns will be cried and set a date." He paused, flashing his most engagingly boyish grin. "By the bye, Reely, you do wish to marry me, don't you?"

"I—I . . ." She opened her mouth, but the words refused to come. She felt the color flood into her face, hurt, embarrassment, and anger warring within her breast.

Everard Ramsey heaved himself to his feet. "This is the outside of enough! Even for you, Justin." His face flushed, Ramsey took an awkward step backward, kicking over Aurelia's workbasket. The contents spilled to the floor, unnoticed by him as he spluttered, "To—to be making Miss Sinclair an offer with me sitting here!" An expression of extreme irritation crossed his fine-chiseled features. "Ah, I see. 'Tis another one of your pranks, Justin. You and Miss Sinclair are making a May game of me."

"Not at all. Aurelia and I are completely serious," Justin said. "Are we not, Aurelia?"

"Y-yes." At least, *she* was. She could not decide who infuriated her more, Justin, with his thoughtlessness, or Mr. Ramsey, who believed the mere idea of Justin marrying her would have to be in the nature of a jest. She started to rise, longing to give both of them a good setdown, but even after all these years, the icy voice of her mother echoed inside her head. *A lady, Aurelia, never loses her temper.*

She took a deep breath to steady herself, counting backward in French.

Ramsey glowered at Justin. "I think you might defer this to a more appropriate moment."

"Completely, unnecessary, sir," Aurelia broke in.

Aye, doubtless the fashionable Mr. Ramsey hoped that, in the meantime, he might be able to prevent his friend's becoming engaged to such a dowdy, unattractive female. She raised her chin to stare defiantly into Ramsey's blue eyes. "Of course, I will accept your offer, Justin. With the greatest of pleasure."

Ramsey's lips compressed into a rigid line of disapproval, which only seemed to deepen when Justin strode over and clapped him on the back.

"Excellent. Then everything is settled. Why put yourself into such a taking, Ev? Reely is not in the least offended by the manner of my proposal, so why should you be?"

"If Miss Sinclair is not offended, then she ought to be. Even in an arranged marriage, there are certain courtesies, certain expressions of sentiment—"

"Don't be ridiculous. Reely and I are old friends. Our estates march alongside each other. Our marriage has been expected for years. Why, Reely is not in the least romantic. She would laugh in my face if I were to drop to one knee and spout a parcel of sentimental nonsense to her, would you not, old fellow?"

Aurelia swallowed before answering with a lightness she was far from feeling. "I don't know. It might prove quite useful if you were to kneel on the carpet. You might chance to alight upon the needle I dropped."

Justin chuckled, turning to flash a triumphant grin at his friend. Ramsey's face settled into a mask of indifference. " 'Twould seem the pair of you are well suited. Permit me to offer my felicitations."

"Too kind of you, I'm sure," Aurelia said with a brittle smile. Her satisfaction in having nettled Mr. Ramsey faded along with all her daydreams that

231

Justin would somehow learn to return her feelings of love. When would she ever learn that romance was not for such a one as she? But maybe if Ramsey had not been present, Justin would have been more . . . No, she feared he would have proceeded in the same graceless manner. Justin would always be Justin, and there was naught that would ever change him. Were not his unpredictability, his lack of regard for the conventions, all part of his charm?

A friendship, a marriage of convenience, was all he desired. She would have to learn to accept that if she meant to be his wife. Fortunately she had never worn her heart on her sleeve. Justin need never know of her love for him. Mayhap she had not enough pride to refuse his offer, but she had enough to conceal that folly from him. She ate a few more chocolates and returned to her stitching, trying to appear as casual about the morning's events as Justin did.

The two men busied themselves righting her workbasket, gathering up the pincushion, thread, and skeins of yarn. Ramsey straightened, examining a small leather-bound volume.

"You astonish me, Miss Sinclair. I would not have thought anyone as unromantic as you proclaim yourself to be would have a taste for Byronic poetry."

With a sinking sensation she realized Ramsey had gotten hold of her edition of *The Corsair*. It must have fallen out when the workbasket tipped.

"Oh, no! I—I mean that belongs to my companion." She snatched it out of his hands just as he was opening the book to the flyleaf.

Ramsey looked considerably surprised when she stuffed the volume behind the sofa cushion, leaning against it. Better that he should think her a bit touched in the upper works than he should read that foolish inscription. How his lip would curl in scorn.

"I shall have to tell Effie to be more careful with her books," she said.

"Indeed." Ramsey hooded his eyes, the look in them unfathomable.

Justin rubbed his hands together. "I suppose I should hasten back to Penborough to convey the glad tidings to my mother and Clarice."

"Yes," Aurelia said dryly. "Only fancy how astounded they will be."

Justin laughed. "Ah, Reely, that is what I like best about you. You are such a jokesmith."

"Truly. I am so amusing, I laugh at myself, sometimes." The words nearly caught in her throat. If only he and Mr. Ramsey would leave. Her smile was feeling strained, and absurd tears were beginning to prickle at the back of her eyes. She prepared to see the gentlemen out, but as she tried to set her needlework aside, she was appalled to realize she had sewn all the way through the linen into the fabric of her dress.

Aurelia nearly groaned aloud. 'Twas as if the Fates conspired this morning to make her appear a total fool. She settled the frame back onto her lap, hoping that neither Justin nor Mr. Ramsey—especially not Mr. Ramsey—had noticed.

"Forgive me if I don't see you to the door," she croaked, "since we do not stand on ceremony here."

Justin smiled, his mind apparently on nothing more than escape. He bent over and placed a chaste kiss upon her cheek, assuring her he would call upon her again very soon. The kiss was so far from what she had hoped for after his proposal that her heart did not even skip a beat.

She felt a surge of relief as he strode toward the door, but Everard Ramsey seemed determined to discomfit her to the last. While she sat with her hands draped awkwardly over the linen, trying to pretend nothing was amiss, the man lingered. Finding another spool of thread, he leisurely replaced it in her sewing basket before ducking into a low bow to make his farewells.

"Thank you for a most, er, interesting morning, Miss Sinclair. I hope we will meet again, soon."

And I hope you choke on your own cravat, she thought. Aloud, she said, "So nice of you to call. Good day, sir."

"Come along, Ev," Justin called from the threshold. "If I cannot ride Trueblood, I may need you to take me up in your curricle."

As though oblivious of Justin's impatience, Ramsey slowly raised one of Aurelia's hands and carried it briefly to his lips. Struggling to appear composed, she dared not move until the music room door closed behind the two men.

"Thank God," she said. No matter how disastrous the rest of the morning had been, at least she could congratulate herself upon having hoodwinked the sharp-eyed Mr. Ramsey. She relaxed, allowing her hands to fall back into her lap. 'Twas then she realized Ramsey had somehow found opportunity for dropping an object on top of the stitchery.

Her lips curved into a rueful smile as her fingers closed over her scissors.

Chapter 2

The curricle's iron-rimmed wheels rumbled perilously near the edge of the ditch. Justin lurched against the side of the open-top carriage, then made a frantic grab for the back of his seat.

"Damnation, Everard! Watch what you are about."

Everard directed an angry sidelong glare at his friend. Gritting his teeth, he slapped the reins against the backs of the sprightly pair of chestnuts between the traces. Fields broken into neat squares by hedgerows and mounds of hay being harvested into tall ricks all flashed by in a blur of green and gold.

Justin stared down at the ditch, bracing himself for the accident to come, but somehow Everard managed to guide the vehicle back onto the road just as the rear wheel careened a hairsbreadth over the edge.

When the curricle resumed its pace down the center of the country lane, Justin straightened. "Blast you, Ev! I'll never know how any man who is so cool and circumspect in the saddle can be such a madman when it comes to handling the ribbons."

"If you don't like the way I drive, you can always walk," Everard snapped, still seething over the embarrassing trick Justin had served him that morning. Forcing him to witness that travesty of a marriage proposal! He urged the horse on faster, sending the curricle rattling through a series of bone-jarring ruts. Mud spattered up over the wheels, just missing the toes of Everard's gleaming Hessians, but managing to bespeckle the hems of Justin's buff-colored trousers.

"By God," Justin groaned. "I believe I would have done better to borrow one of Reely's horses or to have led Trueblood back across the fields." His eyes rolled nervously toward the ditch. "Damn it, Ev. Keep toward the center. That side of the road is completely washed out."

Everard turned a deaf ear to the warning. The devil take Justin, he thought. There was nothing Everard hated worse than being involved in any sort of a scene. For once in his life, Justin might have employed a modicum of decency, of common sense, of—

"Dash it, Ev. Hard to the left. To the left. Ow!" Lord Spencer swore. Lunging forward, he reached across Everard and seized the reins, yanking until the horse halted in the center of the road.

The muscles in Everard's face went rigid with suppressed anger. In carefully controlled tones, he said, "If any other man besides you had dared do that—"

"I know." Justin panted. "You would run him through. Have mercy, Ev. I don't mind attempting to break my own neck, but I very much object to someone else doing it for me."

His teeth flashed into a broad grin, which Everard returned with a stone-faced regard. "You needn't have feared," he said icily. "I would never permit anything to happen to Aunt Lydia's best curricle." He gazed pointedly to where Justin's fingers still gripped the reins. Justin released the leather straps and slumped back in his seat. Everard set the carriage into motion again. Although his irritation with Justin continued to gnaw at him, he managed to keep the chestnuts to a sedate trot.

"So what the devil have I done now to put you in such a bad skin?" Justin asked. "Surely you're not still fuming about that night I paid Moll Periwinkle a guinea to sneak into your bed?"

Everard grimaced at the remembrance of waking to feel bony elbows and knees digging into his back, a mouth reeking of cabbage and garlic nibbling at his ear.

"No, until you mentioned it, I had contrived to forget that particular incident. To be sure, I did not find it half so diverting as the time you put the pepper in my snuffbox."

Justin stretched out his long limbs as much as the curricle would permit, a lazy smile touching his lips at the memory, a smile completely lacking in repentance. Everard heaved a sigh of exasperation. At the age of twenty-eight, he was but two years Justin's senior. Why, sometimes, did he feel as if it were fifty?

"Then I can't understand—" Justin broke off. "Good Lord, you cannot still be grousing over what happened with Reely this morning."

"Not at all. Your affair entirely, old friend. I have only this to say. The next time you propose marriage to some wench, be so good as to leave me out of it."

"I trust there won't be a next time." Justin gave him a playful jab on the arm. "What's come over you, Ev? I have never known you to get in such a pelter over anything so trivial."

"Trivial?" Everard nearly choked on the word. It took great restraint on his part to keep his hands steady. "Oh, aye, the whole affair was so trivial you never thought to warn me what you were going to do. If I had had the least notion, I would have excused myself at once. You place me in a dashed awkward position."

"You live in your own world, Ramsey." Justin chuckled. "You must have been the only person in the shire who did not know the nature of my business with Reely this morning."

"Damn it! Don't keep calling her that! She has a perfectly lovely first name."

Justin gaped at him, but he looked no more astonished than Everard was feeling himself at his outburst.

"Sorry," Everard muttered. "As I said before, entirely your own affair." He shook his head, trying to sift his way through a confusing mélange of emotions. Justin was well within his rights to ask. What *had* come over him? He had been in perfectly good humor when he had first arrived at Sinclair Manor, looking forward to furthering his acquaintance with Miss Sinclair. The woman was an original if Everard had ever met one. Yet his chagrin over what had actually taken place was scant excuse for his present state of agitation.

"I'll tell you what 'tis, old fellow," Justin spoke up suddenly. "You have been rusticating in Norfolk so long, you're getting frayed at the edges. Too many evenings of playing whist for a penny a point with these fat country squires. What you need is to return to town, get back to the tables at Watier's."

"I suppose so, although London would be mighty thin of company at this time of year." Everard forced a smile to his lips, but it continued to disturb him that he had reacted so strongly to the little scene played out before him that morning. Why could he not forget about it?

'Twas most likely because of that damned book. He had had only the barest glimpse of the inscription on the flyleaf: "Aurelia Sinclair loves—" But it hadn't been difficult to guess the rest. In unguarded moments, Aurelia Sinclair's heart surfaced in those remarkable green eyes of hers, revealing a sensitive woman hiding her wounds beneath a veil of wit and jest.

"Damme!" Everard muttered under his breath, cursing the talent he had for discovering secrets. Why was he afflicted with this uncanny perception that saw beyond the facades others presented, probing too deep into their private guilt and pain? 'Twould be so much more comfortable to saunter through life as Justin did, blissfully deaf and blind to his neighbors' heartaches.

Though at the moment, Everard noted wryly, Justin was looking far from being shortsighted. Lord Spencer's eyes nearly bulged from their sockets as he ogled a buxom dairymaid. As they passed the field where the girl led her cows to pasture, she ducked in a respectful curtsy. She put an additional sway into her full hips and blushingly bobbed in Justin's direction. Justin grinned and swept her a salute with his high-crowned beaver hat.

How did they always know, these women, that Justin was so susceptible to a pretty face? Ever since Everard had first become acquainted with Lord Spencer during their days at Oxford, he had pondered the question with no satisfactory answer. 'Twas as if there was some undefinable mutual allure between Justin and any attractive creature in skirts.

Everard slapped down on the reins, urging the horses to pick up speed again, leaving the amply endowed dairymaid behind them. Justin craned his neck for a last look.

"So you are planning to get leg-shackled at last," Everard said sharply to gain Justin's attention. "At least that will put an end to Lady Sylvie Fitzhurst's determined efforts to fix your interest." The thought filled Everard with a sense of great relief. Sylvie Fitzhurst, in his estimation, was a sly, grasping creature, more noted for her dazzling blond looks than her discretion. Any liaison with that baggage would only have led Justin into more trouble.

But Justin's brows jutted upward in surprise at Everard's statement. "What has my forthcoming marriage to do with Sylvie? I am hoping that in the next month or so our flirtation will develop into something far warmer."

"I see you have laid your plans well. A new bride and a new mistress. How damnable convenient and timesaving, too! You can select a wedding gift for Aurelia at the same time as you pick up a few trinkets for Lady Sylvie."

"What a capital notion." Lights of mischief danced in Justin's eyes. "And stop screwing up your face in that manner. You look as priggish as a parson about to deliver a lecture."

"I would if I thought 'twould be of any avail. Have you given one moment's thought as to how Miss Sinclair will feel about this proposed arrangement of yours?"

Justin shrugged. "She would not much care, as long as I am discreet. I've explained to you repeatedly, this is a marriage of convenience, not the grande passion. All Reely expects from me is my title and a nursery full of children."

"Aye. Doubtless, you are correct." Everard grimaced. Most likely that was all Aurelia expected from Justin. But what she might long for, dream of, was entirely a different matter. An image of her flashed through Everard's mind, the curve of her lips quivering into a wistful smile, a wistfulness she quickly concealed behind a too ready laugh.

"You will, I trust, at least remember to take her the ring, will you not?" he asked.

Justin yawned and stretched again. "Oh, aye. I'll remember. Because I know you will give me little peace until I do. The trouble with you, Ev, is that beneath your pose of cynical dandy lurks the heart of a true romantic." His chest rumbled with another deep chuckle. "Lord, after the way you twitted Reely about having a copy of *The Corsair*, how she would laugh if I told her about your own dog-eared copies of Byron, to say nothing of Sir Walter Scott."

Everard felt a tinge of red rise into his cheeks, but he contrived to say lightly, "I beg you will not. I am in enough difficulties without having my reputation destroyed as well."

The laughter swiftly died out of Justin's eyes; his smiling lips set into an expression of unaccustomed somberness. He shifted his gaze away from Everard, appearing to be deeply engrossed by a drainage windmill they were passing, the arms twirling slowly like a lazy giant guarding the land. Lord Spencer cleared his throat. "About your difficulties, Ev, you know I would be happy to lend you—"

"No!" In milder tones, Everard continued, "No, I thank you, all the same. I have not yet sunk to the point of borrowing from my friends."

241

"But you could pay me back—with interest—as soon as your ship comes in."

"My ship." Everard gave a mirthless bark of laughter. "The only way you would recover your loan from my assets on *The Albatross* is if you are capable of holding your breath for a very long time and diving to the bottom of the sea."

"You don't know that for certain. Why, it has only been—"

"One year, ten months, and seventeen days," Everard said flatly. The exact amount of time since he had stood on the dock in Portsmouth and watched *The Albatross*'s billowing white sails skim over the horizon, carrying with her all his hopes, his dreams, and nigh every penny of the modest fortune he had inherited through his grandfather's trust.

"The Folly" his father, Sir Fitzwilliam Ramsey, had dubbed *The Albatross*. "Outfitting merchant vessels for trade with Brazil," he had snorted. "You may as well fling your fortune away on a turn of the cards and be done with it. Didn't you hear what happened to those speculators who put their money in the cargo of *The Royal George*? Scarce enough money left now to buy breeches to cover their privies."

"The Royal George, Father?" Everard had countered in tones of long-suffering patience. "Do you know what cargo they carried? Wool blankets, warming pans, and ice skates! Ice skates to Brazil, for the love of God! We propose to outfit *The Albatross* with lightweight cottons. Brazil has no cotton manufactories."

"I don't give a hang what a parcel of brown-faced heathens have or don't have." Sir Fitz's large peppery mustache fairly bristled with his wrath. Then he uttered his clincher to every argument. "If your brother Arthur had lived, he would never have done anything so foolish."

If Arthur had lived. Everard thought he had heard those words a damn sight too often.

"Ev. Watch out!"

Justin's outcry of warning pierced through Everard's unhappy reverie. He snapped back to the present in time to realize the curricle had rounded the bend and was bearing down upon a pony cart. Everard pulled on the reins, attempting to guide his carriage off to the side. But 'twas already too late. The wheels of the two vehicles slammed together, and Everard's own curses resounded in his ears along with the crack of splintering wood.

The late afternoon sun glinted through the tall windows, sparkling on the silver tea service, but the rich brew tasted remarkably bitter to Aurelia, despite the quantity of sugar she spooned into the delicate Wedgwood cup.

Glumly she regarded the small parcel that had just arrived, delivered by Justin's groom. As she opened the brief note that accompanied it, Justin's bold hand fairly leaped off the page, all but illegible.

> *Reely,*
>   *Everard is still haranguing me about my lack of regard for the formalities, so I thought I'd better dispatch Crowley to bring you the ring posthaste.*

Aye, Aurelia thought with a touch of asperity, since the groom was coming to fetch Trueblood, in any case. Then, scolding herself for her cynicism she read on.

> *Would have brought it myself, but Ev and I suffered a coaching accident on the way home. Not to worry. I have taken no serious injury. As to the ring, Mama thought you might like to have one of the family jewels, so I selected one that you have always particularly admired. Her ladyship has been troubled of late with a touch of the megrim, but shall be calling upon you within the next day or two to set the date for making me the happiest of men.*

> *Yours,*
> *J.*

Aurelia bit her lip as she anxiously perused the note one more time. Wasn't that exactly like Justin to toss out such an alarming piece of news as a carriage accident and then not explain himself more fully? She was forced to suppose from the tone of his letter that all was as he said, that he truly had not sustained any injury. But what of Mr. Ramsey? Justin said nothing of how he had fared.

Her fingers tightened on the brief missive. As if she cared what became of Mr. Ramsey, in any case. Detestable man! Doubtless he was quite unscathed and still laughing to himself over her clumsy error in sewing her gown to the altar cloth. Yet, doubts arose to dispel the unpleasant image. If Ramsey were determined to be amused at her expense, why had he slipped her the scissors, thus sparing her further embarrassment? 'Twas in truth an act of great consideration, not in the least what she would have expected from him. Mayhap her initial impression of the man as an arrogant coxcomb was entirely too harsh.

Still puzzling over Ramsey's actions, she refolded the note and set it down upon her tea tray before turning her attention to the small box. As she undid the wrapping, she stared in disbelief at the gaudy ruby that blinked amid a circle of diamonds and emeralds.

"Good Lord." She groaned. One of the family jewels! 'Twas more like one of the family antiquities. When had Justin ever gotten the notion that she had admired such a thing?

To be sure, she did recall a remark she'd once made upon first seeing the ring amongst the collection of treasures at Penborough Castle. "Upon my word, what a stunning ring. I feel quite stunned just looking at it."

Never had one of her jests been so appallingly misconstrued, Aurelia thought ruefully as she lifted the heavy band from its velvet-lined case. She crinkled her nose in distaste. The ring's hideous vulgarity was not its worst aspect. The most dreadful consideration was that the jewel truly was priceless, an heirloom dating from the time of Henry VIII. How would she ever face Justin's mama if she were to lose it?

So absorbed was she by this gloomy prospect that she scarce noticed when Giddings entered the room, until he coughed discreetly. She looked up to find the elderly retainer's face positively thunderous with disapproval.

"Begging your pardon, miss, but there is a person below stairs absolutely insistent upon seeing you."

"A person?" she repeated. Now who would Giddings describe in such terms? The answer came to her in a rush, sending a blush coursing into her

245

cheeks. Who else but Everard Ramsey? 'Twas past all belief that the man should have the effrontery to call upon her twice in the same day, uninvited. Had he returned to tease her about the dress incident or mayhap to see if there was yet some way to prevent her engagement to Justin?

No, it could hardly be that, or he would not have urged Justin to send her the ring. Nervously, she patted her hair and rammed the large ruby upon her finger. Well, whatever his motives for coming, she would not permit Mr. Ramsey to discompose her so easily this time.

Scarce thinking what she did, she wolfed down one of the tea cakes and said, "Show Mr. Ramsey upstairs at once, Giddings."

Her butler looked as if he thought she had taken leave of her senses. "Why, I did not say a word about Mr. Ramsey, miss."

"Oh." An unexpected sense of disappointment surged through her. "Then who—"

" 'Tis that person who has recently leased Wetherbee Hall." Giddings sniffed. "I put him in the Blue Salon," he added in much the same tones he would have used to describe dropping a dead rat into the refuse heap.

"Mr. Augustus Snape?" Aurelia winced. A gazetted fortune hunter of the worst stamp, Mr. Snape had recently taken up residence in Norfolk, reputedly because he had met with no luck snaring a wealthy bride in London.

"I don't suppose you could simply tell him I died," she said, "or at least have contracted an extremely contagious case of the scarlet fever."

Giddings folded his hands, raising his eyes to the sculpted ceiling. "Certainly, if it is your wish, miss,

I could tell him you had been taken ill. However, in your late mother's time ..."

He left the sentence unfinished, but Aurelia had no difficulty in completing the thought. In her late mother's time, no visitors were ever turned away from Sinclair Manor, not even a man as disagreeable as the oily-tongued Mr. Snape.

"A lady, Aurelia," her mother had always said, "never stoops to subterfuge to rid herself of unwelcome guests. Rather, she receives the visitors and treats them to such a display of chilling dignity, they never dare call again."

Aurelia heaved a deep sigh. "I shall be down directly, Giddings."

"Very good, miss." Giddings made a wooden bow and stalked out of the room.

Aurelia rose and slowly wended her way down the curving red-carpeted stair to the lower floor. She attempted to school her features into an expression of hauteur but gave over the attempt when she caught a glimpse of herself in the hall mirror.

" 'Tis impossible for a woman with a dimpled chin to look chilling," she grumbled. She was tempted to send for Effie. At least the presence of her elderly companion would restrain Mr. Snape from becoming too carried away with his compliments and fawning over her hand. But Effie was still lying down, so overcome had the volatile little woman been by the tidings of Lord Spencer's proposal.

Loath to disturb her companion and berating herself as a coward, Aurelia resolutely shoved open the door and stepped into the Blue Salon. The gangly form of Mr. Snape looked strangely out of place, his plum-colored jacket and apple-green waistcoat

247

clashing with the muted elegance of the blue velvet swag draperies. From above the ornate marble fireplace, the portraits of her parents, her florid, portly father, her reed-thin, hawk-eyed mother, both seemed to regard Snape's presence at Sinclair Manor with extreme disapproval.

Snape stood with one hand held stiffly against his back, while his other cadaverlike hand examined a Sevres vase balanced on a delicate Queen Anne table, his fingernails pinging against the china.

"I assure you 'tis quite genuine, Mr. Snape," Aurelia said dryly.

Snape whirled his head around as fast as his high starched collar and stiff cravat would permit. His pale complexion put Aurelia in mind of the Broadland eels who slithered out of their wintry beds each April.

"Ah, Miss Sinclair. I—I was just admiring this magnificent piece. Your taste is so very similar to that of my third cousin, the Marquess of Scallingsforth."

Aurelia fixed a rigid smile upon her lips and extended her hand with what she hoped was a duchesslike dignity. Snape strode over and pressed cold, thin lips against her knuckles. Aurelia grimaced as she felt the prickles of tiny, stiff chin whiskers scrape against her flesh. Mr. Snape had made a poor job of shaving that morning. 'Twas rumored his valet had run off with the chambermaid a fortnight ago, taking many of the Snape family valuables with them. At least that was the excuse Mr. Snape had given for why there was no silverplate present at the last dinner party given at Wetherbee Hall.

As Mr. Snape was raising his mouth from her

hand, he froze, the facets of the ruby ring sparking red gleams in his narrow eyes.

"Why, Miss Sinclair. What a stunning ring."

"Indeed," she murmured. "Exactly the description I would have chosen myself." Fearing that at any moment, he might begin to drool over her fingers, Aurelia swiftly withdrew her hand.

"Pray be seated, sir, and tell me to what I owe the honor of this visit." She silently congratulated herself upon the frosty accents with which she delivered this speech, but when Mr. Snape pursed his lips together until he resembled an emaciated mackerel, she nigh ruined the entire effect by erupting into laughter.

"I do not know if you will deem this visit an honor or not, when I tell you the reason for it," Snape said in solemn tones, placing one hand over his heart. "But, pray, believe me it is only my concern for your reputation that has driven me hither."

"My reputation?" Aurelia echoed as she settled herself upon the stiff silk cushions of a French sofa. Whatever was the man talking about?

Snape raked bony fingers back through his slick thatch-colored hair, then took a few quick turns before the hearth before stopping to proclaim dramatically, "My dear Miss Sinclair, I fear rumors of a most scandalous nature have reached my ears. It pains me to distress you, but I have been hearing talk in the village of how you, a lady of quality, have been entertaining gentlemen of the most reprehensible character. Rakes, libertines, gamesters!"

Aurelia's mouth twitched. "Dear me. I do not recall receiving any such gentlemen. They must have called when I was not at home. How very disappointing."

Snape fixed her with a reproachful stare. "You

pretend that you have not been visited by Lord Spencer and Mr. Everard Ramsey, when I know for a fact they were here only this morning."

Aurelia stifled an indignant gasp. Of all the insufferable impertinence. Had this odious creature been spying upon the Manor? Let this be a lesson to take care in future whom she spoke to at assemblies, even when someone as unexceptionable as the vicar performed the introduction. She rose to her feet.

"Mr. Snape. I fail to see how it concerns you whom I receive or do not. Now, I fear I am obliged to bid you good—"

She broke off as Snape abruptly changed his tactics. His colorless eyes damp with remorse, he vaulted across the room to her side and began groping for her hands. For one dreadful moment, Aurelia feared he meant to drop to one knee before her.

"Please. Do not be wroth with me, dear lady. If I seemed too abrupt, too forward in my remarks, 'tis only because I find myself so overwhelmed by your numerous charms." Snape sighed gustily, stealing longing glances at the ruby glittering on her finger.

"P-pray, sir, strive for some command of yourself," Aurelia said in a voice that was not quite steady.

But he continued to struggle for possession of her hand. "I know you are far too innocent to realize what the presence of such a notorious womanizer as Lord Spencer—"

Aurelia yanked her hand away. "I must warn you that when you speak of Lord Spencer, you are speaking of the man I am going to marry."

"What!" Snape rocked back on his heels, his countenance waxing even more ghostlike.

Dear God, Aurelia thought. The man looked as if

he were about to swoon, and she had not the least notion where any smelling salts were to be found.

"I am going to marry Lord Spencer," she repeated more gently.

Snape staggered a few steps backward, striking one hand to his forehead. "No, I cannot believe it. Fate could not deal me such a blow."

Aurelia quirked an eyebrow, wondering if, somewhere in Mr. Snape's highly dubious background, the man had trod the boards at Drury Lane.

"I can assure you it is true," she said. "The understanding between Lord Spencer and myself has been one of long duration. You yourself have already remarked upon my betrothal ring."

"But—but I had already informed my creditors —I mean my family—that you and I, that we . . ." Snape stared at her, then slowly lowered his hand. 'Twas as if he lowered a mask at the same time. An ugly red began to seep up his neck, suffusing his thin face, until Aurelia was about to suggest it might be expedient if he were to loosen his cravat.

"So," he growled, "then all this time you have been toying with me, trifling with my affections!"

"I would scarce call dancing with you at the assembly and permitting you to fetch me punch as trifling with—"

"You led me on, you jade." Snape leveled a shaking finger at her. "You permitted me to entertain false hopes."

"I did nothing of the kind! And now, sir, I must really insist that you leave." She strode across the room and yanked on the bell pull one time before Snape bounded after her. He seized her by the wrist and spun her around.

Dropping all efforts to speak with his usual cultivated purr, he shouted, "Oh, no, 'twill take more than that scrawny old butler to toss me out before I've had my say. No one makes a fool of Gus Snape. Especially not after I spent a fortune sending you roses."

Aurelia cried out in shock as much as pain when he twisted her wrist in his bony grasp. She had regarded Snape as nothing more than an ingratiating buffoon. Never would she have guessed him capable of such violence. The man was quite mad, and as he thrust his protuberant nose close to her face, for the first time she detected the odor of sour gin upon his breath.

"I thought a fat old spinster like you would have jumped at the chance to marry me." He sneered. "Never guessed you already had a lord on the string."

Aurelia flushed, raising her free hand almost reflexively, preparing to deal a strong clout to Snape's ear. But beyond her, the frozen stare of her mother's portrait already seemed to be rebuking her for allowing this scene to get so far beyond the bounds of dignity.

Aurelia lowered her arm, striving for icy scorn between clenched teeth. "Sir, I demand you release me at once."

"No country-bred wench gets the better of me. We shall see how high and mighty you are, Miss Sinclair, when I am done with you. I'll have my vengeance. You can bank upon it. I—"

He broke off as the parlor door opened. "Get out of here, you old fool," he snarled, wrenching his head in the direction.

"Giddings," Aurelia cried out, tugging futilely to free herself.

But 'twas not the old man who had answered the bell. The young footman, James, his burly arms al-

252

ready outgrowing his smart new livery, stood silhouetted in the entry. He eyed Mr. Snape, his
mouth splitting into a grin of unholy anticipation
at the prospect of a mill. "Miss Aurelia? Was there
something you was wanting?"

Snape flinched, dropping her arm as if it were a
firebrand.

"Yes, James," Aurelia said, rubbing her bruised
flesh. "I believe Mr. Snape requires some assistance
in finding the front door."

"Right, miss." James doubled two large meaty
fists. Snape stumbled backward, his eyes bulging
as the grinning young man advanced upon him.

"Uh, no, not at all. Quite a misunderstanding.
M-most sorry, Miss Sinclair, to have troubled you.
I—I'll just be going now."

Snape circled around James and bolted from the
room, the man's previous attitude of menace vanishing as rapidly as his flapping coattails.

"Why, what a wretched, cowardly bully!" Aurelia
exclaimed.

"I'll just follow him, miss," James said hopefully,
"and make sure he doesn't get lost."

"That is not necessary. I trust we have seen the
last of Mr. Snape." Aurelia took a deep breath.
"What you could do is fetch me a very large glass of
sherry."

"Of course, miss." Looking considerably crestfallen, James lumbered out of the parlor, leaving
Aurelia to collapse back down upon the French
sofa. The encounter had left her more shaken than
she would have imagined. She had never in her life
been insulted in so vulgar a fashion, let alone suffered any physical abuse from one passing himself
off as a gentleman. How had such a weasel as Au-

gustus Snape ever managed to gain entrée into polite circles?

Her gaze traveled to the portrait of the slender, sharp-faced beauty above the mantel. "Well, Mama, and to think you always told me that I was not the sort that would ever break hearts."

Aurelia emitted a weak chuckle as she raised her hand, staring at the heavily jeweled ring. "In future, I shall have to take care that my abundant charms are not so lavishly displayed." A shudder coursed through her as she remembered Snape's spiteful expressions, the nasty glint in his eye as he had threatened vengeance. What would she do if he persisted in troubling her further?

For a moment, she almost thought of sending for Justin, informing him of Snape's insulting behavior. But she feared Lord Spencer would be driven to deal with Mr. Snape in an exceedingly rash and violent manner, stirring up no end of scandal. Now, a gentleman like Everard Ramsey . . . She closed her eyes. She could easily picture Mr. Ramsey dispatching Snape with cool efficiency, the villain cringing before Ramsey's hard stare, withering under his steel-edged scorn.

Startled by her imaginings, Aurelia's eyes fluttered open. Why had visions of Everard Ramsey popped into her head? 'Twas extremely disloyal and unflattering to Justin to be making these comparisons, though much as she adored Justin, she was obliged to admit the truth of her observations.

'Twas clearly Mr. Snape's fault if her thoughts were so jumbled. She would tell no one about what had happened here today. The man was a coward, full of bluster, his threats not to be taken seriously. In any case, if his affairs were as bad as 'twas ru-

mored, the man would likely lose his lease on
Wetherbee Hall and go back to London where he
came from. She would not waste another moment's
thought upon the horrid creature.

Chapter 3

Everard Ramsey padded across the thick Brussels carpet in his stocking feet, moving closer to the mahogany-framed cheval glass. In the soft glow of wax candles mounted on either side, the mirror reflected back his well-honed body, the lean musculature but scantily disguised by a pair of tight-fitting black Florentine silk breeches and an immaculate white frilled shirt. Bending forward, he began to fold the foot-long tie carefully around his collar. His deft fingers stayed momentarily as he paused to frown at the faint purplish mark lingering on his forehead, all that remained of the enormous goose egg he had sported from the curricle accident of a week ago. Mayhap, he thought with a wry grimace, when even this trace of the bruise disappeared, Justin would no longer plague him with jests about trying to set a new fashion for three-wheeled curricles.

His balding, dapper little valet, Beddoes, scurried about the large oak-paneled bedchamber, picking up the sweat-soaked breeches and shirt Everard had discarded earlier that afternoon after his attempt to teach the son of a local baronet some of the finer points of fencing. Beddoes gingerly reached for the blunted foil, whose steely length glinted brightly against the crimson damask bedcover.

"Did you have good sport with young Master Winchell today, sir?" he asked as he replaced the light sword in its silk-lined case.

"Ummm," Everard replied, raising his chin. He had reached the critical stage of putting the creases into the starched linen cravat. 'Twas rumored that Beau Brummell threw away scores of stocks before one was arranged to his taste. Everard scorned such a waste of time, when perfection could be achieved on the first effort with just a little concentration.

"There," he pronounced when the last fold of the *trône d'amour* stood out in pristine crispness against his shirtfront. "Yes, the bout with Master Winchell went well enough," he replied. "What the lad lacks in skill, he makes up for in enthusiasm. In any event, 'twas far more diverting than spending another day with Lord Spencer upon the river, watching him wreak havoc amongst the mallards."

He wondered if that was how Justin had occupied himself, or if he had gone to call upon Miss Sinclair again, as Everard had suggested. Despite his badgering, Justin had only been to Sinclair Manor twice since the morning of the proposal. Not that it was any of his affair, but he was troubled by an image of Aurelia, standing by her window, day after day, her green eyes clouded as she regarded the empty stable yard below. Damn it, marriage of convenience or not, 'twas shabby indeed how Justin neglected the girl.

"I entirely agree with you, sir."

"What?" Startled, Everard wondered if he had been voicing his thoughts aloud, but Beddoes's next comment reassured him.

"About the hunting, sir. You always were too refined for such sport as only amuses the rustics."

257

"Oh, that. No, I fear hunting mostly bores me because I am a notoriously bad shot." He raised his arms so that Beddoes could help him don a striped marcella waistcoat and jacket of black superfine. "Unlike Arthur, who could kill more birds than any other man in England."

"So your late brother was wont to say, sir." Beddoes gave a contemptuous sniff, then stepped back as Everard smoothed out the lapels. "Perfect, sir. What a pity it must be wasted at a dinner party given for a parcel of country bumpkins."

Everard's mouth tipped upward in amusement. "What a dreadful old snob you are, Beddoes. As it happens, this is a very special dinner party, given by my aunt to celebrate the betrothal of my best friend to a most charming lady. And whatever other social graces Aunt Lydia might lack, I assure you she sets a table to rival anything you would find in town."

Beddoes's brow crinkled, his upturned nose showing that he was singularly unimpressed. "And when, sir, if I might take the liberty of asking, will we be able to return to town?"

Everard's gaze shifted to a small Sheraton writing desk, its lacquered surface littered with thick white envelopes, duns that had followed him from London.

"Not anytime soon, I fear. In fact, you'd best brace yourself to spend the winter in exile."

"Oh, sir!"

"Unless, of course, you choose to abandon me here amongst the barbarians and seek service elsewhere. 'Tis always prudent, you know, to desert a sinking ship before the water gets too deep."

Beddoes eyed him reproachfully. "I shall not even dignify such a heartless jest with a reply, sir."

At that moment, a loud rap sounded on the bed-chamber door. Everard winced. "That would be Aunt Lydia, wanting to know what the devil detains me so long. Beddoes, would you inform my aunt I shall be down directly?"

"Very good, sir," the valet said, expressing his still wounded feelings by the stiff set of his shoulders as he strode over to answer the door. After a brief exchange of murmured words, he returned bearing a large parcel.

" 'Twas not a message from your aunt, sir, but one of Lord Spencer's servants delivering this package from his lordship."

Everard glanced at it with mild surprise. "Well, open it."

But Beddoes handed the parcel to Everard, as if he feared it might explode. "If 'tis all the same to you, sir, I had much rather not."

Everard flung back his head and laughed, recalling Beddoes's dismayed expression at the last parcel that had arrived from Justin: a most handsome dressing gown that the valet had held aloft with delight, only to recoil shrieking from the garter snake that tumbled from the silken folds, hissing its resentment of having its sleep disturbed. Still chuckling at Beddoes's uneasiness, Everard tore off the brown paper, revealing a flat rectangular cherrywood case. He proceeded with extreme caution as he lifted the lid. With Justin, there was no telling. . . .

"What the deuce?" he exclaimed as he stared down at a pair of flintlock top-hammer pocket pistols, the handles inlaid with silver lions and blue steel.

Beddoes, who had been holding his breath, exhaled with relief. "Here is the note that accompanied it, sir."

Everard set the pistol case down upon the bed, then tore open the envelope. He grinned as he perused the first part of the letter.

. . . thought you could use these to get in a little practice. Then, perchance, the next time we go hunting, there will be other wildlife, in mortal danger besides myself.

But as Everard scanned the rest of the page, his smile abruptly vanished.

Regret to say I will not be joining in the festivities this evening. Urgent affairs at my estate at Hoxley demand my immediate attention. I am setting out even as I write this to you. Don't know when I shall return. Look in on Reely for me from time to time.

Urgent affairs? Aye, but not at Hoxley, Everard would have wagered his life upon it. Hoxley was a small manor in the hands of an extremely capable bailiff. Its chief attraction was that it was quite near the country estate of Lady Sylvie Fitzhurst.

"Be damned to you, Justin." Everard crumpled the note and tossed it into the fireplace grate.

Beddoes coughed discreetly. "So Lord Spencer is plotting more of his mischief, is he, sir?"

"The mischief has already been accomplished."

Everard wondered what Miss Sinclair had said when Justin informed her of his plans. Of course, she would have no way of guessing the truth as to why her betrothed could not be troubled to attend a party given in honor of their engagement. She would only know that he was not to be there, that fact alone enough to cast a damper over her spirits, Everard was sure.

"Of all the inconsiderate young fools." He muttered to himself for several minutes in this vein before he realized Beddoes was waiting for him to finish venting his anger and don his freshly blackened Hessians.

"Do you believe this will be a late evening, sir?" the valet asked, warily stepping back as Everard snatched the boot from his grasp. "Shall I wait up?"

Everard jammed one foot inside the stiff leather. "No, Beddoes. Completely unnecessary. I greatly fear this is going to be a very short celebration."

Everard paused on the threshold of the cedar-paneled drawing room, the large, well-appointed chamber almost masculine in its starkness, the tall mullion-paned windows shorn of any draperies, the walls bare except for the occasional painting depicting the hunt. Aunt Lydia could not abide frills.

He raised his quizzing glass to study the company gathered about the fire crackling in the hearth, warding off the early autumn chill. In vain did he seek for the burnished tint of auburn hair, laughing emerald eyes. Aurelia had not yet arrived.

His gaze skimmed impatiently over the local gentry Lady Foxcliff had assembled for this evening's party: Justin's mother, Lady Spencer, the picture of stately elegance as always, her eldest married daughter, Clarice, looking enough like Justin to have been his twin, Clarice's stocky husband, Lord Norton. Grouped further away from the fire, Squire Morley wheezed a laugh at some jest of carrot-haired Winchell Denison; the vicar and his lady conversed earnestly with sundry others whose names Everard did not remember.

But doubtless Aurelia knew every last one of them well, these, the friends and neighbors she had grown up amongst, who would now bear witness to her humiliation this evening. Small wonder that she had not as yet put in an appearance. Most likely a note would arrive at any moment: "Miss Sinclair regrets, but she has been of a sudden taken ill." Everard lowered his glass, silently cursing Justin once more.

"Ha! So you've decided to grace us with your presence at last." The boisterous female voice, accompanied by a sharp jab in the ribs, caused Everard to jump. Rubbing his side, he turned to face his aunt's scowl. Garbed in a plain, straight gown of ecru satin straining across her strapping shoulders, her ladyship put Everard in mind of a tall marble pillar. Her iron-gray curls, done up in a profusion of sausage curls, bobbed with energy as she shook her finger at Everard.

"Confound it, sir, how could it take any man so long to rig himself out? Why, my third husband, Harry, God rest his soul, frequently dressed himself in less than five minutes."

"And frequently looked it, too." With a movement born from long experience, Everard quickly moved the knuckles of his right hand out of range of her ladyship's ivory-handled fan.

"Unlike yourself, dear Aunt," he continued smoothly, "who, as usual, quite puts all the other ladies into the shade this evening." He bent forward and planted a swift kiss upon one heavily rouged cheek.

"Flattering rogue." Balked of the knuckles, Lady Foxcliff dealt a forcible rap to Everard's shoulder, but he could see the trace of pink stealing along her square jawline.

His aunt lowered her voice to tones that were meant to be confidential, but were still quite loud enough for the entire room to hear.

"So, what do you think of this mad behavior of Justin's? Disgraceful, I call it. If I were the boy's mama, I should never have permitted him to go haring off to Hoxley."

"I am sure he wouldn't have, Aunt, without an—an excellent reason." Everard's lips tightened as he gave voice to the lie, but after all, Justin was his friend.

"Humph. Can't be any good reason for leaving Reely in the lurch, to say nothing of ruining my table arrangements. Now I've got one too many females." Her ladyship glared at her guests. "If I had only had some warning, I could have found a way to be rid of one of these dratted girls."

Lady Spencer and Clarice who were well accustomed to her ladyship's outspoken ways kept talking as if they had not heard, but Everard noted with amusement that the vicar's daughter paled with dismay.

"I shouldn't worry about your numbers, Aunt Lydia," he said softly. "For I very much doubt that Miss Sinclair will—"

He never had opportunity to complete the thought, for the door to the drawing room suddenly swung open and Lady Foxcliff's sour-faced butler thrust his head in to announce.

"Miss 'Relia Sinclair and Mrs. Perkins, yer ladyship."

As Aurelia stepped into the room, followed by her elderly companion, Everard became aware of a lull in the conversation behind him, but he could not

263

tear his eyes away from Aurelia. She was garbed in another of those hideous dresses that accented all the worst points of her figure, this time one of dove-gray silk with so much lace and so many rosette trims, Everard longed to get after it with a pair of scissors. But she could have worn sackcloth for all the difference it made to the way she appeared to-night.

Green eyes dancing, a becoming flush in each cheek, she had entwined a single rose of pink silk in her luxuriant hair. Auburn curls flowed loose about her shoulders, the glow of fire playfully captured in each glossy strand. Why, she looks positively radiant, Everard thought with a bemused frown. Mayhap he was mistaken about her feelings for Justin. Surely, not even the most courageous of women could disguise her chagrin over her beloved's defection to that extent.

As if aware of his stare, her gaze swept up to meet his with that direct, honest regard so different from the missish way most females fluttered their eyes. 'Twas both delightful and disconcerting. Scarce thinking, he fumbled for his quizzing glass and wielded it before his eye like a jouster settling a protective shield into place.

"Good evening, Miss Sinclair."

Her chin came up a trifle as she raised a quizzing glass of her own. Her eyes twinkled at him like bright green jewels; her lips widened into a smile of impish challenge.

"And a very good evening to you, Mr. Ramsey." She rolled the syllables off her tongue in precise imitation of his own languid tones.

They stood for a long moment, eye to eye, un-blinking until Everard's gravity was the first to break. He lowered his glass, no longer able to restrain his smile.

"Ah, Miss Sinclair, I see you have adopted my habit of employing a quizzing glass. So useful is it not, for locating small objects, such as—as a pair of scissors."

"Indeed, sir. Or even larger objects, such as a pony cart."

Everard choked, but before he could think of a proper retort, his aunt swooped in, enveloping Aurelia in a hug of exuberant welcome.

"Well, Reely, at least you can always be depended upon to do what's right and proper. Only fancy! Not attending one's own engagement party. Rag manners, I call it."

Aurelia's musical laughter rang out. "Oh, no. Don't tell me Justin is being fashionably late again."

At her words, an awkward silence descended over the guests. The damned scoundrel never told her he was going away, Everard thought as he watched Aurelia's smile waver, her brow furrow with uncertainty as her gaze swept the room.

"Hell's fire!" Lady Foxcliff bellowed, causing the vicar to wince. She glowered at Lady Spencer. "That harum-scarum boy of yours has gone shabbing off to Hoxley and never breathed a word to Reely about it."

"I am sure *my son* left a note to be delivered," Lady Spencer replied in arctic accents. "One of the servants has obviously been grossly negligent."

"Stuff! You know right well Justin never did. He has always been an inconsiderate young brute. If I had my say in the matter, Reely would never have accepted his offer."

While the two women engaged in a heated dispute over Justin's conduct, Everard watched the color fade from Aurelia's cheeks, like a killing frost taking the bloom off a summer rose. The lashes lowered over her eyes concealing their expression. With a gesture that appeared almost unconscious, she reached up and plucked the pink flower from her hair.

Nervously twisting the silk petals between her fingers, Aurelia became aware of the averted eyes of most of the men, of the vicar's wife attempting to conceal her clucks of self-satisfied disapproval behind her fan. Aurelia shrugged, trying to smile, searching for the jest that wouldn't come.

Justin had ridden over twice to see her that week. Twice! she wanted to scream. He had stayed upward of half an hour, laughing and joking as if he truly enjoyed being with her. It had been like old times, when they had romped together as carefree children. The awkward manner of his proposal had been forgotten. Hope of winning his regard had been reborn.

She had dressed herself with such care for this evening, wanting to make him proud to claim her as his future bride, daring to let down her hair from the braids, even daring to fancy that she did look—oh, just a very little bit—pretty. Perhaps even the fastidious Mr. Ramsey would revise his poor opinion of her. She had smiled to herself, slipping the quizzing glass into her reticule, plotting her little jest to meet the man's challenging stare.

What a simpleton you are, she told herself scornfully. 'Tis not necessary for Justin to make a fool of you. You manage so wonderfully all on your own. Imagining yourself to be pretty when you know full well you are not. You don't deserve that Justin should care two pins about you.

She wished she could raise her head and laugh away all her neighbors' whispered comments about "Poor Reely" and their pitying glances. But her mouth felt so dry and she had a terrifying fear she was about to disgrace herself totally by bursting into tears.

At that moment, a cool male voice broke into Lady Spencer's rigid defense of her son against Lady Foxcliff's accusations.

"In truth, Justin's absence must be laid at my door." Lady Foxcliff and Justin's mama ceased their bickering long enough to stare at Everard Ramsey.

Aurelia's eyes flew to his impassive countenance, all her earlier suspicions against the man stirring to life once more.

"Yes," he continued, not batting so much as an eyelash, "I had Justin kidnapped by pirates to get him out of the way."

Lady Spencer looked considerably affronted, but amusement rippled amongst the other guests. Aurelia's chin came up. Was the man attempting to mock her and expecting that she would let him get away with it?

"Pirates, Mr. Ramsey?" she asked. "Here in Norfolk?"

"Actually, I had to import them from the Mediterranean, Miss Sinclair. Shockingly expensive business. Had to spout my watch to do it."

Lady Foxcliff let out a loud guffaw. Ramsey's air of casual nonchalance while rehearsing this outrageous tale caused even Lady Spencer's thin lips to curve reluctantly.

"You see, Miss Sinclair, I knew if I did not proceed to such extremes, I would not have a single hope of being able to partner you at dinner this evening. I trust I am to be rewarded for my pains?"

Ramsey offered her his arm, one dark brow arched questioningly.

Aurelia eyed him for a moment, wondering what mischief lay behind this gallant gesture. His polite smile told her nothing. But his eyes ... An unexpected spark of warmth appeared in the blue depths, not of pity, but of such an uncanny empathy with her feelings as caused a shiver to work its way up her spine.

She lowered her gaze in confusion, hesitating. Yet whatever the man's motives, she could not help feeling grateful for his intervention. His jest had relieved the tension, helped her to regain command of herself.

"I do not see how I can refuse you, Mr. Ramsey," she said. "I always believe ingenuity should be encouraged."

With all the dignity she could muster, she linked her arm through his. His hand came up to cover her fingers, which rested lightly against his jacket sleeve.

How strange, she thought. Strange that a gentleman as coolly elegant as Everard Ramsey should have a hand that felt so warm and strong.

As Effie nodded off on one of the drawing room chairs while waiting for the carriage to be brought round, the mantelpiece clock chimed quarter past midnight. Aurelia started at the sound, astonished that the evening had passed so quickly. She usually found these dinner parties such interminable affairs. What had been so different about this one?

Her attention strayed involuntarily toward Everard Ramsey. With great difficulty she snapped her head back, trying to concentrate upon what Justin's sister was saying.

". . . and I don't know why you wish to marry Justin, Reely." Clarice's pert nose crinkled. "He's the greatest beast in nature. But I am *so* glad you are going to be my sister."

"Clarice. The coach . . ." Her husband stood on the drawing room threshold, yawning and tapping his foot.

"I shall be there directly." Clarice bestowed upon Aurelia a farewell embrace, whispering in her ear, "And I have not even had opportunity to tell you the most exciting news. I am *enceinte*."

When Aurelia offered her delighted congratulations, Clarice gave a trill of laughter. "Only fancy. Soon I shall be as round and plump as—"

The girl broke off in confusion, blushing at her faux pas. Although Aurelia winced, she gave Clarice a wry smile. Justin's sister had never been noted for her delicacy or tact.

After such a blunder, Lady Norton heeded her husband's demand to be gone with alacrity, only pausing long enough to assure Aurelia that she must be the babe's godmother. Clarice would have no one else. Aurelia's quiet acceptance was all but lost as the impatient Lord Norton fairly dragged his wife from the room.

With a deep sigh, Aurelia self-consciously smoothed the folds of her gray silk gown over her stomach, then turned toward the remaining guests. Sir Marcus and Lady Denison were having extreme difficulty tearing their eldest offspring away from his fascinating discourse with Everard Ramsey on fencing. Aurelia marveled at Ramsey's relaxed demeanor, so unlike his usual hauteur. He leaned against the mantel, a graceful negligence in his pose, the arrogant planes of his countenance softened by the light and shadow cast by the flickering flames.

She would have sworn it unthinkable that he would deign to waste his time upon a raw country lad, listening to the boy rattle on about hits, thrusts, and parries. Or that the elegant town beau would have gone out of his way to entertain her at dinner, keeping her on the verge of laughter with his anecdotes of the haut ton, until she had nigh forgotten her hurt over Justin's absence.

I believe I was mistaken about your friend, Justin, Aurelia thought. Given time, I might even learn to like him.

As if she had spoken aloud, Everard's eyes traveled in her direction. Aurelia quickly sank down upon a cherry-striped divan, behaving as if it were a matter of life-threatening urgency if she did not locate her handkerchief inside her reticule.

Lady Foxcliff bounded into the drawing room. Having just bade good-night to Clarice and Lord Norton, she now proceeded to gather up the Denisons. Forcibly pulling Winchell away from Everard, she said, "Well, well. So delightful having all of you here, but no point in wearing out one's welcome, is there?"

The young man scarce had time to make his farewells before her ladyship had propelled him after his parents out of the room.

"Dear me," Aurelia said, "I do hope Morrison has the horses in the traces, or I fear I shall find myself sitting out upon the drive."

Everard drew forth his watch and consulted it. "If your coachman does not bring your carriage round within the next five minutes, I have strict orders from Aunt Lydia to carry you out."

Aurelia joined in his laughter, but stopped when

270

he crossed the room and sat down beside her. The room seemed to grow oddly quiet, except for the crackle of the fire and Effie's gentle snores from the opposite end of the parlor. Aurelia twisted the large ruby weighting down her hand, wondering why these attacks of shyness always beset her at the most awkward of moments.

"You appear to have made quite an impression on Winchell Denison," she said, striving to break the silence. "I believe I have never seen him in anything but buckskins and a frock coat. He was actually wearing a cravat tonight."

"Good Lord. Is that what it was? I feared I must have inadvertently pinked the boy in the throat during our match earlier and his mama had swathed him in bandages."

She chuckled. "But indeed, it was very kind of you to spend your afternoon instructing Winchell, when I am sure there were other things you would much rather have done."

She felt him shrug, the movement causing his shoulders to brush up against hers. Aurelia fought down a blush, inching a little further away.

"I greatly enjoy a little exercise with the foils myself. Alas, it seems to be a dying art, one of the last traces of an age of elegance, before gunpowder came to dominate, with all its dirt and noise."

His voice took on a dreamy quality. "I've often wished I could have learned to wield a real sword, one of those heavy lengths of steel as the knights used to—"

He stopped suddenly. When Aurelia raised her head, daring to look at him, she was astonished to find Ramsey appearing a trifle sheepish, a hint of red darkening his cheeks. He muttered something about running on like a dead bore.

"Not at all, Mr. Ramsey. Do go on." He had disconcerted her so often in their brief acquaintance, she could not resist the opportunity of having some of her own back. "You were telling me you would like to be a knight, riding a white charger no doubt, rescuing damsels in distress."

"Certainly not," he snapped. "I never have the least patience with young ladies who attempt to introduce dragons into polite society."

"You need have no fears about me on that score. I always slay my own."

"Do you, indeed? A most perilous occupation. One runs such a danger of being scorched." His gaze took on that penetrating quality that Aurelia found so unsettling. She barely knew this man, harbored mixed feelings about him at best, and yet he seemed to slip past her barricades of feigned good humor with ease, wandering down the secret paths of her mind where she permitted entry to no one.

"Gracious. I wonder what is keeping my carriage." She fumbled for her reticule and attempted to rise, wanting only to escape those keen blue eyes that saw far too much, but Everard's strong fingers encircled her wrist.

"Aurelia."

Flustered, she tried to assume an expression of haughty reproach at his use of her name.

"Miss Sinclair," he continued, pausing as if weighing each word with care. "About Justin. Sometimes he can be such a heedless fellow. You ought to write and give him a good set-down for his blackguard behavior. 'Twill make you feel much better than if you simply smile and tolerate it."

Aurelia stiffened at Ramsey's blunt criticism of her betrothed. What impertinence! That he should tell her how to deal with Justin, she, who had known Lord Spencer far longer than Ramsey ever had. She jerked her hand away, but she could still feel the disturbing warmth of Everard's touch banding her flesh.

"Justin has a perfect right to do as he likes," she said, "without being made to feel guilty."

Ramsey leaned back against the cushion, folding his arms across his chest. "The right to trample roughshod over your feelings, as though you were a cobblestone? Tell me, Miss Sinclair, do you never get angry with Justin? Do you always feel obliged to conceal your emotions, even from the man you love?"

Aurelia gasped, the color surging into her face. She drew her arms in closer to her bosom, feeling as exposed as if Everard had undone the ribbons of her chemise. Attempting to hide her embarrassment, she examined the lace cuff of her gown and said tartly, "How odd. I don't recall having worn my heart upon my sleeve tonight."

"You never do. I read the inscription in that book that fell out of your workbasket."

"Have you never heard of the word *privacy*, Mr. Ramsey? I have never advocated the practice of book burning before, but in future, I shan't be so liberal."

Completely unperturbed by her rebuke, Ramsey stroked his chin in thoughtful fashion. "I don't mean to offer advice where it may not be wanted, but you intrigue me, Miss Sinclair. You have from the first. If you could get past the point of letting Justin treat you with less consideration than he shows his horse, I believe you are exactly the sort of woman he needs."

"Well, I can't begin to tell you how much your opinion means to me, sir." Aurelia glowered, spanning her fingers along her waistline. "Such a nice, sensible, *solid* sort of woman, is that your estimation?"

"No," he retorted. "Such a lovely, intelligent woman who, for some strange reason, is at pains to hide her beauty behind a silken monstrosity that resembles a rose garden run amok."

"For your information, sir, this happens to be my best gown. And—and roses are my favorite flower." She shot to her feet, all her gratitude for his earlier rescue of her evaporating, her hearty dislike returning in full force. "I fear my appearance will never measure up to your *exacting standards*, Mr. Ramsey." She lowered her voice when Effie shifted on her chair, stirring in her sleep. "What with the shortage of magic wands of late, I shall never be transformed into the belle of the ton."

He also stood, but with a more leisurely grace. "You could be, if that is what you desire. All you need is the right tutor. Place yourself under my direction, and Justin would not be the only man you would dazzle with your charms. Indeed, he would have to mount guard to prevent your being snatched from his arms."

For a brief moment Aurelia was entranced by the picture Ramsey's words conjured before her eyes. How oft had she dreamed of promenading into a ballroom upon Justin's arm, her lithe figure swirled in a gossamer gown that was the envy of all the ladies, Justin darting jealous glances at the men, daring them to approach her.

But reason quickly intruded, in the sharp memory of her mother's voice echoing through her mind. Lady Sinclair had thrown up her hands as she watched Aurelia being garbed for her coming-out party, the corset strings not quite managing to pull tight enough. *God knows I've tried Aurelia, but you will never be a beauty. You take after your father's side of the family, every one of them hopelessly fat. The most we can hope for is that you will learn not to be so awkward.*

"And the most we can hope for," Everard was saying, "is that not too many men will lose their lives fighting duels over you."

Aurelia gave her head a brief shake, dispelling the painful recollection of her mother, along with the rosy haze of her dreams.

"You'll need a different manner of dressing your hair," Ramsey continued. "And some new gowns cut upon straighter, more elegant lines."

"By all means," Aurelia said bitterly. "In case anyone has missed any of the flaws in my figure, let us be sure to accent them."

Ramsey stepped back a pace, studying her curves in expert, assessing fashion. Aurelia's cheeks burned. If he reaches for his quizzing glass, she thought, I'll break it over his nose.

But Everard appeared satisfied with his brief inspection. "No, 'tis not as desperate a case as you imagine it to be. Granted, you will want to trim off a few pounds."

Aurelia thought if she had not been so angry, she would have wept. What ungentlemanly insult would he utter next? Worst of all, he did not speak lightly, as though in jest.

"You must be bored, indeed, Mr. Ramsey. Have you such an urge to play Pygmalion, then?"

"If that is how it pleases you to describe my offer, Miss Sinclair."

"It doesn't please me at all. I am not a statue!"

"Well, who the devil said you were?" Lady Foxcliff bellowed from the doorway, causing Aurelia to jump. She stepped inside the room, scowling from Everard to Aurelia. "Now what has that nevvy of mine been saying to make your face come over all splotchy like that?"

"Nothing. Just a parcel of nonsense." Aurelia spun on her heel and strode over to the Queen Anne chair. She shook Effie awake none too gently.

"Aurelia," Mrs. Perkins murmured sleepily. "Has the carriage come yet?"

"If it hasn't, we're walking home." Ignoring Effie's wail of dismay at her threat, Aurelia hauled her to her feet. Scarce giving the bewildered Mrs. Perkins time to don her cloak, she bundled her out into the waiting carriage.

After Effie was safely bestowed in the darkened interior, Aurelia felt Everard place his hand upon her elbow to help her up the coach steps.

"I am sorry if I've upset you, Miss Sinclair. But I don't take back a word I've said. My offer still stands. You could be as beautiful—"

Aurelia wrenched her arm away, nearly stumbling as she scrambled into the coach. She plopped down onto the squabs, thrusting her head forward for one last glare at Everard Ramsey. Moonlight skimmed his handsome face; his blue eyes were lit with the same brilliant intensity as the North Star. She could not tell if he was serious about this mad proposal or merely mocking her with some outrageous jest.

"Mr. Ramsey, I strongly suggest you go soak your head in a bucket of cold water. You have obviously had far too much champagne."

Not waiting for his reply, she pulled the coach door from his grasp, closing it in his face with a loud slam. Everard stepped back as the coach lumbered off down the gravel drive.

"Well, Ramsey," he said to himself with a rueful sigh. "You handled that with all the finesse of—of a Justin Spencer." Maybe Aurelia was right. Perhaps he *was* slightly foxed. What was he about, making such suggestions to her, meddling in what was obviously none of his concern?

He grunted as, the next instant, his aunt gave him a sharp poke in the back.

"Now, sir. I have never seen Reely in such a taking in all her days, and I've known that girl from the cradle. What was that flummery I heard you a-whispering to her about being beautiful?"

"I made her an offer which she found rather unpalatable."

"An offer, you rogue! You know perfectly well she's engaged to that scamp, Justin Spencer, more's the pity."

"Not that sort of an offer, Aunt." Cursing himself for a blundering fool, Everard started to kick the toe of his boot into the gravel, then stopped. Beddoes would faint in horror if he scuffed the Hessians. When Lady Foxcliff continued to hector him, he explained reluctantly, "I offered her my help in altering her appearance. Aurelia could be a diamond of the first water if she chose to be."

Lady Foxcliff scowled. "You've got maggots in your brain, lad. Why, Reely's a good, sensible girl, the best, in my opinion, but as for beauty—pshaw. I've always had a face that would rival anything in my stables, but I've done just fine, thank you—seen three husbands to their graves."

Although Everard laughed, he immediately sobered. "Aye, but 'tis different for Aurelia, Aunt Lydia. She seems to hold herself in such low esteem."

" 'Tis the fault of that mother of hers. Nasty, dis-

277

paraging tongue Clarabelle Sinclair had. But you won't help poor Reely's esteem a jot by filling her head full of crackbrained notions. Can't make silk out of sackcloth."

Everard felt a twinge of impatience. He was beginning to find all these comments about Aurelia's plainness as irritating as his father's constant references to Arthur's many virtues. "I tell you, Aunt, Aurelia could outshine any woman in England. I would wager a thousand pounds, I could change her—"

"Done!" the old lady shouted, slapping her thigh.

"I could teach her to—I—I beg your pardon?" Everard asked startled.

"I said, 'Done.' I accept your wager."

"Aunt Lydia"—Everard chuckled uncertainly—" 'Twas only a figure of speech."

"What, sir! Are you trying to weasel out of the wager already? And you, with your reputation of being such a reckless gamester!"

Everard eyed her with suspicion. "If this is your way of trying to give me money yet again, Aunt Lydia, I warn you, I won't have it."

"Hoity-toity," her ladyship blustered. " 'Tis you who will end by paying me. You will never win this bet, my lad. Especially considering the look Reely gave you when she slammed that carriage door. Appeared as if she was imagining she had your head caught in the opening. She'll have nothing to do with your schemes."

"Ah, but she will, Auntie. When I desire, I do possess a certain amount of address with the ladies."

"Conceited rogue. Well, we shall see. But I think you've met your match in Reely. Too stubborn by half." With a resounding buffet to his ribs, Lady

Foxcliff made her way back into the red brick Georgian mansion, still clucking her tongue at him.

Grimacing, Everard rubbed his side. Leaning against one of the portico's towering white pillars, he took a deep breath. Although he had no intention of accepting his aunt's wager, he could not allow such a challenge to go unanswered. Aurelia Sinclair, sackcloth? He would show Aunt Lydia what a pearl lay hidden beneath the shell. And Justin, too.

Justin. Everard's mouth split into a grim smile as the thought came to him. Aye, a way to settle a few scores for the snake, the pepper, the bit of muslin slipped into his bed. He would see Justin properly dished this time. Not only would he turn Aurelia into a beauty, but he would make Justin fall helplessly in love with her as well.

Everard's sudden bark of laughter split the still night air.

Chapter 4

A glum silence settled over the breakfast table, broken only by the clatter of forks against the china. Aurelia stared out the bay front window, the brightness of the yellow chintz curtains and the snowbound world beyond dazzling her eyes.

She blinked, shifting her gaze toward Everard's plate, heaped with pressed beef, ham, cold tongue, and then to Effie, munching a muffin dripping with marmalade and honey butter. The tiny woman paused to lick a stray drop of honey from her fingertip in a gesture that was pure torture to Aurelia. Her stomach emitted an angry rumble. Small wonder, when the last time she could remember enjoying a meal of any substance was the night of Lady Foxcliff's dinner party several months ago.

She shoved away her glass of vinegar-and-water, wondering for the thousandth time why she had ever permitted Everard to cajole her into this madness. The day after the engagement party, she'd thought that he had ridden to Sinclair Manor to apologize for his insults. Instead, the man had alternately coaxed and bullied her, attempting to convince her to cooperate with his absurd scheme, flinging out the barb that he supposed she lacked bottom. After all, it took a certain amount of courage to make sweeping changes in one's life. Of course, if winning Justin's devotion was not important enough for her to be bothered . . .

Damn Everard Ramsey! How well the rogue knew where to find the chinks in her armor. But why was he at such pains to do so? She studied his profile as he slowly chewed the last bite of ham. He was, ever, point-device; the frothy folds of his cravat spilled across his navy jacket, and the only thing out of place was one stubborn dark curl that drooped over his forehead.

The man was still an enigma to her. So cool, so meticulous, he looked nothing like the reckless gamester he was reputed to be, wildly flinging his fortune away at hazard, hiding in Norfolk to escape his creditors. He behaved as if he had not a worry in the world, as if nothing were more important to him than trying to turn a dowdy country-bred female into a fashionable beauty.

Boredom, she supposed, could drive a man into doing some peculiar things. And yet, there was not a trace of ennui in the twinkling blue eyes that now looked up at her.

Everard slid her glass back into place, favoring her with a teasing smile. "Eat your breakfast, Aurelia. There's a good girl."

She glared first down at her plate of rice and then at him. "I refuse to eat another mouthful of this detestable stuff. This is pure madness. I don't know why I permit you to torment me in this fashion."

"Because, occasionally, there are moments when you forget yourself and lapse into bouts of being sensible." He patted her arm.

"Don't touch me in that condescending fashion," she said, the sour taste of vinegar lingering upon her tongue. "I'll bite your hand, I swear I will. That is how hungry I am."

"Tush." Everard leaned back in his chair and applied his napkin to his lips with a satisfied smile. "Your diet is more than adequate. Rice and vinegar. 'Twas what Lord Byron ate, and it did wonders for him."

"Lord Byron is a fool. I shall never read *Childe Harold* again."

Effie piped up, "I entirely agree. 'Tis all very well for poets to do such odd things. One expects them to be a little eccentric, but Aurelia is a lady of quality."

She stood up and flounced to the sideboard, pouring out a steaming cup of chocolate. Balancing the delicate saucer and cup in one hand, she extended the dark, creamy brew to Aurelia. "Here, my dear, before you waste away entirely. Ring for Giddings and have that dreadful vinegar mess cleared away."

Aurelia drew in a deep breath, her nostrils assailed by the rich aroma of chocolate. Her mouth watered as she reached for the cup, but before she could raise it to her lips, Everard snatched the china from her grasp.

"We'll have none of that," he said sternly, returning the chocolate to the sideboard. Aurelia moaned, her nails digging into the white linen tablecloth.

"Well, really, sir!" Effie sputtered. She squared off with Everard, her quivering chin not quite reaching as high as the lacy edge of his starched cravat. Ramsey's narrowed eyes glinted down at her with the tolerant amusement of a great dark-winged falcon being twittered at by a small brown wren.

"This state of affairs cannot continue. Aurelia's dear papa would never have approved. Always, I remember how he worried that she did not eat enough, so afraid that she would tend to be of a consumptive nature, like many of her mama's sisters."

"I think it highly improbable that Aurelia will develop consumption," Everard said.

"No, I am more like to die of starvation first." Aurelia poked her fork at the clumps of rice upon her dish, pulling a face at the sight of the tasteless grain. "And what do I have to show for it? I look as much a fright as I ever did."

"That is because you still dress as if you were a display of wares in a mantua maker's shop window. But after the new clothes that I ordered from London arrive—"

"Mr. Ramsey!" Effie's outraged gasp stopped him in midsentence. "Indeed, you have far exceeded the bounds of propriety this time."

"I fear I am forced to agree with her, Everard." Aurelia felt a blush coursing into her cheeks. "For you to be buying me clothes as if I were your—your . . ."

"My mistress?" he supplied, raising one eyebrow mockingly. "I assure you my finances are not in a state to buy so much as a hatpin for a lady, even if I were so inclined."

Aurelia thought she detected a certain edge of bitterness in his voice, but it vanished as he continued, "No, ladies, rest assured all purchases were handled by my sister Philippa with great discretion. The demand for payment will be forthcoming."

Aurelia lowered her eyes, still fidgeting with embarrassment. "You might have consulted me first. I do have my own dressmaker."

"Ah, yes, that half-blind woman from the village who overstocked herself with lace and furbelows."

Aurelia's hand flew to the frills of her lime-green morning gown, the stiff ruffles of the high-necked gown scratching her chin. She wished she could think of a scathing retort to Everard's criticism, but 'twas impossible, when she knew he was right. Her wardrobe was woefully inadequate, especially considering that Justin, in one of his rare communications, had decided they should be married in London. Despite the fact Justin had implored her to name the day that would *make him the happiest of men*, he had set their wedding date himself. Late winter, nay, perhaps spring would be better. Then he would fetch Aurelia, and they could be wed at the fashionable St. George's in Hanover Square. The very thought of such a thing made Aurelia's stomach turn flip-flops.

"Excuse me, Aurelia." She felt Effie tug on her sleeve. Glancing up, she saw that Mrs. Perkins had gone as rigid as the fireplace poker, her lips pursed into a tight white line. "I wonder if I might have the favor of a few words in private, my dear?"

Aurelia sighed. She was in no humor for more of Effie's scolds, but she supposed 'twould be far less mortifying than having the woman rant on in Everard's hearing. Whisking the napkin off her lap, she flung it down by her place setting. "If you will excuse us a moment," she said to Everard.

He sketched her an exaggerated bow, his cool blue eyes impassive as he watched her follow Effie from the room.

Scarce able to contain herself, the little woman rounded on Aurelia as soon as they had crossed the threshold, not even bothering to pull the breakfast parlor door all the way closed.

"This madness has got to stop, Aurelia. 'Tis simply not proper! Bad enough to allow Mr. Ramsey to call upon you nigh every day, with Lord Spencer still away at Hoxley. I am supposed to be your chaperon. I shall be blamed if—"

"Now, Effie," Aurelia broke in soothingly. "I am scarce ever alone with Everard. And he is Justin's closest friend."

"That is another thing," Effie moaned. "What if anyone hears you calling him *Everard*!"

Aurelia caught a glimpse of Everard through the crack in the door, refilling her vinegar glass. "I daresay I shall be calling him much worse than that before this winter is over."

Effie squeezed Aurelia's hand in a distracted manner. "You are such an innocent, my dear. You cannot imagine how people might misconstrue. A single, personable man to be so often at the side of an unmarried lady—and so early in the day, too. At breakfast!"

Aurelia stiffened. "If you are implying that Everard would ever behave in anything less than an honorable—"

"No, no." Effie hastened to disclaim. "I am very fond of Mr. Ramsey myself. The dear boy! He is all that a gentleman ought to be. I realize he simply means to be kind. There is not the least fear that a man so fastidious would find *you* attractive."

"No, he wouldn't would he?" Aurelia fixed a wooden smile upon her lips. "So, why make such a fuss?"

"Because of what others will say. The vicar's wife has already most kindly informed me there has been some gossip in the village." Effie's spiderlike hands fluttered to her cheeks. "Oh, dear, and what if Lord Spencer got to hear of it? How dreadful 'twould be if he were to call Mr. Ramsey out and—and—"

"You have been reading too many Minerva Press novels again, Effie. Since Justin never troubles himself to return to Aldgate, he is unlikely to hear anything. And when he does"—Aurelia thrust out her chin proudly—"I trust he will have more sense than to pay heed to the blathering of narrow-minded individuals who twist an innocent friendship into something sordid."

With that, she spun on her heel and stormed back into the breakfast parlor without waiting to see if Effie would follow her. She plunked back down in her seat, attacking the rice with her fork. She could sense that Everard was regarding her with a puzzled frown, but refused to meet his gaze until he lightly touched her hand.

"Aurelia, if I have offended you in the matter of the wardrobe, I am sorry. I thought you had given me carte blanche to do whatever I felt was necessary."

"Y-yes, I did." She snatched her hand away as if he had scorched her, heat creeping into her cheeks. Plague take the vicar's wife, with her nasty, gossiping tongue, and plague take Effie for listening to her. Aurelia hadn't realized until this moment how comfortable she had become with Everard. Effie's insinuations somehow threatened the understanding that had sprung up between them, making Aurelia acutely aware of Everard's undeniable masculinity beneath the frilled shirts and elegantly cut waistcoats.

She squared her shoulders, straightening in her seat. Such foolish notions could entirely ruin their friendship if she let them. Well, she would not!

"Do not pay the least heed to me," she said with forced gaiety. "The vinegar has soured my disposition this morning. And I am nigh distracted, wondering what new horrors you have in store for me today. No more of those long trudges through the snow, I trust?"

"I would remind you, Miss Sinclair, that I was with you every step of the way, trudging, as you call it."

"Yes, but the freezing temperatures have not the same effect upon someone who has ice-water in his veins."

Everard withdrew the hand that she had shrunk from touching, his expression becoming more withdrawn as well. "I may not be as impervious to the cold as you think," he muttered. Some dark thought appeared to cloud his brow for a moment. Then, as if giving himself a shake, he said in lighter tones, "This afternoon, I propose we have our exercise indoors. 'Tis high time I taught you the proper manner to waltz."

Aurelia felt her muscles tense. The last time she had danced had been at the assembly, with Augustus Snape, when she had been so desperately tired of sitting against the wall. And look what that had brought down upon her head. At least, the dreadful man had finally left Norfolk and returned to London. But stumbling all over Mr. Ramsey's toes was entirely another matter. She had not the least desire to demonstrate to Everard how clumsy she was.

"I don't see how that will be possible," she said. "Unless you propose to hum while we dance."

"Mrs. Perkins will play for us."

Aurelia's gaze traveled the length of the table to Effie's empty chair. "I rather doubt that."

"Because she was a trifle vexed with me this morning?" Everard asked. "I think I can manage to bring her around." His lips twitched, but whether out of amusement or annoyance, Aurelia could not tell.

"Believe it or not, Miss Sinclair. There are a few women who occasionally are susceptible to my charms."

"I daresay," she retorted. "The same as there are women who are extremely susceptible to influenza. However, Effie's constitution may prove tougher than you imagine."

In truth, Aurelia was very much counting upon Elfreda's noted stubbornness to spare her a most uncomfortable and embarrassing exercise. But later, after she returned from consulting with her cook about the day's menu, Aurelia was taken aback to discover Mrs. Perkins and Everard already in the music room, moving back the furniture.

"Oh, good. There you are, Aurelia." Effie clapped her hands together, beaming at Aurelia as if she recalled not a word of their disagreement, nor any of the dire warnings she had issued only an hour ago. "Now we may begin."

Aurelia watched with dismay as Effie skittered over to the pianoforte, arranging her black silk skirts upon the bench. Everard stole a glance at Aurelia, then brushed his nails against his lapel, looking so smugly triumphant, Aurelia longed to shy her workbasket at his head.

He bent over Effie, helping her settle the music into place. " 'Tis prodigiously kind of you, Mrs. Perkins," he said in low, intimate tones. "And such a treat for us. 'Tis not often we are privileged to enjoy your musical talents."

As Effie preened and simpered, Aurelia thought she was going to choke. But why should she be so astonished when Aurelia knew how easy it was to find one's common sense floundering in the treacherous depths of those dark-fringed blue eyes?

Desperately, Aurelia made one last effort to extricate herself from the ordeal to come. "Effie does play beautifully," she said. "What a pity the waltz is not yet danced in Aldgate, and she does not know how to play—"

"Pooh! I have not allowed myself to become as out of date as *some*." Effie began to pound out the three-quarter time of the waltz with the ease of long familiarity.

Aurelia shrank back as Everard advanced upon her with long purposeful strides. Ruefully, she stared down at his gleaming Hessians. Well, 'twas his own fault. The man deserved every scuff mark he was going to get.

"Give me your hand, Aurelia," Everard commanded.

Trembling, she permitted him to take her fingers within the warmth of his grasp. He positioned her other hand so that it rested lightly against his shoulder. Aurelia held herself rigid, standing nigh an arm's length away.

"Relax, Aurelia," he said, "You look as though you were about to visit the tooth drawer."

Her answering retort broke off with a gasp as his strong arm encircled her waist, pulling her so near she feared he must hear the thudding of her heart. Heat rose into her cheeks as she glanced at Effie, half hoping, half fearing her chaperon would intervene. But Mrs. Perkins only nodded in encouragement before beginning to bounce up and down, completely absorbed in her music.

Aurelia scarce comprehended Everard's instructions regarding the movement of her feet. She had never been this close to any man except her father.

Why, Everard might as well have been embracing her. Snatches of her conversation with Effie drifted back into Aurelia's head ... *A single personable man ... no fear Mr. Ramsey would find you attractive ... if Justin got to hear of it ...*

As Everard attempted to whirl her in a circle, she stumbled forward, brushing against the hard plane of his chest.

"Are you all right?" he asked, tightening his arm about her waist.

She nodded, trying to extricate herself. "I knew this would be of no avail. I simply have no sense of rhythm."

He gave her an impatient shake. "Nonsense. You haven't even tried. Now start again and count this time. One-two-three. One-two-three."

Aurelia sighed, making a weak attempt to assimilate all his rapidly barked instructions. "Turn, Aurelia, and for pity's sake, smile. 'Tis customary, you know, to hold some conversation with your partner while dancing."

"I cannot count and talk at the same time."

"And, 'twill be considered excessively odd if you address all your remarks to your partner's waistcoat."

Goaded past endurance, Aurelia's head jerked up, but she realized it was a grave mistake. The fine carved lines of Everard's face hovered but inches from hers, his sensitive mouth quirked into that mocking half smile that was so peculiarly his own.

"Stop holding yourself so stiff. Anyone would think you had never danced with a man before."

"I assure you, sir, I have trod upon far more handsome—I mean—far better—feet than yours."

Everard's deep chuckle rumbled close to her ear.

She fancied that she could feel his breath fanning the tendrils of hair along her brow. Ducking her head, Aurelia missed her footing, tramping down hard upon his instep.

Although she heard him suck in his breath, he made no comment upon her awkwardness. Yet her cheeks burned all the same.

Hopeless, she thought, her lashes batting aside the tears gathering in her eyes. Utterly hopeless, but Everard would never release her until she forced him to acknowledge the fact she was naught but a galloping clodpole.

Determined to show him how clumsy she could be, Aurelia gave over all effort to mind her steps, throwing herself into the waltz with a fierce abandon. The tempo of Effie's enthusiastic thumps along the keyboard struck an answering chord within Aurelia's angry jumble of emotions.

Strangely enough, instead of tripping headlong as she expected, Aurelia found she was moving in perfect harmony with every sway of Everard's polished steps.

"Much better," he said, his lips close to her ear.

As they glided past the piano, Aurelia heard Effie exclaim, "Why, Reely, how quickly you've caught on. I declare I've never seen you dance half so well."

Me? Dance well? Aurelia's startled thought echoed. But indeed she was. She could feel the rightness of her movements in every fiber of her body. Everard's touch became provocatively light now, the fingers skimming her waist, no longer tugging but gently waltzing her the length of the music room.

Waltzing? Nay, 'twas more like floating on air, swirling like a fragile autumn leaf caught in the throes of a powerful wind. An excited wave of merriment bubbled inside of Aurelia. Never before had she felt so light upon her feet, so graceful, so lithesome. When Everard led her into a series of twirls, her senses reeled from the sheer pleasure of it, headier than sipping champagne. The pianoforte, the fireplace, the French window, all spun before her gaze, until her world had only one focus, Everard's deep blue eyes. Even when she began to stagger, she would not permit him to stop, until he nigh lost his own balance.

Panting with laughter, Everard tried to collapse back upon the settee, but Aurelia seized him by both hands, tugging insistently.

"No. Can't stop now," she gasped. "Just getting the feel of it. Effie, keep playing."

Everard permitted Aurelia to drag him back to the center of the room. "Very well," he cried in mock dismay. "But more slowly this time. A little decorum, if you please. I'd look no end a fool if I sprained an ankle dancing."

Giggling like a schoolgirl, she slipped back into his embrace. It took a few moments for her to calm herself enough to catch the rhythm. But by the time they had gone down the room, she moved in perfect step with him, gliding as if she had waltzed with Everard Ramsey every night of her life.

She peered up at him, almost shyly. "I—I can scarce believe it. You can't possibly know how clumsy . . . my mother always despaired that—I mean I never . . ." She floundered, at a complete loss for words to express the wonder she was feeling.

But it was unnecessary. The warm light in his eyes told her that he knew, although he only smiled and said, "Mayhap you simply never had the right partner."

"Mayhap not," she said slowly. "Or mayhap you do have a magical wand about you after all."

When he laughed, it suddenly occurred to her how very much she *liked* Everard Ramsey this way, the cynical lines of his face relaxing, gentled by his smile. No bored mask in indifference, no elegant dandy hiding behind his quizzing glass. Simply a man who looked at her as if—

Aurelia's breath caught in her throat. As if it mattered naught whether she were beautiful. Because 'twas enough that he made her feel as if she were.

Dimly, Aurelia became aware of Effie's excited applause. The woman called out. "Oh, you do waltz beautifully, my dear. 'Tis nothing short of a miracle. Why, Mr. Ramsey ought to be a dancing master."

"Aye," Aurelia laughed happily. "Only fancy how astonished Justin is going to be."

She felt the arm encircling her waist stiffen. Everard jerked her to an abrupt halt. A strange expression crossed his features, an expression Aurelia could only describe as being like that of one slumbering, deep in dreams, being startled awake.

Before she could ask what was wrong, Everard released her, averting his gaze toward the fire. When he looked back at Aurelia again, he had schooled his features into their customary languid expression.

"Shall I play a cotillion now, Mr. Ramsey?" Effie asked eagerly. "Aurelia has always had difficulty with that."

"No," he said. "I believe I have had quite enough exercise for one day. Mayhap another time."

"Y-yes," Aurelia stammered, twisting her betrothal ring, wondering miserably what she had done to break the spell. An image of how she must have looked to Everard surfaced in her mind. A plain, awkward, ungainly female prancing about, tossing her head, imagining herself some sort of a fairy-tale princess. She must have appeared a complete fool. Her face flushed as she said stiffly, "Mr. Ramsey, I do want to—to thank you for the lesson and for spending so much time—"

He started to reach for her hand, then stopped. "Not at all, my dear," he drawled. "What else is there for one to do in this wilderness?"

His words cut her like the lash of a whip. Hurt and confused, she retreated to the fireside, rubbing her arms, feeling chilled, as if the French doors had blown open, letting in the icy blast of winter. She scarce heard his murmured words of farewell to Effie, or the door click as he let himself out.

Chapter 5

Aurelia picked her way through the collection of trunks and bandboxes, resisting the urge to kick pettishly aside one containing a bonnet of green silk trimmed with lilac ribbon. With these constant reminders of her imminent departure for London cluttering her bedchamber, she was beginning to feel much like a watch with its spring wound too tight.

Effie's coos of delight as she lifted the elegant bonnet from its wrapping only further served to irritate Aurelia. Defiantly, she picked up her oldest broad-brimmed hat of straw, decorated with some rather wilted-looking cloth flowers, and rammed it on her head.

Effie didn't appear to notice, so engrossed was she in the packages from London. "Oh, doesn't Mr. Ramsey's sister have the most exquisite taste!" she exclaimed. "I have been longing to tell him I was quite mistaken about the new wardrobe. 'Twas really an excellent notion. Why do you suppose he did not call again yesterday?"

"I haven't the slightest notion," Aurelia said, loath to admit she had been wondering the same thing herself. Everard had been so aloof since that long-ago winter afternoon he had taught her to waltz. When she chanced to meet him in the village or at Lady Foxcliff's manor, he seemed determined to keep her at bay with cynical glances through his quizzing glass, his lips set in an infuriating attitude of detached boredom. It had become a challenge to break through his cool demeanor, set him laughing, but whenever she succeeded, he appeared excessively vexed with her.

Shoving a dressing case aside, Aurelia plopped down upon the downy quilt coverlet spread across her bed and tried to put all thoughts of Everard from her mind, but 'twas exceedingly difficult, when Effie persisted in talking about the man.

"I daresay Mr. Ramsey will call today, dear," Mrs. Perkins twittered as she began to refold the frothy layers of a new petticoat she had been examining. "He knows how very anxious you are getting about the journey to London."

Anxious? Aurelia grimaced. She was petrified at the notion of confronting Justin again in the midst of all his elegant tonnish friends. She hunched her shoulders in an effort to appear indifferent, to both the grim prospect lying before her and Everard's unexplained defection.

"I daresay Mr. Ramsey has found other far more amusing diversions than trying to starve me to death. In any case, you should be pleased." She glowered at Effie. "You were always complaining that he called too often."

"Yes, but I never meant he should stay away altogether." Effie regarded her with reproachful surprise. "Really, Aurelia. How you do take one up. You have been cross as crabs of late. Most unlike yourself."

Aurelia drew in a deep breath, knowing Effie's criticism was fully justified. She had felt strange these past days, alternating between the desire to burst into tears and the urge to smash something. "I—I am sorry if I have been snappish, Effie," she said. "I expect I am light-headed from want of food."

"But the diet has done wonders. That old gray frock of yours positively hangs on you. I thought you were going to give it to the kitchen maid."

"Sally didn't want it." Aurelia self-consciously patted the folds of her comfortable old serge gown.

"And you haven't even tried on any of your lovely new things." Effie held aloft an enchanting high-waisted morning gown done up in a dusky shade of primrose. "Pray, Aurelia, do try at least this one."

Feeling slightly ashamed of her ill humor, Aurelia reluctantly took the gown from Effie. Holding the gauzy lengths in front of her plain gray dress, she stalked over to regard herself in the bedchamber's only mirror, a small gilt-framed oval. She could detect no changes in herself whatsoever from the unattractive woman Justin had blithely bade farewell to last autumn. Mayhap, she was a trifle paler, that was all. And the frolicksome pink of the gown only seemed to accent the dark shadows under her eyes.

With its daringly low décolletage and bright embroidered hem, it would not permit her to blend into the woodwork as she had always managed to do in the past. She tried to imagine how Justin would react when he saw her wearing it, but 'twas difficult to bring into focus the image of his teasing, light gray eyes. Instead, the vision of cool blue ones set beneath mockingly arched dark brows kept intruding upon her thoughts.

"Given the right tutor, you could dazzle the ton next spring, be as beautiful as you desire," Everard had said. Had he ever believed that? It scarce mattered for 'twas obvious that he no longer did. Aurelia could place no other interpretation upon his continued absence. He had given up on her.

Well, she had always known she was a hopeless case. Why did it hurt so much more now that Everard apparently thought so, too? Aurelia dropped the pink gown back into the trunk.

"I haven't any more time for this nonsense, Effie," she said. "I have to pay a call upon one of the tenants before tea."

"But I thought you would wish to change. All these pretty new gowns to choose from." Effie's eyes rounded in horror. "Surely you don't intend to go calling in that hideous old gray sack."

"Old Mrs. McGinty will not care how I look, so long as I am bringing a basketful of her favorite jam."

Before Effie could protest any further, Aurelia seized her drab brown merino cloak and hurried from the room. She longed to escape from the sight of the elegant new clothes that only served to remind her of her own shortcomings, her sense of failure.

Mrs. McGinty's reed-thatched cottage nestled at the very edge of the Sinclair estate, only yards from one of the broads, those clear-water lakes that dotted the Norfolk landscape. In the distance brown-sailed wherries skimmed the silver surface like playful, daring birds defying the whitecaps that threatened to toss them off-balance.

The last of the winter snows had melted, leaving the lakeside path a veritable sea of coffee-colored mud. Yet Aurelia would have enjoyed the walk under other circumstances. As it was, she kept remembering the last time she had passed this way,

Everard tugging on her hand, forcing her to keep up with his brisk pace, laughingly threatening that if she did not cease her grumbles about being hungry, he would chip a hole in the ice and catch an eel for her supper.

Huddling deeper into the folds of her brown cloak, she tipped forward the brim of her battered straw bonnet, shielding her face from the nip of the March wind. She supposed in future she would take all her walks alone. Wandering by the lakeside was not a diversion that would ever appeal to Justin.

Despite the mud, the roads were now quite passable. There was not the slightest reason in the world why Justin could not return to Aldgate and fetch her to London himself instead of waiting for Lady Foxcliff to bring her. Not the slightest, except for the myriad of reasons Justin manufactured in his infrequent letters. The tone of his writing oft reminded Aurelia of a young man trying to avoid having to escort his sister to a ball.

His sister. Of a sudden, Everard Ramsey's well-modulated voice echoed through her mind. *If Justin thinks of you as his sister, 'tis your own fault for never attempting to show him otherwise. But we are going to change all that.*

Why had she ever listened to him? She was far too old to believe in fairy tales.

Listlessly, Aurelia knocked at the cottage door, hoping to keep the visit short, but as usual, it was difficult to escape from the garrulous Mrs. McGinty. The old woman was suffering from a bout of rheumatism again, but that hadn't kept her from her baking, nor from pressing a large chunk of gingerbread upon Aurelia when she finally took her leave. As soon as she was out of sight of the cottage's whitewashed walls, Aurelia stared down at the tantalizing bit of cake fashioned in the shape of a lopsided little man, still warm from the oven. She supposed she could take it home to Effie for tea. But the pale sun had already shifted lower in the sky, casting long afternoon shadows across the shore of the reed-choked lake. By this time, Effie had most likely already stuffed herself with biscuits.

The spicy aroma of gingerbread wafted to her nostrils, warring for dominance over the loamy scent of the mudwashed earth. Aurelia's fingers inched the cake toward her mouth. The sly currant grin of the gingerbread man seemed to mock her as if taunting, "What would Everard say if he caught you thus?" As if it mattered what scathing remark he would utter, Aurelia thought bitterly. No one truly cared how plump she was, not Justin and certainly not Everard Ramsey. In a gesture of defiance, she bit off the gingerbread man's leg.

She chewed slowly, savoring each mouthful with a sense of hollow satisfaction. But before she could take another bite, she was distracted by the sight of a punt making its way toward shore. From beneath the shade of her bonnet brim, she studied the tall man so expertly maneuvering his small craft. 'Twas not one of the cottagers. Even from this distance, she remarked the elegant cut of his trousers, the white shirt shoved up past the elbows, exposing the sinewy muscles of his forearms. He braced his powerful legs beneath him like some bold pirate captain surveying the deck of his ship, while midnight strands of hair whipped across his brow as he shaded his eyes, squinting in her direction.

Aurelia blinked, scarce trusting her vision. No, it could not possibly be!

"The devil," she exclaimed in dismay. What perverse mischance had brought Everard to this very spot, engaged in such an unlikely occupation? She whipped the gingerbread behind her back, entirely forgetting she had just sworn that she did not give a groat for Ramsey's opinion. Stepping backward, she attempted to slink into the line of willow trees, but 'twas already too late. Ramsey raised his hand, calling out her name.

She froze while he poled in to the side, distractedly seeking some way to rid herself of the gingerbread man. She thought of flinging it into the broad. No, Everard would be bound to notice. She ended by slipping the cake figure back into her pocket. Adjusting her bonnet to conceal the guilty flush mounting into her cheeks, Aurelia watched Everard leap to the bank with an athletic grace quite different from his usual languid movements. Proceeding to moor his craft to a low hanging branch of a slender birch, he deftly knotted the rope with the ease of long practice. He lifted a frock coat from the seat of the punt and slung it carelessly over his arm, as usual appearing entirely impervious to the elements.

Aurelia tried not to gape at him as he strode toward her, but 'twas the first time she had ever seen Everard appear other than the picture of polished elegance. Despite his recent exertions, not so much as a speck of dirt marred his whipcord breeches, nor one wrinkle the folds of his plain, buff-colored waistcoat. But he wore no cravat; the top buttons of his shirt were undone to expose the vee of his chest. Aurelia caught herself staring in fascination

301

at the dark hairs curling against the tanned flesh, then blushed more deeply than ever.

"Good afternoon, Miss Sinclair." He bowed with as much aplomb as though greeting her in the manor's most formal dining room.

She placed her fingers instinctively over the area of her cloak where the gingerbread nestled in her pocket. "Oh-h, Everard. How astonishing to meet you here. So unexpected. I would never have imagined that you . . ."

"That I could manage to pole a boat without tumbling myself into the water?" he filled in when she began floundering for words.

"No, I believe I am more astonished that you would wish to do so."

One of Everard's dark eyebrows shot upward in lofty fashion. "My dear Miss Sinclair, occasionally even *I* take pleasure in some of your rustic amusements."

Aurelia's heart sank. So he meant to play the dandy today, when she so longed for but one glimpse of his warm, encouraging smile. She watched unhappily as he rolled down his sleeves, rebuttoned his shirt with deliberate finesse, then shrugged his broad shoulders into his frock coat.

"I must apologize for my appearance," he drawled. "I, too, am finding this meeting most surprising. One does not expect to find a *lady* of such elegance sauntering through this wilderness." He cast a disparaging glance at her floppy-brimmed bonnet and the hem of her gray dress, steeped an inch in mud.

Aurelia hugged her cloak more tightly around her. "Oh, dear, Mr. Ramsey, you have caught me sadly out of fashion. I forgot 'tis all the crack now to wear one's silks and diamonds while trudging knee deep through the mire on one's estate."

"That does not appear to be all you've forgotten." Before she could guess his intent, Everard caught her wrist and wrestled her hand away from her pocket. In the next instant, he had pulled forth the gingerbread.

Aurelia suppressed a groan. She might have known those keen eyes of his would miss nothing. "Oh, that." She cringed under his accusing stare. "Mrs. McGinty gave it to me. I—I was taking it home to Effie."

"Indeed?" Everard whipped out his quizzing glass. Did the man never go anywhere without the damn thing? He proceeded to inspect the gingerbread man with mock solemnity. "Why, the unfortunate chap seems to have lost one of his feet. You don't by any chance have a mouse in your pocket, do you, Miss Sinclair?"

Aurelia bit her lower lip and glared at him, feeling very much like a little girl caught filching biscuits from the pantry. "No," she said chokingly. "If I had, I would have trained it straightaway to bite you."

She attempted to snatch the gingerbread from his hand, but he flung it far out into the broad, where it disappeared beneath the rippling waters with a soft plop. When his gaze shifted back to her, an angry spark flickered in his eyes.

"What the deuce did you think you were doing with that?"

"Well, to the best of my memory, I believe the pastime is called *eating*."

"Damn it, Aurelia. There is less than a fortnight before you leave for London."

"I am as perfectly capable of reading a calendar

as you are, sir," she snapped. "And equally as aware that it matters naught how much time is left."

"Not if you intend to get up to such tricks as this the moment my back is turned."

"I would scarce describe this past month as *a moment*." Aurelia could have bitten out her tongue as soon as the words were out. She had no desire to give Ramsey the impression that she might have missed his daily visits. Aware that he was studying her with frowning surprise, she turned aside. "You may as well concede defeat, Mr. Ramsey. It is perfectly obvious you have given up the ridiculous task you set yourself—"

He caught her by the shoulders, spinning her around. "Whenever I cry quits, Miss Sinclair, you will be the first to know. And I will admit that, right now, the temptation is mighty strong." Despite his chiding words, a note of tender exasperation crept into his voice. "Stand still," he commanded when she attempted to wriggle away from him. Carefully he swept back the auburn curls, which the wind had tumbled about her cheeks, his fingers tangling in the fine strands. Then he forcefully straightened her ancient bonnet, retying the satin ribbon strings with a firm tug.

"There. That's better, but not much. Why are you not wearing any of your new things from London?"

Color spilled into Aurelia's cheeks, not entirely caused by the briskness of the weather. "None of those lovely gowns were meant for me. I feel like the vain crow in Aesop's fable, trying to borrow the peacock's feathers."

"The only time you look in the least like a crow, my dear, is when you run around garbed in these old rags. The next time I set eyes on you, you'd best be properly attired, or I swear I'll dress you my-self."

He took much of the sting out of the threat by lightly chucking her under the chin. "And now," he said softly, "whatever put the idea into your head I had given up on you?"

Aurelia swallowed, suddenly feeling very foolish. "You—you have grown so excessively critical of late. And I have had the feeling you are trying to avoid me."

"Despite what a frippery sort of fellow you think I am, Aurelia, I do have to attend to business occasionally."

She glanced toward the punt. "Indeed, 'tis remark-able how many gentlemen have pressing business upon the broads at the first hint of spring."

She meant the remark to be light, teasing, and was appalled to hear how shrewish she sounded. Justin had been gone months, and she had never penned him so much as one word of reproach. Why, then, was she waxing so peevish with Everard, upon whom she had no claim other than friend-ship? His next words made her feel even more ashamed of her behavior.

"I frequently pole down the stream from Aunt Lydia's, then out here amongst the shallows on the lake, when I want to be alone, when I need time to think through some difficulties."

"Difficulties?" For the first time, Aurelia noted the lines of weariness etched at the corners of his eyes. "I—I had no idea, Everard." Shyly, she squeezed his hand. "Why don't you tell me about them? Mayhap I could help."

Slowly Everard withdrew his fingers from her grasp. "I think not, my dear."

"That hardly seems fair. You know all of my deepest, darkest secrets."

But Everard merely shook his head, ignoring the coaxing note she infused into her voice. He retreated toward the bank, poking the toe of his boot at the green-tipped reeds. "A pity 'twere not later in the spring. I would have picked you some water lilies."

"I detest them. They smell like brandy." Aurelia trailed after him, determined not to let him change the subject. "Is it something to do with *The Albatross*?"

Everard's brow darkened into a frown. "How did you know about that?"

"Lady Foxcliff happened just to mention it one day."

Everard compressed his lips, although he said with forced lightness, "How very disconcerting. I thought the members of my family had all agreed to keep my bouts of insanity a secret."

"Your aunt was not being in the least critical," Aurelia hastened to add. "She has the deepest admiration for what she called a most daring and shrewd investment."

"Well, it seems my most daring and shrewd investment is now bits of flotsam off the coast of Brazil. A letter arrived from my solicitor a few days ago."

"Oh, Everard, I—I'm most dreadfully sorry." To Aurelia, her words seemed dreadfully inadequate. She reached out one hand to touch his sleeve, then allowed her arm to fall helplessly back to her side.

Everard stared out across the lake, his changeable blue eyes shifting with all the turbulence of the choppy waters. "Pure folly," he murmured as if he'd almost forgotten she was there. "Just as my father always said. But then, I've always been something of a fool about ships." She followed his gaze to where the silhouette of a sail scudded around a tree-lined bend out of view. "I was wont to dream of going to sea when I was a lad. Planned to follow in the footsteps of Lord Nelson."

He gave a soft, self-deriding laugh before wrenching his eyes back to Aurelia. "Could you picture it, Miss Sinclair? Me, a sailor?"

"Yes, I could," she said stoutly. Indeed, she suddenly had no difficulty imagining Everard upon the deck of a ship, clad only in dark, tight breeches outlining his powerful thighs, and a lace-cuffed white shirt, repelling hordes of Frenchmen swarming over the sides. Only not with a pistol; Everard would wield a sword.

"You are possessed of far too lively an imagination, Aurelia." She started, hearing a ripple of amusement in Everard's voice, and was once again beset by the eerie feeling that he could read her thoughts.

He continued, "I fear the only deck I will ever command is that of cards, and none too successfully at that."

"Stuff! You only feel that way because your father is forever going on about Arthur—" She broke off at the shuttered look that came into Everard's eyes, warning her she was treading on forbidden ground.

"Aunt Lydia talks a great deal too much. I would never have guessed the pair of you had turned into such gossips."

Aurelia sensed she should let the subject drop, but found she could not. Her words tumbled out in a rush. "Your aunt only spoke of it because she worries about you, the quarrel with your father. I can well understand how you must have disliked your brother—"

"Not at all. I was very fond of Arthur until he was so inconsiderate as to die, leaving me to fill his shoes."

Aurelia summoned up all her courage to make her next suggestion. "Wouldn't it solve all your difficulties if—if you simply went home, made up the quarrel. Imagine what you must mean to your mother and father. Their only living son, their heir—"

Everard's harsh laugh halted her attempt at gentle persuasion. "How much I mean to them? My dear Miss Sinclair, do you know what happened the day after my brother was buried? A neighboring lord dropped by to pay his condolences." A bitter smile touched Everard's lips. "The poor fool thought to comfort my parents by pointing out to them that at least they were fortunate in having one son left to carry on the family name.

"My mother and father both looked at me. I think it was the first time it occurred to either of them that I was now the sole surviving son. My mother burst into tears, and my father poured himself out a very large bumper of whiskey."

Aurelia felt a lump form in her throat. Despite his sardonic smile, she could see a vulnerability in his eyes that she knew all too well, having experienced it herself so often. From out across the lake came the harsh call of a teal, the melancholy sound piercing Aurelia with an aching sense of loneliness, the same loneliness she perceived in the towering man before her. She was beset by an overpowering longing to . . . She retreated a step, feeling confused, not quite knowing what it was she longed for. Unbidden tears welled in her eyes, one trickling down her cheek.

"That tale was meant to amuse you, Aurelia," Everard said, halting the course of the tear with a gentle stroke of his fingertip. "Not to make you look so glum. Don't waste your pity upon me, my dear. I am every bit as worthless as my father ever imagined."

Aurelia swallowed, then whispered vehemently, "No! I believe you could do anything in the world you put your mind to."

The rigid line of his mouth thawed into a half-doubting, half-grateful smile. "Thank you," he said. "If I am ever seeking a situation, I shall certainly apply to you for letters of character. I thought I might make a profession of bedeviling unfortunate young women with a penchant for gingerbread."

Aurelia emitted a watery chuckle. "I could certainly recommend you most heartily for that," she sniffed. "Indeed, if I did not know you were going to be there to bedevil me in London, I think I could scarce face the prospect of making such an exhibition of myself."

A startled expression crossed Everard's handsome features. He looked momentarily at a loss, then said haltingly. "Aurelia, I very much fear you are harboring a false impression. I will not be going to London."

"W-what?" Desperately, she scanned his solemn face, hoping for some twitch of the lips, some twinkle in the eye to indicate he was teasing her. The realization swept over her how much she had come to depend upon Everard. "Oh, n-no. But I thought you said you hadn't given up on me. You wouldn't be so cruel as to abandon me, would you?" She tried to make it sound like a jest, but her voice wavered and her fingers moved of their own volition to clutch at his sleeve.

He covered her hand with his own. "Aurelia, you won't need me. Justin will come to fetch you."

"No, he wrote to say he cannot come. He will meet me in London."

She winced at the sound of some words Everard muttered under his breath, although she only managed to distinguish the half of them that concerned Justin's parentage.

Almost as a form of habit, she rose to her betrothed's defense. "Well, he is extremely busy now that Parliament is in session."

"Parliament. If Justin ever saw the inside of the House of Lords, 'twas because—" Everard broke off in midsentence, looking extremely uncomfortable. "Ah, yes. That's true. I had forgotten Justin's strong interest in—in politics."

The statement was so ridiculous that when they eyed each other, neither could refrain from bursting into laughter. Aurelia was the first to recover, wiping her moist eyes and giving a little shrug.

" 'Tis quite beastly of you to oblige me to admit such things about Justin, but I know perfectly well he is off enjoying himself and has scarce given me a thought all winter. But you promised me you would change all that. How am I to go London without you? I shall make the most dreadful fool of myself at all the ton gatherings, and Justin will be ashamed of me."

"You will have Justin's mama to help you."

" 'Tis too close to the time of Clarice's confinement. I am to travel with Lady Foxcliff and stay at her town house until the wedding. Effie will not even be accompanying me. The London air gives her headaches."

"Well, Aunt Lydia may seem a bit rough in spots, and I fear she will be most lax as a chaperon, but you are a sensible woman and—and she does know her way around London society."

"*I need you,*" Aurelia persisted, her voice catching.

His eyes widened in shock.

"I—I am sorry," she faltered. "I should not have—"

"No, don't apologize," he murmured. " 'Tis just that . . . I believe that is the first time anyone has ever said that to me." She watched his eyes darken, the blue depths clouding as though some mighty conflict raged inside his mind, a conflict that seemed resolved when he raised his head to study her face.

That peculiar half smile crossed his lips again. "Your every wish is my command, my lady. If you truly *need* me when you journey up to London, I'll be there."

"Everard!" she cried, joy and relief mingling in her voice. On a sudden impulse, she flung her arms about his neck and planted a swift kiss upon his cheek. Then she stepped back, appalled by her own boldness, yet not quite sorry, either.

"Goodness, 'tis so late," she said breathlessly. "I'd best get home before Effie thinks I have fallen in the lake and drowned."

Barely giving him time to bid her farewell, Aurelia turned and struck out on the path for home. Everard stared after her until the last glimpse of auburn curls wisping from beneath that absurd bonnet vanished from sight. Then he stumbled toward the punt with movements entirely lacking in his usual grace.

The very devil! What had he done, promising her

he would go to London? His fingers fumbled inside his waistcoat pocket, drawing forth the crumpled letter he had carried with him for days.

Albatross *last sighted going down in bad storm. . . . News has had bad effect upon your credit . . . Writs being sworn out for your arrest. . . . Strongly advise you stay out of London.*

The neat black scrawl blurred before Everard's eyes, the lines paling beside the memory of Aurelia's fiercely uttered words: *"I need you."*

Slowly he tore the letter to bits, casting the pieces adrift along the silver-gray waters of the lake. Nay, he was pledged to the task of helping this reluctant butterfly emerge from her chrysalis. No matter what perils lay ahead, 'twas too late to turn back now.

Everard touched his hand gingerly to his face, still feeling the petal-soft whisper of her mouth against his skin, as though the sensation were branded there. Aye. He grimaced. Far too late.

Chapter 6

Everard paced the length of the small front parlor in his aunt's fashionable London town house, which she had inherited from one of her numerous husbands. Hanging candle lanterns illuminated the parlor's walls of India Japan boards, the lower panels of which were carved with gilt flowers. 'Twas her ladyship's private jest to call the chamber her Smoking Room, for no matter how oft the chimney was cleaned, the flue still never seemed to draw properly.

Everard, however, was in no humor for jests of any kind. He strode to the parlor door, peered out at the circular marble stair curving up to the second floor, impatiently straightened the sleeves of his black superfine tailcoat, then resumed his pacing before the hearth.

"Why the devil isn't Justin here?" he growled. "After abandoning Aurelia all winter, the least he could do is arrive in time to escort her on her first evening in town."

"Pah! Aurelia isn't ready herself yet," Lady Foxcliff said. She shifted slightly on her Indian fanstick chair, then rearranged her stiff mauve skirts over the painted satin cushion. With the heavy diamond necklet glittering about her throat and matching aigrette in her iron-gray hair, she resembled a mighty empress about to hold court, even more so when she glared at Everard with a most royal displeasure.

"Blast it all, Nevvy. Will you sit down before you wear a hole in that carpet? My first husband, Sir Thomas, imported it all the way from China, long before the Prince Regent stirred up the craze for Oriental foofaraw. Can't say it was ever to my taste, but always ahead of the times, my Thomas was."

Everard compressed his lips. In his present humor, he was ready to consign both the late Sir Thomas and his Oriental rug to perdition. His hand crept toward his cravat, and he nearly caught himself running a finger inside his neckcloth, an awkward gesture he never permitted himself to indulge in. He swore, locking his hands behind his back.

Damn folly this! He had told himself that with every turn of the hackney coach's wheels conveying him from his London lodgings to his aunt's town house. He had half expected a sinister shadow to come melting out of each corner, the burly arm of a tipstaff to stretch forth, dragging him off to debtors' prison. He must be mad thus to risk disgrace and ruin before he had opportunity to recoup his losses from *The Albatross*.

Aye, stark, raving mad. And his madness bore the form of misty green eyes alight with a simple faith that took his breath away. Aurelia. How she trusted, depended, upon him. He could not disappoint her, not even if it meant balancing upon the precipice of hell itself.

That, he assured himself, was the only reason he had taken this great risk by coming to London. But even as the thought filtered through his mind, he knew himself for a liar. He had risked his freedom simply because he could not seem to stay away from the woman. The realization that he had fought to suppress all winter refused to be denied any longer. He had developed a strong attraction for the betrothed of his closest friend. How was he even going to look Justin squarely in the eye when he did arrive?

Everard slammed his fist down against the mahogany mantel, his mind filling with self-loathing. Blast it. He had known from the day he had taught her to waltz, felt her brushing against him, so warm, vibrant, that he was courting disaster. And she, in her innocence, had not the least notion what she was doing to him. He should have had the wit to refuse her entreaty to come to London. The temptation increased tenfold each time he was near her. Damn it all, Justin was the rakehell, not he. How could he betray his friendship with both Justin and Aurelia by allowing these unaccountable physical impulses to get the better of him?

"Go back to pacing again." Lady Foxcliff's barked command broke in upon his grim thoughts. "Better for you to wear out the carpets than to be thunking my poor old chimneypiece and pulling all those ferocious faces, as if you'd gone queer in the attic."

Everard spun on his heel to take another look out the study door. He wished Justin would arrive so that he could get this over with. Place Aurelia in Lord Spencer's care, watch her glide off in his arms, thus sweeping all temptation from Everard's path. Then he could return to his normal round of amusements, spending late evenings over the cards at White's. Perhaps he would even take a brief sojourn on the continent, he told himself, steadfastly ignoring the hollow feeling that accompanied the thought.

315

"Damnation," he said irritably. "Where is Aurelia? How can it possibly take you women so long to dress?"

"Humph! You're a fine one to talk. Now, dash it all, sit down before you drive me completely mad."

Before Everard could protest, Lady Foxcliff had seized him by the arm and tumbled him backward into a straight-legged Oriental chair. She rang for a glass of brandy, which Everard impatiently tossed off, scarce tasting the golden liquid. The fiery spirits burned his throat, but that seemed as nothing to the other burning sensations which had troubled him of late, keeping him awake nights, thinking about Aurelia. He set down the glass and proceeded to drum his fingers against the dark lacquered wood of the chair's arm.

Lady Foxcliff said nothing for several moments, but eyed him in a shrewd manner, which added to his discomfort.

"If you have something to say, kindly do so and stop regarding me as if I'd suddenly misplaced my head."

"Your head or your heart?" her ladyship asked. Everard glared at her. What the devil did she mean by that? His aunt's generous mouth split into an infuriating grin.

"Deuced odd. You've become remarkably surly. One minute snarling like a dog who has lost its bone, the next, looking all calf-eyed. If I didn't know better, I'd swear you'd fallen in love."

"Well, you do know better," Everard said curtly. "If I appear to have anything on my mind of late, 'tis money difficulties, not women."

"Dibs still not in tune, eh? Well, you'll come about when I pay off the wager, for I'm ready to concede the bet now. The changes you've wrought in Aurelia! Never seen the like in all my days. Pity she insists upon wasting herself on that scamp, Justin. If she manages to hang on to her wit along with her newfound looks, what a devastating effect she'll have on you poor hapless males."

Everard grimaced. Devastated. Aye, 'twas a fitting description of his present state. Aloud he snapped, "There is no wager. I told you before that I'd called that off. I never had any intentions of taking your money."

Abruptly he stood up and began to pace again.

Lady Foxcliff heaved a gusty sigh. "I expect you might as well finish off my carpet. Reely's already had her whack at it earlier this afternoon."

"If Aurelia is nervous, she's got good reason," Everard said. "You would think that Justin would have called upon her first thing she arrived in town instead of keeping her waiting until right before Lady Carlisle's ball. The devil only knows what sort of mischief Justin has been up to this past winter."

"Did I hear someone slandering my name?" A cheerful male voice spoke up from the doorway. Everard stopped his pacing long enough to confront Justin's broad grin. The butler belatedly announced Lord Spencer's presence as he strode into the room. He planted a hearty buss on Lady Foxcliff's cheek, then proceeded to all but wring off Everard's hand by way of greeting.

"Best watch what you say about me, old fellow. I might be obliged to call you out, and I have no desire to end up on the point of your sword. I know *you* would never choose pistols."

The smile which had been coaxed from Everard froze. If Justin only knew how close he came to having a true reason to call him out.

Justin's eyes widened. " 'Twas only a jest, Ev." He

317

gave Everard a rough clap on the shoulder. "You look as grim as a pallbearer who has misplaced the coffin. Don't tell me you finally wagered your sense of humor and lost that, too."

"Perhaps not lost so much as mislaid," Everard murmured. "How have you been?"

"Oh, in rare form." Justin craned his neck, peering about the room. "So, where's Reely? Have you been taking good care of her?"

"Prodigious good care," Lady Foxcliff said in dry tones, stealing a sly glance at Everard. He was annoyed to feel himself redden, although much of his feelings of guilt began to dissipate at the casual way Justin inquired after his intended bride.

"If you are so concerned about Aurelia's well-being," he said, "I would have thought you might have made some effort to return to Aldgate. 'Tis exceedingly difficult to plan a wedding without the bridegroom."

"Lord, you sound like my mother. There's no great rush. I might as well be—I mean Aurelia should be permitted to enjoy the season first, before becoming leg-shackled." Justin strolled toward the far end of the room. He drew back the delicate gauze curtains, feigning deep interest in the coaches rumbling through Grosvenor Square.

Everard compressed his lips. "My sister Phillipa informs me she has not even seen announcement of the engagement in the *Post*."

"Er, well, I have not exactly found time to arrange that. Been busy, you know. Parliamentary sessions. Farm issues regarding Norfolk."

"Since when has Sylvie Fitzhurst been interested in debating the price of wheat? I hope you—"

Everard broke off when Lady Foxcliff lifted one finger to her lips and shushed him. She smiled at a point beyond Everard. "Good evening, Reely. Glad you have come down before Ev paces his way through the floor. He's been taking on worse than my second husband, Harry, when he was waiting for his favorite brood mare to foal."

Aurelia's silvery laugh sounded in Everard's ear. Spinning around to look at her, 'twas all he could do not to catch his breath. She stood silhouetted in the doorway, her perfect oval-shaped face drained of all color except for one rosy spot glowing in each petal-smooth cheek. Her soft pink lips parted in an apprehensive smile as she nervously twisted that hideous, gaudy betrothal ring.

Slowly, Everard permitted his eyes to wander from the glossy auburn ringlets caressing the slender white column of her throat, his gaze traveling down to encompass full, round breasts and gently curving hips accented by a high-waisted gown of pearl-colored satin. Dainty kid slippers peeked out from under the hem, which was embroidered with garlands of gilt leaves and coral roses. Her trim waist was banded by a belt of narrow gold ribbon.

"Well, my dear, you'll turn quite a few heads tonight, I vow." Lady Foxcliff said. "You'll make all these London wenches look like a parcel of swaybacked mules. Stap me, Ev, you must take the money. Never was a wager so fairly won."

Everard shot his aunt a quelling frown, but Aurelia appeared not to have heeded her ladyship's remark. Her regard never wavered from Everard. He sensed that she was awaiting for some sign of his approval, but he found himself at a loss for words. She was beautiful, dazzlingly beautiful, more so than he had even dared imagine. But her radiance came not so much from the elegant clothes, the transformation in her figure, nor the new coiffure.

The true source of enchantment lay in those expressive eyes of hers that had so captivated him from the very beginning. Tonight they shone like polished emeralds, the glittering facets reflecting all her hidden depths of passion, her fears, her longings, her dreams . . . the eyes of a woman about to fly to the arms of the man she loved.

Everard lowered his gaze as though shielding his sight from a too brilliant sun. From behind him, he heard Justin exclaim in jocular tones, "I say, Ramsey, you sly dog. You have been holding out on me."

Aurelia started, then blushed as if becoming aware of Lord Spencer's presence in the room for the first time. Everard noted how she tensed, her breathless expectation as Justin elbowed his way past Everard. His teeth flashed in his most engaging grin.

"I will contrive to forgive you, Ev, if you present me to this ravishing creature at once."

Everard folded his arms across his chest, supposing that, as always, Justin meant to pull off one of his cow-handed jests. But one look at the rapt expression on Justin's face told him otherwise. Good Lord, the man truly didn't recognize Aurelia.

Justin gave Everard a sharp, eager nudge, hissing under his breath. "What's the matter with you, Ev? Present me."

Everard rolled his eyes heavenward, then said in his driest tones, "Miss Sinclair, allow me to introduce you to a gentleman perishing to make your acquaintance, your fiancé, Lord Spencer."

"How do you do?" Aurelia sank into a curtsy. The moment was too solemn for her even to smile. Everard heard Justin suck in his breath with a great whoosh. He took two faltering steps forward, squinting at Aurelia like an ancient grandsire whose eyesight was failing him.

"R-reely?" All color drained from Justin's face. As he sank back, Lady Foxcliff shoved a chair under him.

"Ha!" She guffawed. "Ring for Jervis to bring the boy some smelling salts. Better yet, have a swig of this." She forced a huge swallow of brandy between Justin's lips, then whacked him vigorously on the back when he began to choke.

"Been waiting years to give you a start like this, you young rapscallion. Did you think I'd ever forget the time you dressed up that sheep in my best nightgown and stuck it in my bed?"

And Lady Foxcliff went off into peals of mirth at Justin's befuddled expression. Everard glowered at the two of them in mounting irritation, before making his way to Aurelia's side. Her smile seemed plastered on her face. Everard didn't know exactly what Aurelia had been expecting from this moment, but he was certain it was not this farce. He started to place his arm about her stiff shoulders, then stopped himself.

"Blast it all, Justin," he said. "She hasn't changed that much, if you'd only had the wit to use your eyes before."

Aurelia's lips trembled, but she managed to reply, "I daresay the problem was Justin never had a quizzing glass."

"Quizzing glass. I'm beginning to think I must need spectacles." Justin staggered to his feet. He peered at Aurelia once more. "I must be dreaming. Someone slap me awake."

"I would be only too happy to oblige," Everard said between gritted teeth.

"This is utterly incredible! Who in his wildest

imagination would ever have thought that—ow."
Justin broke off when the toe of Everard's shoe
crushed down upon his foot. For once Everard's
dark looks of warning penetrated through even
Lord Spencer's thick sensibilities.

"Er, yes. Just so." Justin floundered, straightening his cravat until he appeared to have regained
command of himself. "My dearest Reely ... Aurelia," he quickly amended when Everard's foot found
its mark again. "You look absolutely stunning. Can
you blame me for being so overcome?"

He reached for Aurelia's hand, raising it to his
lips with a practised gesture, holding her gaze for
just the right length of time, infusing his gray eyes
with just the right amount of sincerity. "My beautiful fairy-tale princess, forgive me and say that you
will favor your awkward cavalier with the first
waltz this evening."

Aurelia's reply was all but inaudible, but she
managed to nod. A tremor shot through her slender
frame as she stared down at the carpet like a bash-
ful country girl.

Damn it, Aurelia, Everard longed to scold her.
You look like a queen. Raise your head and carry
yourself regally. The woman still did not realize her
own worth, that she was indeed conferring a great
favor upon the graceless Justin.

Justin linked his arm through hers, and the two
of them strolled from the room, heads bent together, whispering as though not another person
existed in the world. Aurelia did not even so much
as glance back at Everard.

Lady Foxcliff gave her nephew a sharp poke in
the ribs. "Well, you've done it, my boy. Dished
Justin something proper. Congratulations."

Everard made no response; his mouth had gone

suddenly dry. He waited for the sense of triumph he had once expected to feel at this moment, but it was not forthcoming.

'Twas exactly as Aurelia had always dreamed. The ballroom spun out before her, a dizzying array of marble panels, mirrors, floral swags, and great fluted Corinthian pilasters. Crystal chandeliers blazed overhead but were no more glittering than the assembled company, the ladies resplendent in their colorful silk gowns, set off like bright jewels by the more somber black evening attire of the men.

Justin pressed close to her side, smiling down at her with a possessive pride. Exactly like her dream.

Then why did she feel this strong urge to tear herself from Justin's side and run to Everard, cling to his hand like a frightened child? She stole a glance over her shoulder to where he walked behind, escorting his aunt. His features were already schooled into an expression of bored indifference, but he relaxed long enough to give her an encouraging smile that seemed oddly tinged with melancholy.

Aurelia stiffened her spine, trying to concentrate as Justin presented her to their hostess, Lady Carlisle. The vivacious brunette subjected Aurelia to a critical inspection before beginning to fawn over Justin. Aurelia tried to appear at ease, fixing an unconcerned smile upon her face. If only she were not so miserably conscious of all the ladies' eyes trained in her direction, the whispers behind the painted fans. And the men were even worse, ogling her without even attempting to hide the fact. Why, one gaunt, pale fellow by the musicians' platform actually craned his neck.

Aurelia froze, feeling the blood drain from her face. No, it could not be. But there was no mistaking the colorless eyes, the skin stretched taut over angular bones, the thinning hair plastered to the small skull. Augustus Snape. As her gaze locked with his, she saw Snape's mouth go slack with startled recognition. Then he recovered, sweeping her an insolent bow. Although she might have forgotten his existence, she could tell from his smirk he had never forgotten her. Her mind drifted back to that dreadful day in the parlor when Snape had bruised her wrist, threatening her with his vengeance. She shivered.

"Aurelia? Is something wrong?" Everard's voice murmured close to her ear. "You look as though you had seen a corpse." He seemed to sense at once who had disconcerted her and leveled his quizzing glass at Snape's cadaverlike frame. "By God, you have!"

Snape appeared about to approach, but the stony expression on Everard's face apparently made him think better of it. The man melted back into the throng of other guests.

Everard gave a snort of disgust. "The Carlisles were never noted for being particular about whom they invite to these affairs." He glanced down at Aurelia, frowning. "I take it you are acquainted with that walking collection of ill-assorted bones?"

Aurelia nodded, moistening her lips. She suddenly felt very foolish. After all, she knew what a coward Snape was, and the notion that the man could still be harboring some sort of a grudge was pure melodrama. She forced herself to shrug and say, " 'Tis only someone who used to live at Aldgate. No one of any consequence."

She sensed that Everard did not believe her, but before he could pursue the matter further, the orchestra struck up the strains of a waltz. Aurelia's pulses quickened in time to the music. She remembered how it had felt gliding through the steps of the dance in Everard's arms. So warm, so exhilarating.

Justin stepped in front of Everard, giving Aurelia a heart-melting smile. "I believe this is our dance, my dear."

"Oh. Of course." Aurelia turned to excuse herself to Everard, but he was already gone. Her feet felt peculiarly leaden as Justin spun her out onto the dance floor, but she held her breath, waiting for the magic to overtake her. After all, this was Justin, the man she loved, holding her so close to his tall frame. But something was dreadfully wrong.

Justin's arm banded her far too tight. She had scarce room to breathe, let alone move. As she tried to concentrate on her steps, his lips brushed close to her ear. She prayed he was not going to call her "his beautiful fairy-tale princess" again. She had nearly dissolved into hysterical laughter the last time he had done so.

But she had longed all her life for Justin to murmur tender words to her. Aye, tender, she thought, but not ludicrous. Then she felt promptly ashamed of herself for being so critical and dissatisfied. When Justin guided her the length of the ballroom, she stumbled over his feet.

After that first misstep, she seemed incapable of regaining her balance, all that Everard had taught her fleeing her mind. When Justin tugged one way, Aurelia found herself dipping in the opposite direction. Her cheeks burned, certain that everyone present was remarking how clumsy she was. 'Twas exactly like the assemblies in Aldgate, only worse. At home she had not been such an object of curiosity. What was wrong with her? She had danced so beautifully with Everard that day.

Mayhap you simply never had the right partner.

The memory of Everard's words echoing through her head startled her. Justin gasped when she trod down hard upon his instep.

"Ow," he yelped, his newfound gallantry momentarily forgotten. "Hang it all, Reely, between you and Everard, I shall end up lame."

Before Aurelia could ask what Justin meant by his odd reference to Everard, he whirled her around, blundering into another couple. Aurelia stepped on a gold-spangled train.

"I beg your pardon."

"You—you stupid, clumsy . . ." The woman's voice trailed off into incoherent rage that seemed far out of proportion to what had occurred. Adjusting the décolletage of her exceedingly low-cut gown, the blond-haired woman thrust out a pouting red lip. Eyes like pale blue ice chips glared at Aurelia as if . . .

As if she hated me, Aurelia thought in bewilderment. Merely for stepping on her gown?

"Beg pardon, Sylvie," Justin muttered. "Er, I mean, Lady Sylvie."

The woman favored him with a killing glance before she swept her skirts aside, then stalked off the dance floor, leaving her astonished partner to hasten after her. Aurelia started to ask Justin who the extremely choleric lady was, but he twirled her in an awkward circle, hastily beginning to pay compliments about Aurelia's eyes, comparing them to sapphires. He waxed so poetic Aurelia did not have the heart to remind him her eyes were green.

From the shadow of one of the pilasters, Lady Sylvie Fitzhurst glared at the couple. "Clumsy cow!"

Augustus Snape observed the blond beauty's rage with sneering amusement. Smoothing down the straggling wisps of his hair, he wended his way to Lady Sylvie's side.

"Good evening, milady. What! All alone?"

Lady Sylvie eyed Snape with intense dislike. "No. Unfortunately, you're here."

Unperturbed, Snape flicked open an enamel snuffbox, raising a pinch to his thin nostrils. "Ah, I beg your pardon for disturbing you when you are so preoccupied. I see you are extremely taken with Lord Spencer's intended bride."

"That cloddish stick of a female?" Sylvie tossed her head. "So very thin. She looks as though she were dying of consumption."

"But surely you must find her presence in London highly diverting. Or could it be that you had begun to nourish hopes that Lord Spencer would never bring her from Aldgate, that mayhap he had forgotten all about her?"

Beneath the layers of pearl powder and rouge, Lady Sylvie Fitzhurst's cheeks were mottled an unbecoming shade of red. She was not about to admit the fact to a disgusting creature like Snape, but that was exactly what she had begun to hope. The engagement had not even been formally announced in the papers. Aurelia Sinclair's presence at the Carlisle ball had come as a nasty shock, the more so because Sylvie had formed a far different impression of Lord Spencer's betrothed. She had imagined some dowdy country wench whom his lordship was being pressured to marry out of a sense of duty. And men had been led astray from their duty before.

Why, only last autumn Sir Barton Crumm had eloped with his mistress, and now his family found themselves forced to acknowledge her. Sylvie had laid her own plans then, plans that the lovely Miss Sinclair seemed to have put to rout. Of course, she had several other prospects she kept dangling, in case of failure with Justin, but none of them were nearly as attractive as the possibility of becoming a marchioness.

Snape chuckled softly. "So depressing, is it not, my dear? After you invested so much time in Lord Spencer, were so generous with your attentions."

Sylvie's fingers curled until her nails bit into her palms. "Why don't you seek out some company more congenial with your station, Mr. Snape? I am sure you can find any number of stable boys out in the yard."

"Tch, tch, my dear. How unkind, when I only meant to sympathize. When Lord Spencer announced his engagement, my own hopes were quite cut up as well as yours."

Sylvie arched her brows, then emitted a shrill laugh. "You and Miss Sinclair? I find that extremely difficult to believe."

Snape's smiling lips hardened for a moment. He thrust out his thin chest. "Well, I *am* connected to the Marquess of Scallingsforth. And Miss Sinclair was not always the dazzling creature who is now inspiring you to such spasms of jealousy. Only last summer, she was a deal plumper and dressed more like a housekeeper than the mistress of a great estate."

Sylvie sniffed, staring at the whirling circle of dancers waltzing past her. She reflected that it would have been much easier to deal with a plump, plain rival than the auburn-haired sylph who was holding herself so woodenly in Justin's arms. "Then by what miracle was she transformed?"

The muscles of Snape's gaunt face tensed into an expression of brooding. "I don't know. But even miracles run a risk of being undone, my lady. And I have an account to settle with Miss Aurelia Sinclair." His features relaxed into their customary leer. "So you see, Lady Sylvie, you are not alone in your desire to rescue Lord Spencer from what could prove a most disastrous engagement."

For the first time since she had set eyes upon Aurelia Sinclair, Sylvie saw a glimmer of light amongst the dark ruin of her schemes. Her mouth widened into a feline smile. "My dear Mr. Snape," she said, taking his arm. "Do tell me more." They drifted off in the direction of a private alcove just as the waltz was coming to an end.

Strange, Aurelia reflected, when the last chords of music sounded in her ear. Once all she had longed for was to be taken into Justin's arms; now she moved out of them with a feeling of considerable relief. Everything was happening too quickly, she told herself. If only she had time to be alone with Justin, then all would be well. But she scarce had time to draw breath before she found herself surrounded by an army of broad male shoulders crowding forward, clamoring for the next quadrille. Yet the one perfectly starched white cravat she looked for was missing. No mocking blue eyes twinkled down to reassure her; no teasing, sensitive mouth quirked into a half smile. Everard appeared to have completely vanished. Had he already left the ball? The thought made her feel inexplicably weary, but she forced herself to smile at her next partner, a dashing young man whose high, starched shirt collars threatened to wreak havoc upon his earlobes.

Although Aurelia did not quite disgrace herself with Mr. Comstock as she had with Justin, she moved through the dance with more precision than enthusiasm. Were all London men so entirely wanting in conversation?

"I vow, Miss Sinclair," her partner lisped. "You take the shine out of all the other ladies. I can tell you will be the new ornament of the season."

"Ornament, sir? That sounds most alarming. Do you think people will wish to hang me?"

"I—I beg your pardon?" Mr. Comstock's large brown eyes went amazingly blank. Aurelia sighed. As she went down the rest of the dance she amused herself by imagining what retort Everard would have flung back at her.

So this was what it was like to be a much sought after belle, perpetually on display like a waxworks figure, prized only for the molding of one's figure, the elegant clothes bedecking one's back. Aurelia winced, feeling a blister begin to form on her heel. There was something to be said for spending the evening propped against the wall after all.

But, she reminded herself, she had not endured months of starvation to become a social success. She had done so with the idea of winning Justin's love. Firmly excusing herself to the portly baronet bearing down upon her to claim the next cotillion, Aurelia set off in search of her betrothed. She spotted him bending over Lady Carlisle, laughing far too loudly at something that coy beauty had said.

Frowning, Aurelia started in that direction only to be intercepted by a cool, slender hand laid upon her arm.

330

"Pray, Miss Sinclair, don't rush off," a feminine voice cooed. "Our acquaintance has gotten off to such a bad beginning."

Aurelia turned to confront the voluptuous blonde whose dress she had stepped upon during the waltz. What had Justin called her—Lady Sylvie? Her previous ill humor obviously forgotten, the woman was smiling at Aurelia in the sweetest manner imaginable.

"I am Lady Sylvie Fitzhurst, an old, old friend of Justin's."

"Indeed?" Aurelia asked politely, all the while wondering why this old, old friend of Justin's had only moments ago looked as if she would have liked to thrust a dagger through his heart.

As though she guessed what Aurelia was thinking, Lady Sylvie gave a tinkling laugh. "Pray excuse my earlier display of bad temper. Such a crush of people. It does so wear upon one's nerves. I would have left at once but, I have been longing to meet you. Justin has told me so much about you. I had no idea you had been so shockingly ill."

"Ill?" Aurelia blinked in astonishment. She could not recall ever having been sick a day in her life.

Lady Sylvie's soft voice oozed sympathy. "A wasting sickness of some kind, was it my dear?"

"N-no," Aurelia said, beginning to wish she had taken a little more time to study herself in the mirror before she had left her bedchamber. But she had been far too eager to hasten downstairs and gauge Everard's reaction.

Lady Sylvie linked her arm through Aurelia's, pulling her along. "You look so fatigued and so pale. That Justin! Such a careless one. I'll wager he's been too busy flirting with Lady Carlisle and has not been looking after you."

'Twas perfectly true that Justin did seem to be paying an inordinate amount of attention to Lady Carlisle. And only moments ago he had whispered some nonsense in Aurelia's ear about being so dazzled by her brillance that he did not even see any of the lesser stars on the horizon. Aurelia supposed she should be feeling vexed, but her emotions seemed tangled into a hopeless ball of confusion.

"I know you provincials—" Lady Sylvie coughed, then amended, "I mean you ladies from the *country* are not accustomed to supping at such a late hour. You must be perishing for want of food."

As Lady Sylvie steered her in the direction of the dining room, Aurelia was about to protest that she was not in the least hungry, only quite fatigued. But her words faltered at the sight of bewigged footmen in scarlet livery scurrying to lay covers upon a long, narrow buffet table. In the center of the gold and marble chamber stood a table cleverly decorated to appear like a plantation of flowering shrubs. Two silver dolphins arose amidst the greenery, spouting streams of water into a crystal fountain. Clustered around the centerpiece were iced creams, cakes, sweetmeats, and every possible sort of confection Aurelia could have imagined.

She closed her eyes, feeling a surge of weakness coming over her. She had been especially good since that afternoon Everard had caught her with the gingerbread, determined not to disappoint him. But Everard wasn't here. He might have troubled himself to dance with me at least once, Aurelia thought with a sudden stab of resentment. And after he had promised faithfully to support her through this ordeal.

Her fingers closed reflexively over the china plate Sylvie Fitzhurst pressed into her hand. Aurelia stared down into a succulent heap of macaroons and small frosted cakes.

"A little sustenance will do you no end of good, my dear," Lady Sylvie purred. "Can't have you fainting before supper is served your first evening in town. You will need your strength. I am sure you have a long time to go until your wedding day."

Wedding day? The words jolted Aurelia. In the midst of all the preparations, the anticipation of seeing Justin again, she had nigh forgotten her main reason for coming to London, to be married. Nervously, she began to nibble on one of the macaroons.

It scarce surprised her when the plate was snatched from her hand. She had but to take a bite of something sweet for Everard Ramsey to rise up before her like some dark, avenging angel. But rather than feeling discomfited, she was flooded with a sensation akin to relief when his piercing blue eyes regarded her with stern reproof.

"I believe you have forgotten this is our dance, Miss Sinclair," he said in clipped tones.

Her mouth full of coconut, Aurelia could not reply. Sylvie insinuated herself between them. "Why, my dear Mr. Ramsey. I had no notion you were back in town."

She fluttered long, sultry lashes up at him, her eyes devouring his broad shoulders and lean hips with more appetite than Aurelia had for the macaroon that turned dry as dust in her mouth. She swallowed hard as Lady Sylvie dipped closer to Everard. His gaze flicked briefly down her plunging neckline. Aurelia nearly choked. Uncertain of her opinion of Lady Sylvie before, she took a violent dislike to the woman.

With a pretty pout, Sylvie extended one hand to

Everard, clearly waiting for her fingertips to be kissed. "I am inclined to be angry with you, sir. Why ever have you not come to call upon me?"

"Alas," Everard drawled. "I expect it is because I have never liked crowds. There appears to be such a press of other gentlemen departing from your home at all hours."

As Lady Sylvie went rigid with shock, he slowly turned her outstretched hand palm upward and balanced the confiscated plate of desserts upon her hand. With another affable nod at the outraged lady, he seized Aurelia by the arm, dragging her out of the dining parlor.

Aurelia stole one glance over her shoulder at Lady Sylvie. The woman looked very much as though she wanted to fling the dish at Everard's retreating back. "Everard," Aurelia gasped on a half laugh. "That was abominably rude."

"All part of my image. 'Tis expected of me."

"Don't I know it!" Aurelia struggled to pull her arm free from his grasp, remembering that she should be annoyed with him. "I don't recall in the least having promised to dance with you, which is not surprising. I have scarce seen you all evening."

Everard halted under the archway leading into the ballroom. "And you, Miss Sinclair, know full well why I was forced to say that."

"Ah, yes. I was actually about to—heaven forbid—enjoy myself. Tell me, sir. Do you expect me to live on rice and vinegar for the rest of my life?"

"No, I merely expect you to behave sensibly. I didn't devote my entire winter preparing you for this night to have you waste it gorging yourself on sweets."

Aurelia's chin snapped up, her eyes locking with his own smoldering blue ones. "Mayhap what I chose to gorge upon is no longer your concern, sir. You never seem to trouble yourself unless—"

Aurelia broke off, her face flushing as she became aware their quarrel was attracting no little attention. Behind her, an elderly gentleman coughed, waiting to escort a portly dame into the ballroom. Aurelia and Everard squarely blocked the entryway. Everard noticed this embarrassing circumstance at the same moment as she did. Fixing a look of rigid politeness upon his face, he linked his arm through Aurelia's, propelling her forward.

The musicians struck up the notes of another waltz. The melody drifted hauntingly to Aurelia's ears. 'Twas the same waltz Effie had thunked out on the pianoforte that long-ago day. How uncomplicated her life had seemed then. Aurelia sighed deeply, feeling her anger dissolve.

Impulsively she tugged at Everard's sleeve. "Everard." She refused to be daunted by the icy glint when he regarded her. "I—I am sorry for being such a shrew. I believe this is your dance, after all. Do come and waltz with me."

His long, dark lashes lowered, concealing the expression in his eyes. "No."

"Why not?"

" 'Twould utterly ruin my reputation," he explained in self-mocking tones. "Dandies, my dear Aurelia, do not dance attendance upon young ladies at these affairs. Rather they find a convenient pillar to lean upon, cross their arms, and look insufferably bored."

So saying, he located one of the carved pilasters and proceeded to demonstrate. Aurelia smiled coaxingly. "Can you not make an exception this once?"

"I am afraid not. You have no need of me. 'Tis not

as though you were suffering from a dearth of part-ners."

"No, I suppose I cannot complain of that," Aurelia said slowly, although she felt if she were obliged to listen to another set of lavish compliments, she was going to scream. Every man in the room to-night, including Justin, had told her how dazzling she looked, every man that is except for the one whose opinion she valued the most. Everard had not said one word about her appearance. Was he disappointed in her? Had she failed to meet his exacting expectations?

"Aurelia," he cut into her thoughts. " 'Tis going to be exceedingly difficult for me to keep staring dis-dainfully at this rabble if you are going to stand in front of me looking so forlorn. Now, what is amiss?" His voice suddenly sharpened. "Has Justin been saying or doing anything he oughtn't?"

"Oh, no. In fact, he has been making me all man-ner of pretty speeches. 'Tis just . . ." She hesitated, biting her lip. Her finger fidgeted with the neckline of her gown. "You have never said if—if my appear-ance meets with your approval."

Everard's brow furrowed, his hand moving in-stinctively toward his quizzing glass. Aurelia gripped his wrist, halting the movement, forcing him to meet her gaze.

After a lengthy pause, he said, "You look—presentable."

The cold words would have stung Aurelia if his eyes had not told her otherwise. He tried to stare at a point past her, but as though he could not help it, his gaze traced every line of her face, lingering on the silhouette of her curves with an appreciation that appeared increasingly warmer, until Aurelia suddenly felt as though she were glowing. Her hand slipped down his wrist to be crushed within the pressure of his strong fingers.

"I have never yet thanked you," she said softly, "for all you've done for me, for giving me—"

"I've done nothing," he said abruptly, his voice going hoarse. "There is not one thing I gave you that you did not always possess."

A blush heated her cheeks, which none of the flattery she had received all evening had been able to produce.

"So what mischief have the two of you been about?" Aurelia felt Justin's arm encircle her waist almost at the same moment Everard dropped her hand as though it were a live coal.

"What the deuce do you mean by that?" Everard snapped.

Justin gaped from her to Everard and then back again. "Why, nothing in particular. Only that the pair of you looked so remarkably serious when I walked up just now, I—" Justin frowned. "I declare neither of you seem able to appreciate a jest anymore."

Everard's face was oddly tinted with red, but he resumed his position by the pillar, saying in his customary languid manner, "You know I never find anything in the least diverting about these tedious affairs, Justin. Why don't you attempt to amuse Miss Sinclair? I have the distinct impression she would like to dance."

"An excellent suggestion. Reely?" Justin gave her a melting smile. Aurelia permitted him to lead her away, but her heart misgave her. The last thing she desired was another awkward session on the dance floor with Justin. She glanced wistfully back at Everard, who was already engaged in conversation with Mr. Comstock. The gentleman preened, showing off the lapels of his new jacket. Aurelia was not close enough to hear Everard's remark, but from the quirk of his mouth, 'twas obviously something cutting. The young man's puffed out chest deflated.

Justin tugged at Aurelia's hand to regain her attention, but she stepped out of the circle of his embrace. "Please," she protested. "I am so hot. Mayhap we could sit down for a moment."

Justin's eyes gleamed in a manner Aurelia found disconcerting. "Oh, I think we can do better than that," he said. He led her to a small curtained alcove behind one of the ballroom's Grecian sculptures, a statue of Venus. A long French window stood ajar, letting in wisps of cool air that Aurelia found refreshing until she realized how close Justin stood next to her.

They were now quite alone. But this was the very thing she had always wished for, wasn't it? He turned her slowly to face him.

"I thought I would never wrest you away from all your other admirers. I have been waiting for this all evening," he said huskily.

"Truly?" she asked, swallowing the urge to comment that it had been excessively kind of Lady Carlisle to entertain Justin while he waited. But it seemed a remark likely to destroy the romance of the moment. She was secluded with a most handsome man, the man she loved, she reminded herself. Beyond the dark panes of glass, a silver crescent of moon skated across the night sky. And she was about to receive her first kiss.

Aurelia stared as Justin's bronzed features bent closer, waiting for the wild thumping of her heart, the racing of her pulses she'd always expected.

His lips a breath away, Justin paused. "Umm,

Aurelia, 'twould help considerably if you would close your eyes."

"Oh. Sorry," she mumbled, promptly complying with his suggestion. She felt the warmth of his lips press against her own. The sensation was interesting, she decided, and not altogether unpleasant.

Justin drew back, and Aurelia risked a glance at him. His brow was puckered with anxious concern and a shadow of chagrin. Aurelia felt she ought to apologize, but she was not quite sure for what. 'Twas unfortunate the moment she had longed for most of her life should occur when she felt so utterly drained by the confusing emotions she'd experienced this evening.

She wrapped her arms around Justin's neck, trying to spark more enthusiasm into their next kiss. His lips crushed down harder, more demanding this time. The physical aspects of love must be greatly overrated, Aurelia decided sadly. All kissing did was make one's front teeth ache. Something to be endured, just as her mother had always told her. She had so hoped that for once her mother would be proven wrong.

As she searched her mind for some polite way to indicate to Justin she felt suffocated, the sound of a muttered oath grated upon her ears. Aurelia wrenched her head away from Justin's lips and twisted toward the alcove's entrance. Everard stood, one hand frozen upon the curtain, his features pulled taut into an expression of stone. He might have been a statue except for the storm-shadowed depths of his eyes.

Aurelia yanked free of Justin's arms, pressing her hands to her heated cheeks. The agonizing moment seemed to drag out forever until Everard's mask of impassivity settled back into place. Addressing himself to Justin, he said, "I am sorry. It appears we both had the same idea. I mean," he added hastily, "about getting a breath of air."

Justin gave him a lazy grin. "Quite all right, old fellow. Don't distress yourself over it."

Everard nodded curtly. Spinning on his heel, he strode out of the alcove without saying a word to her. Aurelia's spirits plummeted. Had she shocked Everard with her behavior? Surely 'twas no sin to kiss one's own fiancé. Why, then, did she feel she had done something terribly wrong?

Justin began to draw Aurelia back into his arms. "Now what were we about? Oh, yes . . ." But as his lips drew near hers again, Aurelia quickly buried her face in his jacket. She closed her eyes, the image of Everard's tense features seeming branded upon the lids. "Justin," she said in muffled accents, "C-could you please take me back to Lady Foxcliff's? I—I have the most splitting headache."

Just beyond the curtain, Everard caught one last glimpse of Aurelia nestling herself against Justin's shoulder, molding to his friend's tall frame as though she had always belonged there. Everard spun on his heel and strode across the ballroom, seeking out the one room he'd avoided all night.

Inside the spacious drawing room, groups of men gathered about the small green baize card tables. When Lord Carlisle beckoned him to join them, Everard compressed his lips, taking a seat. But for the first time in his life, when he cut a deck of cards, his fingers trembled. He scarce saw the black spades, the hearts, or diamonds staring up at him, did not know whether he held aces or deuces. All he saw was Aurelia locked in Justin's arms, fervently returning his embrace. He relived the moment over and over again, the memory piercing him with sword-point swiftness. As the queen of hearts fumbled from his hand, landing face up before his opponents, he realized the true nature of his folly regarding Aurelia. Not friendship. Not physical attraction. Damn it all to hell, he was in love with the woman.

Chapter 7

Aurelia awoke to the sound of iron wheels and horses' hooves ringing on the cobblestone pavement beneath her bedchamber window. She groaned, stuffing her head under the feather-tic pillow. During the fortnight she had been in London, she had yet to accustom herself to the perpetual bustle of the streets. Nor to the infernal sounds of the charleys making their rounds all night long, singing out, "Three o'clock and all-ll is wee-eell."

But all was not well, Aurelia thought irritably. Her head throbbed, and her mouth was stuffed with cotton waddings. She touched a finger experimentally to her lips. No, 'twas not cotton. 'Twas her tongue. Flinging the pillow aside, she rolled over with another small moan. Bright sunlight streamed past the silk hangings, telling her that the hour was well advanced. She forced her stiff, aching muscles out of bed, surveying the room with bleary eyes. The airy, well-appointed chamber was decorated with a parchment-colored wallpaper, hand painted in a delicate design of young trees, with tiny birds nesting here and there in the fragile branches. But the bucolic scene did little to soothe the pounding behind her temples.

She rang for her maid, then shrugged painfully into a linen wrapper, easing her feet into a pair of velvet mules. Padding across the carpeted floor, she squinted into a bamboo-framed mirror. Dark-ringed eyes that seemed overlarge in her pale face peered back at her; her auburn curls drooped dejectedly about her shoulders. So this was what one looked like the morning after a night spent in dissipated merriment, sipping too much champagne in an effort to appear gay and carefree. She could have passed for an orphaned waif or—or a woman completely down on her luck, who had lost her last friend.

If not her last friend, then certainly her dearest. Aurelia glanced toward a small cabriole-legged vanity, where her tortoiseshell brushes were all but buried beneath an avalanche of invitations and calling cards. Not one of the elegant gilt-edged rectangles of vellum had come from Everard Ramsey.

Aurelia bit down on her lip to keep it from trembling. At least, she had once thought Everard was her friend. But friends did not desert one simply because—because ... Aurelia could not think of a single reason why Everard should do so. Had it anything to do with his strange reaction to her kissing Justin at the ball? Everard might be something of a stickler about the proprieties, but he was not that old-fashioned in his notions, nor in the least a prude.

More likely that now he was no longer *buried in the wilds of Norfolk*, as he put it, he could return to his former amusements amongst the dandy set. Doubtlessly, he presumed all her time to be taken up with Justin. Which, of course, was exactly how it should be, Aurelia reminded herself, wincing at the red glare of her engagement ring.

The door to the bedchamber slammed open. Aurelia grimaced, feeling the loud sound reverberate, sending waves of pain to the very roots of her hair.

"Wallis," she hissed at her maid.

"Beg pardon, Miss Aurelia." The apple-cheeked young woman closed the door with another excruciating thud. "Oh, miss," she exclaimed, the ribbons on her mob cap flying, "I was just making haste to wake you. Lord Spencer is already below stairs waiting."

Aurelia stared at the girl in surly silence. What of it, she wanted to ask, entirely forgetting, in her present misery, that at one time she would have sold the hair off her head to receive such tidings.

Wallis's cheery manner withered under Aurelia's glare. "Will—will miss be wanting her glass of vinegar this morning?"

"No!" Aurelia said emphatically. Her stomach turned over at the very thought.

While Wallis filled the wash basin and tiptoed about to lay out her clothes, Aurelia undressed herself with deliberate slowness. She had no cause to complain of Lord Spencer's inattentiveness these days, she told herself morosely. He was forever at her side, escorting her to the routs, the theater, the park. Although his ardor was extremely gratifying, 'twould have been pleasant, just once, to enjoy a quiet cup of tea without feeling Justin's arm stealing about her waist. Couldn't he ever simply say that he loved her without subjecting her to one of those rib-bruising embraces?

As she splashed cool water over her face, Aurelia was tormented by words her grandmother had once spoken to her. *Be careful what you wish for, child. It might be granted.* She shook off the disturbing memory as she toweled away the droplets of moisture from her skin. Nay, she was out of sorts this morning because of a surfeit of champagne, not Justin. All her wishes were coming true and she *was* happy. She adored Justin, and he seemed to be devoted to her. What more could she desire? Declining to pursue that question any further, she stood stiff as a statue while Wallis flung a cambric gown of sea-green muslin over her head, then slipped on Roman sandals with crisscross lacing over her silk stockings. Barely giving the maid time to dress her hair, Aurelia trudged out of the bedchamber, not so eager to greet Justin as she was to escape the disconcerting thoughts that lurked in the solitude of her room.

Justin awaited her in Lady Foxcliff's Oriental drawing room. He stared out the bay window, frown lines marring his handsome brow, his hands jammed into the pockets of his beige-colored riding jacket.

When he continued unaware of her presence, she snapped, "Good morning, Justin."

He turned at the sound of her voice, his grim features relaxing into a smile. "Ah, Reely. I mean, Aurelia. Good morning, or perhaps we should say good afternoon."

"Well, if you had not kept me up dancing until all hours, mayhap I would have been ready when you arrived."

"I was not complaining, *ma belle*." Justin crossed over to her side, lifting first one of her hands, then the other, to his lips. Was it her imagination, or was there a certain perfunctoriness in the gesture?

"You look absolutely radiant this morning," he murmured. "Like spring violets newly washed with dew."

Since she felt more like a wilted dandelion, his

remark only served to irritate Aurelia. Scowling, she noted that his cravat had gone askew.

"I wish I could return the compliment." She tugged at the linen about his neck, nigh choking him in her efforts to straighten it. "Truly, Justin, how can you go abroad in that careless manner? Everard would never do so."

"So you have informed me any number of times this past week."

"Pray, forgive me. I had no notion my conversation had begun to bore you." She gave the cravat one final sharp tug.

"No, not in the least, my dear. 'Besides"—he inched closer—"with such tempting lips as yours, the words scarce matter."

Aurelia quickly sidestepped his encircling arms, then glowered at him in total exasperation. What was the matter with him? The Justin she remembered would never have uttered such foolish remarks to her. Could he not be in love and still speak to her in the old comfortable way?

"Why are you here so soon?" she asked.

"I thought I would take you for our drive in St. James's much earlier than yesterday. You grumbled so about all the crush of carriages when we went at five."

"Oh, did I?" Aurelia asked innocently, while inwardly she cringed. She remembered perfectly well complaining that there was hardly any point in going for a promenade in the park. One could scarce see the flowers for the herds of fashionable people trampling down the grass. What was the matter with Justin? she had asked herself. Nay, what was the matter with *her*? She was behaving like an absolute termagant, almost as though she were aching to provoke a quarrel with him. Feeling slightly ashamed of herself, she averted her gaze from Justin and strolled over to an occasional table carved of Jamaican mahogany. She pretended to examine the small tissue-wrapped parcel left lying there. More chocolates. Justin would insist upon bringing her a box of sweetmeats each day, despite the number of times she had begged him to stop. Everard would never have subjected her to such temptation. She suppressed a sigh of self-disgust. Why must she always be comparing the two men?

"I suppose I have not accustomed myself to town ways as yet," she said, turning back to Justin. She could not quite keep a touch of acid from her voice when she added, "When one is left *alone* so much in the country, one develops a penchant for solitude."

Justin replied cheerfully enough. "Aye, 'twould seem that this 'penchant' must be contagious. Ev has not been of the most sociable disposition since he returned from Norfolk, either, though I daresay he is too taken up with that new gaming hell, er, establishment that he's found."

Gaming hell? The casually dropped words sent a cross-bolt of alarm shooting through Aurelia.

"Is that where he has been spending his time—gaming? And he, already in such difficulties. Justin! You're his friend. How can you permit it?"

Justin gaped at her in astonishment. " 'Tis scarcely my place to interfere if Ev wants to—"

"*He* would if your positions were reversed. Everard would never permit you to ruin yourself."

Justin threw back his head in a hearty laugh. "There's hardly any likelihood of ruin, my sweet, not when you consider the pile of money he's come into."

Aurelia's lips parted to deliver another rebuke, but instead she faltered, "P-pile of money?"

"Aye. 'Twould seem you haven't acquired a knack for town gossip, either. Why, I would have thought Lady Foxcliff would have spoken of it. Ev's poor old *Albatross* came limping into harbor two days ago. The venture was a smashing success. He's now as rich as Midas."

Aurelia slowly sank down upon a cross-legged ottoman. *The Albatross* limped in two days ago? Everard rich, and more important than that, his judgment vindicated. Yet he had never come to tell her about it. Such an important event in his life, and she was left to hear about it by chance. Stark feelings of betrayal slashed through her. Her friend, she thought with bitter scorn of the words, *her dearest friend*.

Her eye fell upon the box of sweetmeats. Of a sudden she seized it, ripping off the lid. Damn you, Everard Ramsey. She began popping the chocolates in her mouth, one after the other, swallowing with difficulty past the knot of tears in her throat.

Justin observed her in bemused astonishment. "There is no need for you to eat in such haste, Reely. We can bring the chocolates with us if you like."

But by the time her maid had fetched her pelisse, and Justin's tiger brought the high-perched phaeton around, the box was empty. Justin whipped his team of grays in the direction of St. James's. Aurelia sat beside him in glum silence, feeling completely miserable over Everard's defection. As the phaeton's great sprawling wheels rattled past the park's stately line of elms and flourishing lime trees, she scarce heeded Justin's constant stream of remarks. Good Lord, couldn't the man ever sense when one wished to be silent?

"Look, there's old Jack," he said, drawing the

phaeton near the pond known as the Long Water. "Queen Charlotte placed him here in St. James's herself. Dreadful nuisance. He's drowned several dogs, to say nothing of pulling a little boy into the water."

Aurelia flicked a desultory glance toward the shimmering blue surface and the elderly man who was feeding a flock of wild ducks at the shore's edge.

"He looks a harmless enough old gentleman to me," she said.

Justin roared with laughter. "You knew I meant that large, rather nasty looking swan, not old Mr. Peterborough." Still chuckling, Justin eased his hand down to squeeze her knee. "Ah, Reely, in some respects, you will never change."

"Nor will you, I fear." She seized his hand and flung it back at him. "Will you kindly stop behaving like a cake and tend to your driving."

His smiling good humor quite vanquished, Justin did as she requested, though she heard him mutter. "Aye, in many respects, you haven't changed. You still behave as though you were my older sister."

Aurelia winced, but she knew she deserved the remark. In truth, she was behaving most unfairly. 'Twas Everard that angered her, with his Turkish treatment of her since they had come to London. One would have thought their friendship would have meant a little more to him than that. Yet Aurelia was feeling entirely too wretched to apologize to Justin for making him the brunt of her ill-humor.

Instead she said, "Justin, I should like to go home."

"Home? But we just got here—"

"I mean *home* to Aldgate. I have had rather enough of London."

Justin relaxed his concentration upon the avenue ahead long enough to shoot her a glance of complete incredulity. "Enough of London? In the midst of the season?"

"I—I don't belong here. Quite out of my milieu," she said for her own benefit as much as his. Of course, her sudden desire to escape to the security of her own home had nothing to do with Everard's recent callous behavior. Yet her explanation did not satisfy Justin any more than it truly convinced her.

"Hang it all, Reely." He scowled. "We can't go haring back to Norfolk now. 'Tis deadly dull there this time of year."

"But I did promise Clarice to return in time to stand godmother to her baby."

"Plague take Clarice. Why can't she bring the baby to London? Then we could all—"

"And," Aurelia continued stubbornly, "I would as lief be married at Aldgate Church. I do so detest all these fashionable crowds. I'm sure it would better please your mother to be spared the journey."

Justin's mouth opened as though he meant to argue the point; then he compressed his lips in a taut line. "Whatever you wish, my dear. After all, 'tis *your* wedding."

He said little for the rest of the drive, leaving Aurelia to note with exasperation that Justin still had not outgrown his habit of sulking when he did not get his own way. The only time he smiled was when they chanced upon another carriage. Despite the fact 'twas not the fashionable hour, there were others taking the air in the park, and a goodly number of them ladies. It did not help Aurelia's depressed spirits to note that whilst she might not be inclined

350

to flirt with her betrothed, many other women appeared more than willing to oblige, chief amongst them Lady Sylvie Fitzhurst.

Her ladyship strolled along the park's green expanse of lawn, twirling her parasol in such a manner as to attract attention. Her face wreathed in smiles when Justin tipped his high-crowned beaver hat in passing. The sultry blonde stood fluttering her handkerchief long after the phaeton rolled out of sight.

"Did you remark how the pair of them were sitting?" Sylvie gloated to her companion. "So stiff and miserable. I declare, something must already be amiss between Justin and his precious Miss Sinclair."

Augustus Snape slunk from behind the shadows of a gnarled elm tree. He shrugged. "A lover's tiff. Nothing so remarkable in that."

"Pooh, I tell you 'tis a favorable sign. I shall have him back soon. You'll see." Lady Sylvie gazed ruefully in the direction of the iron gates through which the phaeton had disappeared. "If only I could have got them to stop. Without Everard Ramsey to intervene, I might have induced that sow to stuff herself upon some of St. James's syllabubs."

Snape's pale eyes regarded her with contempt. "In truth, Lady Sylvie, I had hoped you would conceive of a more clever plan to disrupt Lord Justin's engagement than merely attempting to wreak havoc upon Miss Sinclair's waistline."

"Well, it's been nigh two weeks since her arrival in London." Sylvie pouted. "I haven't heard you putting forth any scheme of surpassing brillance, either."

"I have been biding my time. Now, I believe, the

moment for action approaches. I shall be escorting you to Vauxhall Gardens tomorrow evening."

Sylvie flicked her parasol over her shoulder, staring disdainfully down her nose. "And what, pray tell, makes you think I would be seen at Vauxhall with you?"

"Because Lord Spencer and Miss Sinclair will also be there."

"How in the world do you know that?"

"I have my ways."

Sylvie shrugged. "I still do not see what is to be gained by my spending another evening watching Justin and that—"

"That is because you are so lacking in imagination," Snape purred. His thin lips parted in a secretive smile. "There are so many interesting dark walks at Vauxhall. Anything can happen there, my dear Lady Sylvie. *Absolutely anything.*"

The candles in the silver-carved sconces burned dangerously low, their attempt to dispel the night's shadows from Lady Foxcliff's heavy-velvet-curtained library growing more feeble by the moment. Aurelia thought of ringing for fresh candles, but it seemed hardly worth the effort. Surrounded by four walls of books in the small room, she had as yet to find a volume capable of diverting her unhappy thoughts. Restlessly thumbing row after row of musty leather-bound texts, Aurelia finally settled on a copy of Defoe's *Robinson Crusoe*.

She flopped down upon the comfortable cushions of an overstuffed chesterfield, kicking off her slippers and tucking her stockinged feet beneath the hem of her ancient gray gown. Catching a glimpse of herself in the broad gilt mirror above the fireplace, she took a grim, almost vicious satisfaction in how dreadful she looked. She had promised Everard she would burn the dress. The much-mended dull frock now had a scorch mark on the hem where she had nearly complied. In an agony of nervous apprehension, she had rescued the faded cotton from the flames at the last moment. And a very good thing she had! The somber color not only exactly suited her mood this evening, but 'twould render her most unappealing to any gentleman who might chance to call upon her, especially if that gentleman was prone to study her disdainfully through a quizzing glass.

Not that she expected Everard to call. Apparently 'twas only she that remembered a certain early spring afternoon by the lake shore, his hand pressing hers, murmuring assurances; *If you truly need me, I'll be there.* But that was all before Mr. Everard Ramsey had become a man of wealth and importance. Now he clearly had no time for old friends.

And as for Justin, her beloved had very cheerfully departed for Lady Martingdale's supper party without her. She supposed he was still wounded because of what she had said to him that afternoon. Not that Justin has sulked for long. When they chanced upon Lady Carlisle about to ride her spirited black mare into the park, Justin had reined in the phaeton and immediately begun making a cake of himself over her. Lady Carlisle was so much more receptive and adept at flirting than Aurelia could ever hope to be.

Men! Aurelia thought, turning a page of her book so forcefully she nearly wrenched the paper from its binding. Perfidious creatures, every one of them. Especially ones with waving dark hair and treacherous blue eyes. She sniffed. Robinson Crusoe had no notion how fortunate he was. A desert island populated by no males of any kind sounded a wonderful proposition in her present humor. She would even have driven the faithful Friday into the sea.

A soft knock sounded at the door. For a brief second, Aurelia forgot about the solitary bliss of an island, her heart lurching with sudden hope. After all, one would think that Everard would at least take the time to call upon his aunt.

Her ladyship's butler entered, bearing a small parcel for Aurelia. Aurelia sank deeper into the sofa as she accepted it, her spirits plummeting once more. From the shape of the box she could tell it was only another supply of chocolates sent by Justin.

When the library door had closed behind the manservant, Aurelia halfheartedly examined the accompanying card. It contained Justin's curt wishes that the contents might "sweeten" Aurelia's disposition and render her more reasonable about remaining in London. Sighing, she began tugging at the wrapping strings. So Justin had not completely given up hope of prevailing upon her to . . .

Her lips parted in an "ohh" of astonishment as the lid from the box clattered to the floor. 'Twas not more chocolates. Cradled within a nest of tissue paper was a large pink rose, its petals and green leaves all wrought of glistening sugar. Aurelia stared at the delicately shaped confection, which looked almost too beautiful to eat, an odd sensation of melancholy sweeping over her.

No matter what she might think about Justin's lack of perception, he knew her quite well. Beneath all the fine trim and feathers, she was naught but a little country mouse pining for a nibble of sweets. Was it any wonder Justin was already turning his gaze so blithely toward another lady? Oh, she might have dazzled him briefly, but she was still much the same plain creature she had always been, lacking in all feminine charm. She could almost hear her mother's voice echoing with brittle laughter at Aurelia's folly in imagining she could ever be otherwise.

Feeling more than a little sorry for herself, Aurelia leaned back against the cushions, her book sliding to the floor. At one time in her life, she would have devoured the confection, eagerly seeking consolation in the sweet taste of the sugar dissolving upon her tongue. But, surprisingly, she found she would as soon have set the rose aside. Clutching the confectionary box between her hands, Aurelia wearily closed her eyes.

A wry smile tugged at her lips. She had as yet to taste of the rose, but this was usually the moment she could count upon Everard to rise up before her, as swift and ominous as an avenging spirit summoned by a wizard's spell. She could picture exactly how he would look, the lean contours of his face rigid with disapproval, dark brows arched thunderously over furious blue eyes, his sensitive mouth set into a forbidding line. He would stride forward to snatch—

The floorboards in the library creaked in a manner far too vivid even for her imagination. Aurelia's eyes fluttered open. Garbed in immaculate black evening clothes and frothy white cravat, the object of her fantasy stood glowering over her, his hands pressed against his hips. He looked so much like the image she had conjured up herself only moments before, Aurelia sat up slowly. Cautiously she poked at the vision's exposed wrist. Warm flesh jerked beneath her fingertip.

With a rueful sigh, Aurelia raised her eyes to confront Everard's angry stare. Her hand moved almost reflexively to conceal the sugar rose. How could he possibly always know? There was something not quite natural about the man.

"Are—are you some sort of a warlock?" she croaked.

The hard expression on his face did not waver as he ignored her foolish question. "I did not intend to startle you. Reeves told me where you were, and I knocked at the door before I came in. When you didn't answer, I thought you had fallen asleep."

"Oh no, I wasn't sleeping. I—I—"

" 'Tis quite obvious what you were doing."

"I—I was reading." Aurelia scrambled about looking for her book, then brought herself up short. Why should she always permit Everard to make her feel like a guilty schoolgirl?

A defiant smile hardened her mouth. "And I was just about to partake of this delightful surprise Justin sent me. You know how dreadfully fond I am of roses. Would you care for a piece?"

She extended the box, half expecting Everard would dash it from her hand.

"No, thank you." He flicked the sugar rose a derisive glance before stalking away to lean one arm up against the mantel. The box trembled in Aurelia's fingers as she settled it back upon her lap.

"Pray be seated, Mr. Ramsey," she said. "This is a most unexpected pleasure. Whatever has pulled you away from your cards so early? Did you draw a jester, and it reminded you of me?"

Her forced gaiety was met with silence. Aurelia studied the stone-carved lines of his profile with dismay. He seemed so much farther removed from her than just the width of the room. Had she only

356

imagined that day by the lake when she had felt so close to him, as though she had finally slipped past his elegant facade and drawn nigh to touching the heart of this bewildering, infuriating man? Aye, she must have, for the coolness of his eyes entirely mocked that belief. His gaze swept a disparaging path from her toes peeking out beneath her faded gown to the disheveled auburn curls that she now attempted to brush back from her eyes.

With great difficulty, Everard resisted the urge to rush at Aurelia and shake her. He had just spent a hellish two weeks trying to forget how much he loved this woman. Night after night, gaming until all hours, at the card tables at White's, shooting hazard at a less reputable establishment. What a bitter irony it had been to rise from the tables, a perpetual winner, *now* when all that mattered was the filling of his empty hours.

How he had ached for just one glimpse of Aurelia, to see the way her mouth quivered with laughter, the militant sparkle in her eye when she was about to level him with her wit. Then to find her looking like this! So pathetic, surfeiting her misery upon sweets. And from whence she had dredged up that old gray rag? He should have burned it himself.

He could guess what had inspired such behavior. Playing at whist with Lord Martingdale in his private study, Everard had glimpsed Justin arriving for the supper party, but not with Aurelia upon his arm. Sporting a new set of diamonds that had never come from her clutch-fisted husband, Lady Carlisle had draped herself over Justin in a way that was positively shameful. But Aurelia's response, hiding out here, reverting to her old habits, infuriated Everard as much as Justin's lack of fidelity. When would the woman ever learn she deserved better treatment from her betrothed—but far more important than that, better from herself?

"I met my aunt at Lady Martingdale's, and she told me you were ill." Everard laced his voice with sarcasm. "I can see you are in a worse case than I had feared."

"Not at all. I have never felt better." Her smile overbright, Aurelia broke off a large leaf of the sugar rose and paused, eyeing him. Was she deliberately trying to provoke him? Everard clenched his hands into fists.

"Then why didn't you accompany Justin tonight?" he asked.

"Ennui." She heaved a gusty sigh. "I'm beginning to find these affairs a crashing bore." Slowly, ever so slowly, she began raising the confection to her lips, giving Everard ample opportunity to prevent her.

He forced his hands to relax, folding his arms across his chest. "If you are waiting for me to stop you, Aurelia, you are going to be sadly disappointed. I am no longer interested in acting as your nursemaid."

Although her cheeks reddened, Aurelia defiantly rammed the section of rose in her mouth. She appeared to swallow with great difficulty. "Ummmm, delicious. No, I didn't in the least expect you to keep bothering about me. A man with your important business interests, the untold responsibilities of wealth—"

She paused long enough to break off another piece of the rose. Everard gritted his teeth.

"If I had only known *The Albatross* had come in, I would have sent you a box of chocolates to celebrate. Oh, but, silly me." She laughed hoarsely. "I forgot you don't care for sweets. But I could have eaten them for you if only you had told me."

"It didn't seem important enough," Everard said, even though he remembered how the news had filled him with unspeakable joy. He had rushed to the dockside to gaze upon the tall-masted ship with his own eyes, drink in the sight of her battered hull, her windswept sails. The moment had not been spoiled, until his solicitor, a dry little man who had known Everard since he was in short coats, had coughed and said, "Most miraculous, Master Ramsey. But I hope you do not intend to immediately plunge into another venture of this kind?"

Everard had emitted a happy bark of laughter. "Rest easy, Mr. Quincey. My speculating days are over."

The solicitor had nodded in approval. "Time to settle down on an estate, young sir. Offer your heart to some fortunate lady and set about providing your father with a grandson."

The old man's kindly meant advice had effectively robbed Everard of all delight in *The Albatross*'s return, and had brought back the feelings he had been trying to suppress. Aye, he was wealthy enough now to take a bride, but he could not *offer his heart* where it was not wanted, where the fortunate lady in question had already made her choice, and that choice his closest friend.

Everard wrenched his mind back from the bright, sunlit harbor and focused on the wax candles guttering in their silver sconces. The light from the tiny flames flickered over his features, but the glow was not enough to dispel the pale shadows, the careworn lines etched about his eyes. Yet Aurelia was far too caught up in her own unhappiness. She scarce noted the slump of broad shoulders normally carried so gracefully erect. Her throat ached with misery. Was Everard truly going to stand there and permit her to devour the entire rose?

"Not important enough to tell me?" she echoed his description of *The Albatross*. "Your pardon, sir. I have never detained anyone from affairs they consider more important. I am sure at this very moment you have other weightier—"

She nearly jumped from her seat when Ramsey slammed his palm against the mantel and said in a voice taut with control, "Go upstairs and get dressed, Aurelia. I am taking you to Lady Martingdale's. To Justin. Where you belong."

Although her heart was thudding, Aurelia settled back on the sofa with every impression of ease. She forced herself to eat another leaf of the rose, although the cloying sugar coated her tongue, all but sickening her. "I am quite comfortable where I am, Mr. Ramsey."

"While you are being quite comfortable, *Miss Sinclair*, Lady Carlisle and Sylvie Fitzhurst are at this very moment battling over whom your betrothed will take in to supper. I thought you came to London to win Justin's heart, not to sample all the confectionaries."

Aurelia affected a careless shrug. "I scarce see what I could do about the situation. I cannot take on both Lady Carlisle and Lady Sylvie. Mayhap when I get more up to my fighting weight—"

Her words broke off in a gasp when Everard charged across the room. Seizing her wrists in a painful grasp, he hauled her to her feet. The box containing the sweetmeat tumbled to the carpet, the rose shattering into myriad sparkling sugar crystals.

"Damn you, Aurelia! I am tired of your sitting around in a corner weeping, feeling sorry for yourself."

She twisted her hands, trying to yank free. "I don't sit in a corner. When I weep, I am quite brazen about it. I do it in the center of the room. Now let me go!"

Fear mingled inside her with a peculiar sensation of triumph in having breached his icy reserve. She had never seen Everard so furious before. His lips were pinched white with his anger, his eyes blazing like blue embers of fire.

"Did you learn nothing about yourself this past winter besides the fine art of self-pity?" he grated. "I suppose the new clothes, the diet, were not enough if you still believe you can be bested by women the likes of Sylvie Fitzhurst. At the first sign of any difficulty, you go diving for a box of chocolates."

"At least, 'tis far less expensive than diving for a deck of cards," she shot back.

For a moment, she thought she detected a flash of pain in his eyes, but 'twas quickly gone, replaced by a furious glint. He gave her a brisk shake. "Don't change the subject. How do you expect Justin or—or anyone else—to care about you when you do not care enough about yourself? You could be a queen, but you persist in acting as though you deserve to be treated like a scullery maid."

Aurelia yanked her hands free with a mighty pull. Retreating a step, she blinked back angry tears. "Mayhap your lessons were incomplete, Mr. Ramsey. You never taught me how to swish my skirts and bat my eyelashes."

Aurelia swept into a mocking curtsy, furiously fluttering her eyes, speaking in a too-sweet falsetto. "Ohh, la, sir. I vow you will quite turn my head with your compliments. I am nigh ready to swoon at your feet."

Everard's mouth clamped into a tight hard line. "I never thought you desired lessons in how to act like a fool."

"But my accomplishments are quite lacking, sir." Aurelia simpered, continuing to goad him. "Why, you never even taught me the proper way to kiss."

The instant the words were spoken Aurelia flushed, regretting them. Her statement seemed to crackle in the air between them, charging the room with a stifling tension. Everard's eyes narrowed to points of steel.

"Then by all means," he said, his voice low, dangerous. "Allow me to complete your education."

Before she could move or cry out in protest, his arms were around her, crushing her against him, the expanse of his chest unyielding beneath the layer of black silk, the frothy lace of his shirt front. His hand shot up, gripping the nape of her neck, forcing her head back. His mouth hovered above hers for the barest instant, before crashing down to claim her lips. Aurelia was too stunned to put up more than a token struggle before she became lost in the bruising, sensual tempest of Everard's kiss.

The stiff awkwardness she had known in Justin's arms quite vanished. Her body swayed against Everard's lean frame, melting to him in a way that was positively shameful. Sparks of fire snapped through her veins. Her struggles ceased altogether, her lips clinging to his, her heart thundering in her ears.

She staggered when Everard thrust her away, breaking the warm contact of his mouth, leaving her feeling bereft. His features ashen, she saw the muscles in his jaw working as he struggled for control.

"Aurelia," he said "I—I don't know what the devil got into me. My abominable temper . . ."

"Oh, no, Everard, please." She flushed to the roots of her hair. " 'Twas—'twas all my fault. I provoked you. I have been behaving like such a fool tonight. Can you ever forgive me?"

"Damn it, Aurelia. Don't you dare apologize. You have every right to be angry. You should slap my face, claw my eyes out."

A quavery laugh escaped her. "I don't want to scratch your eyes out. You would have wasted such a dreadful amount of money on quizzing glasses." Her words coaxed no smile from his lips. He continued to look so stricken with self-reproach, as though his sense of honor had been shaken to the very core, as though he had betrayed—

Justin. The name slammed into Aurelia's consciousness with the impact of a fist driving between her breasts. But all feelings of guilt were entirely overridden by her fear as she observed the strange look settling over Everard's features. He looked like—like some noble highwayman about to place his neck in the noose to compensate for his crimes. She could almost feel him putting distance between them.

"I hope that such a ridiculous quarrel will not spoil our friendship," Aurelia stammered. "Please. Can we not simply forget this ever happened?" She extended her hand toward him in a tentative gesture.

Everard stared out the library window for a moment, the night beyond the latticed panes as dark as the shadowed expression on his face. "Aye, forget," he murmured. He slowly took her hand. Aurelia thought he meant to carry it to his lips, but instead he proffered a wooden handshake. Then he flashed her his odd half smile, bade her good evening, and was quickly gone, forgetting to close the door behind him.

Somehow Aurelia's shaking limbs carried her to the portal. She clicked the door shut, leaning heavily against the smooth-grained oak surface. Raising her fingers, she touched her trembling lips, the hot, sweet fury of Everard's mouth still lingering there. Now why couldn't Justin—She tried to shove the treacherous thought aside.

"Aurelia Sinclair loves Justin Spencer. Aurelia Sinclair loves . . ." she repeated, clinging with desperation to the remnants of her childhood dream. Being in love with Justin was such a comfortable prospect. She had known him forever. So convenient.

She winced. Since when had she started thinking of her affection for Justin in such terms as comfortable and convenient?

But 'tis true, whispered a voice inside her that refused to be stilled. What could be more secure than falling in love with a man whom one is already bound to marry? So much safer than launching upon deep, uncharted waters, waters as blue and unfathomable as Everard Ramsey's eyes.

Aurelia pressed her hands to her burning cheeks. No, she could not be that fickle, to be so swayed by one kiss. But it was more than the kiss, she had to acknowledge. It was waltzing in a pair of strong arms that knew just how to hold her. It was the scolding, the badgering, the caring, that had forced her to bring forth the best in herself. It was the shared laughter, the moments of companionable silence, when there had been no need for words.

Stumbling across the room, she stooped to gather up the remains of the broken rose. But the pent-up emotion, the tears she had denied for so long, refused to be contained. They overflowed, splashing down her cheeks, one crystal droplet dissolving the particles of sugar in her hand.

What an idiot she was. Five long years she had had to think before becoming engaged. And now! Now, when it was far too late, she discovered she had betrothed herself to the wrong man.

Chapter 8

Everard linked his arm through Lady Foxcliff's, impatiently threading his way through the throng of happy fools meandering along Vauxhall Garden's Grand Walk. The avenue shimmered with a thousand colored lanterns rivaling the glow of the starlit spring sky; the crisp night air was adrift with the hush of rustling leaves, the gurgle of the fountains, and the lilting music of violins.

Everard attempted to block out the babble of mirthful voices. The gay sounds were an affront to his dark mood and the dull ache in his heart, as he reminded himself over and over that he could never see Aurelia again.

"Don't look so glum, Nevvy," Lady Foxcliff said, her almost masculine stride kicking up the gravel as they passed under one of the triumphal arches bestriding the path. "Smile, man. Enjoy yourself. After all, 'tis your last night in London. Though why you are in such a hurry to go haring off is beyond me."

"Business," Everard said curtly. "I should have been gone long since." Aye, gone long before anything like that kiss ever happened. He cursed himself silently. Why hadn't he followed through on the resolve he had formed when he first realized he loved Aurelia? To stay away from her, to drive this hopeless passion from his heart. But both were equally impossible as long as he remained in England, continued to walk the same shores that she—

"Ramsey!"

Everard drew in a sharp breath as his aunt's fan whacked him on the knuckles. "Mind your steps. You nigh plastered my nose against that fellow's loincloth."

Everard snapped back to his surroundings long enough to stare up at a towering figure of Apollo, his bulging white biceps and disdainful stone eyes seeming to dare all mortals to set one foot off the walkway into his private glade.

"Sorry," Everard muttered, guiding his aunt back onto the gravel path.

"I declare." The feathers on Lady Foxcliff's gold silk turban shook vehemently. "Much more of these wool-gathering looks and I'll be getting the impression you don't want to have a bite of sup with your poor old auntie."

Everard shot a wry glance at the tall woman whose strapping shoulders rivaled his own, but he said politely. "Not at all, Aunt Lydia. There is no one I would rather be with."

"Hah, Liar!" Lady Foxcliff's eyes narrowed, an expression of shrewdness lurking in their depths that Everard found annoying.

" 'Tis only that I do not understand why we had to come to Vauxhall," he continued. Raising his quizzing glass, he studied the crowd. Rowdy shop clerks bumped elbows with even more boisterous noblemen. A shameless lightskirt squealed, plunging down one of the narrower dark paths, pursued by a leering gent Everard recognized from one of his gaming halls.

"This place is too vulgar by half."

Lady Foxcliff halted in her tracks. "Stuff and nonsense. 'Tis exceedingly romantic. This is where I proposed, er, where my first husband asked me to marry him."

She sighed gustily at the memory. "Of course, it created the most dreadful scandal. You see, *I was already betrothed to Lord Wyburton at the time*. But when one falls in love, all other considerations seem of no importance."

"Indeed," Everard said glumly. How well he knew the truth of that.

"Don't you agree with me, Nevvy?"

"Agree?" Everard repeated blankly.

"Aye!" Her ladyship stamped her foot. "Don't you think 'tis better to have the scandal of a broken engagement rather than condemn two—mayhap—three people to a lifetime of misery?"

Although ashamed of his inattentiveness, Everard shrugged. He was in little humor to listen to Aunt Lydia's reminiscences about her long-dead husbands, but he tried to frame a suitable response. "There are always questions of honor to be weighed—"

"Bah!" The ostrich feathers quivered as her ladyship gave him a glance of withering scorn. "Exactly like you to have such crack-brained notions rattling in your head. I feared as much.

"And pay attention!" Lady Foxcliff dealt him a sharp rap on the shoulder. "I've no objection to you ogling the Cyprians. 'Tis something you men can't seem to help. But for heaven's sake, show a little discretion."

Everard started, realizing for the first time that while he had been attempting to sort out his aunt's disjointed conversation, he had been staring absently at a buxom blonde mincing her way toward the curving sweep of the supper boxes set within one of the groves. He stiffened when Lady Sylvie Fitzhurst waggled two gloved fingers at him by way of greeting, her lips parting in a sly smile. She walked arm in arm with that bony, slick-haired fellow whose appearance had so disconcerted Aurelia at the Carlisle ball.

"Who is that? My lady Sylvie?" Lady Foxcliff snorted. "She's certainly come down a peg, being seen with that Snape fellow. Rum customer, if there ever was one. Course she ain't much better. Always puts me in mind of a mountain valley."

Scowling, Everard barely acknowledged Lady Sylvie's and Snape's pointed stares. "A valley, Aunt Lydia?"

"Aye, her gowns dip down so low, 'tisn't difficult to get a good view of the peaks."

A reluctant laugh escaped Everard when he guessed from the sudden firing of Lady Sylvie's cheeks that his aunt's booming voice must have carried.

He raised Lady Foxcliff's hand affectionately to his lips. "Aunt Lydia, you truly are the most outrageous old woman. I vow you even put me to the blush sometimes."

Her ladyship gave his fingers a crushing squeeze. "I'll do more than that, sir, if you give me more trouble about who is to pay the shot for supper this evening. This is to be my treat. Don't care if you have become a nabob."

Her feathers seemed to tremble with proud satisfaction. "Besides, I still insist that I owe you the money on our wager over Reely. After all you won fair and square, working so hard, badgering the poor girl until you turned her into such a belle."

369

Everard quickly shushed his aunt, his smile fading. He would not find it amusing if Lady Sylvie or anyone else were to overhear that. Even the hint that such a wager had ever existed would stir no end of gossip, cause Aurelia a deal of embarrassment. He noted with relief that Lady Sylvie and her companion had moved on, disappearing behind one of the colonnades that depicted the ruins of Palmyra.

"Well, Aunt Lydia," he said with forced cheerfulness, turning back to her ladyship, determined to make up for his previous ungracious behavior. "Are you ready to assay some of Vauxhall's famous ham?"

"Aye, I am ready to drop in my tracks for want of food. And a large quantity of rack punch, too."

But despite her ladyship's claims of near starvation, she showed a perverse tendency to linger, studying the occupants of the small covered dining areas. When Everard impatiently tried to steer her toward their own supper box, she balked. "Don't be in such a dratted haste. Can't come to Vauxhall and snub all of one's acquaintances."

Everard resisted the urge to fling up his hands in exasperation. Aunt Lydia was being damnably difficult this evening, insisting on dining at Vauxhall, asking him peculiar questions, behaving in a manner that seemed far too whimsical for her usual forthright nature. Her expression was oddly eager, yet at the same time almost secretive.

He was at a loss to account for it until they passed one of the supper boxes situated near the end of the grove. A small oil lamp illuminated the faces of the young couple lingering over their supper. A couple remarkable for the fact that in the midst of all the gaiety and romance surrounding them, they sat a distance apart, looking extremely morose.

But the lady would have been remarkable in any case, Everard thought, experiencing a sudden pang near the region of his heart. Aurelia's loosely dressed auburn tresses hung freely about her shoulders, satiny waves cascading against the snowy whiteness of neck. Her long, dark lashes spilled against her pale cheeks; her delicate mouth and jawline were so lacking in animation she might have been a portrait instead of the vivacious woman whose sparkling green eyes had captured Everard's heart. Her high-waisted gown of daffodil silk clung to the gentle curves of her breasts in such a way as to stir Everard's senses, despite how manfully he tried to suppress his feelings.

"Damme," he muttered under his breath. He forced his gaze to shift to Justin. Lord Spencer's mouth drooped with what Everard had always termed his "hangdog" look. Everard had seen the same martyred expression a dozen times when his friend had been forced to attend one of his mother's afternoon teas. The only time Justin's slumped shoulders perked to attention was when another set of skirts happened to rustle by the supper box.

A bitter surge of anger washed through Everard. Blast Justin! How could he be so blind, gazing at other women, when Aurelia sat only a heartbeat away, the velvet texture of her lips positively begging to be kissed. The fool didn't appreciate what love was his for the asking, didn't deserve to wed Aurelia.

Everard ground his fingers against his temples, appalled at the direction his thoughts were taking. Nay, he was simply trying to find excuses for his own selfish wishes. For, in truth, it mattered naught whether Justin deserved Aurelia or no. She loved him, Everard reminded himself hollowly. *She loved him.*

Tugging on his aunt's arm, he tried to melt back into the line of trees before Aurelia or Justin looked around. Much to his dismay, Lady Foxcliff broke free of his grasp and strode forward, hallooing in a voice loud enough to capture the attention of half the grove.

"Justin! Reely!"

Everard had no choice but to steel his features into what he hoped was his customary expression of cynicism and trail after her ladyship. Justin leaped up at their approach, appearing glad of any diversion, but Aurelia dove beneath the folds of a China crepe shawl, looking very much as though she wanted to pull it over her head.

"Well, I declare." Lady Foxcliff beamed as she pushed her way through the door at the back of the supper box. "Such a pleasant surprise!"

"Surprise?" Justin echoed. "But you gave me permission to bring Reely to—ooff." He broke off with a pained gasp as her ladyship's elbow found the tender part of his stomach.

"Everard and I were just strolling the grounds, merry as grigs," she continued, "when I said to him, 'now doesn't that look like Justin and Aurelia over there?'"

"Yes, doesn't it?" Everard repeated dryly. He began to eye his aunt with dawning suspicion. All her irrevelant chatter about broken engagements and love being worth the scandal began to make sense. While knowing that Aunt Lydia's meddling must be inspired by her affection for him, Everard was not about to permit her ladyship to ride roughshod over Aurelia's feelings.

Aurelia rose shakily to her feet. Everard was painfully aware that she avoided glancing in his direction. So much for her brave little speech about forgetting the insult he had offered her last night. A rush of emotion swept through him—love, tenderness, despair—all of which he hoped his countenance did not reveal.

"Justin and I had just begun our supper. Won't you join us?" Aurelia congratulated herself that she managed to extend the invitation without her voice squeaking. She half hoped, half feared Everard would decline, but he scarce had any say in the matter. Lady Foxcliff leaped at the suggestion with alacrity, settling herself next to Justin.

With perfect gallantry, Everard held Aurelia's chair for her while she reseated herself. She fixed her gaze upon her plate, not daring to let him see into her eyes. One look and he would know she had spent half the night sniffing into her pillow, resolving that Everard should never be burdened with the knowledge she had fallen in love with him.

He eased himself into the chair beside her, taking care not to brush against her skirts. Aurelia could not refrain from stealing one glance at his face. How embarrassed he looked. How uncomfortable. *She had done this to him.* The kiss that had awakened her to these feelings of love had destroyed something very precious. They could never be friends again.

She could read that in the rigid line of his mouth ... the same mouth that had moved over hers in such demanding fashion, stirring such flames, the same flames which now flared into her cheeks until she felt her flesh must burn more hotly than one of the garden's lanterns.

Aurelia snatched up a napkin, fanning herself. If

she did not stop this, she would never be able to behave naturally with him. She would have them all staring at her.

"Are you not hungry, Everard?" she croaked when he made no move to fill his plate. "The—the food is excellent." Her gaze traveled involuntarily back to the warm curve of his mouth. "You should try the chicken lips. I—I mean the thighs," she stammered, her eyes locking on the lean musculature of his legs, outlined by the tight-fitting silk breeches.

"Would you like some ham?" she finished, blushing more hotly than ever. This was absurd. She had fought and jested with this man all winter; now she was behaving like a perfect widgeon.

"No, thank you."

Was that a note of disgust she heard in his voice? Nay, he only sounded weary, so unutterably sad that she longed to reach out to him and—

Aurelia caught herself before she'd actually touched his sleeve. Grabbing up her fork, she attacked a wafer-thin slice of ham.

"Pig's already dead, Reely," Justin's jovial tones carried across the table. It was one of the few comments he had volunteered all evening. Aurelia glared at him. For someone who had appeared so glum only moments ago, he was looking unaccountably merry.

But the retort she had been about to utter died on her lips. How could she even think of rebuking Justin, when she sat here at his table, betraying him in her heart. Overcome with guilt, Aurelia permitted her fork to clatter into her plate, lapsing into a silence as deep and painful as Everard's.

All conversation was left to Justin and Lady Foxcliff, which they managed with a rollicking good humor, making Aurelia long to gag them both. The pair of them chattered and laughed, all the while stewing their own chicken in a china dish over the lamp in such boisterous fashion, Aurelia thought it was a mercy they did not set the supper box afire. She felt considerably relieved when the meal had ended and her ladyship suggested they stroll toward the orchestra rotunda to hear the new singer.

"For I simply dote on music," Lady Foxcliff said, addressing her remarks principally to Justin. "I always say there's no finer way to pass an evening than watching some great fat dame shaking like a blancmange, caterwauling out some tunes by that Handey fellow."

"Handel," Everard said wearily. "Aunt Lydia, I don't think—"

But Justin jumped up eagerly. "That's a capital notion. I'm dashed fond of 'Handey' myself. What a great gun he was for churning out those ditties."

The next instant Lady Foxcliff had linked her arm through Justin's, and the pair of them charged off down the lantern-lit pathway with as much enthusiasm as though they were bound for a race meeting.

An awkward silence ensued. For the first time that evening Aurelia raised her head, daring to meet Everard's eyes. Although he was looking slightly vexed, his mouth twitched as he struggled in vain to maintain his gravity.

"Well, Aunt Lydia's tastes in music have taken a most surprising turn. She once vowed to me the sweetest melody she'd ever heard was the braying of her hounds when they'd run a fox to the ground."

Aurelia's own mouth began to quiver. "A-aye, and I'd always believed that Justin's entire range of musical experience consisted of the time he severed the strings in his sister's pianoforte so that she was unable to practice."

Everard's deep chuckle swelled into a laugh, a laugh that Aurelia heard her own voice echoing. She felt some of the constraint between them beginning to dissolve. How good it felt to be able to laugh with Everard again. Like a burst of sunshine after a dreary drizzling rain. Mayhap there was hope after all. But what she hoped for Aurelia scarce dared allow herself to think.

"I'd expect we'd best hasten after them," Everard said. "I don't know whether Madame Vivani will be quite braced to find two such enthusiastic admirers amongst her audience."

He reached for her arm. "In any case, it will put us in an excellent position for when the fireworks begin."

As his strong, tapering fingers skimmed the sensitive underside of her arm, Aurelia felt as though the fireworks had already begun. The warm pressure of his hand next to her flesh seemed to set a skyrocket bursting inside her.

Fretting the ends of her shawl to disguise the tremor that shot through her, she permitted Everard to escort her from the supper box. Deeply conscious of his broad, well-formed shoulder brushing so close to hers with every step, Aurelia stared down at the ground as though nothing were more fascinating than the stride of his boots across the gravel. His every movement seemed the very embodiment of masculine grace.

She stifled a sigh. If only she had met Everard sooner . . . Then what? a mocking voice inside her cried. Did she dare to presume that such a connoisseur of feminine beauty, such a stickler for perfection, would ever have cherished a tendre for her?

She, whom all the silks and jewels in the world could not transform into anything other than the plain, awkward creature that she was, let alone the sort of elegant lady that Ramsey would be able to love.

Caught up in her grim self-disparagement, Aurelia did not see the skeletal form of Augustus Snape approaching until it was too late. Lurking in the shelter of one of the arches, he fairly leaped out at her like some scrawny cat about to pounce upon its prey, his pale-colored eyes narrowed with malevolence.

Dismayed, Aurelia halted in her tracks. She had been dreading such a confrontation ever since the night of the Carlisle ball. She wondered what had taken Snape so long.

"Good evening, Miss Sinclair. I have been looking for you. So distressed to think of you being left all alone in the middle of Vauxhall Gardens." An oily smile bedecked Snape's ferretlike features.

Before Aurelia could muster her startled wits to make reply, Everard asked sharply, "And pray tell, sir, why would you expect to find Miss Sinclair unescorted?" He leveled his quizzing glass as Snape, conveying the impression that some new and highly undesirable species of reptile had just slithered from the bushes.

Snape purpled beneath Everard's stare, his tongue snaking nervously across his lips. He straightened, making a visible effort to recover his manner of sly insolence. "But of course, my dear, I should have realized you would waste little time finding another to take Lord Spencer's place."

"What the deuce do you—" Everard began, but Aurelia hastily interposed herself between the two men.

"In fact, we were just going to look for Lord Spencer. If you will excuse us, sir." She tugged at Everard's arm, which suddenly felt as rigid as though carved of stone.

"No great rush, Aurelia," Everard said. "I believe 'tis time I made this *gentleman's* acquaintance."

The words were spoken pleasantly enough, but when Aurelia glanced up at Everard's face, her heart turned over in alarm. His eyes bore the look of flint striking steel.

"Oh, n-no. Some other time, perchance. I could not bear it if—Good evening, Mr. Snape."

She yanked at Everard's hand, dragging him off the Grand Walk toward one of the darker, less frequented paths, scarce pausing to see if Snape dared follow them. Everard voiced a faint protest, but Aurelia took to her heels, frantically pulling at his hand. Low-hanging branches slapped at her face, tugged at her skirts, but still she refused to stop, determined that Everard should not be put to any further trouble because of her.

When he finally caught both of her arms, forcing her to a standstill, they had come some ways in from the main path and were now well entangled in a maze of dark lanes where the bright glare of the lanterns did not seem to penetrate.

"Hold, Aurelia." Everard panted. "Good Lord, woman, we've come far enough to outdistance the devil."

Aurelia drew in a deep breath, trying to still her pounding heart. Everard's hands lingered upon her shoulders, slowly kneading her tensed muscles beneath the shawl. "Why did you bolt like that? Who *is* that blackguard."

"Snape is—is merely an unpleasant man I once

snubbed back in Aldgate. But you looked so fierce. I did not want any sort of embarrassing scene."

"I'm not Justin." The words came low, clipped.

"I know," she whispered sadly. How painfully aware of that fact she was.

"What I mean is," he chided her gently, "don't you know I would never do anything to cause you distress?"

Aurelia hung her head, her panic subsiding. "I—I am sorry," she faltered. "You must think me half mad, dragging you off like that."

His rich chuckle sounded in her ear. "Not at all. In fact, if I had known 'twas the custom for beautiful women to pull gentlemen off into the bushes, I would have visited Vauxhall more often."

Aurelia felt the heat rise into her cheeks and was glad of the concealing night shadows. She became suddenly conscious of how very much alone she was with Everard and how very close he was standing.

" 'Tis exceedingly poorly lit in this part of the gardens," she said.

"Aye." His voice had suddenly turned husky. "The Dark Walk is not one of the more respectable areas of Vauxhall. A place fit only for rogues—and lovers."

"I suppose we must fit into the former category."

Aurelia meant to sound light, but her words came out scarce above a whisper. She began to wonder about the way Everard had kissed her last night. Mayhap she had but imagined most of his effect upon her. There was no point in her being this miserable if she were not sure she was hopelessly in love with him. If he would only repeat the gesture again . . .

Scarce thinking, she tipped her head back.

Everard's shadow-skimmed features swam before her, his eyes as distant and mysterious as the starlight peering between the tree limbs. His hands trailed slowly down the length of her arms until he caught her fingertips in a firm warm clasp.

"Aurelia. There is something I must say to you."

"Yes?" she asked breathlessly, her heart bounding with wild, impossible desires.

His dark head bent forward as he began to raise her hands to his lips, the vulgar glare of her engagement ring not dimmed even by the pale moonlight. Everard froze, then released her with such a sudden, almost violent movement, Aurelia stumbled backward.

"I am going away," he said, as though the words were wrung from him.

Going away? Aurelia drew her trembling fingers beneath the security of her shawl.

"You—you mean you are going home to see your family?"

"No. I have arranged to set sail upon *The New Wind* tomorrow. To check out some new investment opportunities firsthand in—in Jamaica."

"Jamaica!" To Aurelia, it sounded like the ends of the earth. "You c-could be gone years."

"Very likely. If I like it well enough, I . . ." Everard paused. Turning away from her, he snapped a silver-tipped oak leaf from a low-hanging branch, then continued in a voice which was almost inaudible. "I may not return to England at all."

Aurelia huddled deeper within her shawl. She watched numbly as his graceful fingers shredded the leaf to bits. "So you see, I will be finally realizing my wish to become a sailor, and you will be marrying Justin. We shall both realize our childhood dreams."

Aurelia could not find her voice to reply. Aye, but dreams had a sad way of changing, shifting so that they were still forever tantalizingly out of reach.

"Were you not even going to come bid me farewell?" she asked.

"I thought after what happened that—" He broke off suddenly at the crackling of twigs underfoot and the murmuring of other voices. Even through her haze of misery, Aurelia noted the way Everard's shoulders stiffened. He parted one of the branches, peering into the distance, the set of his mouth going white, hard. Whirling on his heel, he caught Aurelia by the elbow.

"This is no place for you. We'd best be getting back. Lady Foxcliff will be worried."

He began pulling her from the secluded glade, but Aurelia hung back, listening. "But—but Everard, that sounds like . . ."

"No, it's not Justin!" he snapped. "You are mistaken. Now come with—"

Aurelia wrenched her body around, craning her neck in an effort to peer through the line of trees. Despite all of Everard's efforts to block her view, she caught a glimpse of another couple. The man was undoubtedly Justin, and the woman draped all over him was Lady Sylvie Fitzhurst. Justin's hands spanned the waistline of her ladyship's thin gown, while Lady Sylvie hung about his neck, crushing her mouth against his as though she would devour him.

"Oh," Aurelia said softly, though, deep down, she found she was not all that surprised. But she did feel very much a fool being witness to such a scene, knowing that Everard was regarding her with pity.

381

She ought to be crushed, finding her betrothed in the arms of another woman. Yet, in truth, she did not care a jot. Now if it had been Everard . . . Sharp pangs of jealousy gnawed her at the mere thought, which was completely absurd, considering he was not hers to be jealous of. After tomorrow, she would never even see him again.

Suddenly she was overwhelmed by the painful knowledge. In another moment, she would be bursting into tears.

"I—I should like it very much if we could find Lady Foxcliff. Indeed, I am not feeling quite the thing."

Everard nodded and hastened to escort her back to the Grand Walk. He was grimly silent most of the time, although right before they located Lady Foxcliff by the music pavilion, he made an attempt to assure her everything would be all right. Aurelia scarce heeded his words, concentrating all her will on avoiding a bout of hysterics in the midst of the crowd at Vauxhall Gardens.

Lady Foxcliff looked less than pleased when Everard pulled her away from a very agreeable flirtation she had struck up with an elderly gentleman of her acquaintance.

"Reely wants to leave now? But we shall miss the fireworks. And what of Justin? That ridiculous Mr. Snape came rushing up awhile ago, howling that Sylvie Fitzhurst is missing. Justin went to help look for the blasted wench, and now he's gone and lost himself somewhere."

"You look after Aurelia." Everard ground out. "I will deal with Lord Spencer."

Justin deeply regretted he had ever agreed to help Augustus Snape discover Sylvie's whereabouts, but it had seemed an excellent notion at the time. Not that he had ever shared Snape's apprehension that his former mistress was in any sort of danger, but any activity seemed preferable to listening to Madame Vivani screeching fit to break a man's eardrums.

However he had never expected Sylvie to pounce upon him out of the darkness, then cling like a lymphet. Ardent kisses he'd once found exciting were now downright embarrassing. Eyes seemed to peer at them from behind every bush, and once he was almost certain they'd been spotted. He had to get away from this lunatic female. Faith, she was even attempting to undo his waistcoat buttons, without the slightest concern who might come upon them.

"See here, Sylvie," he spluttered.

"Oh, Justin," she crooned, grinding her bosom against his chest. "It has been forever since we were alone together. I know you have been longing for this as much as I."

"But dash it all, Sylvie. No, don't do that! Someone is coming!"

He tried to thrust her away as two drunken sailors staggered past on a nearby path.

"Eh, look there, Fred. It's a gent in distress. That 'er gel looks fit to rape 'im."

"Be happy to save yer virtue, m'lord. Just send that hot wench over here."

Justin groaned, feeling himself turn red. He pulled Sylvie back farther into the trees until the sailors staggered on their way, their coarse laughter ringing in his ears. Shaking loose from Lady Sylvie, Justin attempted to make a dash back to the Grand Walk. But he had not gone far, when

Sylvie was upon him again, pressing hot, moist kisses all over his cheeks.

"Damn, Sylvie, you must stop this. Oh, Lord, I think someone else is walking this way."

"Where?" Sylvie asked. Still clinging to him, she peered eagerly behind her. Blast it, one would think the silly wench wanted to make an exhibition of herself. Everard had warned him this one would cause him trouble.

"I don't see anyone." Sylvie pouted, nestling closer. "Besides, what do you care if she—I mean whoever—sees? Isn't it about time we put an end to all pretense?"

"Pretense?" Justin frowned, trying to salvage the remains of his cravat from her groping fingers. "Sylvie, please. My mother will have my head if I create any sort of a scandal this close to the wedding."

"Aye, that is exactly what I am talking about— your engagement to that little country nobody. You cannot seriously be intending to go through with it."

"Well, I . . ." Damnation! Sylvie was behaving like a madwoman, easing the fabric of her bodice lower across her ample bosom. In another moment—Justin made a frantic grab for the silk, awkwardly trying to halt its downward slide. Sylvie buried her hands in his hair, trying to draw his lips downward toward her exposed flesh.

"Sylvie! Will you please—Now, stop it and help me with this dress."

"I never knew you to require such assistance before." The cold, clipped male voice seemed to cut through the darkness, startling Justin like the slash of a hickory switch. Sylvie relaxed her hold enough for him look up at Everard. Justin had never congratulated himself that he was good at reading other people's expressions, but he could tell that Everard was definitely not amused. In fact, angry seemed too mild a word for the look of accusing fury twisting Ramsey's normally impassive features.

Justin became acutely aware of his disheveled cravat, his hand gripping the front of Sylvie's bodice.

"Damn it, Ev, I know how bad this looks, but I swear to you, for perhaps the first time in my life, I'm innocent. Sylvie, tell him—"

Justin never got to finish his appeal before Everard's fist cracked into his jaw with bone-shattering force. The sound of Sylvie's piercing shriek mingled with that of renting silk. The bodice ripped away in Justin's hand as he went flying backward to land with a dull thud in the dirt.

He sat up slowly, raising one hand in wonderment to his swelling jawline, then stared at Everard, a dazed expression in his eyes. Everard rubbed his throbbing knuckles, a little stunned and even more appalled by his own action. Only months ago, he would have judged himself incapable of such barbarism. Yet he had but to remember the agony on Aurelia's face when she'd glimpsed Justin kissing this witch, and fury surged through Everard anew. Both his hands knotted into fists.

"Damn you, Justin," he hissed. "You shall never serve Aurelia such a trick as this again, not if I have to flay you alive to prevent it."

But as he took a menacing step in his friend's direction, Justin made no move to defend himself. He sat grinning up at Everard like the village idiot.

"Stap me, Ev," he gasped in awed tones. "Who'd

ever have imagined *you* to have such a punishing left?"

Before Everard could demonstrate what his right was capable of as well, another male voice called out, "What the deuce is toward here?" Branches thrashed as Augustus Snape's gangly form fought its way into the clearing. He gaped from Everard down to the sprawled limbs of Lord Spencer.

"I believe these two gentlemen are fighting over me," Lady Sylvie smirked, clutching the remnants of her torn bodice. But the simper on her face disappeared at one murderous glance from Everard. She skittered over to hide behind Snape.

"Tut, tut, Mr. Ramsey." Snape's lips pursed with sneering disapproval. "Such uncivilized behavior. And you a gentleman of supposed refinement."

"Go to the devil," Everard snarled. Turning his back on both Snape and Sylvie, he seized Justin by the collar, hauling him to his feet.

"Damn, Ev . . . choking me," Justin said, struggling to get free. "No need for . . . no harm done."

"No harm done!" Everard gave Justin such a savage shake, Lord Spencer's teeth clattered together. "You damned fool. *She saw you.* Aurelia saw you fondling that whey-faced trollop."

Lady Sylvie's delighted trill of laughter quickly changed to a gasp of outrage. "How dare you," she shrieked, rushing over to thrust her angry red face within inches of Everard's and the wriggling Justin's. "I am not whey-faced. I mean, I am not a trollop. Ohhhh, Justin, Mr. Snape. Will you permit this varlet to insult me so?"

"Madam, you have exactly two minutes to remove yourself from my sight." Everard tightened his grip on the back of Lord Spencer's neck, totally ignoring Justin's outcry of "Ouch! Damn." "Or," he continued, eyeing her with loathing, "not that there is any question of you being a lady, but I may well forget you are a woman."

Sylvie Fitzhurst's eyes spit venom, but 'twas Augustus Snape who answered for her. Strolling over to the furious woman's side, he said, "Mr. Ramsey! I really must protest."

As Everard glowered at the pair of them, a sudden thought clicked into his mind. Strange . . . exceedingly strange that Snape, the man whose presence so disquieted Aurelia, should be the one to have sent Justin looking for Lady Sylvie. Stranger still that Snape had appeared to know exactly where Justin and Lady Sylvie were to be found. Everard's eyes narrowed. He began to smell something deuced rotten about this entire business, other than the heavy odor of Lady Sylvie's perfume.

He released Justin so abruptly, Lord Spencer all but fell to his knees.

"And what is your interest in this affair, Mr. Snape?" Everard demanded.

Snape ran his thumbs beneath his jacket lapel, thrusting forward his thin chest like a bantam rooster. "Justice, sir. Besides being a good friend of Lady Sylvie's, I deplore hypocrisy. You are in no position to be chastising Lord Spencer or anyone else. Didn't I see you slipping off into the bushes with Lord Spencer's intended?"

"What, the virtuous Miss Sinclair?" Sylvie chortled with glee.

"The devil you say!" Justin cut in. "Everard would never! Nor Reely either."

Consciousness of his own guilt rendered Everard momentarily speechless as Justin added hotly, "Especially not Reely, no matter how she happened to feel. She's the most perfect lady I ever knew."

Snape sneered. "It pains me to disillusion you, sir. How little you know about your betrothed."

"And you, sir, claim to know the lady better?" The softness of Everard's voice masked all the barely leashed fury roiling beneath the surface.

"Oh, prodigiously better. The lady and I spent a great deal of time together in Norfolk. We became intimate friends, most intimate."

"Why, you—" Justin gasped. Everard sensed he was about to lunge, but he moved more quickly than Lord Spencer, dealing several open-handed slaps across Snape's gaunt cheeks. The man staggered backward, his eyes watering.

"You villain," Sylvie shrieked at Everard. "You shall meet Augustus for this."

"N-no, he shan't," Snape gasped, regaining his balance. "Things—getting out of control. My—my apologies. All a jest, sir, about Miss Sinclair."

"Coward! You *will* meet me," Everard said, cracking the back of his hand across Snape's mouth again, until a thin smear of blood appeared. "Unless you desire to be beaten insensible here and now."

Justin thrust himself in front of Everard, his eyes rounding in alarm. "Now, Ev, this has gone far enough. I'll admit he is a smarmy-faced little weasel but—"

Everard shoved Justin aside, his gaze never wavering from Snape. "My second will wait upon yours at your earliest convenience, sir."

"He accepts," Sylvie hissed, "with pleasure."

What little blood he possessed drained from Snape's countenance. "Shut up, you silly doxy. This was no part of my plan."

"You have but to name who will act for you,"

388

Everard continued inexorably, "And your choice of weapons."

"Pistols," Sylvie blurted, her eyes gleaming with vicious satisfaction. "He wants pistols."

"Be quiet, Sylvie," Justin shouted. "Who made you Snape's blasted second?"

"Pistols will be entirely satisfactory," Everard said, his lips tightening.

"Have you run mad?" Justin yelped. "Now I want everyone to calm down and—"

But Everard did not pause for the rest of Justin's frantic speech. He sketched Snape a brief, ironic bow before striding from the clearing. The fury that had driven him to act in a manner so unlike himself slowly drained, leaving him feeling empty and hollow as a well. He smoothed down his coat sleeves, attempting to regain his aura of detachment, which had always served him so well in the past.

Footsteps rustled behind him, but he did not turn around, not even when Justin seized him by the arm.

"Ev, what the devil has gotten into you? You cannot seriously mean to fight Augustus Snape. Why, the little rotter is not even a gentleman. Besides, you know 'tis me you really want to murder."

Everard shrugged. "Mayhap that is so, but 'tis excessively ill-bred to kill one's friends, no matter what the provocation."

Lord Spencer did not return his wry smile. Beads of sweat stood out upon Justin's forehead, and he looked more agitated than Everard would ever have thought possible.

"But—but pistols!" he moaned. "You know Sylvie deliberately primed Snape to choose those. Everyone knows what a bad shot you are. Why, with your notions of honor, Alvaney and Montmorten have had a long-standing bet at the club as to whether you would die being shot in a duel or by a curricle accident."

"How gratifying," Everard drawled, "to be the object of such kindly interest."

He and Justin both started at the sound of a loud report. Overhead, Roman candles suddenly exploded. Everard tipped back his head, staring at the shower of sparks spilling across the inky night sky. He slowly hunched his shoulders. A bullet through his head or a slow, lingering voyage taking him farther and farther from Aurelia. What odds did it make?

Chapter 9

It had taken Aurelia the better part of a sleepless night to reach her decision, most of the morning to summon the courage to act upon it. Facing Justin across the palatial-like crimson-and-gold salon at Spencer House, she squared her shoulders against the stiffly ornate back of the Louis XIV chair.

"Justin, I—I have come here this morning to—to tell you that I cannot marry you."

To Aurelia, it seemed as though her low-spoken words echoed off the gilt ribbing of the high coved ceiling. She waited nervously for Lord Spencer's reaction. Poor Justin was looking decidedly haggard already, as though he had not slept much, either. His brow, normally as untroubled as a babe's, crinkled with deep lines of anxiety; his mischievous gray eyes were dulled by the shadows cast beneath them. An enormous bruise purpled one cheek, making Aurelia wonder what sort of carousing Justin had been engaged in after she left him last night. But despite his disreputable appearance, after she had explained the purpose of her visit, his face brightened, the grim set of his mouth relaxing into a broad grin.

"Try not to be too devastated," she said tartly. "If you continue to look so brokenhearted, I shall be quite overcome with remorse."

His grin erupted into a laugh. "This is wonderful, though not entirely unexpected. I only trust it may not be too late."

Aurelia scarce gave more than a moment's consideration as to what on earth Justin meant. She felt far too annoyed with his lighthearted acceptance of a decision that had cost her a great deal of agonizing. The breaking of an engagement was no small matter, even if it did not involve the breaking of Justin's heart. She was setting aside the plans of both their families, a promise made and accepted in good faith. It was more than slightly dishonorable, in her opinion. But there would be even less honor involved in wedding one man whilst she was hopelessly in love with another.

Stiffly, she inched the betrothal ring from her finger.

"Oh, no," Justin protested. "You may still keep the ring."

Aurelia regarded the vulgar ruby in dismay. "I couldn't possibly. 'Tis a family heirloom. Your mother would never—"

"Oh, Mama wouldn't mind. Consider it a gesture of, er, friendship."

"No, please. You must take it back."

"Don't be a goose, Reely. 'Tis completely unnecessary."

"I insist!" Aurelia leaped up and seized his hand, slapping the ring into his open palm.

Justin shrugged cheerfully, pocketing the ring. "Oh, very well. If it will make you feel better . . ."

Aurelia sank back onto her chair's slick cushion. Nothing, she thought, would ever make her feel better. With what great ease the gentlemen in her life seemed able to dismiss her existence. Justin obviously experienced not so much as a pang of regret, and Everard would set sail today without once looking back. No! She had sworn she would not think about that.

Pressing her knuckles against her lips, Aurelia fought back the sense of despair that had threatened to engulf her ever since her parting with Everard at Vauxhall. Surely he would come to see her one last time before—

"And we should have known years ago we would not suit," Justin was saying. "I expect that is why I have been dragging my heels over the wedding. You have turned into something out of the common way, a real beauty. But, dish me! When I kiss you, 'tis still like embracing my sister."

"I suppose that is because I am lacking in the art—" Aurelia stopped herself. Those were almost the same words she had spoken the night Everard had kissed her. Everard, who had made her feel she was *something out of the common way* long ago, when she well knew she was not.

An anxious note crept into Justin's otherwise complacent voice. "I hope you are not angry with me, are you Reely?"

"Angry? About what?" 'Twas she who was ending the engagement.

A hint of embarrassment spread across Justin's cheeks. "About what happened with Sylvie last night. 'Tis so unfair. I truly was innocent. I wish someone would believe me."

"It scarce matters. That is not the reason I decided to—"

"Oh, I know that. 'Tis because you have fallen in love with Everard."

Aurelia regarded Justin with an expression of horrified astonishment. For most of the time she had known Lord Spencer, he had always been blithely imperceptive, never guessing her secret feelings. Why did he have to begin now?

"Justin, I—I am so sorry," she stammered, unable to deny his words. "How did you—how could you possibly—"

"I'm not quite so thick-skulled as you might believe. You have done naught but sound out the man's virtues for the past week. If I did not know Ramsey so well, I would swear from your description of him, he was a combination of Sir Galahad, Saint Peter, and—and Admiral Lord Nelson."

Justin gingerly touched the ugly swelling along his cheekbone. "I have also had a few other hints as to how matters stand between you and Everard."

"You mustn't put any of the blame upon him," Aurelia said quickly. "The fault is all mine. He doesn't even know about my decision to break the engagement. 'Tis none of it his doing."

"Oh, no, indeed. I daresay I just imagined Everard planted me a facer last night. Mayhap I can even begin to imagine it doesn't still ache like the very devil."

Aurelia could not have felt more stunned than if Justin had yanked the chair from beneath her. "Ev—Everard hit you?" she gasped. She tried to picture the cool, imperturbable Everard so far gone in fury as to be capable of such a ruffianlike behavior—tried and failed.

"Why would Everard do a thing like that?"

Justin regarded her with a look of fond exasperation. "For the same reason knights were wont to charge off in defense of their fair damsels. I suppose I may consider myself lucky Ramsey doesn't own a lance."

When she continued to stare at him uncomprehendingly, Justin chuckled, "The man's head over ears in love with you, you silly peagoose."

"Oh, no—no, he couldn't possibly be." Aurelia shook her head, but was unable to quite still the sudden leaping of her heart. "He simply couldn't. Could he?" she asked wistfully.

"Well, why else would he behave like such an idiot—knocking people down, preparing to fight a duel—" Justin broke off, then groaned, "Oh, Lord!"

"A duel?" Aurelia whispered, the word sending a trickle of ice along her spine.

Justin stood abruptly, then busied himself jabbing the poker into the empty fireplace grate, stirring long-dead coals. "Forget I said that. A jest, merely. In very poor taste."

But Aurelia stared at the broad expanse of his back, feeling as though her worst nightmares were about to come true. "You—you and Everard are going to fight a duel!"

"Good God, no!" Justin straightened, dropping the poker. "Ramsey is my closest friend and—and he isn't going to fight anyone—But if he were, it wouldn't be me."

With great difficulty, Aurelia restrained the urge to leap at Lord Spencer and throttle him. She managed to keep her voice calm, as though reasoning with an exasperating child.

"Then if this duel that is not going to be fought did take place, who _would_ Everard's opponent be?"

"No one. No one at all, my dear." Justin flashed her his most disarming smile, but Aurelia shot to her feet. Fists clenched, she advanced on Lord Spencer.

"Justin, I swear if you do not tell me at once, I shall give your left cheek such a thump, it will match the other side."

"Damme, you're as mad as Ev." Justin retreated behind a backless Egyptian couch covered with embroidered silk. He stretched out one arm as though to ward her off. "Calm yourself, Reely, and sit down. I—I will tell you everything, though, the Lord knows, I shouldn't." He sighed. "The whole affair has been driving me nigh distracted, and that's the truth."

Although Aurelia scarce drew any comfort from his words, she forced herself to be seated upon the settee. Justin plunked down beside her, folding his arms across his chest.

"I am waiting," Aurelia said when he continued to be silent.

Looking as guilty as a small boy about to confess some misdeed, Justin said, "Everard is set to meet Augustus Snape tomorrow morning."

"Snape!" Aurelia clutched Justin's sleeve.

"Aye." Justin nodded miserably. "The rogue made some rather insulting remarks about you. Ev should have let me pound the fellow into the ground, but instead he needs must challenge the little weasel. Gone completely off his head, Ev has.

"And Sylvie," Justin continued, "what must the spiteful wench do but put it into Snape's head to ask for pistols. Pistols!" Justin groaned, permitting his head to sag against his hands. "If it were swords, Ev could fight an entire regiment. But pistols! A blind man would have a better chance."

"Then the duel must be stopped." Aurelia was astonished her voice sounded so cool, when her emotions were in such a turmoil of fear and panic.

"Don't you think I haven't wracked my brains for a way to do so? But Ev completely refused to listen to me." Justin raked his fingers back through his sun-streaked hair. "He's supposed to be always getting me out of scrapes. 'Tis damnably disconcerting to have to be the sensible one."

He drooped his head dejectedly back against his hands. Aurelia ignored his obvious despair, her own lips hardening into a firm line of resolve.

"If Everard cannot be reasoned with, then we must use physical force to stop him. Even if you must render him senseless. We will kidnap him, force him to sail upon *The New Wind* as he'd planned."

Justin's eyes rounded in horror. "We cannot do anything like that, Reely. Why, Ev would never speak to me again. He has to go through with the duel. It's a question of honor."

"Honor!" Aurelia snapped. "Where is the honor in Everard's setting himself up like a wafer in a shooting gallery?"

"You don't understand, Reely, and there's no sense trying to make you."

"None whatsoever. I can see no good reason in the world for Everard to risk his life in this fashion. Why, I would not even put it beyond Augustus Snape to attempt to cheat."

"Impossible! I'm Ev's second. I would never permit any cheating. Besides," Justin added gloomily, " 'tis completely unnecessary for Snape to do so. He's accredited to be a fair shot. I hope he will prove skilled enough to maim Ev and not accidentally kill him."

But Aurelia found little consolation in such a hope. Choking back an unladylike oath, she rose briskly to her feet. 'Twas obvious Justin was not going to be of any help whatsoever. And she knew instinctively appealing to Everard would be to no avail. The devil take these men and their ridiculous notions of honor! Wouldn't she give Everard a blistering scold when this affair was over!

Over . . . A dreadful image rose before her eyes—Everard sprawled out upon the ground, the pristine lace of his cravat streaked bright red, Augustus Snape's sneer of triumph, his smoking pistol . . .

No! Aurelia shuddered. Not whilst there was breath left in her. No wretched toad like Snape was going to endanger the man she loved. With or without Justin's help, she would put a stop to this duel nonsense, no matter what she had to do. Aurelia clenched her hands into tight fists. *No matter what.*

Augustus Snape stared morosely at the evening shadows creeping up the plaster walls of his shabby lodgings, then poured himself another glass of gin. Blue Ruin, the local denizens of this down-at-the-heels part of London called the stuff, but the vile-tasting liquid could not prove more ruinous than last night's excitement at Vauxhall had been.

He raised the glass to his lips, wondering yet again if it would not be wiser to have bolted from London long before the sun rose tomorrow. Much as he had enjoyed the prospect of making mischief for Aurelia Sinclair, it had never been any part of his plan to risk his own precious hide. Plague take Everard Ramsey. Underneath those cool manners and unruffled gentlemanly appearance lurked a raving lunatic. Who would blame Augustus if he did not appear at Hyde Park tomorrow?

Everyone came the harsh answer. Snape took a huge gulp of the gin, grimacing as it burned his throat on the way down. Defaulting on a duel. Unforgivable offense, that. The story would be bound to leak out. He would lose forever what tenuous hold he had on the fringes of polite society and with it any chance of ever making a wealthy marriage.

Snape's bony hand slammed down against the wobbly pockmarked oak table. What a damned predicament. 'Twas that Fitzhurst bitch's doing. He should have rammed his fist down her throat. Prodding him along into accepting Ramsey's challenge! He should have known better than ever to get involved with the scheming creature. But when he'd seen an opportunity to punish Aurelia Sinclair for spurning him, the temptation had been irresistible. Damn it all, he was the third cousin to the Marquess of Scallingsforth, no matter what anyone thought. He had Miss Sinclair to thank for his present wretched circumstances. He could have been comfortably married by now. All that time he had wasted courting her, when he should have been scouting out another heiress. She had known all along she never intended to become Mrs. Augustus Snape, already had her sights upon being Lady Spencer. Well, he had vowed to make her rue the day, show her a thing or two about her precious Justin.

Draining his glass, Snape lolled his head against the top rail of the hard ladder-back chair. When had his plans begun to go awry? The scheme at Vauxhall had seemed simple enough. Lady Sylvie was to lure Lord Spencer off into the bushes, engage him in some compromising activity. Then Snape had but to maneuver Miss Sinclair into position so that she would have a good view of the proceedings. Exceedingly simple, but effective. How he had looked forward to savoring her humiliation when she caught her fiancé virtually flagrante delicto with Lady Sylvie.

But he had not counted upon Everard Ramsey's

presence at the scene. Blast him! Snape scowled. There were some pretty smoky doings between Ramsey and Aurelia Sinclair. He was sure of it. Why else would the man go about slapping complete strangers, simply because they made chance remarks about the lady's virtue? In any event, Ramsey had completely put "paid" to his scheme for revenge. When Snape remembered that, he thought he would take great pleasure in putting a hole through the interfering jackanapes. If that was the way things turned out. Snape ran his finger nervously beneath his grime-ridden collar.

Lady Sylvie assured him that Ramsey was a notoriously bad shot. And although he had never crossed the sacred portals of White's himself, Snape had heard something of the jests about Ramsey's lack of skill with the pistols. Pouring himself another glass of gin, he kept reminding himself of those jests over and over again, trying to force his tensed muscles to relax.

But when a sharp rapping came against his door, he nearly shot through the cracks in the plaster ceiling. Feeling his heart thumping beneath his rib cage, he snarled, "Who is it? What the devil do you want?"

The door creaked open an inch, and his jowl-faced landlady thrust her nose into the room, each greasy coal-black hair upon her head seeming to bristle with indignation.

"Lady belowstairs," Mrs. Wiggins bit out. "Insists upon seeing you."

Lady? Snape rocked back in his chair. He knew of no woman, lady or otherwise, who would be tempted to call upon him in this district, just off Butcher's Row. Surely not even Lady Sylvie Fitzhurst— With a loud thud, Snape let the chair fall forward. He was about to tell Mrs. Wiggins to send the unknown female to perdition when curiosity got the better of his surly humor. Lurching to his feet, he strode out to the staircase landing to have a look at this creature bold or desperate enough to call upon a man at his lodgings. Mrs. Wiggins followed behind, her heavy jowls waggling with disapproval. "I run a respectable establishment here, Mr. Snape. If you be thinking of holding any sort of assignations under my roof, you can just think again."

Snape ignored her high, whining voice and studied the woman pacing the entryway below. Of medium height, her features were concealed by a heavy white veil, but along her back, he caught the gleam of one auburn curl. Snape's eyes narrowed, his tongue slithering across his lips.

"Ah, Mrs. Wiggins," Snape purred. " 'Tis a cousin of mine. She has come to bring me funds so that I can pay the arrears I am owing you."

Although Mrs. Wiggins sniffed with suspicion, greed won out over her sense of dubious propriety. She ambled down the steps to escort the lady above. As Aurelia Sinclair followed the plump landlady, she hugged her dove-gray skirts close against her, already regretting her reckless action in coming here. Only the thought of Everard's dark-fringed blue eyes closing in agony kept her feet moving up the thread-bare carpeted treads.

Snape awaited her at the top of the stairs. "Good afternoon, my dear." With one white hand, he indicated the door to his apartment, a too-wide smile splitting his mouth. Feeling very much like a harried fly winging near the web of a gangly-legged spider, Aurelia stepped inside.

Snape all but slammed the door in the face of his

inquisitive landlady. Aurelia fingered her reticule, as she took in the sparsely furnished sitting room, the narrow alcove beyond which housed a rumpled four-poster bed. Studying the faded floral wallpaper and the holes gnawed in the wainscoting, Aurelia would not have been in the least surprised to feel rats whisking against the toes of her Roman sandals.

But then, she thought, as she forced herself to turn and face Snape, rats came in many forms and sizes. She would have preferred the kind that crept along the floor to the tall, slick-haired man who all but rubbed his hands together with glee.

"Well, well, well. Miss Sinclair. What an unexpected pleasure."

She started at his instant recognition, fought down the feelings of uneasiness and revulsion prickling along her skin as Snape stepped closer. With slow deliberation, she raised her veil, trying to steel her fingers from trembling. She had a part to play, and she must do it well. Everard's life depended upon it.

"Good afternoon, Mr. Snape," she said. "I trust I have not called at an inopportune moment." Her gaze shifted to the empty glass upon the table, and she crinkled her nose at the strong smell of spirits in the room. "If it were not the matter of utmost urgency, I should not—" She broke off with a gasp when Snape's clammy fingers closed round her own. Snatching her hand back before he could raise it to his moist lips, she struggled to keep the disgust from her eyes, all the while assuring herself that her maid and coach were just in the street outside. If Snape should so far forget himself as he did upon his last visit to Aldgate Manor, she could rush to the window and shout for her coachman. Snape was naught but a cowardly bully. Indeed, 'twas his cowardice she was pinning all her hopes upon.

"Now, Miss Sinclair, you've no call to be nervous with me. I know some harsh words once passed between us. Let bygones be bygones, I always say."

"I entirely agree with you, sir." With great difficulty Aurelia mustered a smile. "Which is why I risked my reputation to come here to warn you."

Snape appeared more absorbed in groping for her hand than in paying heed to her words. Aurelia retreated a step closer to the window, but halted in her tracks when he chortled, "Why Miss Sinclair, whatever happened to your engagement ring?"

Flushing self-consciously, Aurelia whisked her hand behind her back. Trust Snape to notice a thing like that. His eyes glinted with malicious satisfaction. "Broke off the betrothal, did you, my dear? Cannot say as I blame you after Lord Spencer's behavior last night."

"I have not come here to discuss Lord Spencer."

"Ah, then perchance you have changed your mind about me, come to regard my attentions with more appreciation since you have discovered Lord Spencer's perfidy."

Aurelia shuddered, fearing she was going to be ill at the mere suggestion of such a thing. "No, sir. I have come here to save your life."

"My life?" Snape broke into cackling laughter. He strolled over to the table and poured himself another glass of gin. "And pray tell, Miss Sinclair, what inspires you to such tender solicitude upon my behalf?"

"I know all about the duel tomorrow. I had hoped to save you from Everard Ramsey."

"Save me? That's rich, upon my word. You appear to take a strong interest in that gentleman's doings, Miss Sinclair, what with taking him for guided tours of Vauxhall's dark walks and all. Mayhap 'twas not *you* who broke off the engagement."

Aurelia flushed, her lips tightening at Snape's insinuations, but she forced herself to remain calm. If she gave the odious man so much as a hint of her feelings for Everard, he would see through the fabric of lies she was about to weave. She affected a careless shrug, then lowered her veil as though about to leave.

"Alas, Mr. Snape, I did come, in all fairness, to warn you. But if you are not in the least particle interested to know what mortal danger—"

"Hah. Don't try any of that nonsense on me. I am quite familiar with Ramsey's reputation as a marksman. Why, they're giving five-to-one odds at White's that Ramsey will die as a result of the duel."

"Aye, that he will die, but those that place the wagers never mention how. But I quite see I am wasting my time talking with you. Regrettably, your mind is made up. Farewell, Mr. Snape."

Aurelia started for the door, but she had not gotten far when Snape caught her by the elbow. His eyes narrowed with suspicion, but his smirk had begun to waver.

"What do you mean—the wagers never mentioned how? How else would he die but by my shot?"

"There is always a hangman's noose." Aurelia firmly uncurled Snape's fingers from her sleeve.

"What are you talking about, you silly chit? Why, I know the law regarding dueling, but no one has ever actually received the death penalty."

Aurelia infused a mournful note into her voice. "Aye, but I fear, this time, Mr. Ramsey will have ex-

hausted the good humor of the magistrates. Three
men killed in less than two years. How will
Everard—I mean Mr. Ramsey—ever explain away
a fourth?"

She flung up her hands, affecting a startled gasp.
"Oh, dear, I should never have told you that. His
poor family hushed up all the others, kept his
dreadful secret for so long, even putting about the
rumors of his poor marksmanship so that no one
would believe—But I suppose I needn't worry." Grimacing beneath her veil, Aurelia forced herself to
pat Snape's skeletal hand. "I daresay you will not
be in a position to tell anyone after the morrow."

"What foolery is this?" Snape growled, but a fine
mist of sweat began to bead upon his brow. "I know
damned well Ramsey cannot shoot. I was told—"

"By whom, sir?"

"By Sylvie Fitzhurst." Aurelia could see some of
Snape's confidence begin to fade with mere mention
of the name.

"Lady Sylvie. I am sure the lady is well noted for
her—her circumspection and keen judgement. The
only testimony I have to offer you is the graves of
three men who believed as you do."

Aurelia wrung her hands together in an implor-
ing gesture, fearing she might be overdoing it, but
a nervous tic had begun along Snape's jawline.

"I entreat you, Mr. Snape. If you have no regard
for your own life, at least consider poor Mr.
Ramsey's family. Even if he is not hung, this time
he will surely be obliged to flee the country."

Snape swallowed, looking very much as though
something were stuck in his gullet. He gave an uncertain laugh. "What—what a parcel of folderol. I
don't believe a word of it. Now that you have lost

Lord Spencer, you are obviously bent upon marrying Ramsey. That's why you want to stop the duel."

"Not in the least. I have no desire to live in France or be wed to such a madman. Who can say whom he will take it into his head to shoot next?"

Taking care to conceal her trembling fingers, Aurelia reached for the doorknob. "My conscience is now clear. I have never borne you any ill will, Mr. Snape. At least, I feel I have done my Christian duty by warning you."

She slowly opened the door, glad that Snape could not see the perspiration trickling down her own cheeks beneath the veil. The man was looking decidedly shaken. When he raised his gin to his lips, the glass clinked against his teeth. She turned to fire one last parting shot. "I would be happy to do you one more favor, sir. Where does your mama live?"

"My mama?" Snape gaped at her. "In Cheapside. Why the deuce should you wish to—"

"I would be happy to call upon her"—Aurelia lowered her voice to a tender hush—"after . . ."

The glass dropped from Snape's hand, shattering into a hundred pieces. With a gentle curtsy, Aurelia let herself out of the room. She scarce drew breath until her coachman was handing her into the safe confines of her own carriage.

Before the vehicle lumbered away, she stole one last glance up at the dirty panes that comprised Snape's window. Was he peering at her from behind the curtain even now, wondering, doubting? Had she played her part well enough? If only he had given her some definite sign that he was indeed terrified enough not to meet Everard on the morrow.

Aurelia bit down hard upon her lip. She had done

her best, but she could not risk Everard's life on the mere chance that she had managed to frighten Snape away. No, she needed an alternative plan, something more direct. Something decidedly more desperate.

She shivered, her fingers tightening on her reticule as a dreadful notion popped into her head. No, she couldn't. Both Justin and Everard might hate her for it, but the more she considered the idea on the long ride back to Grosvenor Square, the more she became convinced there was no other way.

Chapter 10

The click of the surgeon's case being snapped open broke the early morning stillness of Hyde Park. Everard ground the toe of his boot into the dew-soaked grass and watched with an air of strange detachment as the portly, moon-faced doctor began to arrange his instruments in readiness. Justin, however, winced with the sight of every sharp blade the cheerful little man drew forth.

"Fine morning for your meeting, gentlemen," the doctor said, patting the ends of his bristly mustache. "I remember the dreadful rain when Lord Mifflin met Mr. Harbottle. Mr. Harbottle's blood soaked everywhere. O'course 'twas nothing compared to when Sir Norton challenged the Honorable Mr. Shaw. The sun was far too bright that day. Each shot the other, with Sir Norton's kneecap blown clear off. I thought I heard the bone crunch beneath my feet as I ran to him, but it turned out to be a piece of broken glass. Ha-Ha!"

Justin's features washed gray, nigh the same shade as the overcast sky. Everard gave his friend's shoulder a reassuring squeeze, at the same time wishing Snape would arrive so he could make an end to this affair. Slowly, he eased himself out of his double-breasted jacket of sapphire-blue superfine and tossed it carelessly to the ground.

Justin emitted a loud groan. "Blast it, Ev! I told you to wear something black, with small buttons."

Everard adjusted the hem of his red-and-white striped marcella waistcoat. He jutted one eyebrow upward with a faint trace of his customary self-mockery. "Black for morning wear, old fellow? The mere suggestion of such a thing is enough to chill my blood."

"But this is a duel, damn it. Not an—an al fresco breakfast." Justin raked his hand back through his hair, a gesture he had indulged in repeatedly since arising. "And that starched cravat. You might as well have painted a bull's-eye upon yourself and be done with it."

"I have arranged my cravat to perfection every morning since I can remember. 'Tis the one thing I do well." Everard's mouth crooked into a wry half smile. "You would hardly expect me to leave off now."

"I would expect—oh, what the devil's the use in talking to you?" Justin tore at his hair again. The ends were beginning to bristle up in such a fashion as made him appear as if he had just crawled from his bed. Everard would have found the effect amusing, but for the anxiety and fear he saw mirrored in his friend's eyes. 'Twas curiously touching to see the carefree Justin so troubled upon his behalf. He shook Justin's hand in a firm clasp.

"Justin, in case I have neglected to tell you, I am dashed grateful for—"

But Justin jerked away from him. "No! No, blister it! Don't talk as if you were going to . . . You will dispatch that varlet Snape, and we will soon be making merry at breakfast. I firmly believe that."

And some otherwise sensible folk believe in the second coming of King Arthur, Everard thought, but did not voice it. Justin was looking miserable enough. As for himself, he felt nothing at the imminent prospect of the duel, only a kind of emptiness. He reviewed mentally all the preparations he had made, attempting to determine whether he had forgotten anything. He'd left instructions with his solicitor regarding his will, a letter to be delivered to his parents, in case Snape's aim proved too accurate. And a message for Aurelia as well.

With her image shimmering in his mind, some of Everard's feelings of impassivity began to waver. How he had longed to see her one last time, hold her, tell her . . . No, even faced with the prospect of his own death, there was nothing he could tell her, nothing that he had the right to say. It had taken the better part of the night for him to compose a simple farewell letter. In the end he could pen naught but a single line, "God bless you, my dearest friend—and keep you."

Justin jostled against Everard as he drew forth his pocket watch. "Snape is late. I told you he was no gentleman. I think we should leave and forget—"

"Your timepiece is too fast. In any event, I believe that is my worthy opponent arriving now." Everard indicated an open-topped carriage rumbling through the gates of the park's brick enclosure. But as the coach drew nearer, the only discernible passengers were a heavily veiled woman accompanied by her maid.

"I would wager there goes a lady of most passionate disposition," Everard remarked in languid tones after the carriage had rumbled past, disappearing behind a line of trees. " 'Tis passing early to be abroad on an amorous adventure."

"It wouldn't surprise me if it were Sylvie," Justin

said. "She is vindictive enough to enjoy watching you—" He swallowed, allowing the grim thought to remain incomplete.

"Well, your mistress did go to great lengths to arrange this entertainment. I trust she will not be disappointed."

"Harpy! She's no mistress of mine. I'll have no more to do with the wench."

"I am glad to hear that," Everard said softly. "Especially for Aurelia's sake."

"I don't know how much it would matter to Reely. Now that the engagement is off." Justin turned his gaze back to the doctor. He crinkled his nose in distaste. "Plague take it. That fellow's brought enough of those gruesome instruments with him to operate on half of Wellington's army."

But Everard scarce heeded the last part of Justin's speech. His hand clamped around Justin's wrist in a viselike grip. "What did you say?"

"I said that fellow has enough blades to—"

"No, I mean about the engagement."

"Oh, didn't I tell you?" Justin said, his manner a trifle too casual. "Reely's called it off."

"Called it off? Damn you, Justin! How could you let that happen. Didn't you apologize to her for what happened last night?"

Justin managed to free himself from Everard's bone-crushing grip. Grimacing, he rubbed his wrist. "Well, I tried, but she didn't care about me and Sylvie. That's not the reason she doesn't want to marry me. She—" He broke off, giving Everard a wary look. "She'd have my head if I told you the real reason, and between the pair of you, I don't know which is the more dangerous. I had hoped that after this was over . . ."

"You had hoped what?" Everard asked sharply.

His one consolation in going through with this affair with Snape had been the knowledge that although Aurelia might grieve a little for him, she would soon be safely wed to Justin.

Justin shuffled his feet. "Reely made me promise I would not tell you, but, oh, hang it all! You've a right to know before you face Snape. She's fallen in love with you, Ev."

"That's nonsense! 'Tis you she loves—has loved all her life."

"As a brother, perhaps." Justin shrugged. "I did try to tell you there was nothing romantic between us."

Everard opened his mouth to protest, then closed it again. He could scarce credit what Justin was telling him. It was such a dangerous hope. Already his heart was soaring with it; he was beginning to imagine all sorts of impossible things.

He compressed his lips sternly. "Justin, if you are feeding me another of your Banbury tales . . ."

"Upon my honor, 'tis true. Reely told me so herself. Do you think I would tell you such a thing in jest?"

Everard slowly shook his head. "No, but I can still scarce believe it. Why—why would she . . ."

"Prefer you to me?" For the first time that morning, Justin grinned. "Hanged if I know. I think it has something to do with the way you tie your cravats."

Everard gave a shaky chuckle. Aurelia free of her engagement and possibly in love with him? Was he dreaming? Of a sudden, he had difficulty meeting Justin's eye. "I—I suppose you have guessed my feelings for her. I never meant it to happen, to betray our friendship in this manner."

"Don't be such a clunch, Ev. Why, I couldn't be

happier if you had fallen in love with my own sister. In fact. I wouldn't have wished Clarice upon my worst enemy. The only betrayal I will feel is if you don't ask me to stand up with you at the wedding."

Wedding? It occurred to Everard that Justin was speaking of *his* wedding—his wedding to Aurelia. He tipped back his head, staring at the dull gray clouds scudding by. Never had the English skies appeared so blue to him, the sun so brilliant. Laughter rumbled deep in his chest, which Justin's voice echoed. Justin dealt him a playful buffet on the shoulder, which he returned, all the while trading quips about finally losing one's heart and slipping one's neck into the matrimonial noose. Everard felt almost drunk with the joy flooding through him.

The sound of curricle wheels upon the gravel path doused his high spirits like a cold-water bath. He glanced around, his smile freezing upon his lips at the same time he saw Justin's grin fade.

Augustus Snape had finally arrived.

From her place of concealment behind the broad-based trunk of an oak tree, Aurelia stared through the haze of her veil at Justin and Everard. Her stomach tensed until she thought she was going to be ill when she saw the surgeon preparing his scalpel. As Everard and Justin began laughing, playfully slapping each other on the back, Aurelia thought she could have gladly shot them both herself. How could they be romping like a pair of schoolboys out on a lark, when Everard might soon be fighting for his life? She was relieved when they both became more somber, relieved until she noted what had put an end to their mirth.

Like a tall, thin shadow creeping across the grass, Augustus Snape marched toward Everard. Aurelia pressed her hand against her breast, feeling iron bands of fear tighten about her heart. Her scheme had not worked. Snape had not believed her. Frantically she glanced toward the park's iron gates. But it was obvious no other source of help was coming. She was forced to revert to her final, most desperate plan. Her hand inched inside the voluminous pocket of her drab brown cloak weighted down by the pistol. She eased her sweating palm around the smooth wooden handle. The weapon was primed and ready. Had she loaded it correctly? She prayed she had, prayed she wouldn't actually be forced to use it.

She stepped out of her place of concealment and began walking slowly toward the group of men, who were as yet unaware of her presence. Her heart thudded with every step. She expected at any moment to see Everard distance himself from Snape, their seconds handing them the weapons.

Their seconds . . . Aurelia halted in midstep. But Snape had arrived alone. She was not completely clear on the codes of dueling, but she was certain both combatants were required to have a second present. Otherwise, the meeting could not take place, could it? Renewed hope began to flicker inside of her. She waited. Yes, something of a peculiar nature definitely was taking place.

Aurelia eased her grip on the pistol. Even from this distance, it was not difficult to see that Snape was fawning over Everard, rubbing his bony hands together, cringing in an almost servile manner. 'Twas almost as if Snape were . . .

"Apologizing." Aurelia breathed, but she dared

not feel any sensation of relief, for Everard stood rigid, staring at Snape's outstretched hand.

Please, Everard, I beg you, Aurelia silently prayed. Accept his apology. Accept it.

The minutes seemed to stretch into hours. Her gaze never wavered from Everard's unruly dark hair, the unyielding cast of his aquiline profile. With that uncanny sense of his, he suddenly turned and stared straight in her direction, as though she had called his name aloud.

Then slowly he favored Snape with a curt nod and touched his hand in reluctant acknowledgement.

"Thank God!" Aurelia choked on a half sob. All the tension, the fear, rushing out of her system left her feeling nigh giddy, but she managed to keep her knees from buckling beneath her. Even from this distance, she could sense Everard's eyes upon her, the softening of his expression, the slight tremor of his sensitive mouth as it tipped into his half smile.

She drew in a tremulous breath, her pulse quickening as Everard started toward her across the lawn. For a brief moment she saw nothing but him. Then the pounding of horse's hooves penetrated her consciousness. She shifted her gaze long enough to note a burly constable dismounting. He and two other officials bore purposefully down upon Everard and Justin.

"Oh, no!" Aurelia moaned in dismay. "Not now, you silly fools."

She started to race forward, to tell the officers to go away, their intervention was unnecessary. But 'twas already too late to halt what she had set in motion the evening before.

The beaming constable had seized an astonished

Everard by the arm. "In the King's name, I command you gents to set aside your weapons and come peacefully with me. You are all under arrest."

Seated across from Lady Foxcliff in the cozy little parlor at the back of her ladyship's town house, Aurelia slumped down on the divan. Dolefully she finished her tale of how she had broken her engagement with Justin and then taken steps to put a stop to the duel.

". . . and then when I wasn't sure if I had frightened Snape away, I laid information against Everard with the magistrate. I tried to tell the constable I was mistaken about the duel, but what with the surgeon being there and and the pistol case, he wouldn't listen. Both Everard and Justin have—have been taken away."

Aurelia waited, certain that her ladyship would look justifiably vexed to hear that her favorite nephew had been arrested. Instead, Lady Foxcliff flung back her head and guffawed so hard, she appeared likely to fall off the thin-legged Chippendale chair upon which she perched.

"Lord, 'tis better than a farce at Drury Lane. Serves him right. What was the boy thinking of to be dueling in Hyde Park! I would give a monkey to have seen Ramsey's face when that beef-witted constable hustled him off."

"Neither he nor Justin looked too pleased with me." Aurelia sighed. "Though I don't think Everard was quite so angry until the pistol in my pocket went off and nearly shot him in the foot."

Lady Foxcliff stomped her foot and clutched her sides, tears of mirth streaming from her eyes. Her ladyship's laughter was infectious. Despite herself, Aurelia's lips curved into a reluctant smile, al-

416

though she complained, "It did seem quite unfair of Everard. He was most eager to stand up and deliberately let Augustus Snape try to wound him, but when I almost did the same by accident, he was furious."

Her ladyship swiped at her moist eyes. Her chuckles abated long enough for her to deal Aurelia a hearty reassuring smack on the shoulder. "Now, my dear, don't fret yourself. I know how these affairs go. The magistrate will wink one eye and deliver some long-winded homily on the evils of dueling. Ramsey will be back here to plague you before the cat can lick its whiskers, so you run along upstairs and put on your prettiest frock and settle down to wait for the scamp."

Aurelia opened her mouth to protest, then blushed under the knowing look her ladyship was giving her. Much reassured by Lady Foxcliff's attitude toward the disconcerting turn of events, Aurelia whisked upstairs to her room to obey. It took her the better part of an hour to select a gown, dismissing first this one and then that, until she nigh drove her maid to distraction. Finally she settled upon a day dress of dark green satin with goblet-shaped cuffs, embroidered at the hem in a geometric pattern of pale pink.

But the morning stretched into late afternoon with no sign of Everard. By the time tea was laid out in the parlor, Aurelia had rearranged the delicate Sevres cups and silver spoons upon the mahogany serving table at least a dozen times. Her ladyship's cook had served up a platter of the most delectable strawberry tarts. Although Aurelia's stomach was knotted with tension, she felt the old desire to ease her nervous pangs by gobbling up every last one. She inched the plate closer, then resolutely shoved it aside. No, Everard would be excessively disappointed if he found her giving way to temptation. Who knew what havoc she might have already wreaked upon her figure since coming to London?

Anxiously she hurried over to study herself in one of the pier glasses set between the tall windows which opened out into the gardens. For once, she set aside her habit of self-criticism and tried to see herself as Everard would when he walked in the room.

There was a soft glow in her eyes she'd never seen before, and the glossy auburn curls framing her face enhanced the creaminess of her skin. Perhaps it was all owing to the elegance of the gown, which made her look supple and slender.

She raised one hand, tentatively touching her flushed cheek. "I—I am almost beautiful, am I not, Everard?" she whispered. Mayhap it was not so absurd to think that he could be in love with her, as Justin insisted. She thought back to all the time he had spent with her last winter. Why else would he have taken such pains with her, scolding, encouraging, setting aside all his customary pursuits? She had been a fool not to realize it before. Everard *did* love her.

She stood a little taller, confidence fluttering to life inside her like a butterfly testing its wings for the first time. Her heart began to thud with anticipation when she heard a footfall upon the carpeted hallway outside the door. With a slight spring in her step, she sat back down by the tea tray, gracefully arranging her skirts, and settled her hands primly upon her lap.

Her ladyship's surly butler stepped inside long enough to announce, "Lady Sylvie Fitzhurst."

Before Aurelia had time to protest, Lady Sylvie swept into the room and the butler closed the door behind her. Aurelia stared at the woman with less than cordiality. Lady Sylvie's eyes were darting daggers back at her, despite the feline smile fixed upon her ladyship's face.

"Good afternoon, Miss Sinclair."

Aurelia rose to her feet with slow dignity. "You astonish me, Lady Sylvie. I would not have thought that even you would be bold enough to come where you must assuredly know you will not be welcome."

Aurelia was astonished by the chilling accents of her voice. If only her mother could have heard her. Lady Sylvie flinched, but she stepped further into the room. An angry titter escaped her.

"I daresay you are wroth with me over what happened at Vauxhall. I—"

"Not in the least. I never overly concern myself with such *trivial* matters."

"But you and Lord Spencer are still engaged?"

"Is that what you have come here to discover?" Aurelia arched one eyebrow mockingly, while feeling an inner sense of triumph. She had learned more than she realized from Everard this past winter. She only regretted she did not have a quizzing glass. "I should hate for you to perish from curiosity. We have indeed broken off the betrothal."

Lady Sylvie's smile widened, only to vanish as Aurelia continued, "But it had naught to do with you. Heavens! If one became angry every time Justin decided to kiss another pretty wench, er, I mean lady . . ." Aurelia indulged in a silvery laugh. "Not that this information will be of any use to you, my dear Lady Sylvie. I doubt your charms will be enough to tempt Justin again, especially considering you did your best to endanger the life of his closest friend."

Aurelia permitted her gaze to rove over Lady Sylvie's frame in disparaging fashion. The woman's ample bosom quivered with suppressed fury, an unbecoming red mottling her cheeks. Aurelia was half tempted to examine her own hands to see if she had sprouted velvet claws. Never in her life had she treated another woman in such cutting fashion, but then, never had one so threatened the man she loved. She half expected Lady Sylvie to hiss like a furious serpent, then storm out of the room.

But with great visible effort, Lady Sylvie checked herself. She sat down upon the divan, and began to pour out a cup of tea.

Aurelia gently removed the cup and saucer from her grasp. "You won't have time for that. You're leaving now."

Lady Sylvie's eyes spit venom. "I talked with Augustus Snape earlier and heard how you frightened him off from the duel. I suppose you are feeling rather clever at the moment."

"Yes," Aurelia agreed affably. "I did think it was rather a brilliant stroke upon my part."

Sylvie sniffed. "One wonders how such a *clever* woman can permit a man like Everard Ramsey to make a fool of her." She picked up a butter knife and began to tool it between her fingers. "For you will look a fool, Miss Sinclair, when the story of Ramsey's infamous wager leaks out."

Aurelia feigned a yawn. "Mr. Ramsey has a penchant for involving himself in so many wagers. I can scarce be expected to keep track of them all. To which one are you referring?"

"The one where he wagered he could turn some poor dowdy creature into this season's belle. How fortunate you must feel that he chose you. But, of course, it never does a lady's reputation any good to be the vulgar object of a bet."

"W-what are you talking about?" Aurelia felt some of her confidence begin to waver, but she shook off the sinking feeling. She would be a dolt to believe anything Sylvie Fitzhurst had to say. 'Twas obvious the woman, having been balked in the matter of the duel, was seeking some new form of spite.

Lady Sylvie's eyes narrowed. She gave a throaty laugh. "Why, my dear, can it be you did not know? Everard Ramsey made a wager with his aunt that he could turn even you into a beauty. Of course, to my mind, the degree of his success is questionable, but I have heard that Lady Foxcliff was satisfied enough to concede the bet."

"Neither Lady Foxcliff nor Everard—" Aurelia began, then halted, her mouth suddenly going dry. An unwelcome memory surfaced in her mind of her first night in London as she had nervously prepared for the Carlisle ball, then presented herself in the drawing room for Everard's inspection. Her ladyship had laughingly remarked, *"Stap me, Ev. You must take the money. Never was a wager so fairly won."* Everard had promptly shushed his aunt. Aurelia had been too anxious for some sign of Everard's approval to question the strange comment then. But now . . .

She gripped the back of the divan, wanting to refute Lady Sylvie's hateful words, wanting to, but unable. Why did it make so much more sense, why was it easier to believe that Everard's attentions were the result of a wager than his being in love with her? How had she ever dared to fancy such a thing? Herself beautiful, desirable. Bah!

She felt as though Lady Sylvie dealt her a blow

to the stomach instead of an insidiously soft pat upon the hand. "Perhaps you should sit down, Miss Sinclair. You don't look at all well."

Aurelia wrenched her hand away, a sharp driving sense of anger suddenly taking possession of her, leaving her shaking from head to toe. How dare Everard Ramsey! *How dare he* sweep into her world, make such unsettling changes in her existence, and all for a wager, for sport, for his own amusement. She'd been perfectly content as she was in the old days. If not content, at least she had still had her pride, her sense of humor. The knowledge of this stupid wager somehow robbed her of both in one fell stroke. Tears of fury burned in her eyes; her hands were clenched into tight fists until her nails nigh drew blood from her palms.

'Twas at this unfortunate moment that Everard Ramsey strode down the hallway to the parlor. Feeling more nervous than he could ever remember, he paused just outside the door, patting his waistcoat to make certain the ring was still safe. He was determined to make a better job of his proposal than he had seen Justin do.

"Your guardian angel, Ev," Justin had laughingly referred to Aurelia, and he was right. 'Twas certain that she had had something to do with Snape's withdrawal from the duel, though how she had accomplished it, Everard couldn't begin to guess.

His mouth tilted into a soft smile. To perdition with all the fancy phrases he had been rehearsing. His heart was too full for that. He would sweep her into his arms immediately and be done with it. Turning the knob, he stepped quietly into the room.

Aurelia had her back to him, her auburn curls tumbling in charming disarray along the graceful curve of her neck. He noted with great tenderness that she was trembling.

"Aurelia." He breathed her name, covering the distance between them in two quick strides. Slowly, she turned.

His arms closed about her before she looked up at him, bracing the heels of her hands against his chest. As he bent to kiss her, it occurred to Everard, his angel appeared to have twin devils burning in her vivid green eyes.

He hesitated, repeating more uncertainly this time, "Aurelia?"

"Is it true?" she asked tersely.

"Is—is what true?" Everard sensed some impending disaster about to overtake him, but had not the least notion what. Was she still upset over something involving the duel?

"Is it true that there was a wager between you and your aunt as to whether you could turn me into a beauty?"

The guilty flush spreading across Everard's cheeks condemned him before he could even reply, "Well, yes, but—"

He never had opportunity to finish. She drew back her arm and cracked him with the full force of her open palm across the jaw. Everard staggered back in astonishment, raising his hand to rub his stinging cheek. What the deuce? Then he noticed they were not alone in the room. Lady Sylvie Fitzhurst had retreated to the window seat and stood watching, a malicious smirk upon her face, as though waiting for the curtain to ring up upon some choice bit of entertainment.

It took no great stretch of the imagination for Everard to guess what had happened. That night at Vauxhall, Lady Sylvie must have overheard his aunt's unfortunate remarks about the wager. But God knows how devilishly the woman had twisted the facts when repeating the tale to Aurelia. Everard straightened. Well, he had no intentions of putting on a performance to satisfy Sylvie Fitzhurst's warped sense of malice. He would settle this with Aurelia privately.

"Aurelia, my dear," he began patiently. "If you will strive to compose yourself, we can—"

"I don't want to compose myself. Tell me, Mr. Ramsey, how much did you win? I should like to know exactly how much I was worth to you."

"Stop it, Aurelia." He spoke more sternly this time, trying to capture her hands. She whipped away from him with an expression of revulsion that hurt him more than the slap had done.

She gave a bitter, strangled laugh. "I suppose to a gentleman with your penchant for gaming, the whole thing was trivial, just another lark, but I trust you won enough to have made it worth your while. You were put to such pains to achieve your effect."

Everard froze, his hand half-extended toward her in a gesture of appeal. It would not have surprised him for his father or anyone else to believe him capable of conducting such a heartless wager, but for Aurelia to do so and on the mere word of a viper like Sylvie Fitzhurst! He lowered his outstretched hand slowly back to his side.

Aurelia was too far gone in her own misery to note the flash of pain in Everard's eyes before he hooded their expression. If only he would deny he had done this dreadful, hurtful thing, instead of standing there looking so cold, so remote.

"I—I am waiting for your explanation," she said.

He hunched his shoulders. "What explanation is

necessary? Lady Sylvie appears to have already told you everything you need to know."

His casual dismissal of her pain cut Aurelia worse than the fact of the wager itself. He was not even going to attempt to apologize. She fought back the tears that threatened to spill down her cheeks at any moment.

"Oh, how I despise you." She choked. "I—I wish I had never met you. I wish I had shot you myself. I—I . . ."

"There is no need for you to elaborate further." Everard interrupted, his eyes flintlike, his features appearing carved from stone. "You have made your feelings abundantly clear."

Turning on his heel, he strode from the room, slamming the door behind him. Aurelia's shoulders began to shake. She sank down upon the divan, pummeling the bolster as tears of impotent rage spilled down her face, rage at herself as much as Everard. How could she have been foolish enough to think she had fallen in love with such a cold-hearted man?

She completely forgot Lady Sylvie's presence in the room, until the woman clapped her hands together, calling out mockingly, "Bravo, Miss Sinclair."

Aurelia swiped the moisture from her cheeks as her ladyship glided over to her. She clung desperately to her anger, for she knew when it was gone, the pain would begin. She could feel the dulling edges of it tugging at her heart already.

"There, there, my dear," Lady Sylvie cooed. "Forget the worthless man and enjoy your tea."

With a sneer upon her lips, she handed Aurelia a china plate bearing a large strawberry tart. Aurelia sniffed, staring at the succulent pastry, feeling she had come full circle. Once again, the only consolation in her life seemed to be food. And what did it matter to anyone what she looked like? Certainly not to Everard Ramsey.

Aurelia's fingers clamped around the plate. Damn Everard Ramsey! It did matter. It mattered to someone very important. It mattered to Aurelia Sinclair.

"Go ahead, my dear," Lady Sylvie prodded. "After what you have been through, you deserve to indulge yourself a little."

Aurelia drew in a shuddering breath, then stared up at her ladyship. "You're absolutely right. I do."

No, Aurelia! She could almost hear her mother's voice. *A lady would never—* But for the first time in her life, Aurelia gave little credence to her mother's dictums.

She scooped up the delicate pastry and crammed it against Lady Sylvie's face. The woman tried to gasp, but was choked by the crumbs and flowing red berries dripping down her chin into the neckline of her low-cut bodice.

As Aurelia stalked out of the room, she could still hear Lady Sylvie's muffled shrieks.

Chapter 11

Justin watched with an expression of baffled dismay as the last of Aurelia's portmanteau was slung on the back of the chaise-and-four.

"But—but Reely, you cannot be set upon leaving this way, not even giving Ev a chance to explain."

"When I last saw Mr. Ramsey, he evinced no desire to explain anything," Aurelia said in taut accents. Nearly a week had passed since her quarrel with Everard. For all she knew or *cared*, she thought fiercely, he might have sailed off the end of the world. She glanced around the stable yard, pretending to ascertain whether Wallis had forgotten to hand up her smallest dressing case, in reality taking a moment to conceal the tears swimming in her eyes.

"Well, blast it all, you did tell the man you never wanted to see him again."

But he didn't have to be so quick to believe me, Aurelia thought, but she halted the forlorn slump of her shoulders. She said briskly, "Lady Foxcliff has promised to send on the rest of my things later. So I believe that takes care of everything."

Justin scowled. "No, it doesn't. Not by a long shot, and you know it."

"Did Everard send you here to act as his emissary?" Despite herself, Aurelia could not suppress the hopeful quiver in her voice.

"No, but—"

She sighed, then thrust out her hand. "Then let us part friends, Justin, and say no more about it before we end by quarreling, too."

Reluctantly he took her hand. "But, Reely, all I wanted to say was—"

"It should be lovely in Norfolk this time of year." She spoke up, deliberately interrupting him. "I shall call upon your sister and write you a full report on how your new nephew is doing."

"Aurelia!" Justin's fingers crushed down around hers. "Hang it all, will you please listen to me for but five minutes?"

She shook her head. "No, Justin, please. I—I have had Lady Foxcliff haranguing me all morning."

"Then she must have explained to you about the wager."

"She did, but it makes no difference."

Justin gaped at her in bewilderment as Aurelia struggled to put into words what she did not quite understand herself, the feeling that she was as much to blame for the quarrel as Everard. Her old self-doubts had gotten the better of her, making her incapable of believing that she was worthy of being loved. Even if she could change that, 'twas too late. She knew she had said some things to Everard that were unforgivable.

"There—there are some fences that cannot be mended," she said, swallowing back her tears. "Now, please Justin, just bid me farewell."

Justin looked more as though he would have liked to shake her, but instead he bent down and lightly brushed his lips against her cheek. After he

428

had seen Aurelia and her maid bestowed safely in the coach, he could not resist one final appeal.

"But, Reely, Ev doesn't even know that you are going away. What shall I tell him?"

"Tell him"—she sighed wearily—"tell him anything that you like."

The coachman whipped up the team and the chaise rumbled out of the stable yard. Scowling, Justin stood staring long after it had vanished from sight. If this wasn't the damnedest situation! When two of the most sensible people he knew could behave in such absurd, mule-headed fashion, why, they might as well unlock the doors of Bedlam and let all the lunatics loose.

Justin raked his fingers back through his hair. He would soon be bald at this rate. 'Twas a novel experience for him, this business of becoming so deeply involved in other people's problems. Uncomfortable and exasperating! He wanted simply to forget the whole thing. Leave Ev and Reely to sort it out on their own. But neither of them seemed capable of doing so.

Damn! He'd never have any peace until this was settled. But now with Reely haring off back to Aldgate, what was he going to say to Ev? Nothing would induce Ramsey to go after her. The fellow was like to choke on his pride.

"Tell him anything you like," Reely had said. Hah! Tell him anything . . . Justin blinked, as the glimmer of an idea came to him. But no, he couldn't tell Ev a thing like that. Why, Reely would flay him alive.

The corners of Justin's mouth upturned in a grin of pure mischief. Ah, but what reproach could she make? She *had* given him permission.

* * *

Everard's dapper little valet wrung his hands, tears all but springing to his eyes as he watched his master don his new suit of clothes.

"Oh, sir, that I should live to see this day!" Beddoes moaned.

Ignoring the man's wails, Everard faced himself in the cheval glass. He deftly tied his cravat in a plain style to match the severe cut of his navy jacket of fustian and the unremarkable somberness of his waistcoat and breeches.

Beddoes sniffed. "If you have no regard for your own reputation, sir, then think of mine."

Despite his gloomy frame of mind, which quite matched the apparel, a reluctant smile tugged at Everard's lips. "Do not distress yourself unduly. I shall make it clear to all and sundry you had no part in this."

"But why, sir? Why are you doing this? You, the most elegant gentleman in England, saving only Mr. Brummell."

"It is high time I earned a reputation for something besides being a frivolous coxcomb and the way I cut a deck of cards." His mouth set into a hard line, Everard turned back to face his reflection in the mirror. Then, Miss Sinclair, he thought, perhaps you will have a higher opinion of me than to believe . . .

Suppressing the rest of the notion, he attacked his unruly mane of dark hair with a comb, attempting to whip it in line with his new, more sober image. 'Twas a hopeless task, but at least it gave him something to concentrate his energies upon. His emotions had run the gamut this past week, bitterness, anger at Aurelia, despair. He had almost responded to her doubts the same way he always had to his father's. By indulging in a wild round of gaming to show her how right she was. But something held him back. He was growing too old for such boy's tricks.

He would shed his ne'er-do-well image if it killed him. Hadn't Aurelia once told him he could do anything he put his mind to? Well, he would prove to her how serious-minded he could be. And then . . . A gleam of gold on the dressing table caught his eye. He slipped the engagement ring he had bought Aurelia inside his waistcoat pocket. It would stay there, he resolved, until the day she would be proud to wear it upon her finger. He began to brush down his lapels, trying not to grimace at the sight of the dully clad figure the mirror reflected back, when a loud banging sounded on the door to his lodgings.

Dispatching Beddoes to get rid of the impertinent caller who came bothering him at this hour of the morning, Everard fought down the urge to reach for his quizzing glass and attach it round his neck.

The door slammed. He heard Beddoes's muffled cry as Justin shoved his way into the room.

"Ev, thank God I've found you in."

Everard turned slowly to face his friend. It occurred to him that Justin was looking more distressed than he had the morning of the duel. His hair practically stood on end, but he halted in midstride, looking considerably taken aback as he studied Everard from crown to toe.

"Stap me, Ev! Who has died?"

"No one." Everard's lips tightened in annoyance. "What the deuce do you mean by bursting in here like—"

Justin seemed to snap to attention as though remembering the purpose of his errand. "It's Reely,

431

Ev. She . . ." He trailed off, glancing significantly in Beddoes's direction.

The valet sniffed. "If you will excuse me, sir. I shall go see about procuring more champagne for the boot blacking. I trust we are still going to keep our boots polished?"

At Everard's frowning nod, the small man favored Justin with a dignified bow before quitting the room.

"Now what is this nonsense about Aurelia?"

"She's run off, Ev. Left your aunt's house this morning."

Everard steeled his features to remain impassive. "She most likely had decided to return to Aldgate. 'Twas always her intention."

"No! She has gone off with Snape!"

"What!" Everard arched one eyebrow, regarding Justin as though he had taken leave of his senses. His friend paced about the room with all the grace of an agitated bear.

" 'Tis true. They are going to be married. You must go after her before 'tis too late."

But Everard crossed his arms over his chest. "Now where did you get such a humbug tale as that? Why would Aurelia ever consider wedding Augustus Snape?" he asked sharply. Sometimes Justin's jests went beyond the bounds of good taste. But there was an earnest look in his friend's eye that began to make Everard feel uneasy.

"Because she promised him, that's why." Justin stopped his pacing. "The woman's so mad with love for you, she'd do anything."

"I fail to follow the logic of that. If Aurelia is so much in love with me as you say—"

"Blister me! When was there anything logical where women are concerned?" Justin seized Everard by the shoulders. "I tell you, we don't have time to stand here talking, you great dolt. We both wondered why Snape suddenly decided to apologize and call off the duel. Well, I feared when Reely left me that day, she was going to do something desperate to save you. She promised to marry that sniveling fortune hunter."

Everard slowly uncrossed his arms. "But—but how did you discover all this?"

"She left me a note, but her maid delivered it too soon. Reely begged me to try to make you understand. That was why she quarreled with you that day." Justin sighed, staring down at the carpet. "She thought if you hated her, it would make matters easier."

Everard felt the color draining from his face. "Easier!" he said chokingly. "To see her the wife of that miscreant! I'll see Snape in hell first!"

Striding to the door, Everard bellowed for his valet, then tore about the room in search of his boots. Aurelia and Snape! The mere thought was enough to make his flesh crawl. As he began ramming on his boots, he commanded Justin, "Give me her letter. She must have left some clue as to their destination."

"Er, no! She didn't! I—I mean in my haste to find you, I forgot the note. But I believe they are going to Aldgate."

"Aldgate?" Everard checked in the act of putting on his boot to stare up at Justin.

"You cannot think Reely would ever stand for being wed over the anvil at Gretna Green. No, I am almost positive her letter said something about a special license."

"A special license! Then they could well be married before I . . ." Everard left the horrible thought

433

unfinished. It didn't matter, he told himself grimly. Even if she was wed, Aurelia would be a widow before the sun set tonight. Not waiting for Beddoes, he flung some of his belongings haphazardly into a valise.

"I shall have to hire a vehicle," he groaned. How much precious time had he lost already?

"No, you take my phaeton and head toward Aldgate," Justin said, firmly steering him toward the door. "I'll obtain another coach and follow the North Road, just in case I have guessed wrong."

Everard nodded in grim agreement. When Justin saw the frantic light glittering in Ramsey's blue eyes, he almost relented. And when he saw the reckless fashion in which Everard whipped up his team of horses and tore down the narrow cobblestone street, Justin experienced more than a small twinge of conscience.

Mayhap he had gone too far this time in playing one of his little jests. For a full minute, he worried about the consequences of what he had done. Then he shrugged. What could possibly go wrong? Ev would overtake Reely on the road. They would fall into each other's arms, and all misunderstandings would be cleared away. They would both thank him for this later. Justin drew in a deep breath. It was a fine spring morning, promising to be a beautiful day. Mayhap he should call upon the voluptuous Lady Carlisle and see if she would care for a drive in the park. Whistling cheerfully, Lord Spencer strolled off down St. James Street.

The baby's squalls only increased in volume as Lady Norton proudly handed her offspring into the vicar's outstretched arms. Aurelia shifted wearily from foot to foot, her eyes wandering past the small gathering of friends and neighbors as she gazed about the light, airy interior of Aldgate's tiny church. Then she caught herself and focused her attention back upon the babe, trying to look deeply interested in the proceedings. She had arrived home only yesterday and had not expected to be faced with a christening ceremony. But Lady Norton had been adamant. Even though Aurelia had shown the good sense not to wed her tiresome brother, Clarice insisted that Aurelia still stand as little Stephen's godmama.

At least, Aurelia thought, it was a diversion from being at the Manor. She had no notion her own house was going to depress her so, with the thought of the empty years stretching out there, a lonely future without—She stiffened, sternly refusing to allow herself to whisper *his* name, even in her heart.

As the vicar moved closer to the baptismal font carved with figures of smiling cherubs, Aurelia eyed the red face of her godchild with considerable sympathy. His tiny fists flailed in a futile attempt to turn his head aside from the frills framing his bonnet.

Aurelia felt equally uncomfortable, although her misery did not stem from her garb, but more from the icy regard of Justin's mama as she inched her way forward for a better view of her grandson. No matter how the rest of the family might feel, Lady Spencer obviously was not accepting the broken engagement with becoming grace.

Aurelia longed for the christening to be over so that she might escape her ladyship's reproachful frowns. The vicar's voice droned on, all but drowned out by young Stephen's howls of disapproval. They had reached the part for Aurelia to utter her own solemn pledges of care for the child when the door at the far end of the church was flung violently open.

"Stop!" A familiar male voice shouted. "I forbid you to proceed any further."

The startled vicar nigh dropped the child into the font. Aurelia turned with the others to stare in the direction of the chancel. Sunlight filtered through the stained glass windows, so that the figures of Saints Brigid, Catherine, James and Lawrence appeared to regard with mild astonishment the wild-eyed man rushing toward the south transept.

Everard! Aurelia blinked to make certain she was not imagining things. Nay, it was Everard, although in such fashion as she'd never seen him before. His cravat was all but hanging from his neck, and his plain-cut jacket torn and travel-stained. But the ravages to his clothing were as nothing compared to his face. Ramsey's cool, well-bred features were streaked with sweat, his brow knit into the thunderous expression of a man about to commit murder.

Among the astonished assemblage, the vicar was the first to find his voice. "Sir, what is the meaning of this interruption?"

" 'Tis a friend of my brother's." Lady Norton bounded forward a few steps to intercept Everard. Scarce looking at her, Ramsey thrust the young woman out of his path.

Nothing daunted, Clarice demanded, "Everard, why did you not tell me you were coming to attend the christening?"

Lady Spencer muttered something about "scarcely suitably attired."

"Christening?" The word escaped Everard in a strangled choke. Before Aurelia could react, he

436

strode forward and seized her by the shoulders. His blazing fatigue-rimmed blue eyes roved wildly about the baptistry.

"Where is Snape?"

Still somewhat dazed by his sudden appearance, Aurelia realized she was gaping. Closing her jaw somewhat, she stammered, "I—I haven't the slightest notion."

"You haven't the—" Everard stopped, his lips tightening into a thin white line. Then he let loose such an astonishing string of curses that Clarice shrieked, covering her ears.

"Are you drunk, Mr. Ramsey, or mad?" Lady Spencer spluttered.

"This is a house of God, sir," the vicar said, looking as wrathful as he could with the squirming infant in his arms.

"The devil!" Everard hissed. Seizing Aurelia by the wrist, he began dragging her down the aisle. Her first impulse was to resist, but after one sidelong glance at Everard's savage expression, she decided it might be best to humor him. She heard Clarice wail before he hauled her through the church doors, "But who is to be godmother for my baby?"

Outside, Everard flung her unceremoniously onto the seat of an ancient farm cart. He leaped up beside her, slapping the reins down against the backs of a pair of dapple-gray horses. Aurelia clutched the side of her seat, but the plodding mares did not look as though they would have charged forward even to please Satan himself. Despite all of Everard's efforts, they trotted through the sleepy village of Aldgate at a very sedate pace.

Aurelia waited until the last straw-thatched cottage was left behind before she dared risk a glance at Everard.

He looked more in control, but a muscle still twitched along his jaw. His dark hair clung to his brow in such achingly familiar disarray, it was all she could do not to brush the silky midnight strands away from his eyes. She had no idea why he had come, but only that her madly pounding heart was excessively glad that he had.

He finally reined the farm horses to a halt, but stared across the flat panorama of hedgerows and stubbly corn fields, not speaking to her. When the silence stretching out between them grew unbearable, Aurelia summoned up the courage to say meekly. "I—I know young Stephen is not the most prepossessing child, but to interrupt his christening—"

"I knew nothing about the babe"—Everard glared at her—"I thought you were about to be married to Augustus Snape."

"You—you thought . . ." Aurelia gasped. "Have you gone completely out of your mind, Everard Ramsey?"

"I do believe that I have. How could I ever have been so taken in! Damn that Justin! I'll roast him alive." Everard stopped muttering curses under his breath long enough to explain. "He told me you had run off with Snape and I, fool that I am, believed him. I've been pursuing you since yesterday, but I smashed up Justin's new phaeton. Serves him right," he added savagely. "Then I could not find another vehicle to hire except this wretched contraption. I have been going half-mad imagining you in Snape's arms."

Aurelia tensed indignantly, her cheeks flushing. "You believed I would marry that—that disgusting toad—permit him to touch me. Indeed, sir, you certainly have a high opinion of my character."

"As high a one as you have of mine, to think I could be guilty of that wager."

Aurelia returned his glare as they both squared off for several seconds. Everard was the first to avert his gaze.

"I believed you were marrying Snape because you had pledged to do so. I couldn't think of any other way you could have prevented him from continuing with the duel."

"Then you are obviously not gifted with as much imagination as Mr. Snape. I painted for him a very grim picture of all those other men you killed."

"Those other . . . what other men?"

"Those three men in Norfolk you shot through the head in duels," Aurelia said tartly. "I daresay there have been so many, it has slipped your memory."

"I—I daresay." Some of the rigidity about Everard's mouth relaxed. His eyes softened, studying her in such a way as caused Aurelia's pulses to flutter. She began to have great difficulty remembering she was angry with him.

Another long moment passed before he asked, "Aurelia, can you truly believe that everything that passed between us was the result of a wager?" He tried to make the question sound offhand, but she could sense how much her doubts had pained him, were hurting him still.

"No." She swallowed. It was impossible for her to be less than honest. "Yes, at first I did. You see, 'twas so much easier to believe that than—than . . ."

"Than what?" he prompted.

"Than to believe you could—could have any other reason for wasting your time upon me." Staring down at the wagon's floorboards, she gave a shaky laugh. "You remember me from the old days last winter. Better than anyone else, you should know what I am."

"Yes, I better than anyone." A strange huskiness filled his voice. He seized her in his arms, crushing her hard against his chest. "You are a . . . beautiful . . . exasperating . . . enchanting . . . infuriating little fool." He punctuated each word with a trail of kisses along her hair, her brow, her cheek, until his mouth finally captured hers.

Although she longed for nothing more than to surrender herself to the fierce, sweet pressure of his lips, Aurelia forced herself to draw back, determined to finish her explanation.

"Oh, Everard," she whispered. "I never meant to hurt you that day. It wasn't that I have such a bad opinion of you, but—but of myself. I can't believe that you could—"

"Love you? Desire you? Then I shall prove it to you, if it takes the rest of my life."

His lips covered hers again, slowly at first, as though he would savor every moment, then becoming more demanding. Aurelia thought she should protest his scheme to throw his life away in this fashion, but with the world spinning so dizzily about her, she could only cling to Everard. When he followed up one kiss with another, she began to abandon all notion of persuading him to give up this folly. And by the next kiss, she was firmly convinced herself of the nobleness of Everard's plan.

Long moments later, when she nestled comfortably against his shoulder, she heard him mutter, "Damme, I am nearly as forgetful as Justin."

She felt his arm shift beneath her as he struggled to retrieve something from his coat pocket.

"Here it is." Triumphantly he pulled forth a small ring. Fashioned in the shape of a rose, its petals were delicately wrought of gold polished to a pink hue. "I searched all of London to find it." He smiled tenderly. "You see I did not forget your penchant for roses."

" 'Tis—'tis beautiful," she said. When she raised her hand, he gently slid the ring onto her trembling finger.

"I—I mean, you do wish to marry me, don't you, Aurelia?" Everard groaned. "Lord, what a mull I am making of this. I mean that I am in love with you—"

She laid her fingers against his lips, her eyes brimming with tears and laughter. " 'Tis all right. I do not know when I have had a more charming proposal. Not since—"

"You little witch." With a throaty growl, Everard jerked her back into his embrace. But the sudden movement tumbled over his valise at the bottom of the cart. The contents spilled out, falling across Aurelia's feet. She broke off their kiss long enough to stare in puzzlement at the objects strewing the floor. Before Everard could prevent her, she bent down to right the valise.

Amusement quivered at the corners of her mouth. The case contained nothing but an assortment of cravats, and a well-worn deck of cards. She raised the latter, fixing Everard with a look of teasing accusation.

One dark eyebrow jutted upward. "Well, madam, I did pack in some haste."

He took the deck from her, then with a laugh, threw it into the air. The cards fluttered down the lane unnoticed, as Everard pulled her back against him for another long, lingering kiss.